CONSENT TO KILL

CONSENT

TO

KILL

VINCE FLYNN

**SIMON &
SCHUSTER**

London · New York · Sydney · Toronto

A CBS COMPANY

First published in Great Britain by Simon & Schuster UK Ltd, 2006
A CBS COMPANY

Copyright © Vince Flynn, 2005

3 5 7 9 10 8 6 4

Simon & Schuster UK Ltd
Africa House
64–78 Kingsway
London WC2B 6AH

Simon & Schuster Australia
Sydney

www.simonsays.co.uk

A CIP catalogue record for this book is available from the British Library

ISBN 0 7432 6874 1
EAN 9780743268745

Printed and bound in Great Britain by
The Bath Press, Bath

To my brothers and sisters—
Daniel, Patrick, Sheila, Kelly, Kevin, and Timothy . . .

and

in loving memory of Lucy Flynn, whose smile, love, and grace live on
in Lauren, Connor, and Jack

ACKNOWLEDGMENTS

To Emily Bestler and Sloan Harris, my editor and agent, I can't believe it's been seven books. Thank you again for all of my guidance. To my publishers, Judith Curr and Louise Burke, once again you've done a great job. To Jack Romanos, Carolyn Reidy, and the rest of the Simon & Schuster family, thank you for all of your hard work and support. To my publicists, David Brown and Hillary Schupf, I really appreciate your efforts in a very difficult job. To Sarah Branham, Jodi Lipper, and Katherine Cluverius, thank you for making sure things run so smoothly. To Tanya Lopez and Alan Rautbort at ICM, thank you for all of your diligence on the TV front.

One of the best parts of my job is the research. It's what stokes the creative flames. Along the road I get to meet a lot of interesting people, and quite a few of them work for the CIA. At the top of that list is Rob Richer. The men and women of the Directorate of Operations have a near impossible job, but they do it stoically while enduring immense criticism from people who almost never have all the facts. Their successes are kept secret, but their failures end up on the front page of every newspaper and the lead item of every news talk show. I am in awe of your commitment and sacrifice and am grateful for all that you do.

To Sergeant Larry Rodgers of the St. Paul Police Department, thank you for taking the time to answer my sophomoric questions about explosives. To Eric Prince and the rest of the folks down at Black Water, you have my respect and appreciation for the difficult mission you perform. To Mary Matalin—I don't know where to start. As my wife likes to say, "You're a rock star." To Tom Barnard, who in addition to making me laugh, makes me think. I appreciate your helping me out with a couple of the finer points in the book. To Senator Norm Coleman, for his public service and much more.

To Paul Evancoe, a top-notch warrior and a good man. To Chase Brandon, for our monthly talks. To Joel Surnow, Bob Cochran, and Howard Gordan, for letting me look behind the curtain of my favorite TV show, *24*. To the El Cantinero crew, who always make my trips to New York such fun. To Carl Pohlad once again, for his generosity and friendship. To my Aunt Maureen, for helping me with some of the translations in the book. If there are any mistakes they are mine. Lastly, to my phenomenal wife, Lysa. None of this would be as much fun without you.

CONSENT TO KILL

PRELUDE

To kill a man is a relatively easy thing—especially the average unsuspecting man. To kill a man like Mitch Rapp, however, would be an entirely different matter. It would take a great deal of planning and a very talented assassin, or more likely a team, who were either brave enough or crazy enough to accept the job. In fact, any sane man by definition would have the sense to walk away.

The assassins would need to catch Rapp with his guard down in order to get close enough to finish him off once and for all. The preliminary report on his vigilance did not look good. The American was either hyperalert or insanely paranoid. Every detail of their plan would have to come together perfectly, and even then, they would need some luck. They'd calculated that their odds for success were probably seventy percent at best. That was why they needed complete deniability. If whoever they sent failed, Rapp would come looking, despite their positions of great power, and they had no intention of spending the rest of their lives with a man like Mitch Rapp hunting them.

1

Rapp stood in front of his boss's desk. He'd been offered a chair, but had declined. The sun was down, it was getting late, he'd rather be at home with his wife, but he wanted to get this thing taken care of. The file was an inch thick. It pissed him off. There was no other way to describe it. He wanted it gone. Off his desk so he could move on to something else. Something more important, and probably more irritating, but for now he simply wanted to make this particular problem go away.

His hope was that Kennedy would simply read the summary and hand it back to him. But that wasn't how she liked to do things. You didn't become the first female director of the CIA by cutting corners. She had a photographic memory and a hyperanalytical mind. She was like one of those high-end mainframe computers that sit in the basement of large insurance companies, churning through data, discerning trends, risks, and a billion other things. Kennedy's grasp of the overall situation was second to none. She was the depository of all information, including, and especially, the stuff that could never be made public. Like the file that was on her desk right now.

He watched her flip through the pages with great speed, and then backtrack to check on certain inconsistencies that he had no doubt were there. Preparing these reports was not his specialty. His skill set had more to do with the other end of their business. There were times when she would read his work with a pen in hand. She'd make corrections and jot down notes in the margins, but not now. This particular file could turn out to be toxic, the type of thing that would ruin careers like a tornado headed for a trailer park. Kennedy knew when he came to her office, either early in the morning or late in the day, and refused to sit, that it was a good idea to keep the cap on her pen. She knew what he wanted, so she kept reading and said nothing.

Kennedy wanted final review on things like this. Rapp wasn't so sure that was a good idea, but she had a better grasp of the big picture than he did. She was the boss and ultimately it was her pretty little neck on the chopping block. If the pin got pulled, Rapp would jump on the grenade without hesitation, but the vultures on the Hill would want her hide too. Rapp respected her, which was no small thing. He was a loner. He'd been trained to operate independently, to survive in the field all on his own for months at a time. For some people that type of work would be unnerving. For Rapp it was Valhalla. No paperwork, no one looking over his shoulder. No risk-averse bureaucrat second-guessing his every move. Complete autonomy. They had created him and now they had to deal with him.

Guys like Rapp didn't do well taking orders unless it was from someone they really respected. Fortunately, Kennedy had that respect, and she had the clout to make things happen, or as in this case, simply look the other way while he took care of things. That's all Rapp wanted. What he preferred, actually. He didn't need her to sign off or give him the green light. She just needed to give him the file back, say good night, and that would be the end of it. Or the beginning, depending on how you wanted to look at it.

Rapp had the assets in place. He could join them in the morning and be done with it in twelve hours or less if there weren't any surprises, and on this one there wouldn't be. This guy was a moron of the highest order. He would never know what hit him. The problem was in the stir it might create. The aftermath. Personally, Rapp couldn't care less, but he knew if Kennedy hesitated, that would be the reason.

Kennedy closed the file and removed her reading glasses. She set them down on her desk and began rubbing her eyes. Rapp watched her. He knew her well. As well as he knew anyone. The rubbing of the eyes was not a good sign. That meant her head hurt, and in all likelihood the discomfort was due to the pile of crap he'd just dumped on her desk.

"Let me guess," she said as she looked up at him with tired eyes, "you want to eliminate him."

Rapp nodded.

"Why is it that your solution always involves killing someone?"

Rapp shrugged. "It tends to be more permanent that way."

The director of the CIA looked disappointed. She shook her head and placed her hand on the closed file.

"What do you want me to say, Irene? I'm not into rehabilitation. This guy had his chance. The French had him locked up for almost two years. He's been out for six months, and he's already back to his same old tricks."

"Have you bothered to think of the fallout?"

"Not really my forte?"

She glared at him.

"I've already talked to our French colleagues. They're as pissed off as we are. It's their damn politicians and that goofy judge who let the idiot go."

Kennedy couldn't deny the fact. She'd talked to her counterpart in France at length about this individual and several others, and he was not happy with his country's decision to set the radical Islamic cleric free. The counterterrorism people in France didn't like it any more than they did.

"This guy is a known entity," Kennedy said. "The press has written about him. They covered his release. If he turns up dead, they're going to jump all over it."

"Let them jump. It'll last a day or two . . . maybe a week at the most, and then they'll move onto something else. Besides . . . it'll serve as a good message to all of these idiots who think they can operate in the West without fear."

She looked back at him, her eyes revealing nothing. "What about the president? He's going to want to know if we had a hand in it."

Rapp shrugged. "Tell him you don't know anything about it."

Kennedy frowned. "I don't like lying to him."

"Then tell him to ask me about it. He'll get the picture, and he'll drop it. He knows the game."

Kennedy leaned back in her chair and crossed her legs. She looked at the far wall and said, more to herself than to Rapp, "He's a cleric."

"He's a radical thug who is perverting the Koran for his own sadistic needs. He raises money for terrorist groups, he recruits young impressionable kids to become suicide bombers, and he's doing it right in our own backyard."

"And that's another problem. Just how do you think the Canadians are going to react to this?"

"Publicly . . . I'm sure some of them will be upset, but privately they'll want to give us a medal. We've already talked to the Mounted Police and the Security Intelligence Service . . . they wish they could deport the idiot, but their solicitor general is hell-bent on proving that he's Mr. PC. We even have an intercept where two SIS guys are talking about how they could make the guy disappear."

"You're not serious?"

"Damn straight. Coleman and his team picked it up this week."

Kennedy studied him. "I have no doubt that our colleagues will privately applaud this man's death, but that still doesn't address the political fallout."

Rapp did not want to get involved in the politics of this. He'd lose if that's where they ended up going. "Listen . . . it's bad enough when these religious psychos do their thing over in Saudi Arabia and Pakistan, but we sure as hell can't let it happen here in North America. To be honest with you, I hope the press does cover this . . . and I hope the rest of these zealots get the message loud and clear that we're playing for keeps. Irene, we're in the middle of a damn war, and we need to start acting like it."

She didn't like it, but she agreed. With a resigned tone she asked, "How are you going to do it?"

"Coleman's team has been in place for six days watching him. This guy operates like clockwork. No real security to worry about. We can either walk up and pop him on the street, in which case we might have to hit anyone who's with him, or we can take him out with a silenced rifle from a block or two away. I prefer the rifle shot. With the right guy, the odds are as good and there's less downside."

Her index finger traced a number on file and she asked, "Can you make him disappear?"

"With enough time, money, and manpower I can do anything, but why complicate things?"

"The impact will be significantly reduced if the press doesn't have a body to photograph."

"I can't make any promises, but I'll look into it."

Kennedy began nodding her head slowly. "All right. Number-one rule, Mitch, don't get caught."

"Goes without saying. I'm very into self-preservation."

"I know . . . all I'm saying is if you can come up with a way for him to never be found, it might help."

"Understood." Rapp reached down and grabbed the file. "Anything else?"

"Yes. When you get back I need you to meet with someone. Two people, actually."

"Who?"

She shook her head. "When you get back, Mitch. Meanwhile, you have my consent. Make it happen, and call me as soon as you're done."

2

Mecca, Saudi Arabia

"I want a man killed."

The words were spoken too loudly, in front of far too many people and in a setting that hadn't heard such frank talk in decades. Twenty-eight men, bodyguards included, were standing or sitting in the opulent reception hall of Prince Muhammad bin Rashid's palace in Mecca. Rashid was the Saudis' minister for Islamic affairs, a very important position in the Kingdom. The palace was where he liked to hold his weekly majlis, or audience, in the desert sheik tradition. Some came to ask favors, many more came just to stay close to the prince, and undoubtedly there were a few who came to spy on behalf of Rashid's half brother King Abdullah.

With the utterance of this blunt request any pretense of discreet eavesdropping, normally an art form at these weekly audiences, was dropped. Heads swiveled in the direction of the prince as words hung on lips half spoken.

Prince Muhammad bin Rashid did not look up, but could feel the collective gaze of the men around him. He had felt only the briefest discomfort at his friend's brazen request, and it wasn't because it involved killing. Rashid had expected that. For some time now he'd been feeding his friend the information that would incite this desperate plea. In truth the only thing that annoyed him was that his old friend would be so reckless as to utter such a thing in front of so many who could not be trusted. The Kingdom had become a very dangerous place, even for a man as powerful as Muhammad bin Rashid.

Rashid clasped the kneeling man's hand and carefully considered his reply. The request, and what was said next, would be repeated all over the Kingdom and possibly beyond by sunset. There was a division in the House of Saud. Brother had been pitted against brother, and Rashid knew he needed to be very careful. Royal family members had already been killed and many more would die before it was over. His chief adversary was the king himself, a weak-kneed leader who all too often lent his ear to the Americans.

Resisting his cultural tendency toward bravado he chided, "You must not speak of such things, Saeed. I know the loss of your son has been difficult, but you must remember Allah is mighty, and vengeance is his."

The man replied angrily, "But we are instruments of Allah, and I demand my own vengeance. It is my right."

The prince looked up from the pained face of his old friend, who was kneeling before him, and gestured for his aides to clear the room. He then reached out and touched the knee of a man sitting to his right, signaling for him to stay.

After the room was cleared, the prince looked sternly at his friend and said, "You lay at my feet a very serious request."

Tears welled in the eyes of Saeed Ahmed Abdullah. "The infidels have killed my son. He was a good boy." He turned his anguished face to the man Rashid had asked to stay: Sheik Ahmed al-Ghamdi, the spiritual leader of the Great Mosque in Mecca. "My son was a true believer who answered the call to jihad. He sacrificed everything while so many others do nothing." Saeed looked around the large room hoping to direct some of his anger at the privileged class who talked bravely, threw around money, but gave no blood of their own. He'd been so immersed in his own pain he hadn't even noticed they'd all left.

Sheik Ahmed nodded benevolently. "Waheed was a brave warrior."

"Very brave." Saeed looked back to his old friend. "We have known each other for a long time. Have I ever been an unreasonable man? Have I ever burdened you with trivial requests?"

Rashid shook his head.

"I would not be here now asking for this if the cowards in Riyadh had honored my simple request and stood up to the Americans. All I asked for was the body of my youngest child, so that I could give him a proper burial. Instead, I am told he was defiled by Mitch Rapp so as to intentionally bar him from paradise. What would you expect me to do?"

Rashid sighed and said, "What is it you ask of me?"

"I want you to kill a man for me. It is no more complicated than that. An eye for an eye."

He studied his friend cautiously. "That is no small request."

"I would do it myself," Saeed said eagerly, "but I am naïve in such things, whereas you, my old friend, have many contacts in the world of espionage."

For eight years Rashid had been Saudi Arabia's minister of the Interior, which oversaw the police and intelligence services. Then after 9/11 he was shamefully dismissed by his half brother, the crown prince, who had caved into pressure from the Americans. Yes, Rashid had the contacts. In fact he had just the person in mind for the job. "Who is this man you want killed?"

"His name is Rapp . . . Mitch Rapp."

The prince concealed his joy. Rashid had been planning this moment for months. It had started when his friend had asked him to find out what had happened to his son, who had left the kingdom to fight in Afghanistan. Rashid had used his sources in the intelligence community and discovered a great deal more than he ever revealed. Slowly, he fed his old friend the information that he knew would lead him to demand nothing short of vengeance.

"Saeed, do you know what you ask of me?" The prince spoke in a well-rehearsed and dire voice. "Do you have any idea who this Mitch Rapp is?"

"He is an assassin, he is an infidel, and he is the man responsible for the death and defilement of my son. That is all I need to know."

"I must caution you," Rashid said very deliberately, "this Mitch Rapp is an extremely dangerous man. He is rumored to be a favorite of the American president and the king as well."

"He is an infidel," the bereaved father repeated as he turned to the religious man. "I have listened to your sermons. Are we not in a war for the survival of Islam? Have you not told us to take up arms against the infidels?"

What little face that could be seen through the thick gray beard showed nothing. The sheik simply closed his eyes and nodded.

Saeed looked back to the prince, his old friend. "I am not a politician or a statesman, or a man of God. I am a businessman. I don't expect either of you to publicly or privately support what I am going to do. All I am asking, Rashid, is that you point me in the right direction. Give me a name and I will handle the rest."

With the exception of Saeed's public proclamation, Rashid couldn't have been more pleased with how things were proceeding. He had predicted his friend's response almost perfectly. He sat stolidly, not wanting to appear too eager. "Saeed, I know of a man who is very skilled in what you ask. He is extremely expensive, but knowing you as well as I do, I doubt that will be an issue."

Saeed nodded his head vigorously. He had easily made billions, first by putting up phone and power lines around the kingdom and other countries in the region and now by laying thousands of miles of fiber-optic cable.

"I will send him to see you, but you must make no mention of our meeting here today to him or to anyone else. I share your anger, and I wish you success, but you must give me your word as my oldest friend that you will never speak of my role in this to anyone. The Kingdom is a very dangerous place these days, and there are brothers of mine who would not be as sympathetic to your plight as I." Rashid's reference to Saudi Arabia's pro-American government was obvious.

Saeed sneered. "There is much I would like to say, but as you said the Kingdom is a very dangerous place these days. You have my word. I will speak of this to no one. Not even to the man you send."

"Good," smiled Rashid. He stood and helped his friend to his feet. The two began walking across the cavernous room, leaving the cleric sitting alone. "Because, my friend, if you succeed in killing Mr. Rapp, and the Americans find out you were behind it, the king will cut off your head. If you fail, and Mr. Rapp finds out you were behind it . . . he will visit you and your family with more pain than you can imagine."

Saeed nodded. "How will I recognize the man you send?"

"He is a German. There will be no mistaking him. He is infinitely capable. Just tell him what you want, and he will take care of the rest."

3

MONTREAL, CANADA

Rapp arrived the next morning on a Falcon 2000 executive jet leased through a front company in Virginia. A certified pilot, Rapp was the acting copilot on the flight and was dressed accordingly. With the uniform, and a well-used, but fake passport, he breezed through a cursory customs inspection at the private airport and hailed a cab to the hotel where the team was staying. It was Saturday morning. The team's seventh day. There were four of them, including Coleman. Their history with Rapp went back a decade and a half. Each knew how the others operated, and they all trusted one another, which in their line of work was no small thing.

Coleman was waiting for him in the hotel room, ready to bring him up to speed on the tactical situation. The other three men were out keeping an eye on the target. The former SEAL was about an inch shorter than Rapp. He normally kept his blond hair close cropped, but he'd let it grow out, so it spilled over the top of his ears and touched his shirt collar in back. There was a wave to it with a slight curl. He was lean and athletic, but had a relaxed way about him that could be very deceptive. Confident in his abilities, he no longer felt the need to prove anything. He had done it all, survived some really nasty stuff, and lived to keep his mouth shut. That was the way of the SEALs. They might exchange war stories with each other, or other operators, but that was as far as it went. They were a tight fraternity—one that didn't like braggarts.

Rapp set his flight bag down on the one bed and looked down at the map spread out on the other one.

"Here's the hotel, here's the mosque"—Coleman pointed to one spot and then the other—"and here's his apartment."

Rapp looked down at the map of downtown Montreal and the surrounding neighborhoods. "How long does it take him to walk from the mosque to the apartment?"

"He averages five minutes and twenty-three seconds. Quickest time is four minutes and eighteen seconds. He was late for prayer and in a hurry. Longest time was just over ten minutes. He stopped to talk to someone along the way."

"Any signs of surveillance by the police or the intelligence service?"

"Nothing."

Rapp frowned. "That's strange."

"I thought so at first, but then I got to thinking that maybe they've got someone on the inside."

"A fellow worshiper?"

"Yeah." Coleman pointed to an eight-by-ten surveillance photo of the mosque. "We've picked up some chatter. Not everyone agrees with his radical interpretation of the Koran."

Rapp's right eyebrow shot up in surprise. "You've got the mosque wired?"

"No. We've been able to monitor the worshipers as they come and go using parabolic mikes. Caught a couple older guys yesterday after Khalil delivered his Friday afternoon sermon. They think he's a cancer in their community. A bad influence on the kids. Filling their heads with all of this talk of jihad and martyrdom."

This did not surprise Rapp. The overwhelming majority of Muslims did not agree with what these terrorists were doing in the name of Allah. Rapp just wished they were more vocal about it.

"Anything else?"

"Yeah. He's a real pious bastard, this one. We got into his apartment yesterday during the afternoon sermon. The whole building empties out, so we figured it was pretty safe. We took a look at his computer." Coleman extracted a memory stick from his pocket. "Copied his hard drive for you."

Rapp grinned and took it. "Thank you."

"It's filled with porn."

"No way?"

"Dead serious. A lot of really kinky shit. Mostly bondage."

Rapp studied the memory stick. "You just never know with these idiots, do you?"

"Nope, but it doesn't surprise me one bit."

"Yeah, I suppose you're right. They're all running from something. What else?"

"Best spot to hit him is obviously between the mosque and the apartment. Five round trips a day. Before sunup, just after noon, late afternoon, just after sunset, and then my favorite . . . his ten o'clock trip."

"Why not early in the morning?"

"It would work," said Coleman, "but the sunrise call to prayer has double the attendance that the evening one does. By the time he heads home it's almost eleven, and the streets are empty."

"He walks alone?" Rapp asked, still not believing the intel report he'd received earlier in the week.

"Yep."

This guy was a real moron, but pretty typical when you looked at his early years. Khalil Muhammad, Egyptian by birth, had grown up in the clutches of an offshoot of the Muslim Brotherhood, indoctrinated into the strict unyielding brand of Islam perpetuated and funded by the Wahhabis out of Saudi Arabia. At the age of fifteen he and a group of peers stoned a reporter to death for writing an article that was critical of the madrasa they attended. The religious school he attended had sent every single one of its graduates off to fight in the Afghani war against the Soviets. It was rumored that many had been sent against their will.

While the others stood trial for the stoning, Khalil fled to Saudi Arabia, where he received further religious instruction at the hands of the Wahhabis. In his early twenties he completed his studies and became an Imam. At twenty-six he immigrated to Canada with the express purpose of building a new mosque and spreading the Wahhabi faith to North America. His mosque grew rapidly and as a reward he was granted funding to build a second mosque in France.

Khalil's comings and goings went unnoticed for the most part. Until 9/11. After that everything changed. When Khalil was finally arrested by the French it was due to his involvement in a plot to pull off a Madrid-style train bombing in Paris. He had recruited six young men, none of them over the age of seventeen, to act as martyrs. Khalil had promised them great rewards in paradise. They would be purified and exalted. They would be remembered as heroes and their families would be taken care of and given great respect. His recruits would do all the heavy lifting.

Khalil would remain in the shadows. It would have worked, but the CIA was already on to Khalil. The hackers at Langley were breaking through firewalls as fast as they could in an effort to track the money the Saudis were sending overseas. They stumbled across Khalil and alerted the French DST.

When the authorities went to raid his apartment they came up with nothing incriminating. But the dogs that had come along on the raid seemed unusually interested in a separate apartment down the hall. They broke down the door and found suicide vests and enough explosives to level the building. Khalil went to jail along with the six boys. They all kept their mouths shut and there they sat for over a year while the intelligence services tried to figure out how much they could tell the police without giving away the family jewels. By the time the case ended up in front of a judge, Franco-American relations were near an all-time low. The judge was appalled by the lack of hard evidence put forth by the state. In the case of Khalil, no crime had been committed. He was a religious man who was guilty of nothing more than association with some bad apples. The judge ordered his immediate release. The six boys were charged with possession of dangerous materials and given a paltry sentence. Khalil was sent back to Canada. Within a week he was back in his mosque calling the young men to jihad and decrying the very authorities who protected his right to do so. The French judge had infused him with a false sense of invincibility.

In truth Rapp had bigger problems to worry about, but this guy had gotten under his skin. Three weeks earlier in Afghanistan a car had smashed into a barricade outside a U.S. facility. When the guards approached they found a rock on the gas pedal and a semiconscious boy chained to the steering wheel. The car was filled with explosives which thankfully didn't go off due to a faulty detonator. The boy was cut free and soon afterward began telling his story to anyone who would listen. He said that his parents had immigrated to Canada from Yemen when he was a child. Sheik Khalil Muhammad had arranged for him to go to Saudi Arabia for religious instruction, but upon arriving in Mecca he was bound, gagged, and knocked unconscious. The next thing he remembered was being pulled from the car by American soldiers.

All of this information was passed on to the Canadian Security Intelligence Service who in turn tried to question Khalil about the boy's kidnapping. Khalil became instantly belligerent and got his lawyer and the Muslim Council of Montreal involved. Canada's solicitor general, a wimp if there ever was one, balked at the specter of being labeled intolerant, and yanked on the Intelligence Service's chain. They were told to stay away from Khalil and his mosque. People went missing all the time the world over. Just because the kid got grabbed did not mean Khalil had a hand in it.

Rapp was not so trusting. He put Marcus Dumond, his best hacker, on the case and within thirty-six hours Dumond was coming up with all kinds of irregularities in Khalil's banking records. He was still up to his neck in Wahhabi money, and he had also sent two other boys to Saudi Arabia for religious instruction. Thus far they had not been able to verify if the kids were actually in school, but the parents had confirmed that they had not heard from their children in several months. They had been told it would probably be a year before they would hear from them due to the strict religious regimen of the school. Rapp smelled a rat, and the rat was Khalil Muhammad.

There were worse offenders out there, to be sure, but this one was too close to home. Too brazen. Who knew what he would try next if he was left unchecked? No, it was better to deal with him now. Make an example of him. Kennedy wanted him to disappear, but Rapp had an even better idea. The more he mulled it over the more he liked it.

Rapp walked over to the window, looked out at the gray sky, and said, "All right, here's what we're going to do."

4

I t was a cool, crisp evening and perfect walking weather, so that's what
Rapp did. He wanted to get his blood flowing. The collar of his black
leather coat was turned up, and a worn Montreal Canadiens hat sat
on his head. He'd picked up both at a thrift store as well as a pair of jeans
and hiking boots. He paid in cash and was grateful there weren't any surveillance cameras. The jacket was perfect, at least in terms of what he was
looking for. It had big square oversized pockets in the front. Good for
holding weapons. No flaps. Good for extracting weapons. There was a
tear on the left shoulder seam, but that was all right. He wouldn't be
hanging out at the Ritz. Both the mosque and Khalil's apartment were in
a rundown part of town. It was a pity he couldn't keep the jacket, but
there was a pretty good chance he was going to get blood on it. This one
was going to be messy. When it was over everything he was wearing
would be thrown into a garbage bag and tossed into the St. Lawrence
River.

Rapp kept his hands stuffed in the oversized pockets and his chin
down. In the left pocket was a tactical Rip Cord knife, and in his right
pocket a silenced 9mm Glock 26. He'd brought both weapons into the
country concealed in the false bottom of his flight bag. Since the
CIA, through a subsidiary, leased a large portion of the private airport
in Virginia, it was easy to get the bag past security, and upon landing in
Canada he did not have to worry about having his flight bag x-rayed.
The gun was there as a precaution. The knife would be the instru-

ment of choice. The intent was to send a message. Actually several messages.

He'd seen all the photographs, memorized the street maps, noted the vague patterns of the police squads that patrolled the neighborhood. Compared to most of the ops he'd run, this one ranked pretty low on the risk meter. When Rapp told Coleman what he wanted to do, the former Navy SEAL took it in stride. He asked a few questions, and tried to poke a hole in the plan, but didn't try too hard. The plan was solid, the target was a lamb. That's what they called guys like Khalil. Guys who couldn't bite back. The only real concern was the police, but they weren't very aggressive in their patrols. Once an hour at the most.

Coleman knew better than to argue with Rapp. There were more than a few people back in DC who would flip if they knew he was planning on exposing himself like this, but unlike them, Coleman had seen him in action enough to defer to the younger man's expertise. Rapp was the perfect balance of athleticism, grace, and skill. Coleman had worked with the best, and he was one of them himself. The tight fraternity of Special Forces operators was made up of men who were pushed and trained to the absolute limits. He'd known a few guys who were better shots than Rapp, a few more who were stronger, and maybe only one or two who could match his endurance. But they all lacked Rapp's experience, which is the one thing training can never fully substitute for. His operational instincts were unsurpassed. He could take a look at a tactical situation and dissect it in seconds, coming up with the most efficient way to get from point A to B.

So there was no arguing. Rapp would be the man on the ground. Coleman and his team were manning the surveillance, and in place for backup in case anything went wrong. No one argued with Rapp's deployment of assets. In truth the men were bored. Six days of surveillance on a guy who was this careless got old real quick. Coleman and his team were restless. The sooner Rapp got it over with the happier they'd be. They'd go back to America. They'd get paid in cash, and they'd get on with their families, friends, and jobs.

Rapp was not trying to prove anything. He didn't need to. Especially to these men. They'd seen him handle far more difficult situations. There was nothing brave or bold about what he was about to do. It wasn't like he was charging a machine-gun nest or taking down a building with men shooting back at him. But in the interest of expediency he was going to handle this one. He wanted it done a certain way, and didn't want to have to explain it to Coleman and his men. It was just better if he did it himself.

Rapp entered the alley from the east. He was wearing a tiny wireless earpiece and Coleman was giving him updates.

"That's the one. Turn left."

Rapp didn't reply. He simply turned and started down the dirty alley. He was in a two-story canyon of bricks and mortar. At the street level on each side were dry cleaners, video rental, restaurants, an electronics store, and a menagerie of restaurants and the other businesses that dot the urban landscape of any big city. The second stories consisted of offices and a few apartments. Coleman and his team had done a good job. This was a perfect site for the takedown.

Rapp stepped around a foul-smelling puddle of liquid and checked the windows on the second story. Only two lights were on. They were both near the middle of the block. The street lights at both ends had been taken care of earlier in the week along with seven other lights in the neighborhood. One of Coleman's men had walked around with a .22-caliber silenced pistol and shot them out. It was Urban Espionage 101. Their way of prepping the battlefield. They'd monitored the police scanner while doing it to make sure no one had called it in. In a big city like this it would take months before the lights would get fixed. And in the meantime someone like Khalil would have a few days to adjust to the change in his environment.

Coleman reported that they'd watched Khalil walk home that first night after they'd shot out the lights. He didn't even notice the change. Rapp couldn't believe it. This guy was incredibly stupid. Had no concept of the gravity of the situation he'd involved himself in. Here he was recruiting young men to go off and fight for his extremist arcane view of Islam, and he honestly thought he was safe just because a liberal Canadian official was afraid of being labeled intolerant.

Rapp was a soldier in a war, and this Khalil was an enemy combatant. No, that wasn't right. If he'd gone into battle himself he would've been a combatant and maybe Rapp could have given the man an ounce of respect. Like suicide bombers. Politics aside, calling them cowards couldn't be further from the truth. It took a pair of balls to strap on a vest filled with explosives, walk into a crowd, and blow yourself up. It also took a sick, twisted, and warped mind, but they weren't cowards.

Rapp would not lose any sleep over this one. Not that he normally did anyway. Khalil was a coward. He stood up in his *minbar,* the pulpit in a mosque, every Friday and spewed his vitriolic hatred for the West and especially America. He poisoned the young minds of impressionable men and duped them into joining his jihad. Then he and his fellow cowards enslaved these young men and turned them into human bombs. Khalil risked nothing, and Rapp would feel nothing.

Rapp reached the other end of the alley. It was perfectly dark. A sliver of a moon was rising in the east, barely adding to the ambient light of the city itself. The wall where he wanted to stage the incident was just as Coleman had said. A good ten feet of brick and then a Dumpster. The concealment was ideal. Even a worthy adversary would have little chance against an ambush like this. Of course if it was a worthy adversary, he'd skip the knife and use the silenced gun. Rapp's eyes adjusted to the extremely faint light. He squatted down to get a better look at the ground and found a soda can and several beer bottles. He quietly picked them up with his gloved hands and set them under the Dumpster. The last thing he needed was to kick something like a beer bottle and alert the target that he was behind him.

Rapp settled in against the brick wall. Any minute now. He'd timed his arrival so he wouldn't be left standing around exposed for too long. Coleman's voice came over his earpiece and announced that Khalil was locking the front door to the mosque. Several men were standing outside talking to him. Nothing unusual, reported Coleman. Now Khalil was on the move and headed Rapp's way.

Rapp leaned against the wall. Flexed his legs and hands. Cracked his neck to the left and then the right. The blood was flowing, his heart rate was right where he wanted it to be. He was at that perfect equilibrium between being too loose or too tight. He was poised on the balls of his feet, ready to get it over with.

The first sign of trouble came almost immediately. Coleman's gravelly voice came over Rapp's earpiece with a tone of frustration. "We've got a problem. He's not alone."

Rapp's eyes stayed fixed on the brick wall opposite his position. A small mike was pinned to the collar of his jacket. He whispered, "How many?"

"Our guy plus two."

"Shit," Rapp muttered under his breath. "Do we have an ID on the other two?"

"Negative."

Rapp pictured in his mind how it would play out. One additional guy would be okay. One quick pistol butt to the back of the neck and he'd be out cold. A leg sweep on Khalil and he'd be on his back before he ever knew what hit him. Three, though, was a problem. It would take less than a second to shoot all three in the back of the head, but killing the two unknowns was not an option. Not Rapp's style. If he tried to knock the other two out and then take Khalil it could get messy. One of them might get away or at least scream and alert some of the neighbors. Or worse, if they were armed, one of them might shoot him.

"I think we should abort," said Coleman.

"Negative. Let's see how it plays out. How much time do I have?"

"Approximately three minutes until he reaches you."

Rapp nodded to himself. Three minutes was a long time. He played a few more scenarios out in his mind. They all came up short. The problem was how he wanted it to look. He could easily shoot Khalil and tell the others to run, but then he'd end up with the exact mess that Kennedy wanted to avoid. Maybe he'd just follow the idiot right into his apartment and cap him.

"One of the guys just peeled off," Coleman said.

"Good," said Rapp. "We're back on. Everyone look sharp. Two isn't a problem. Hold your positions unless I give the word."

Rapp flexed his hands again and edged over to the corner. He looked left then right. The street was empty. No pedestrians. No cars. Coleman and the others relayed the position of the two men like it was a countdown for a shuttle launch, but instead of using seconds they were using blocks. Rapp's pulse picked up a bit as they neared. Nothing unusual, just the body getting ready for action. The adrenaline would begin to kick in a bit, and then he'd have to move or he'd get that lead in the boots feeling. They were getting close. Rapp shifted his weight from one foot to the other and then bounced from side to side like a boxer stepping into the ring.

There was a minivan with tinted windows parked thirty feet away. In the cargo area one of Coleman's men was watching intently, ready to pop the door at the first sign of trouble. He was armed with a silenced pistol. No need for anything more powerful. At the opposite end of the block, Coleman would now be taking up position with the second van. If anything should go wrong three separate rallying points were already set.

If things went well, they'd simply dispose of Rapp's clothes, and head back to the hotel, catch a few hours of sleep, and fly out first thing in the morning.

Rapp could hear them now. They were speaking in Arabic. He could hear their footfalls on the cement sidewalk. There were two men. Rapp could tell by the noise. One of them dragged his feet and the other one was a heel-to-toe walker. Coleman's calm voice came over the tiny earpiece.

"Khalil is closer to you. The other man is walking on the street side. Both of them have their hands in their pockets."

Rapp pictured them in his mind. He had no idea if either man was armed, but with the element of surprise on his side it wouldn't matter. He actually preferred that they had their hands in their pockets. If it was someone with more experience it would worry him, but not with these two. Khalil truly was a moron. Anyone with half a brain would vary the route he took to and from the mosque. He would notice that the streetlights that were working a week ago were now out. He would step out onto the street when approaching a blind alley. He would be aware of his surroundings. But this guy wasn't.

They were close now. Coleman was counting down their approach, and Rapp could clearly hear their conversation. They would appear in just a few seconds. Rapp turned toward the sidewalk and dropped to a crouch, ready to spring. He had decided to keep his left hand free. He held the gun in his right. He saw their long shadows appear, cast from a streetlight down at the other end of the block. Time slowed. All of his senses heightened. At the other end of the long, dark alley he heard the rattling engine of a late model car as it passed by. He was perfectly concealed in the dark canyon. His entire body coiled, ready to strike.

They appeared side by side. Rapp held his position. Let them pass so their peripheral vision would not be able to detect him. He slowly rose up, but only a foot. He took his first silent step, and then his second. He was exposed now, and he moved quickly, still in a crouch. At the last second he stood to his full height. He was up on the balls of his feet, his weight leaning slightly forward. Both men were within reach and neither of them so much as flinched. Rapp's right hand came crashing down, the grip of the pistol striking the unknown man on the back right side of his neck. Rapp had rethought his original plan. Instead of using a leg sweep, he planted his left foot, spun to the right, dropped down a few feet and delivered a hammerlike blow to Khalil's right kidney.

Rapp continued through the move, looking to his right to make sure the other guy was out of commission. The man was falling face-first to the sidewalk, his hands limp at his sides. He was already unconscious. Khalil's mouth was open, gasping for air. His back arched, his hands reaching for the area where he'd been hit. His neck was completely exposed. He might as well already be dead. Rapp's left hand shot up and clamped down on the terrorist's throat like the jaws of some lethal carnivore. Rapp was now eye to eye with Khalil, positioned as if they were dance partners doing some intricate move. The man's eyes spoke of pure fear, which was probably the same expression worn by the young boys when they realized they were strapped behind the wheel of a car filled with explosives.

With the man's neck firmly in the grasp of his gloved hand, Rapp forced Khalil's chin up and began driving him back into the shadows of the alley. A basic tenet of hand-to-hand combat is that the body goes where the head goes. Khalil wrapped his hands around Rapp's forearm, but it was already too late. His larynx half crushed, his body completely off balance, Khalil could do nothing but watch in absolute horror as the final seconds of his life played out before him like some awful nightmare. It was the perfect justice for a man who had preached terror and hatred for over two decades.

Rapp accelerated his move, wrenching Khalil's head back as far as it would go. The man was beyond stumbling. He was on his way down, and there was nothing that would keep him on his feet. Rapp used Khalil's weight against him. At the last second he thrust his left arm out like a piston and slammed the back of Khalil's head into the hard unforgiving pavement. The man's entire body went limp a split second after impact. There was a good chance the blow was fatal, but Rapp wasn't about to leave anything to chance.

He wasted no time. He put the gun back in his pocket, spun, took a few steps, and grabbed the feet of the other man. Coleman and his team were under specific orders not to get out of their vehicles unless Rapp called for them. Rapp dragged the unknown man into the alley and deposited him next to the Dumpster. Next, he grabbed Khalil under the arms and propped him up against the brick wall of the building. Everything was done without hesitation and with great efficiency. Rapp grabbed the knife from his left pocket, pressed the button and heard the spring-loaded blade snap into position. Standing off to the right, Rapp placed his right hand on Khalil's forehead and stuck the blade into the man's neck just beneath his right ear. The hard steel went in with little trouble. Rapp then gripped the knife firmly and drew the weapon across Khalil's neck, slicing him from one ear to the other.

5

At first glance the man appeared to fit in. He was wearing the traditional garb of a Saudi businessman. A white *thawb*, or robe made of cotton, was draped over his shoulders and stopped short of his ankles, and his sandy brown hair was covered with a *ghutra* and tied with an ornamental rope to keep it in place. Upon closer inspection, though, there were telltale signs that he was not native to the Arabian Peninsula. His skin was tan, but not the right shade, he was clean shaven and wearing heavy-soled black dress shoes instead of sandals, and above all else, his eyes were a muted blue, almost gray color. At the moment, however, those eyes were concealed behind a large pair of black sunglasses.

It was only 9:00 a.m. in Riyadh, and the temperature was pushing 100 degrees. Erich Abel didn't mind the heat, though. He actually preferred it. Having grown up asthmatic, he found the dry arid climate of Saudi Arabia's capital far preferable to the humid weather of the coastal cities on the Red Sea. Abel had a genuine interest in Saudi Arabia. Not because of the climate, really, or even because of the people. It had more to do with how it would soon shape history. It was an exciting place to conduct business.

The former East German spy believed in going native. It was the only way to really understand a culture. In truth, though, that was only part of the reason he wore the traditional Arab garb. The reality was, Saudi Arabia had become a very dangerous place for Westerners. Kidnapping was of course a constant possibility, but anyone dumb enough to grab him would return him as soon as they found out who he worked for, and then they would beg forgiveness at the foot of Prince Muhammad. The real problem was the increase in random killings by the crazed Wahhabis. There was great unrest in the desert kingdom, and it was very important to be as inconspicuous as possible.

If Abel had a true talent in life it was predicting change. When he'd worked for the Stasi, the ruthless and much feared East German Secret Police, he'd been the only one in his office to predict the collapse of communism and the fall of the Berlin Wall. He'd passed his reports up the chain of command, and they'd all told him he was too young to know what he was talking about. Just twenty-nine when the wall fell, Abel was looked upon as an overeducated intellectual by the cold-blooded ranks within Stasi headquarters in East Berlin. The Stasi prided itself on a certain crass ruthlessness that Abel lacked. Truth be told, he would have fit in better with the British foreign intelligence service, MI6. Abel had great respect for the Brits. They ran creative operations and took great joy in outwitting their adversaries. The Stasi was more like a very efficient and ruthless American organized crime family. At any rate, no one wanted to hear his predictions that their reign of terror was drawing to an end.

Abel had been a sickly child, in and out of hospitals. When he was out, he spent much of his time in bed with barely the strength to read. While the other kids advanced physically, he advanced intellectually. He graduated from university early, at the age of twenty and with dual degrees in math and economics, and was recruited by the Stasi. The employment opportunities in East Germany in the early eighties were not good. That fact combined with the idea of doing some bullying after being picked on for much of his youth appealed to him in a perversely satisfying way.

For the first three years with the Stasi he pushed to get transferred from the analytical side to the operations side, but his delicate appearance always prevented him from reaching his goal. Abel stood five feet ten inches tall, but back then he weighed just 145 pounds. Slowly, he put on weight and spent every moment of his free time working out in hopes that he could pass the physical requirements needed to get out from behind his desk.

He was rewarded in his fourth year by a transfer to operations and began taking part in the systematic kidnappings of Westerners who traveled to East Germany. Abel would help identify targets and sometimes even lure them into traps. His baby face and slight stature meant he could pass for a young teenage boy. Homosexual businessmen who traveled to the east were easy targets for blackmail. Abel would loiter on the appropriate corner, or park, or bar and wait for a man to come along and make a lewd request. He'd give the proper hand signal and the other members would swoop in, throw the man into the back of a van, then dump him in an interrogation room. The man would then be told he could choose between jail and public humiliation, or he could buy his freedom. Abel recalled, all these years later, that all of them but one chose to buy their freedom. That stubborn son of a bitch was eventually taken to an extremely harsh location where after a month of beatings he was strangled to death by a very sadistic and homophobic Stasi officer.

Each kidnapping would usually yield several thousand marks. The Stasi had contacts in almost all of the western banks and they would do their homework before they named the price of freedom. His ultimate catch was a West German noble who brought in $500,000. The man was in their custody for less than twenty-four hours. Abel estimated that his unit alone had brought in over five million dollars in a two-and-a-half-year period.

After that he was promoted to counterintelligence, which gave him reason to travel to West Germany more frequently. He was just getting involved in some serious spycraft when everything fell apart. He'd been warning his superiors for months that the signs were there, but they were too busy shuttling back and forth to Moscow kissing the asses of their KGB bosses. The last thing they wanted to do was tell the autocrats at the KGB that they were losing control of the Soviet Union's westernmost European satellite. Such news was likely to get them marched out back and shot in the head.

Abel had studied the economics of East versus West. He knew the numbers manufactured by the governments in East Germany and Russia to be false. As a general rule, he divided them in half in order to recalibrate for exaggeration and deception. The West, however, was a different matter. The evil capitalists had these things called corporations, and these corporations had a fiduciary responsibility to be honest with their shareholders. An amazing amount of data was public information. Every time Abel ran the numbers he came away with the same conclusion. They were getting their asses handed to them by the West, and they were about to collapse under the weight of their lies and economic inefficiencies. The empirical economic signs were right there for anyone who opened their eyes. The data on its own should have been enough, but Abel saw something else that was equally alarming.

The communist dictators stayed in power by using two tools. The first was intimidation. Through a network of secret police, phone taps, and informants the populace lived under constant fear that if they said anything critical of the government they would be snatched from their beds in the middle of the night and disappear forever. The other tool was not physical in the painful sense, but rather mind-numbing. It was the state-controlled media. The dull thrum of propaganda that George Orwell himself had predicted so eerily in his monumental novel *1984* was churned out day after day on state-run TV and radio and in the newspapers. Abel saw the rise of the information technology age for what it was and knew the German Democratic Republic was about to lose its monopoly on the news and thus on people's thoughts. A full year before the wall came down, unification had become a moot point for the young spy.

More than a decade and a half later, Abel got that same feeling when he visited Saudi Arabia. Change was afoot, and there was no stopping it. It wasn't whether it would happen or not, it was a matter of when. The hugely uneven distribution of wealth itself was forcing the country toward a boiling point. Add to that the supercharged religious component and Abel was willing to bet his life that Saudi Arabia was headed for serious upheaval.

The worldwide economic implications of such an event were staggering. Change for most people was stressful, but for Abel, it presented opportunity. He'd already made millions, but at forty-seven he had grander plans still, and large multinational corporations, international banks, investment houses, commodities firms, and even a few governments were listening to him this time. They were all paying him adequately for his services, but that wasn't enough for a man like Abel. Like a true German he believed one must always strive for efficiency and perfection in order to obtain complete self-realization. He'd built into all of his consulting contracts large bonuses that were contingent on his global predictions coming to pass. Some of those contracts were due to expire in the coming year, and Abel didn't like the idea of being right, but late. The revolution was going to take place. It was inevitable. He might as well profit from it.

Abel stopped in front of Abdullah Telecommunications and stared up at the benign, monolithic six-story building. As someone who grew up in Leipzig, a city famous for its Renaissance architecture, Abel couldn't have been more unimpressed. As much as the former spy tried to embrace the Saudi culture, its architecture was one thing that as far as he was concerned had no redeeming value whatsoever.

After checking with the man behind the large block of stone that fronted for a reception desk, Abel was told politely to wait. No more than thirty seconds later a very anxious man exited an elevator and walked stiffly and quickly across the lobby. The man extended his hand, and in English presented himself as one of Abdullah Telecommunications' senior vice presidents.

Knowing how Arab businesses worked, Abel was unimpressed with the title. A company like this was likely to have dozens if not hundreds of senior vice presidents—almost all of them related somehow to the main man, Saeed Ahmed Abdullah. They all collected sizable checks, maintained generous offices, and with the exception of a handful of Abdullah's most talented relatives, stayed out of the way of the Western consultants who ran the company's day-to-day operations. Abel and his escort took the elevator to the top floor, where Abel was walked through three separate sets of gold-plated doors. He was reverently deposited in a room that oozed Arab masculinity.

The mahogany-paneled walls were covered with the heads of exotic animals. In the center of the room, no more than ten feet away, a spotted leopard was staring him down with his glass eyes. The beast was mounted in a permanent state of agitation, which was conveyed through a snarl that fully exposed the deceased animal's jagged teeth. A large oil painting of a desert landscape hung above the granite mantelpiece of a fireplace that Abel assumed was never used. The entire room was intended to convey virility and strength. That was obvious. How far Abel should read into all of this he was not sure. Some of these Arab men used such decorations as a way to make their position in the pecking order crystal clear, while others did nothing more than pay an overpriced French interior decorator to do what he'd done for some other member of the royal family. They were not big on original thought or content.

A door at the far end of the room opened. Abel turned to see an older man dressed in traditional fashion come striding in. There was a look of tension on his face. Abel met him halfway, by the sneering feline.

"I am Saeed Ahmed Abdullah." The right hand was extended.

Abel was not surprised to hear the man speak English. It was the language of business in the Kingdom. "I am Erich Abel." The German took Saeed's hand. "Prince Muhammad asked me to come see you. He tells me the two of you are very dear old friends."

"We have known each other since the age of nine." Saeed gestured for his guest to sit. "Would you like something to drink?"

"Coffee would be fine, please." Abel sat on one of the long couches.

Saeed pressed a button on the nearby phone, rattled off instructions in Arabic, and then sat on a different couch. Almost immediately, a service cart was wheeled into the room by two Indonesian men in crisp white jackets. They served coffee and left small plates of delicious-looking pastries in front of each man, then vanished as silently as they'd entered.

"Prince Muhammad has been a very good friend to me." Saeed took a sip of coffee. "I think he has been treated unfairly by his brother the king."

Abel immediately thought the man a bit reckless for offering such a frank opinion to a stranger. Always cautious he replied, "I have great respect for Prince Muhammad."

Saeed reached for a pastry and then decided against it. "Did he explain to you my tragedy?"

It was obvious to Abel that his host was very anxious. "No, he merely told me that you were a dear friend, and he would consider it a favor if I would see you."

Saeed clasped his hands together and looked up at the painting of the landscape.

Abel took a sip of his coffee and then set it down. "Mr. Abdullah, let me be blunt. I am not a squeamish man. I doubt that you could shock me. Tell me why you seek my services, and I'm sure we'll be able to come to an agreement."

Saeed looked the German in the eyes and said, "I want a man killed."

Abel nodded casually, signaling that the request did not surprise him. "And who is this man that you would like eliminated?" he asked as he reached for his coffee.

"He is an American."

Abel took a sip of the rich coffee as his interest increased. "Continue."

"He works for their government."

The plot thickens, Abel thought to himself. "His name?"

Abel noted sweat on Abdullah's forehead as he waited for the answer.

"Mitch Rapp is his name."

Abel stopped in mid-sip, and carefully placed his cup back on its saucer lest his host notice his hand beginning to shake. "Mitch Rapp," he said coolly.

"Have you heard of him?"

"I'm afraid so. I doubt there is anyone in my line of work who hasn't."

Impatient and nervous, Abdullah gave him no time to think. "So will you take the job?"

Abel could feel the pace of his heart begin to race. He held up a hand. "Slow down, Mr. Abdullah. To kill a man like Mitch Rapp is no small undertaking. There are many things to discuss. Many details to work out, and even then I am not so sure I would be willing to take the job."

"Is it your fee? Tell me what you would demand for such a job. Let us begin to negotiate."

Abel dug his right thumb into his left palm in an attempt at self-acupuncture. A man was a man after all, and with enough preparation anyone could be killed. "It would be very expensive."

Saeed leaned over and pressed the intercom button. He said something quickly in Arabic and a moment later two unusually large Saudis entered the room carrying large black briefcases. The men set four cases on the table facing the German, opened them, and left the room.

"Five million dollars cash upon accepting the job. Five million more when you complete it."

Abel stared at the money, increased the pressure on his palm, and began running all the permutations through his mind. In mere seconds he concluded that it would be difficult, but not impossible. Someone else would of course do the heavy lifting. The details could and would be worked out later, so his mind settled on the fee. He'd been involved in contract killings before, but had never heard of a ten-million-dollar fee. Rapp had done something personal to Abdullah, that was obvious. It was difficult to measure the wealth of these Saudis, but as best he could figure, Abdullah was worth in excess of two billion dollars. Ten million dollars was play money.

He knew there was no turning back from something like this, and as crazy as it sounded he had no desire to. To kill a man like Mitch Rapp would be the ultimate statement of tradecraft. Suddenly almost euphoric with excitement over the prospect of such notoriety, Abel decided he would take the job, but first he would work on the already ample fee.

"Contract kills in America are a very difficult thing these days, and to go after someone like Mitch Rapp presents an entirely unique set of problems."

"Name your fee, Mr. Abel," the Arab said calmly.

"Twenty million dollars. Ten now . . . ten on completion."

Abdullah stuck out his hand. "Twenty million dollars."

Abel shook the man's hand. "We have a deal."

"How long will it take?"

"I will get to work on it immediately, but I wouldn't expect any results for at least a month."

"As soon as possible, Mr. Abel," the Arab said in a dire voice.

His hatred of Mitch Rapp was palpable. "Do you mind my asking, Mr. Abdullah, what Mr. Rapp has done to cause you such obvious pain?"

"He killed my son."

Of course he did, the German thought. *Of course he did.*

6

Rapp called them at the appointed time, and told them he was across the street. This seemed to both unsettle and irritate them, which was just fine with Rapp. The most difficult part had been deciding to sit down with them in the first place, and then there was trying to find a place they could all agree on. They wanted him to come to one of their offices. They were the type of men who were used to getting their way, and on top of that Rapp trusted neither of them, so he flat-out told them no. They wanted the meeting which meant he would set the conditions, and the sooner he got it over with the better. This was a favor to Kennedy and nothing else.

It took little imagination to envision at least one of them trying to record the conversation. People bugging each other was a fact of life in Washington, DC. The problem for Rapp was that he no longer trusted what little tact he had left. He'd grown so callous, he was capable of saying anything. The one man, he was ambivalent about, the other, he despised. With nothing to lose, Rapp knew the odds of things getting heated were better than even. In truth, the thought of getting a few things off his chest was what appealed most to him. That was more of an afterthought, though. The real reason he had agreed to meet these men was Kennedy. He'd called her first thing on Sunday morning and left her a message. The problem was no longer a problem. Nothing more specific than that.

As of Sunday morning there had been no news of Khalil's body. That was Sunday, however, and today was Monday. The story was everywhere now, and Kennedy wasn't happy. There wasn't much she could do though, until he was standing in front of her in her spacious corner office in Langley. Things like this were not discussed on the phone no matter how secure you thought your lines of communication were. So in an effort to forestall that confrontation, and hopefully give her some time to cool down, he had called up the two men she wanted him to meet with, and here he was in a part of town that he rarely visited, getting ready to meet with two men he had no respect for.

There was very little, if anything, that was soft about Rapp. His angular jaw was set in a very determined way and his dark brown eyes could portray a frightening intensity. They were the type of eyes that missed nothing, and revealed, only to those alert enough, that the man behind them was extremely dangerous. His jet black hair was starting to gray a touch at the temples, and his face was lined with a ruggedness that came from spending long hours outdoors exposed to the elements. A thin scar ran down his left cheek and along his jaw, a constant reminder of the dangers of his trade. He stood six feet tall and weighed 185 pounds—almost all of it solid muscle. He possessed the rare combination of strength and quickness that was usually reserved for strong safeties in the NFL, but instead belonged to a cunning and calculating killer.

Rapp had no problem admitting it, even if those around him didn't want to. Contrary to what many might think, he slept like a baby. What he did was not complicated. He killed terrorists, plain and simple. Men who had either slaughtered innocent civilians, or had very publicly sworn to do so. It was not a job he had sought. He did not grow up pulling the wings off butterflies or torturing kittens. His life had been family, school, friends, lacrosse, football, and a suburban smattering of religion, which meant they went to church twice a year—Christmas and Easter. The thought of killing someone had never entered his mind until Pan Am Flight 103 was blown out of the sky over Lockerbie, Scotland. On that cold morning 259 innocent souls had perished, thirty-five of whom were fellow Syracuse University students, and one of whom was the love of Rapp's life. Shortly after that, and unknown to him, his recruitment into this mysterious and treacherous world of international espionage had begun.

Rapp was dressed in a gray flannel suit, white shirt, and striped tie, all of which his wife had picked out for him. As always, he was armed. Rapp had gone over the room thoroughly with his BlackBerry. The small device doubled as a mobile phone and Internet browser. In addition to that, the Science and Technology people at Langley had retrofitted the small black box to detect and scramble listening devices. The eight-by-twelve-foot room was clean. Rapp sat in one of the six wooden chairs, put his feet up on the table, and clasped his hands behind his head.

The two men arrived five minutes late, which was good since Rapp had told them he would wait no more than ten minutes past the appointed hour. Upon hearing the door handle turn, Rapp rose and casually slid his left hand under the fold of his suit coat. To the untrained eye, it looked as if he was smoothing his tie. The move was reflexive in nature and not done out of fear. In his line of work you never knew who was coming through the door, and it was much easier to draw a gun standing than sitting.

The two men were an unusual pair. One tall and bone-thin, with a hawkish nose, the other short and round, with the nose of a boxer who had lost one too many fights, which according to his bio, Rapp knew to be the case. Senator Bill Walsh was six and a half feet tall and hailed from Idaho. He was the chairman of the Senate Intelligence Committee. It was Rapp's guess that it was he who had requested this meeting. Though infinitely more appealing than the other man in his demeanor, he was also very difficult to get a good read on. His companion was Senator Carl Hartsburg of New Jersey. Barely five eight, Hartsburg grew up in Hoboken, where at one point he was the local Golden Gloves champ. The story on him was that he wasn't that great a fighter, but he could really take a beating, hence the missing cartilage in his nose. Both men were in their mid-sixties, almost thirty years Rapp's seniors.

Hartsburg spoke first and a bit testily. "The Congressional Library. We could have just as easily met across the street in my office."

Rapp had picked one of the many study/meeting rooms at the Congressional Library on Capitol Hill.

"Neutral turf is more appealing," replied Rapp.

Walsh extended his hand. "Thank you for taking the time to meet with us."

Rapp shook Walsh's hand and when he was done didn't bother to extend it to the surly Hartsburg, who returned the favor. After taking a seat, Rapp pressed a series of buttons on his BlackBerry before laying it flat on the table.

Hartsburg looked at the device. "What in the hell is that for?"

"To make sure you're not recording me."

"A jamming device?"

Rapp nodded.

"Good," Hartsburg growled, "because I can tell you right now the last thing I want is a record of this meeting." Under his breath he added, "I'm not even sure I wanted this meeting period."

Rapp folded his arms across his chest and studied the senator, wondering if his grumpy mood was real or an act. Turning to Walsh, he asked, "So why in the world would two big shots such as yourselves want to meet with someone like me?"

Hartsburg frowned and said, "I keep asking myself the same question."

"Carl," Walsh said in a disapproving tone to his colleague. Looking across the table at the no-nonsense Rapp, he cut to the chase. "We are concerned, Mitch . . . concerned that with all of this rhetoric, and the expansion of Homeland Security and the new director of National Intelligence, that we're not doing enough to protect America."

"You won't get any arguments from me."

"We didn't think so. That's why we wanted to meet with you." Walsh flattened his palms on the table and hesitated. "What is your frank opinion on the restructuring of the intelligence community, and the creation of the new director of National Intelligence?"

Rapp took a moment to gauge the sincerity of the senator's question. He doubted they were going to get an honest answer from anyone else so he said, "I think it's a misguided, ill-conceived, overreaction brought on by a bunch of politicians who are in a hurry to act like they're doing something . . . anything . . . so that when the next attack comes they can say they did everything in their power to stop it, when in reality all they did was get in the way of the people who were really defending the country."

Hartsburg scoffed, "You think it's easy . . . our job?"

"Easy doesn't factor into it for me, Senator. I'm talking about right and wrong."

"Well, I'd like to see you go on national television and stand up to pressure from groups like the 9/11 widows. See how far you get with your black-and-white attitude." Hartsburg wagged an accusatory finger at Rapp. "The press would eat you alive."

Rapp raised an eyebrow. "Did you bother to tell those widows that their husbands died because none of you had the balls to order Osama bin Laden's assassination? Did you tell them that your two parties have spent so much time trying to embarrass each other over the past two decades you've turned the CIA into another inefficient, money-sucking Washington bureaucracy?"

Hartsburg glared at the man from the CIA. "That's a bunch of crap. You clowns out at Langley have squandered billions, and it sure as hell isn't our fault."

"You think they died," Rapp ignored the senator's attempt to shift, "because we didn't have a director of National Intelligence?"

"The CIA . . ."—Hartsburg pointed an accusatory finger at Rapp— "and the rest of the damn alphabet soup is a disaster."

"And whose fault is that? You two have each been in Washington thirty-plus years. Your job is oversight. You know that little part in the oath you took . . . to protect and defend? It's your job to lead and make sure the damn alphabet soup works. Not to criticize them after the fact, especially when all you've done is distract them for the last decade and a half by forcing them to implement your politically correct social projects."

"Your corner of the universe is tiny." Hartsburg held his thumb and forefinger in front of Rapp like the pincers of a hermit crab. "You have no concept of the big picture."

"That's where you're wrong, Senator," Rapp said with anger creeping into his voice. "There is no bigger picture than National Security. You guys want to legislate social change . . . go do it over at the Department of Education or Health and Human Services, but don't *fuck* around with Langley."

Hartsburg tapped his finger on the table. "Have you seen Langley's budget lately? We're talking billions of dollars, and I'd like to know what in the hell we're getting in return."

Rapp threw his arms up in frustration. "You guys amaze me. You bitch about the money that's being spent, and then your solution to the problem is to add more bureaucracy . . . more layers . . . slow things down even more. Spend more money. Stovepipe the shit out of everything, so twenty different supervisors and department heads have to sign off on each bit of intelligence before the president even has a prayer of seeing it. You think that's going to solve our problems?"

"I think the CIA is a monumental waste of federal tax dollars, and something has to be done to wake them up."

A sudden calm came over Rapp's face. He leaned back and said, "Senator, this might surprise you, but I couldn't agree with you more."

Rapp's admission left both men silent. The two politicians shared a brief expression of confusion and then Walsh asked, "What's your biggest beef with Langley?"

"Three thousand people are killed in one morning and no one loses their job. . . . Are you fucking kidding me?" Rapp looked at one senator and then the other. "Guilty or not, people should have lost their jobs. And I'm not just talking the CIA. I'm talking FBI, Pentagon, National Security Council, White House, Capitol Hill . . . across the board. The entire 'cover your ass' culture you guys and your politically correct cronies have created needs to be turned on its ear."

"Well, now it's my turn to agree with you," Hartsburg said to Rapp, giving Walsh an accusatory look.

"We made a decision," said Walsh defensively, "that we weren't going to scapegoat anyone for what happened. Nine-eleven was a long time in the works and both parties share the blame."

"I'm not talking about your precious political parties. I'm talking about the dead weight who got in the way of the people trying to do their jobs."

"I know that, and I know you don't have any stomach for politics, but that deal had to be made or the two parties would have destroyed each other in the aftermath."

Rapp frowned. "And that would be a bad thing?"

"Contrary to what you think, Mr. Rapp," said Hartsburg, "we care about this country. I can assure you that is the only reason I'm sitting in this room with you right now."

"If you could right the ship," said Walsh, sounding more eager than when the meeting had started, "how would you do it?"

Rapp studied the senior senator from Idaho with suspicion. "You're asking me . . . a person who has absolutely no experience in management, and no desire to join the club?"

"Yes, but you've got more practical experience in the field than perhaps anyone else in Washington."

Rapp considered the question carefully and said, "Well, it's not very complicated. You've got a top-heavy bureaucracy over there. An inverted pyramid. Less than one percent of the people on the payroll do real field work. Hell, before 9/11 you had more people working in the Office of Diversity than you had on the bin Laden Desk."

"So what's the solution?"

Rapp shrugged. "You do what IBM or GE or any other well-run corporation does. You get rid of the deadweight. You tell every department head their budget is going to be cut by ten percent. You offer early retirement, you give people severance packages, and you wish them good luck. And then you start to rebuild the Clandestine Service from the ground up."

"As much as it pains me to admit it . . . you and I," Hartsburg said as he pointed at Rapp and then himself, "see more eye to eye than I would have ever liked to admit."

"So what's holding you guys up? You run the damn committee. . . . You hold the purse strings."

"We're working on it, but trying to change an entrenched Washington bureaucracy is not easy," Walsh said. "In the meantime we're more concerned with a short-term solution. A stopgap measure, if you will."

"Like what?"

Walsh shared an uncomfortable look with Hartsburg, started to speak, stopped, and then made one more effort at it before he looked again to his more blunt colleague for help. Hartsburg retrieved a copy of the *Washington Post* and laid it down on the table. Beneath the fold on the front page was a story about the brutal murder of an Islamic cleric in Montreal. The senator stabbed his stubby finger at the article and asked, "Did we have anything to do with this?"

Rapp's face didn't change a bit. "Not that I know of."

Hartsburg leaned in and with a look of fire in his eyes said, "That's too bad."

Rapp didn't show it, but he couldn't have been more shocked by the senator's words.

7

LANGLEY, VIRGINIA

Kennedy was standing by the conference table, her arms folded across her crisp white blouse, one leg in front of the other, her front foot tapping the floor like a Geiger counter. The closer he got the faster the foot tapped. He closed the heavy soundproof door. This was not good. Kennedy was by far the calmest person he knew. She was unflappable. Professional to the core. This was the way his wife greeted him when she was mad.

Rapp decided to start the conversation out cautiously. "I went and met with those two like you asked me." He stopped well short of where she was dug in. He unbuttoned his suit coat and put his hands on his hips. The black handle of his shoulder-holstered FN pistol was visible.

"We'll talk about that later." She gestured to the conference table.

Rapp looked at it. Four newspapers were spread out on the shiny surface of the wood table. The *New York Times,* the *London Times,* the *Montreal Gazette,* and the *Washington Post,* which he had already seen. The murder of Khalil was on the front page of each newspaper.

"What in the hell happened?"

Rapp read the bold headlines. This was better than he had hoped.

"The *Montreal Gazette* says he was nearly decapitated."

Rapp glanced at his boss. "That's an exaggeration."

"And how would you know?" Kennedy had ordered Rapp that others were to do the dirty work.

Rapp decided that to say nothing was his best move.

"Left in plain sight for all the world to see," she continued.

"Well . . . that's true." Rapp nodded.

"I'm confused." Her face twisted into an uncharacteristic frown. "I thought we had come to an agreement. This"—she opened her hand and gestured toward the newspapers—"is exactly what I wanted to avoid."

"I know that, but let me explain myself."

She crossed her arms and began tapping her foot with renewed vigor. "I'm waiting."

Rapp let out a sigh and looked back at the papers. "The only one I've read is the *Post*. It didn't say anything about us. Made some reference to him being an international terror suspect and serving time in France, but that was it."

"That was today. Trust me, tomorrow morning, we'll be mentioned. The phone over in public affairs is ringing off the hook. I've already fielded five calls relating to it. This thing is going to mushroom."

"I don't think so."

"And why is that, Mr. Media Expert?"

"Because the press is playing catch-up right now. The Montreal police are keeping their mouths shut, but that won't last long. In fact I'd be willing to bet the specifics on the scene of the crime are already being leaked. This story is going to end up nowhere near us."

Her brow furrowed and she studied him for a moment. "What did you do?"

"Let's just say we made it look like a crime of passion rather than a professional hit."

"Details." It was a command, not a request.

"What the press doesn't know yet was that Khalil was found with a wad of cash stuffed in his mouth and the word *munafiq* scrawled in his own blood on the wall of the building he was propped up against."

"Hypocrite," Kennedy translated the word aloud. "I don't get it."

"Coleman found out some interesting stuff last week. Not all of Khalil's worshipers were happy with him. There was a growing dissent in the community over his call to jihad and his recruiting of young men to go overseas and fight. And there was one other thing. Something Muslims, among other people, find deplorable."

"What's that?"

"He was a porn freak."

"What?"

Rapp pulled the memory stick Coleman had given him out of his pocket. "Scott snuck into his apartment and copied his hard drive. The thing was filled with porn. A lot of bondage, S&M, and some underage stuff that could have got him in major trouble."

"You're not serious?"

"Of course I am." Rapp held out the stick. "Plug it in. Take a look at it."

Kennedy closed her eyes. "I'll take your word for it."

"He also had magazines. A lot of really sick stuff."

"And you think the police and the press will automatically rule us out because of some porn fetish?" She shook her head. "I don't know, Mitchell, it sounds pretty thin to me."

Rapp glanced at the floor and then looked out the window. "There's one more thing."

"What's that?"

"His body was, uh . . ." Rapp let out a sigh, "hacked up a bit."

Her hands moved to her hips and a deep frown covered her face. "Why?"

"I didn't want it to look so professional."

She shook her head.

"Irene, trust me. I know how cops think. This thing will be classified as a revenge crime. They're gonna think that asshole defiled some guy's daughter, which by the way he probably did. We stuffed the money in his mouth and left him there with multiple stab wounds. Details like that will eventually get leaked to the press, and no one in a million years is going to think we had anything to do with it."

Kennedy turned and walked to the seating area at the far end of her office. A long couch and two armchairs were arranged around a rectangular glass-top coffee table. Rapp waited a bit and then followed.

She stood with her back to him looking out the window at the bright fall colors of the Potomac River Valley. After a long moment she shook her head and asked, "How was your meeting?"

Rapp, relieved that they were off the subject, said, "Unusual. Why didn't you tell me what they wanted?"

"I wanted your honest reaction."

"You wanted them to catch me off guard," Rapp corrected.

"You could say that," replied Kennedy. "You seem unusually calm. I half expected you to come marching in here and bite my head off."

Rapp was looking out the window, staring off into space. The fact that he and Senator Hartsburg had agreed on a pivotal issue was enough for him to question his senses, but that was only the beginning. The proposal that the two men had floated his way was mind-boggling. It had been the last thing he'd expected.

"You don't think they're trying to set you up?" she asked.

"No." Rapp kept staring out the window. "They might hate me, but I can't imagine them going through all of this just to take me down." He paused and then added, "Plus, they know I'd kill them before I'd ever let them string me up at some hearing."

Kennedy wasn't sure if he was kidding or not, which she supposed suited Rapp's purposes perfectly. The urban lore regarding Rapp's exploits had grown far beyond reality.

"I could maybe see Hartsburg being zealous enough to set me up, but not Walsh."

"I agree." She set her cup down on the coffee table. "I know what you're going through. I went through the same thing last week when they came to me. You spend all of this time in an adversarial relationship with them and then when you end up on the same side of an issue, it causes you to stop and question your own judgment."

Rapp looked at her. "That's exactly it. Kind of a thanks, but no thanks . . . do me a favor and get off my team."

"There's a key to understanding their motivations. Have you figured it out yet?"

"No."

Kennedy had seen it right away and was surprised Rapp hadn't. "I'm guessing you had a nice quiet drive from Capitol Hill out to Langley. What have you been thinking about?"

"How to structure it . . . how to fund it . . . how to kill them if they double-cross me."

She nodded slowly, deciding he really did mean that he'd kill them if they set him up. "I don't think they're going to double-cross any of us."

"I wish I could share your confidence, but I just can't bring myself to trust Hartsburg."

"The bomb changed everything, Mitch."

Rapp gave her a skeptical look. The bomb she was referring to was part of a plot by Islamic radical fundamentalists to incinerate Washington, DC. If it hadn't been for Rapp and a handful of dedicated government employees, Senators Walsh and Hartsburg and the majority of their colleagues would have been killed by the detonation of a fifteen-kiloton nuclear weapon.

The tumblers fell into place for Rapp and he said, "Self-preservation."

"It's their strongest instinct."

Rapp thought about that for a moment. Politicians were an amazingly resilient breed. He supposed on some Darwinian level she was absolutely correct. "Whatever works. I just want them one hundred percent on board."

"So what do you think of their proposal?" Kennedy picked up her cup for another sip.

"It's basically an expansion of the Orion Team. Which as we've discussed has been greatly underused."

The Orion Team was a covert operations unit that had been founded by Kennedy's predecessor, Thomas Stansfield, some twenty years ago. The idea was that the unit would operate in secret, independent of the CIA or the rest of the national security apparatus. The team allowed Stansfield to circumvent the leviathan of politics and get around small impediments like the executive order banning assassinations. It allowed him to do things that the more civilized crowd didn't have the stomach for. Rapp had been the group's star operative almost from the day he started at the age of twenty-two. He'd spent significant amounts of time in Europe, the Middle East, and Southwest Asia collecting intel and when the situation called for it, dealing with threats in a more final manner.

"Except this time we would have them on our side." By them Kennedy meant Hartsburg and Walsh.

"I might be missing something here, but explain to me why that's a good thing."

"I was part of the Orion Team," Kennedy began, "for eighteen years. Six of which I spent running it." She gave him a forced smile. "In addition to spending most of my time trying to keep you out of trouble, the next most difficult task was trying to scrape together the money to sufficiently fund the operations. With Hartsburg and Walsh on board the funding will no longer be an issue, and more importantly, we won't have to worry about them launching any investigations. Your job will be much easier."

Rap nodded. "I see your point. I just want to make sure they are beholden to us, and not the other way around."

"Absolutely." Kennedy brushed a strand of hair back behind her ear. "Any ideas?"

"Yeah, one." Rapp held up his BlackBerry. "Mutually assured destruction."

"MAD."

"Exactly." Rapp pressed a few buttons and began replaying the conversation that had taken place in the Congressional Library. After a few seconds he stopped the recording and smiled. "I hope you're not disappointed?"

"I would have been disappointed in you if you hadn't."

Rapp snapped the BlackBerry back onto his belt clip. "And I don't want any armchair quarterbacking."

"I already explained that to them."

"And how did they take it?"

"Listen, Mitch, you have a certain reputation in this town that has grown beyond even your own remarkable achievements. The secrecy regarding your past, the untimely death of two politicians who were involved in blowing your cover . . . it has all added up to an almost mythical reputation. When people mention your name they do so in whispers, and then only after they've looked over both shoulders. You get credit for things I know for a fact you had nothing to do with."

"How can you be so sure?" Rapp gave her a devious look.

"Because I know you weren't even on the same continent let alone in the same city when some of this stuff happened. But nonetheless people like a good conspiracy and you play into that perfectly." Kennedy rolled her eyes. "Rugged good looks, a beautiful wife who works for NBC, and none other than the president of the United States as your biggest champion. Add to that the aforementioned deceased politicians and what they leaked to the press, the press referring to you as an assassin . . . our first line of defense . . . and there isn't a person on Capitol Hill who doesn't get a little nervous around you."

"Good." Rapp far preferred his old anonymity, but if some of the less-than-savory politicians in this town were afraid of him, that wasn't such a bad thing. "Here's the bottom line. I'll do this, but I'm going to do it my way. I'm going to pick the targets of opportunity, and I'll take suggestions from you and only you. If they have any suggestions of their own they can give them to you and I'll take them under advisement, but I will hold veto power. If I think something is too risky or not important enough . . . I'll pull the plug."

"I can make them live with that. What else?"

"I'm going to handpick all my people."

Kennedy nodded. She had assumed he would make both requests.

"And we're going to do more than just take out known terrorists."

"How so?" Kennedy asked curiously.

Rapp smiled. "I've been working on something, but I'm not ready to show you yet."

"Would you like to give me a hint?"

"Let's just say that I'm planning on fighting this war on more than one front, and I don't plan on playing by anyone's rules."

"Like your little operation you just ran north of the border?"

Rapp nodded.

Kennedy knew him better than anyone, and that included his wife. She gave him a concerned look and said, "Let me give you some advice. Be very careful about what you do when it involves our allies. Nothing short of getting caught here in America by the FBI will get you in trouble quicker than raising the ire of one of their foreign intelligence services."

Rapp grinned. "I don't plan on getting caught."

"No one ever does, Mitch." She shook her head. "No one ever does."

"I know . . . I know. But I've managed to get by all these years . . . I don't plan on screwing up now."

"Just be careful and move slowly."

Rapp shook his head. "Time is a luxury we don't have. Senator Hartsburg is a hack, but he's right about one thing."

"What's that?"

"We have to hit them before they hit us."

8

The identification in his wallet said his name was Harry Smith. It was not his given name, simply a standard precaution. He'd watched the target for the last forty-eight hours, day and night. He slept after the man went to sleep and woke up before the target got out of bed. He was younger, in far better shape, and had the element of surprise on his side. He'd trained himself to last days on end with little or no sleep. He was acutely aware of his physiological needs, and this job wasn't even close to taxing them. The job, in fact, was beginning to bore him.

The target was a Turkish financier with a penchant for high-risk ventures—especially those involving illegal arms sales. He owned several banks in his native country and held minority interests in another half dozen banks around Europe. Lately the man had been spending a lot of time in London, and the assassin had a pretty good idea why. There was barely a street corner left in the increasingly Orwellian city that wasn't monitored by a camera. In the world of contract killers, a business where your anonymity was your currency, London was a town that was bad for business.

This particular part of London had an unusually high concentration of surveillance cameras. The Hampshire Hotel was situated on Leicester Square just a short hop from a cluster of government buildings with serious security needs. They included the National Gallery, the Ministry of Defense, Parliament, and Westminster Abbey. He reasoned the Turk had picked this hotel for that very reason. The area was saturated with police and other security types. The assassin, however, was not deterred for even a second. The men and women charged with securing these sites were worried about terrorists, not businessmen. All he had to do was look the part, don the urban camouflage, and he could come and go unnoticed.

His partner didn't quite see things his way. She wanted to turn down the job, but he had been insistent. Virtually every city of note in the world was adding security cameras by the droves. To survive in the industry they had to adapt. She preferred retirement to adaptation, but they were too young for that. Harry was thirty-two and Amanda was just thirty. Amanda was not her real name, but for the sake of operational security it was the only name he'd used for the last week. The key to longevity in their line of work was the details, little things like high-quality forgeries, dummy credit card accounts, and the discipline to stay in character whether you were alone or not.

At the current pace of business it would take another five years before they reached the financial level he deemed appropriate for retirement. They already had several million, but he was not interested in merely getting by. He got into this line of work because he was drawn to it, because he could be his own boss, and because, if he played it smart, he would make a lot of money. He had the talent, but talent alone was never enough. When the stakes were this high, skill had to be accompanied by an ardent drive—a need for perfection.

He was not only drawn to this work, he enjoyed it. Yes, he enjoyed it, and he had never admitted that to anyone, not even her. When talk turned to getting out of the business, he always stressed that they needed to make more money first, but he knew a big part of it was that he wasn't willing to let go. His greatest fear was not of getting caught. He was too confident in his talents for that. His greatest fear was of losing her because he wouldn't be able to walk away. Like a gambler drawn to the craps table, he had become a slave to the thrill of the hunt.

Excluding the current job there was normally an exhilaration to stalking a man that was unmatched. The sheer level of training and expertise it took to even enter the arena at this level was mind-boggling. He was an expert marksman with both the short and long barrel. He knew exactly where to stick the blade of a knife to obtain the desired result, which was usually death, but occasionally his contract called for maiming the person and nothing more. He knew how to use his fists, elbows, knees, feet, and even forehead to incapacitate or kill. He could fly both fixed-wing and rotary aircraft, and he was a predatory genius when it came to surveillance and countersurveillance.

Now here he was standing across the square from the Hampshire Hotel, bored out of his mind. A $200,000 contract was on the table that he was an hour or less from fulfilling and he was yawning. He looked at the front entrance of the opulent hotel, stifled yet another yawn, and said, "Come on, fucker. Let's get this over with."

He spoke with a British accent, even though he wasn't a subject. The "fucker" he was referring to traveled extensively, and he appeared to have no problem spending money. He did, however, have a problem paying his bills, which the assassin reasoned was why a price had been placed on his head. For a man who had pissed off the wrong people, he was acting unusually calm. Especially when the people he had offended were Russian Mafiosi. The assassin had been working on his Russian over the last several years, and found the language by far the most difficult of the five he spoke fluently. He did not prefer to operate in the former Soviet Union, but the old communist country and its satellites were the largest growth market in his line of work. They were ruthless bastards willing to kill anyone who screwed them on a deal no matter how illegal or legitimate it may have been. They wanted a guaranteed return on their investments, and when a deal didn't perform, the paranoid thugs immediately jumped to the conclusion that they'd been double-crossed. He guessed that was what had happened with the Turk. He didn't know for sure. To find that out would have involved asking a few questions, and as a general rule, he asked only what he absolutely needed to know.

He and his partner had used a medium-range parabolic microphone to listen in on the Turkish man's phone calls as he went for his midmorning walks. The man had told a friend yesterday that the Russians were simpletons, but that they weren't crazy enough to try to kill him in London. The comment struck the assassin as pure idiocy, and it caused him to wonder how the Turk had lasted as long as he had. The man was fifty-eight years old and had been involved in this type of stuff for twenty-plus years. Underestimating one's enemy was a classic tactical mistake—one that was usually born out of stupidity or arrogance or both.

He leaned against the street lamp and checked his watch, careful to keep his head tilted down. There was a camera pod mounted on the light above him. It was twenty after ten. He was dressed in business attire with a long black trench coat and fedora. His black hair had been lightened to a sandy blond, special contacts made his brown eyes appear hazel and they were further concealed by a pair of black-rimmed glasses with clear lenses. An umbrella dangled from the crook of his left arm that held a twice-folded copy of the *Times.* The sky was gray and looked as if it might bring rain at any moment.

Two days in a row the Turk had appeared at ten in the morning to take his walk to the park. He donned an earpiece and the entire trip, there and back, he talked on his phone and smoked cigarettes. He was oblivious to the fact that he was being watched, which, when one looked at his comments, was not surprising. Like the majority of the men the assassin had killed, the Turk was a man of habits. He always stayed at the Hampshire when in London, and, weather permitting, he took daily walks to St. James Park, went back to the hotel for lunch, then to the bank where he kept an office and then afternoon tea at Browns.

Something was throwing him off his normal schedule this morning and the assassin was beginning to worry. Yes, it looked like it could rain at any moment, but the weather was no different than the previous two days. There was a fine line between rushing a job and sitting on it too long. Long surveillance periods could lead to boredom, hesitancy, and sometimes inaction. They also increased the chances that someone would notice you. On the other hand, rushing a job before you had a complete sense of the overall tactical situation could be even more disastrous. Maps had to be memorized, schedules scrutinized, and multiple modes of transportation put into place. And in London one could never forget about the omnipresent security cameras.

The assassin was beginning to doubt that the Turk would show. He would either have to dispatch him when he was coming out of his afternoon tea or wait another day to kill him in the park. As he was weighing his two options the Turk stepped out under the wrought-iron-and-glass canopy of the hotel and the doorman handed him an umbrella. Pleasantries were exchanged, the Turk lit a cigarette, and he was on his way. The assassin had thought about this part very carefully. He was already positioned in front of his subject. If the police ever got around to reviewing the tapes, they would be looking for someone who had followed the Turk to the park and would in all likelihood not bother to see if someone had been in front of him every step of the way.

The assassin had also found a hole in the way the security cameras were set up. He would take a slightly different path to the park and avoid having his movements recorded. The park itself was a bit of a problem.

There was usually a bobby or two loitering about, a fair amount of state workers, and one particularly pesky camera pod that was in close proximity to the spot where the hit would take place. He was disguised enough that the cameras would never get a clear shot of his face, but they could begin to build a profile. In addition to that he would prefer the act itself not to be recorded. Such footage had a way of galvanizing those who were in charge of solving violent crimes. The assassin had been struggling with this problem the day before when a solution popped into his mind.

He reached up and touched the side of a tiny wireless Motorola headset affixed to his right ear. A second later he could hear her phone ringing.

"Amanda Poole speaking." The voice had a crisp British accent.

"Amanda, I'm going to take a walk. Would you swing by and see if our friend is going to join me?"

"I'd love to, Harry."

The assassin rounded the corner, careful to keep his chin down. There was a tendency in his line of work to overthink things. Much of this stemmed from the fact that most of the people were either former intelligence operatives or military. In Harry's case it was the latter. When you worked for a big government the resources were vast. Field equipment was tested and retested under every conceivable condition, billions of dollars worldwide was put into the development of new ways to communicate and better ways to encrypt. The problem as Harry saw it, though, was that as much—or more—money, was spent on new eavesdropping technology and vastly powerful and complex decryption systems. The National Security Agency of America alone had dozens of satellites circling the planet that were designed to do one thing—record people's conversations. They had the world's most powerful computers ensconced in football-field-size subterranean chambers under their headquarters in Maryland.

These Cray supercomputers churned away day after day, night after night, sifting through e-mails, radio transmissions, and phone intercepts. Highly specialized programs were written so the computers could home in on the key words *bomb, gun, kill,* and *assassinate* in every foreign language of interest. Certain types of transmissions were prioritized. For America, anything coming out of Iran, North Korea, Iraq, Afghanistan, or Pakistan, for example, was kicked to the top of the queue. Anything intercepted in those countries via secure and encrypted modes was further kicked up the queue. And so it went, with the programs designed to focus on the methods used by people who were trying to keep secrets.

All of this left Harry with a simple question. If superpowers, with nearly unlimited financial resources and brainpower, could not keep secrets from each other, what hopes did a two-person operation have to stay up on the technology and out in front of those spending billions? The answer was easy. He couldn't, so the only solution was to go in the opposite direction. The spy agencies around the world didn't care about inane conversations by business associates or lovers. The trick was to stay with the herd. Use the same mode of communication everyone else used and stay away from any discussion of the real business at hand. Consequently, upon arriving in London, they had purchased new phones. They signed a yearlong contract even though the phones would be used for a week at the most.

He walked quickly but calmly down St. Martin's Street and then cut over to Whitcomb. A few minutes later he was walking along the north end of the park. The Turk would be a few blocks behind him at this point. They would enter the park from different spots and meet where the older man liked to stop and feed the ducks while chattering on his phone. At Marlborough Road he came upon a small black delivery van, which his partner was driving. He stuffed his folded copy of the *Times* under his armpit and popped the back cargo doors. Reaching in with a gloved hand he grabbed a sash of balloons and closed the door. The delivery van drove off without a word while he crossed the street to the park.

This part made him a bit nervous. A man dressed in business attire with a long black coat and hat carrying a cluster of balloons was not your everyday sight. He was sure to catch a few stray glances, but like most things in life it was a trade-off. He kept the collar of his coat turned up, his chin tucked against his chest, and his shoulders hunched. All he had to do was make it one block with the balloons.

His eyes swept the surrounding landscape, looking out from under the brim of his hat for the bulbous cap of a bobby or any other patrolmen that might be about. The light post he was interested in was situated just past a park bench. It offered a commanding view of the park and it was easy to see why the authorities had decided to mount cameras on it. As he neared the device he slowed a bit and then extended his left hand far above his head while letting the helium-filled balloons rise into the air. They were tied off in a concave shape so that the middle balloon was shorter than the other six. They formed a perfect basket, and settled in gently around the tinted shield of the camera pod.

The assassin never broke stride. Never looked back. The Turk was already in sight coming toward him from a little more than two hundred meters away. Harry reached the main path that ran east-west and turned to the left. The Turk was now less than two hundred meters away and he was stopping to buy some warm pistachios from a street vendor. Harry watched him take a stale bag of crackers to feed the ducks just like he'd done the two previous mornings. *Good,* he thought to himself. *Keep your routine and everything will turn out just fine.* Sure enough, the Turk continued on for a bit and then left the path for the lake. He stood near a willow tree and began spreading the stale crackers about, popping pistachios into his mouth and talking on his phone.

Harry reached up and tapped his Motorola earpiece once, which redialed the last call he'd made. A second later his partner answered.

"Amanda Poole speaking."

"Amanda, it's Harry. How is everything?"

"Everything is just fine. Your party favors came in and they work perfectly."

That meant the balloons had stayed in position. "Good." He stole a peek over his left shoulder. "Is anyone else coming to our gathering?"

"Everyone who was invited has replied."

The distance was now just under a hundred meters. He turned off the path and started walking toward the lake. "What about crashers?"

"Not a one on the horizon, but if I hear anything I'll let you know immediately."

"Good." As he ducked around a hedgerow his left hand slid between the folds of his coat and retrieved a silenced Walther PPK 9mm pistol. The weapon was quickly placed inside the folded newspaper. He clutched the paper and covered gun to his chest and with his right hand slid one rubber band and then another over the outside of the paper. The assassin started his turn before he reached the water's edge and brought the newspaper up as if he were reading it. "Any other calls this morning?"

The woman responded, "None that I can remember. The rest of the morning is wide open."

"Let's hope it stays that way." He looked over the top of the newspaper and sighted the Turk a short distance ahead.

His heart was not racing, his gloved hands were dry, and his senses were highly alert. He heard every noise, saw everything ninety degrees in each direction, and had a complete mental picture of what was going on behind him. The distance was now less than twenty meters and no one else was near the target. His pace quickened slightly to take advantage of the man's isolation. At ten meters, he could hear the Turk clearly. He had decided on this angle because he wanted the Turk to see him coming. This would seem normal, whereas if he sneaked up behind him he could end up alerting his quarry.

He glanced over the top of the paper and made brief eye contact with the man he was about to kill. Casually, he pretended to return his attention to the paper. He glanced across the lake and then to the left. There were a few people about. None of them were close and he doubted they were paying attention. He was now only steps away, and he could see from his peripheral vision that the target was turning away from him. Humans, the only animals in all of nature who willingly turned their back to a potential predator. Harry was almost disgusted with how easy this was going to be.

Stepping toward the target, he followed him quietly for a few steps as the man walked toward the weeping willow. This was turning into a joke. The tree with its drooping wispy branches was the closest thing the park had to a dark alley, and the Turk was headed right for it. He stopped just short of the outer ring of branches and started to look toward the lake, undoubtedly expecting to see the pedestrian who had interrupted his privacy continuing on his way.

The assassin did not extend the newspaper-encased weapon. He was too practiced for anything so obvious. He merely tilted the paper forward until the angle matched the trajectory that he wanted the bullet to travel. He squeezed the trigger once, and stepped quickly forward. The hollow-tipped bullet struck the Turk directly in the back of the head, flattening on impact, doubling in circumference, and tearing through vital brain matter until it stopped, lodged between the shredded left frontal lobe and the inner wall of the skull. The impact propelled the financier forward. The assassin had his right hand around the man's chest a split second later. He glanced down at the small coin-size entry wound as he went with the momentum of the Turk's dying body. The newspaper-laden hand cut a swath through the dense branches of the weeping willow, and two steps later he laid the dead man to rest at the foot of the tree. Harry quickly checked himself for blood even though he was almost positive there would be none. The bullet was designed to stay in the body and cause only a small entry wound.

With everything in order, he left the dead body and the shelter of the tree and began retracing his steps. A hundred meters back down the foot-path he asked his partner, "Are you free for an early lunch?"

"I am, as a matter of fact."

"Good. I'm done with things here. I'll meet you at the usual spot in a quarter of an hour."

"I'll see you there."

On the way out of the park Harry walked past two of London's finest. They were standing under his bouquet of balloons staring up in consternation and talking with some higher-up back at the station house via their shoulder-mounted radios. When the taller one of the two tried to jump up and grab the strings, Harry had to stifle a laugh. It was the most amusing thing he'd seen all morning.

9

Rapp sat in a worn leather chair, his mutt, Shirley, at his feet and a pen in his left hand. He'd been writing furiously for the past hour, page after page, idea upon idea. Many were crossed off, others were circled and connected like some strange flow chart. The dry birch in the fireplace crackled and popped as he jotted down his sixth page of notes. At least as many pages had already been torn from the pad and thrown on the pyre. He was not writing down his thoughts for the sake of keeping a record, but rather to help play out the potential pitfalls of the job that lay ahead. The opportunity he had been given was fraught with potential problems, but the prospects were impossible to resist. Like everything else he did, the key was to not get caught. The difference this time, though, was that everything was on a much bigger scale. Instead of targeting individuals, he would be targeting groups. The expanded operation needed to be approached like a battle plan—looked at from every vantage point, and then tested and retested to make sure he hadn't missed something. And there could be no hard copy of anything. That's what Thomas Stansfield had taught him.

The deceased former director of the CIA was famous for not carrying a pen, and was known to admonish subordinates who took notes during high-level meetings. He liked to tell his people, "We're in the business of collecting secrets, not giving them away. If your mind isn't sharp enough to remember what was said, you're in the wrong line of work."

Stansfield didn't really fear America's enemies. He respected them for their tenacity and despised them for their ruthlessness, but he always knew capitalism would defeat communism. What Stansfield feared were the opportunists on Capitol Hill, the politicians who eagerly awaited any chance to take the stage and act out another drama. They were the real enemy. The enemy from within. Men who could ruin your career and reputation with one theatrical sound bite. Stansfield had many maxims and one of them was that it was impossible for a man with an inflated hubris not to have an Achilles' heel.

Rapp had heard a rumor once that Stansfield used a network of retired OSS and CIA people to run surveillance on key senators and colleagues. These were men who had fought alongside Stansfield against the Nazis, and then the Russians during the height of the Cold War. Men who hadn't lost an ounce of their conviction, and were bored with retirement. Men who were happy to practice their trade on such easy targets. The files that Stansfield had amassed were rumored to be extremely damaging. They were his insurance policies against those who chose to put their own careers ahead of national security. Rapp made a note to talk to Kennedy again about their old boss's files and a separate note to take out a similar insurance policy.

Stansfield's other precaution involved eliminating any paper trail. When conducting operations that ran afoul of the American legal system he liked to tell those around him, "Notes are the noose that will be used at your execution. If possible, record nothing, and burn everything."

Rapp took those words to heart and many others that the WWII vet had handed down. Stansfield had been a member of the famed Jedburgh teams that were infiltrated behind enemy lines in Norway and France in order to collect intelligence and harass the Nazis. That was exactly what Rapp planned on doing. They needed to adopt a more multipronged attack. Direct action, assassination, seizing funds, placing pressure and demands on states that were less than vigilant in the fight, that was all fine, but to truly confuse and harass the enemy would require a full-blown clandestine operation. An operation that only Rapp would know the full extent of.

He tore off another sheet, crumpled it in his hand, and tossed it into the fire. Not even Kennedy would be fully briefed on what he had in mind. It was time to knock the enemy off balance and get them to doubt themselves. Get them to turn on each other. An extension of what they'd just done in Canada. Expose the pious hypocrites for who they were. Undermine the authority of the zealots and get them to think they had spies in their own camp.

Shirley lifted her head from the rug and a second later Rapp heard a noise outside. He checked his watch, as Shirley ran over to get a look at the source of the noise. It was a little before eight in the evening. That would be his wife returning home after one of her marathon workdays. As the NBC White House correspondent, she started her days early with the morning news and ended late with the evening news. As long as nothing dramatic was going on at the White House, the middle of her day tended to be pretty easy. She usually took an hour to work out and was not afraid to take long lunches that usually involved shopping. Rapp didn't think it possible for one woman to own so many pairs of shoes, handbags, outfits, necklaces, and anything else to do with fashion, but then again he'd never known anyone quite like Anna. She was the most beautiful "bag lady" he'd ever laid eyes on. The closet in the guest room was overflowing with purses designed by people with foreign names that he'd grown to think of as fashion terrorists.

He'd asked her once the price of one of the bags and she replied a bit defensively, "I don't ask you how much your guns cost, do I?"

Rapp had responded that unlike her, he used his guns more than once, and unlike the purses, the guns tended to stay in style for more than a season. He remembered being very proud of himself right up until she gave him that look. Anna Rielly had the greenest eyes he'd ever seen. They could be as calm and enticing as a mountain lake on a hot summer day and as angry and violent as a rogue wave bearing down on an unsuspecting boat. Her father once told him it was her Irish temper. Whatever it was, Rapp liked receiving the first look and dreaded the second. It didn't take long for him to figure out that his wife didn't think him anywhere near as funny as he found himself. He'd also learned that winning these little skirmishes with witty lines inevitably led to him getting his ass kicked in the major battles. This conclusion brought about a new creed: When Anna was happy, he was happy. When Anna was mad, life was less than fun. When Anna was mad at him, life was miserable.

Rapp glanced over his most recent page of notes and stabbed his pen at a certain line, tapping it over and over. He heard the key in the door but didn't look up. He could tell by Shirley's soft bark and the excited tapping of her paws that it was Anna. Tomorrow morning he had a meeting with Kennedy, and he wanted to get this figured out before she began dissecting his operational plan. He heard the handle turn and looked up in time to see his wife enter with her large, striped Kate Spade shoulder bag. It was the only bag she used on a regular basis, which was a good thing, because it cost more than any handgun he owned—even the custom-built ones. In her other hand was a purse and a shopping bag.

"How was your day, honey?" he asked.

"Fine." She dropped her large bag on the floor and stuffed the shopping bag in the front hall closet.

Rapp shook his head. He could tell by the pastel color of the bag that whatever she had bought wasn't for him. "Got a little shopping in?"

"No." She took off her jacket and gave him a wry smile. "Kill anyone?"

"Not today, honey, but I've got a few hours left. What's in the bag?" He pointed toward the closet. Rapp wasn't going to let her lame attempt at hiding her habit go unnoticed.

She was already halfway into the living room. She stopped and gestured at the front hall closet. "That bag?" She folded her arms across her chest. "I called you two hours ago. Why didn't you answer your phone?"

Changing the subject was the first sign of guilt. He knew because he did it all the time. "I've been working on something." Rapp pointed at the legal pad on his knee. "What's in the bag?"

"Did you forget that we had a meeting tonight with Philip?"

Philip was their interior designer. A confused expression fell across Rapp's face. "I didn't know we had a meeting tonight." Even as he said it he began to have a faint recollection of some such thing.

She put her hands on her hips. "For a spy you're a terrible liar."

Rapp felt the table being turned. "Anna, I'm not lying. I didn't know."

"Don't say you didn't know. It's on the calendar," she pointed to the kitchen. "I told you before I left this morning, and I left you a message on your phone an hour before the meeting."

Now he remembered. "Oh, that meeting."

She gave him the look.

"I'm sorry," he said sincerely. They were building a house in Virginia, just outside the beltway on two very private acres, and it had become a full-time job that he didn't have the time for. "What did I miss?"

"Carpet selections. That's what's in the bag, by the way."

Rapp stood. "Sorry." His instincts had failed him. He walked over and gave her a kiss. "You know I'm not very good at that stuff. I trust you. Whatever you and Philip think is best, I'll go along with it."

She gave him a doubtful look. "Like the tile in the bathroom you hated, and the paint color for the dining room that you said reminded you of vomit."

Rapp looked up at the ceiling as if the whole thing sounded very unfamiliar to him.

"You don't need to say anything. As your loving wife I'm going to tell you how we're going to proceed. You are going to open a bottle of wine for us, because I need a drink something fierce. Then we are going to go through the carpet samples, and you are going to help me make a decision, and then we're going to sit down in front of the fireplace and you're going to rub my shoulders."

Rapp put his hands on her shoulders and said with a mischievous look, "And then we're going to have wild sex."

She shook her head. "I am tired . . . my feet hurt . . . I feel gross . . . I have to get up at five, and I'm not so sure I should reward your forgetful behavior."

"I'll make it up to you." He started kissing her neck.

"We'll see. Now go get my glass of wine."

Rapp continued to work on her lovely neck until she pushed him away, laughing. He grabbed a bottle of cabernet from the wine rack and began opening it. As he looked up he saw his wife standing in front of the fireplace holding his legal pad. Her expression was intent as she tried to make sense of his notes. He'd have to start writing in Arabic. That would drive her nuts. He calmly walked back into the living room and yanked the notepad from her hands.

"I was reading that," she said in an indignant voice.

"Really . . . did you ever think it's none of your business?"

Anna smiled. "But we're married, darling. We're not supposed to keep secrets from each other."

"You are so full of it." Rapp tore off the top sheet and threw it in the fire. "When was the last time you let me look at your notes for a story? You're in the wrong line of work. You should have been a spy."

"Really," she said in a hopeful tone. "There's still time for a career change. I'm young."

Rapp went back into the kitchen and finished pulling the cork from the bottle. He poured two glasses. "You'd hate it. You'd never be able to handle the scrutiny from those jackals in the press."

"They're real bastards, aren't they?"

"The worst." Rapp handed her the glass of wine.

Anna swatted him in the butt, and said, "You're bad. Now go get those carpet samples and get to work."

"Only if it means I get a little love later."

"You're on probation for the evening. Don't push it."

Rapp walked to the closet, dreading the mundane task that lay ahead. His thoughts were already returning to his notes. There were a lot of things to consider. In a perfect world it would have been nice to bounce a few things off Anna, but it just wasn't an option. Especially this stuff. Operations like this were designed to never see the light of day. That's why they were called black ops. The Freedom of Information Act would have no effect on them. No records would be kept, and the men and women who were involved would go to their graves silent to their very last breath.

10

Erich Abel drove his brand-new silver SL 55 AMG Mercedes up the switchback road with a heavy foot. Abel had been eyeing the car for sometime. It was not that he couldn't afford it, it was just that, financially, he was an exceptionally conservative man. His BMW Series 7 had been only two years old and he had decided to wait another year before trading it in. In his mind, delaying gratification was in many ways the ultimate form of self-discipline. His recent contract with the bereaved Saudi father, though, had changed all that, and after all, he spent a fair amount of time in his car driving back and forth between Zurich and Vienna.

While in Riyadh, Abel had made precisely seven phone calls. Ten million dollars in cash, while it was very appealing to the eye, presented certain problems that Abel did not want to deal with. He instead told Saeed Ahmed Abdullah that he would prefer the funds wired to five separate banks in Switzerland. Abel wrote down the instructions and called his contact at each institution telling them to let him know as soon as the funds were received. Within an hour all five men had confirmed that Abel now had ten million dollars in very liquid assets to add to $1.4 million in cash he had strategically placed at various institutions around the world. There was another two million in real estate and securities, but in Abel's line of work one always needed a stash to draw from in the event one needed to disappear for a while.

The sixth call was made to the Mercedes dealership in Zurich. He did not bother to haggle with them over the $125,000 price tag of the world's top performance sedan. Abel told them he would be in to get the car the next afternoon. The seventh, and last call, was to someone for whom he had great respect. Dimitri Petrov still lived in Moscow and still smoked two packs a day of his stinky Russian cigarettes. The smoking habit was the only thing Abel didn't like about the man. Petrov was a prince among thieves. A true professional who garnered respect from friend and foe alike, and in all likelihood the only fellow professional who Abel would talk to about his new business opportunity.

It was noon in Moscow by the time he called his old KGB friend, and the Russian's voice sounded as if he'd awoken him from a dead sleep. The two exchanged pleasantries for less than thirty seconds, which for them meant they insulted each other. Abel used a more deft approach, while Petrov initiated a full-on assault that eventually ended in a stream of creatively linked obscenities. The brief discussion reminded Abel of how much he missed his old friend. Getting down to business, Abel told Petrov he needed to see him immediately. When Petrov hesitated, Abel assured him he would be plied with fine food, expensive wine, excellent cigars, and $10,000 for his time. Intrigue alone would have more than likely induced him to make the trip, but Abel was hungry to complete his task. There wasn't a day to be wasted. He sweetened the pot by suggesting they meet at his Alpine house near Bludenz, a little over an hour from Zurich just across the Swiss border in Austria. Petrov loved its majestic views and solitude. The Russian mumbled something about his expenses, Abel assured him they would be covered, and told him to catch the first flight out in the morning.

Abel accelerated through another switchback and then pressed the gas pedal to the floor on the straightaway. The 493-hp engine launched the sedan up the mountain road like a rocket. Abel allowed himself a brief smile. The vehicle was a testament to West German engineering. More than a decade later he still drew the line between East and West. The country he had grown up in could never have produced such an exquisitely powerful and utterly dependable machine. And it wasn't just an East German problem. There wasn't a single communist country capable of such greatness. Abel had abandoned his country of birth and tried his best not to return. There were a myriad of complicated reasons. First and foremost he did not like the constant reminder that he had been on the losing side of the twentieth century's great Cold War. Reunification had helped East Germany greatly, but it still had a ways to go before catching up. The scars caused by the neglect of communism ran deep. Years of tarnish had to be removed before the prideful luster and German efficiency could be fully restored.

Abel had lived a lie the first thirty years of his life, and he refused to waste a single day continuing to do so. He was now a Swiss citizen, and like his new country he had adopted a neutral, more businesslike attitude toward the world. Wars came and went, commerce was constant, and when the two collided great opportunity presented itself. Abel was simply a facilitator. A specialist in risk assessment, and sometimes when it was called for, like now, risk removal.

Abel approached the second to the last switchback and slowed quite a bit. This one was sharper than the others. Through a gap in the lush spruce trees he caught a glimpse of the local ski resort. It wasn't set to open for another month. From Abel's Alpine house it was a twenty-minute drive down into the village. The pristine, high mountain air was good for his asthma, and the solitude was good for both his mind and his business.

He had hesitated just briefly before calling Petrov. In his line of work everything had to be analyzed through the prism of risk/reward. There was always a trade-off. Abel had more than adequate resources when it came to the standard job, but this one called for something special. He needed fresh talent. Someone who was extremely good, but not yet known to all the usual suspects. As a general rule, the fewer people involved the better, but for a job of this level, he had no one in his Rolodex who he felt confident giving the assignment to. Petrov would know of someone, though. He was sure of that.

Abel swung around the last switchback and then turned onto his driveway which went back down the slope slightly parallel to the mountain road. The long driveway was lined with tall, skinny spruce and after a fairly steep initial descent it leveled out. Abel swung into the parking area in front and parked next to a rental car. He noticed his friend's suitcase sitting on the porch next to the front door, and got out of the car. He walked around the wraparound porch to the left and found Petrov sitting in a chair, his eyes closed, basking in the sun.

Without bothering to open his eyes, the Russian asked in mildly accented English, "How long were you going to have me wait, you ungrateful Nazi?"

Abel smiled and noted the gray wool topcoat spread across Petrov's lap like a blanket. With his silver hair he looked like a retired person on a sea cruise. A pack of cigarettes sat on one armrest and a well-used brass lighter on the other. "I have been watching you for over an hour, you old Stalinist dog. I thought you were either dead or napping . . . which considering your age, are both distinct possibilities."

One of the eyes on the broad face shot open and Petrov began cursing Abel in Russian. Abel's Russian had never been great, and had gotten much worse, but he got the gist of what his friend was saying. There was something about dogs fornicating and his lineage and then more of the standard Nazi stuff.

He laughed enthusiastically and then said, "Are you so old you can't stand up to greet an old friend? Should I help you?" Abel put his hands out in an overly dramatic fashion. "Should I call a nurse?"

"I will break your pretty little nose if you lay a hand on me," Petrov growled and yanked himself from the chair with surprising swiftness.

The two men embraced, and Abel once again tried to slap his Russian friend on the back as hard as he was being slapped. It was never enough, though. The two men were roughly the same height, both just under six feet, but the Russian had him by a good fifty pounds. Petrov was sixty-one and didn't look a day under seventy. His silver hair, smoking, love of food and spirits, and undoubtedly the stress of his job had not been kind to him.

"Come," said Abel, "let's go inside. I stopped at the market and got all of your favorite things." The two men walked around the porch and Abel unlocked the front door. "You know where your room is. Go in and get settled, and I'll take care of everything else."

Abel brought his own suitcase in and then unloaded three bags from the trunk. The first thing he did was take the bottle of Belvedere vodka and place it in the freezer. There was a better than even chance that his friend would polish off the entire bottle before they went to bed. Always aware of his asthma, he cracked a few windows to let some fresh air in. Next he threw a six-pack of Gösser in the fridge along with a six-pack of Kaiser. If that didn't keep Petrov busy, there was a well-stocked wine cellar in the basement. He then placed the pickled herring, smoked ham, sausages, vegetables, and cake box in the fridge.

Petrov appeared right on cue, and Abel handed him a bottle of Gosser. He grabbed himself a Kaiser and held up his bottle for a toast. "To old friends and free markets."

Petrov nodded and took a big swig. He was about to say something, but decided to take another drink. "I've been waiting for that all afternoon."

"Sorry I didn't get here earlier, but I just flew in this afternoon." Abel looked at the clock. It was almost five.

"Where were you?" asked the Russian between swigs. The beer was already half gone.

Abel was about to tell him, but caught himself. "The better question would be where haven't I been." He opened a container of mixed nuts and placed them in a bowl on the counter. The key with Petrov was to keep feeding him.

"You've been busy doing OPEC's dirty work."

The Organization of Petroleum Exporting Countries was headquartered in Vienna and was by far Abel's biggest client. "Everybody needs to collect intelligence." Abel held up his beer. "Even the Russian Mob." The comment was a direct shot at Petrov's sometime employer.

"Yes, well, the glorious experiment of communism has ended, and we are now left to fend for ourselves."

"To freelancing and capitalism." Abel raised his glass.

"I'll drink to freelancing, but never capitalism. Those pigs have flocked to my country like vultures to pick at its carcass and prey on the weak."

Abel laughed. "And what did the communists do?" This was a common argument between them, and Abel had never lost it. Capitalism was far preferable. If it was brought up again later, after Petrov was drunk enough, he could get him to admit it. The Russian would threaten to kill him if he told anyone, and then he would launch into a tirade about the corrupt communists and how they ruined a perfectly good idea.

Petrov was mumbling something about greed and the destructiveness of organized religion. Abel cut him off and said, "Go outside and have a cigarette. I'm going to get dinner ready. Here, take the herring. I brought it just for you."

Petrov eagerly took the jar of salty pickled fish and then asked in a genuinely concerned tone, "What about cigars? Please don't tell me I flew all this way and you don't have cigars."

"I have cigars. Don't worry. They're for after dinner." Abel shooed him away and began preparing the meal.

Petrov came in to check on him periodically and shouted insults at him from the open porch door. By the time they sat down to eat, the six-pack of Gösser was gone. Petrov had only one Kaiser and immediately announced it was a girly beer. Too light. The bottle of vodka was placed in the center of the table and the bet was on as to whether or not it would last to see the sun rise. Petrov said absolutely not and Abel agreed.

Abel was not a meek eater, but his Russian friend made him look like a sparrow. Soon all of the sausage and ham were gone, as well as the fried potatoes, and the lion's share had gone to Petrov. Abel placed the dobosh torte on a platter and watched as Petrov's eyes dilated as if someone had hit him over the head. The cake, a confection of layered chocolate sponge and chocolate buttercream covered with caramel, was mouth-watering. Abel had one piece to Petrov's three, whereupon the Russian announced that if he didn't get up and leave the table he would eat the whole thing. Abel was sure he'd be back in around midnight to finish the other half.

Finally, they retired to the porch and a starlit evening. Abel brought out two heavy wool blankets to ward off the cool air. There wasn't a sound other than Petrov's various attempts at aiding his digestion. Abel broke out the box of Montecristo cigars. He kept one and handed the box to Petrov.

"Yours to take home with you." Abel rolled the cigar under his nose taking in the fine aroma.

"Thank you, my friend." The Russian opened the box and looked eagerly at his bounty.

Abel would have only one cigar, and he would smoke it very carefully. The only time he chanced it was when he was in the mountains and even then he had to see how he was feeling. With his asthma he had to be very cautious. He would savor the moment, smelling the cigar for up to an hour before lighting it.

"I need some advice, Dimitri."

Petrov snatched a cigar from the box, bit off the end, and lit it. After several heavy puffs, he said, "I was wondering when you would get around to business."

"Always after dinner. You know that."

Petrov pointed his cigar at his German friend. "You should be careful. You're becoming far too predictable."

Abel didn't like the sound of that, and made a mental note to review his habits. He withdrew an envelope from his jacket and handed it to Petrov. "Your fee."

The Russian hesitated while grimacing. "I don't like this. I have done nothing."

"I have confidence in you."

"Ten thousand dollars." He shook his head. "We are friends."

"Yes, we are." Abel slapped the money into his hand. "And I am being compensated very well. Think of it this way . . . it is not my money . . . it belongs to the man who hired me. You are a subcontractor."

Petrov placed the envelope in his pocket. "Now that I have been hired, what is it you need?"

"A name."

"What kind of name?"

Abel had already decided under no circumstances would he reveal the identity of his target. "I need someone killed."

Petrov shrugged nonchalantly. "You know plenty of people who specialize in such things."

"Yes, but this job requires someone who is better than your average plumber."

Petrov's brow furrowed in thought. "Can you tell me about the target?"

Abel shook his head.

"You must give me something to work with. Do you need it to look like an accident? Do you care about collateral damage? What theater will they need to operate in? What fee will they be paid?"

"I need the best. I need a real professional. Someone who looks at their craft as a higher form of art."

"Ahhh . . ." sighed Petrov. "You want one of the crazy ones. The kind that treat the kill like it is a religion. And you want the best?"

It was obvious that Petrov was thinking of some names. "Yes," said Abel, "I want someone who not only thinks they are the best, but someone who is hungry to prove they are the best." Abel had thought of this distinction carefully. There was a good chance that a seasoned contract killer would turn down the job as soon as he learned the identity of the target. He needed someone who was on their way up. Someone who would want to mount Mitch Rapp like that leopard in Abdullah's office.

"Your target must be someone very important."

"I wouldn't say that necessarily."

"Someone who is well guarded?"

"Not necessarily."

Petrov threw back a shot of vodka and puffed on his cigar. "I hope you are not working for those damn Saudis."

"I never reveal my clients, you know that. But out of curiosity, why do you dislike the Saudis so much?"

"As bad as the communists were, they pale in comparison to the Saudis."

Abel laughed. "How so?"

"The Saudis think that God is on their side, and people who think God is on their side are capable of the most inhumane acts."

Abel was intrigued. He'd never heard his friend talk about religion this way. "Correct me if I'm wrong, but the great leaders of Mother Russia—Comrade Lenin and Comrade Stalin—managed to kill twenty million people, and as far as I know, they were atheists."

"That number is greatly exaggerated."

"Cut it in half then. A mere ten million."

"I will not defend Lenin and Stalin. They were awful creatures, but these Saudis and their maniacal brand of Islam will be the end of us all."

Abel did not want to wander too far from the task at hand. If there was time later they could continue their jousting. "I will tell you one thing and one thing only about my client. His motivation is as pure as it is rotten and is as old as man himself."

"Your client is a prostitute?"

Abel smiled. "No."

Petrov reached for the vodka. "Revenge."

"Yes."

After his glass was full Petrov asked, "Revenge for what? Did someone dare gaze upon one of his daughters without her veil on?"

"I never said he was a Saudi."

"Why does he want revenge?"

"Someone killed his son."

"Someone important?"

Abel shook his head. "Someone who is very dangerous."

"Ahhh . . . I think I see. You need a killer to kill a killer."

"Precisely." Petrov seemed finally satisfied. Abel wondered if his old friend was getting a conscience in his old age.

"And this person is good."

"Yes."

"Anyone I've ever heard of?"

"I am done answering questions. I have already told you too much.

Give me my name and then we can get back to talking about the atrocities committed by communism."

Petrov snarled at him like an old dog who had been poked by a stick. "I have a name and a phone number for you. A woman will answer. She is French. I am told she is quite beautiful. She will act as the go-between."

"And the shooter?"

"I know very little about him. I like it that way, and I assume so does he. My source tells me he is relatively young and very well rounded with the various tools of the trade."

"Would you say he's aggressive or cautious?"

"I would say aggressive," laughed Petrov. "He's done three jobs for me in the last seven months and God only knows how many others."

11

The motorcade turned off the highway and passed the lone, white guard post that had been added in 1993 after several employees were killed on their way into work. The two Suburbans and black armor-plated Cadillac limousine continued onto the narrow tree-lined drive and over a rise without slowing. They appeared to be in a hurry. Once over the rise, an intimidating security checkpoint came into view. All visitor traffic was directed to the right by large, easily readable signs. Other signs warned people that this was their last chance to turn around without risking arrest and prosecution. If they missed the signs, the men in black Nomex jumpsuits carrying submachine guns provided further warning that this place was not part of the local sightseeing tour.

The motorcade stayed to the left and came to an abrupt stop in front of the yellow painted steel barricade. Men with guns were everywhere and there were more of them behind the greenish tinted bulletproof Plexiglas of the blockhouse. Three of the guards who had been talking when the surprise visitors came over the hill immediately spread out. No one had to tell them; it was part of their training. Clusters made for easy targets. This wasn't Hollywood. There was no racking of the slides and flicking of safety switches. When these men were on duty they were hot, which meant they had a round in the chamber, and the only safety was their forefinger.

The motorcade was immediately flanked on one side by four of the black-clad men. Despite the gray overcast morning they were all wearing dark shooting glasses to cover their eyes. Their weapons remained point-

ing down, but fingers caressed trigger guards while eyes tried to peer beyond the heavily tinted windows of the vehicles. These types of motorcades were commonplace, but they were always expected—on the list
and fully vetted. This one was not, and the men and women of the security force did not like surprises.

A captain came out of the blockhouse with a look of slight irritation
on his face and approached the passenger side of the lead vehicle. The
tinted window came down only to reveal a tinted pair of sunglasses. The
captain, an eight-year veteran of the force, asked in a not-so-friendly
tone, "May I help you?"

The man pulled out a black leather case and flipped it open to reveal his credentials. "Secret Service." He jerked his thumb back toward the limo and said, "We have Director Ross. He's here on official
business."

The captain nodded and folded his hands behind his back. "Did you
guys forget your manners?"

"Huh?" the agent asked, not getting the question.

"Simple protocol . . . call ahead . . . let us know you're coming." The
captain rocked back and forth on his heels while he assessed how far he
should push this.

The agent gave him the courtesy of lowering his glasses an inch so
the top two-thirds of his eyes were visible. "The director is a busy man,
but I hear you loud and clear. The problem is we didn't even know we
were coming out here until five minutes ago. We were leaving the new
counterterrorism facility and he told us to come straight here. I'm just
following orders."

The answer seemed plausible. "All right. Roll the windows down, get
your creds out, and we'll make this as quick and painless as possible." The
captain pointed at the lead Suburban and three men appeared from the
blockhouse, one with a dog. The dog and his handler began circling the
vehicle while the two men began inspecting credentials. The captain hesitated for a second and then went back to the limo. He waited patiently
by the back passenger window for a three count, staring at his own reflection. He waited two more seconds and then rapped on the window
with his knuckles.

The window came down revealing two white men talking on
phones. One was in his fifties and the other appeared to be about ten
years younger. The captain recognized the older man as Mark Ross, the
new director of National Intelligence.

The younger man placed his phone flat against the lapel of his suit coat and said, "Could we speed this up, we're on a tight schedule."

"Absolutely," replied the captain. "Who is the director here to see?"

"I'm afraid that's privileged information."

The captain could already see this suit was going to be real fun to work with. "I need to see IDs, and we need to check the trunk. Then I'll have you on your way."

The man gave him a look that said, are you kidding me? "I said we're in a hurry."

The captain stayed calm and polite. "If you'd called ahead some of this could have been avoided, but unfortunately you didn't. Identification please." The captain stuck out his hand and waited. He collected the younger man's ID and wondered whether or not to push it with Director Ross. He decided not to when he realized Ross was talking to the president. He took the single ID back to the blockhouse to make a copy and run a quick check, while the men continued searching the vehicles. He didn't like any of this, but technically, he supposed the new director of National Intelligence was his boss. Less than a minute later he came back out, looked briefly at the limo, and then spoke to the agent in the lead vehicle.

"You guys under high alert or something?"

"Why do you ask?"

"You've got a lot of muscle with you to be driving around DC. Four guys in each Suburban and two more in the limo. That's about what the president travels with when he comes out here."

The agent pulled his glasses down again and said, "I don't ask questions . . . you know what I mean?"

Smiling, the captain replied, "To a point. I'm going to have the Suburbans wait over here in this parking lot on the right, and the limo may proceed to the main building."

"That'll work for me."

KENNEDY REMAINED ABSOLUTELY unreadable as Rapp went through his pitch. He had seen her stoic behavior unnerve subordinates, especially the younger ones—the ones who needed constant feedback and supervision. Rapp needed no cheerleading. He and Kennedy had been doing this for a long time. Normally, she would have been a bit more responsive to what he was proposing, but Rapp had brought someone to the meeting, so she remained her polite but professional self.

"The Pentagon, State . . . they're all throwing money around like a sailor in a whorehouse. We need to do the same thing."

Kennedy glanced at the other man in the meeting, who happened to be a retired naval officer, and then looked back at Rapp. "Throw money around like a horny sailor?"

"Absolutely." Rapp smiled. "The more money the better. That'll make it harder for the General Accounting Office and all those oversight pukes to track what we're really up to."

"Could you possibly come up with a better metaphor than the sailor/hooker one?"

"I agree," said the retired officer.

"How about a Marine in a whorehouse?" Rapp looked at the blond-haired man sitting next to him. "Does that work for you?"

"Absolutely. Marines are pigs." Scott Coleman laughed. The former Navy SEAL was in an unusually good mood, and it had everything to do with what Rapp was telling them.

Kennedy ignored the banter and got back to more pressing issues. "So, in essence, what you're advising is that we take Scott's company and use it as a logistical front for the new and expanded Orion Team?"

"Yes."

"That's been tried before and it blew up in the CIA's face."

"When?"

"The Vietnam War. You've surely heard of an outfit called Air America."

"I was in diapers at the time. Different time, different war, different world."

"I'm not so sure," Kennedy persisted.

"Air America got busted, because they got too big, and a couple of corncob generals at the Pentagon didn't like the CIA having their own air force. That combined with the press, the general mood on Capitol Hill, and the public's attitude toward the war . . . it all contributed to their cover being blown."

Kennedy raised an eyebrow. "And how exactly has anything changed?"

"Everybody, including and especially the Pentagon, are using civilian contractors, and they're not just hiring engineers to build bridges, schools, and hospitals. They're hiring firms left and right to provide diplomatic security, food prep services, cleaning services, trucking . . .

you name it, and if it doesn't involve actual combat, the Pentagon is using private contractors."

"Scott?" Kennedy asked.

"I've seen my business grow from about two million a year to over twenty."

"Tell her about Black Watch." Rapp was referring to the private security firm that had been started by one of Coleman's fellow SEALs.

"They're going to do over two hundred and fifty million in business with the government alone this year. They have six thousand acres down in North Carolina that they've turned into a Disneyland for shooters. They have a race track to teach defensive driving, they have a state-of-the-art sniping range and shooting house, their own airstrips, planes, helicopters, armored personnel carriers . . . you name it. They have equipment that is forward-deployed around the globe. They've even built a damn lake to train SEALs on the underwater delivery vehicles."

"Their philosophy," interjected Rapp, "is that they can do it better and in a more cost effective way than the federal government."

"That wouldn't be difficult."

"Well, they're the first people to really try it, and they are succeeding."

Kennedy knew about Black Watch. The CIA already used them to protect certain assets abroad. There was a very liberal, antiwar minority in Washington who thought of the group as nothing more than a bunch of overpaid mercenaries who were eventually going to give America a black eye. Kennedy thought those people tended to have a naïve view of the world. To them, anyone who carried a gun was bad. Even cops.

"So, where I'm going with this," said Rapp, "is that we begin to use a series of companies to . . ." Rapp didn't get to finish his sentence because the door to Kennedy's office opened. He turned to see two men entering.

"Don't bother getting up," announced the new director of National Intelligence, Mark Ross. Ross was tall, thin, and well dressed, and exuded an air of importance. He marched across the long office trailed by a second, shorter man.

Rapp looked over his shoulder with undisguised irritation. He'd been in countless closed-door meetings in this office, and when the door was closed it was for a good reason—especially this morning. This was a first. People did not simply barge in on the director of the CIA unannounced.

"Irene, sorry to intrude, but I was in the neighborhood and decided to drop by." Ross reached the area where they were sitting and let his gaze fall on Rapp. "Mitch," he said, placing his left hand on Rapp's shoulder and extending his right hand. "Good to see you as always."

Rapp nodded. He'd only met the new intel czar twice, both times when Ross was in the Senate. Kennedy had warned him to be cordial to their new boss. Rapp recalled her being unusually cautious about the former senator. Kennedy had explained that it wasn't Ross as much as it was his new job. No one in Washington was quite sure how the new position of director of National Intelligence was going to play itself out, and that uncertainty had caused the political gamesmanship to begin. At the mere mention of politics Rapp tuned her out. He was more concerned about who Ross was and where he'd come from. If Ross was going to politicize intelligence they would butt heads big-time.

The skinny on Ross was that he had a firm grasp on national security issues and knew how to motivate people. It also helped that after graduating from Princeton he'd actually worked at the CIA in the Directorate of Intelligence. His claim to fame at the Agency was that right before leaving to get his law degree at Yale he prepared a report on a fringe Iranian religious figure known as the Ayatollah Khomeini. Ross predicted that Khomeini's religious fervor and growing following was likely to lead to a full-blown revolution in Iran. He was one of the only people in the government who read the tea leaves correctly. On the surface Ross had an outgoing manner about him that was interpreted by some as self-assured and by others as arrogant. Rapp assumed that like most men who had been members of America's most exclusive club, the U.S. Senate, Ross was a bit of both, depending on the situation. Now Rapp sat uncomfortably in the chair, with the man's hand still on his shoulder, wondering if the former senator had any idea how much he hated being touched. He glanced down at the offending hand and briefly envisioned snapping one of the fingers.

"I see that pretty wife of yours on TV every day," Ross continued. "You're a lucky guy." He took his hand off Rapp's shoulder and looked at the third party in the room. It was obvious by the square jaw and athletic build of the man that he was not your average Langley bureaucrat. He appeared to be a Nordic version of Rapp, and Ross suddenly found himself wondering what he, Rapp, and Kennedy had been discussing.

"Mark Ross," he introduced himself to the blond-haired man. "Director of National Intelligence."

Coleman nodded. If he was impressed he didn't show it. "Scott Coleman."

"You work here at Langley?"

"No, my IQ is too high." Coleman gave him his best shit-ass grin.

Ross laughed. "I don't think there are too many people in this town with an IQ as high as Doctor Kennedy's, but I'll go along with your explanation for now. You look ex-military to me. What branch?"

"Navy."

"SEALs?"

"That's classified."

Ross hesitated for a second, and Rapp thought he noticed a flash of anger just beneath the surface. Ross quelled it and looked to Kennedy. "Definitely a SEAL. Nowhere else in the military do they breed such contempt for authority."

Rapp was the only one in the room who laughed. Kennedy never found such banter very funny, and Rapp knew Coleman well enough to know he was having an internal monologue as to the merits of blindly respecting authority versus real leaders who earned respect.

Before Coleman could respond Ross placed his hand on the back of the man he'd come in with and said, "This is Jonathan Gordon, my new deputy. He's going to be my point man on all coordination between Langley and National Intelligence."

"Nice to meet you, Jonathan," replied Kennedy. She took off her glasses and set them on the leather folder in front of her. Her body language revealed nothing.

Gordon was a half head shorter than his boss and looked to be in his early forties. Rapp tried to size him up, but got nothing.

"Again, sorry for interrupting," said Ross as he clapped his hands together. "I'm trying to get up to speed as quickly as possible. I'll let you three get back to whatever it was you were discussing. I'm going to go check in on a couple of my old intel buddies, and then I'll pop back up here in about thirty minutes." Ross checked his watch. "Will that work for you, Irene?"

"If you give me a few minutes to finish up here, I'll show you around myself."

"No, don't bother," Ross insisted. "I still remember my way, and besides you're too valuable to be giving tours." He started to back away, and in a quieter tone said, "I'll stop back up in a bit. There's a few things I'd like to discuss with you." Ross and Gordon then left the corner office as quickly as they'd arrived.

When the door was closed Rapp turned to Coleman and asked, "Why do you have such a problem with authority?"

Kennedy shook her head. "Mr. Pot, leave Mr. Kettle alone and let's get back to where we were."

ROSS, GORDON, AND the two bodyguards approached the bank of elevators. Ross stopped and folded his arms across his chest. He looked back toward Kennedy's office and appeared fixed on a particular thought. As the elevator doors slid open Ross whispered to Gordon, "I want you to find out everything you can about Mr. Coleman." Ross stepped into the elevator.

"I'm already on it." Gordon retrieved a Palm Pilot from his suit and went to work.

Ross stared at the backs of his thick-necked bodyguards and then tilted his head toward Gordon and, still whispering, said, "Rapp makes me nervous enough as it is. I don't think there's a person in this town who can control him."

"Not even the president?"

"Especially not the president. Rapp's saved the man's life twice." Ross held up two fingers to punctuate his point. "You remember Valerie Jones, the president's chief of staff, stepping down this past summer?"

"Yeah."

"That was Rapp. He and Jones were like a frickin' ferret and a snake. . . . I mean, they hated each other. Rapp gave the president a choice. Me or Jones, and the president chose Rapp."

Gordon appeared impressed. "I've heard the man is very talented at what he does."

"He is. Don't get me wrong, he's the best, but guys like that need to be kept on a short leash. No, strike that. They need to kept in a cage in the basement and the only time you let them out is when there's a murderer in your house."

Gordon flexed his knees. "He doesn't strike me as the type who's going to let you put him in a cage."

"There lies the problem, my friend. We have to rein in all these damn agencies, most of whom can't stand each other, and get them to cooperate. I need them to follow my orders. I need everyone playing off the same sheet of music and looking at me, the conductor. I can't have Rapp running around banging on his war drums doing whatever the hell he wants."

The elevator doors opened. "There are people in this town, Jonathan, who would love to see me fail. People who would give a lot to see me embarrassed, and I don't like to be embarrassed. Rapp makes me nervous, and if you can't figure out how to put him in a cage, you'd better at least find a way to put a leash on him."

They exited the elevator and started down the hall. "And find out the bona fides on that smart-ass Coleman. There's no way he and Rapp are up to anything good."

12

Erich Abel leaned against a light post and stared at the pretty woman sitting across the street. He'd arrived early and walked the neighborhood, doubling back from time to time and making sure he was familiar with at least two potential escape routes. He made a few small purchases: a gift card and an antique pen. Both stops allowed him to pause and make sure he wasn't being followed. The gift card would end up in the garbage, but the pen he would keep. It was an ivory Mont Blanc fountain pen with inlaid silver bands and shirt clip. It would be the fifty-sixth pen in his collection.

He doubted he had anything to fear this afternoon, but discipline was what kept a spy alive. That and the ability to deal with boredom. The truth about spycraft was that ninety-plus percent of it was utterly mundane. It involved a lot of standing around and waiting. Just like he was doing now, but with his new millions spread across a series of banks he felt more secure than he should have, and he allowed his mind to wander.

Abel was wondering why one of the world's most beautiful and dynamic cities gave him a sense of melancholy. He thought perhaps it was because Paris was the heart of France, and he had some time ago come to the conclusion that France was a country whose greatest moments had come and gone.

Their embarrassingly futile effort to defend themselves against the Germans at the start of WWII had left a permanent scar on the country's identity. The tiny country of Finland, after all, had stopped Stalin's Red

Army for three months at the onset of the war, while France had barely lasted two weeks against the Nazi blitzkrieg. In the end it took foreign armies to win their own country back for them, and while it was preferable to living under Nazi occupation, their national pride had been dealt a serious blow. This was, after all, the country of Napoleon, who had once dominated all of Europe. In less than a century they had gone from one of the world's preeminent powers to a country incapable of putting up a fight.

The French were a proud people, and Abel reasoned that to protect their collective psyche from the truth, they had decided that leisure and intellectual refinement were more important than economic and military might. Abel could not deny the worth of intellectual and artistic pursuits, but they were nothing without secure borders and a strong economic engine to fund such lofty endeavors.

The government had instituted a thirty-five-hour work week, and two-hour lunches were a coveted tradition. On top of that almost all workers were guaranteed nine weeks of vacation every year. The country was inching closer to socialism with each election cycle, and the disincentive to work was beginning to take its toll. If you can't, or won't, create on your own, the next best thing is to steal what someone else has created. Abel had seen firsthand how the Soviet bloc countries had used industrial espionage to try and keep up with the West. Similarly, the French intelligence services had become notorious for picking the pockets of visiting executives. So much so that many foreign companies had a standing order forbidding their executives from taking laptops or any other crucial data with them while doing business in France.

Abel came to the sad conclusion that he was watching a once-great civilization slide toward the abyss. The masses wanted the state to provide for them in every way, and the politicians who promised the most largesse were the ones who were elected. They in turn gave the people what they wanted, which then placed an ever-increasing burden on the most productive members of society. This was, he supposed, democracy's Achilles' heel. It struck him at that moment that socialism was far more insidious than communism. In East Germany there had been nothing voluntary about communism. It was simply the only option. But the people of France, through their own selfishness, were choosing this road to ruin.

Abel wondered if there was an investment opportunity to be exploited. Possibly a long-range trend in the financial markets? He made a mental note to talk to several of his clients about the possible implications. The dirty work he performed for his clients was extremely lucrative, but it was also inherently dangerous. In light of the advance for the Rapp job, Abel had started to think about shifting his focus to more legitimate work.

Abel looked across the street at the woman and smiled. He was fooling himself. Going legitimate would be boring. Besides, spying was one of the fastest growth industries in the world, and if Abel was to be honest with himself, there was no other professional fraternity that he would rather belong to.

One thing he would like to partake more in, though, was the company of women. The problem was that he was both too busy and too choosy. He liked intelligent women, but not too bookish, beautiful but not gorgeous, confident but not too extroverted, and they absolutely had to be classy in an austere way. He also wanted a woman who could enjoy silence. Talking was overrated, and Abel believed less was almost always more.

The woman he was currently eyeing seemed to fall into many of his favored categories. She was average in height with black wavy hair down to her shoulders, an oval face with a delicate upturned nose, and a clear milky complexion. He wished he could see her eyes, but she was wearing large black sunglasses, the type worn by movie starlets in the sixties that had recently come back in style. She was in designer black from her coat to her form-fitting, spike-heeled suede boots. Her style was fashion-savvy without being ostentatious. It was the perfect form of urban camouflage for Paris in the fall.

Abel was standing off to the side of a newsstand where he had just purchased a copy of the French magazine *Nouvel Observateur.* He was wearing a dark brown three-piece suit and had a reversible trench coat draped over his left arm. The woman was sitting at an outdoor café across the street. Abel had spoken to her only once, and it had been brief. She'd been polite but had asked him immediately for an e-mail address. Abel complied and then waited patiently by his computer for two hours before her e-mail arrived in his in-box. The first thing she wanted to know was how he had heard about her. Not wanting to name names, he gave her a description of Petrov and vaguely referenced the work she and her partner had done for him over the past year. She asked a few more questions that might trip him up, but Abel knew Petrov too well. Once she was satisfied that Abel was serious, she put forth her terms. Her "firm," as she called it, charged a nonrefundable retainer of $25,000 to get things started. For that initial payment they would consider any job transmitted to them via e-mail. If he'd like to conduct business via a dead drop it would cost him $50,000 and a face-to-face sit-down would run him $100,000. All retainers, she reiterated, were nonrefundable. This woman was no socialist.

Negotiating a job like this via e-mail was out of the question. While the dead drop was tempting, there was simply too much on the line. A sit-down was the only prudent way to handle it. Abel wired the money to the offshore account and she gave him a specific list of instructions, which he had followed with only one exception.

Those instructions led him to where he was now—standing next to a newsstand on the Rue du Mont Cenis in the Montmartre neighborhood of Paris. He had come alone, as instructed, and had purchased the magazine she'd specified. She was sitting at the designated café, just as she said she would, with her Burberry umbrella saving his seat. She'd been sitting there for fifteen minutes and Abel was enjoying making her wait. That was part of his plan. He would go only so far in letting them set the tone and tempo of this new, and hopefully successful, business relationship. They had $100,000 of his money. They could wait a little bit.

If she got up and left, that would be even better. That way he could follow her and learn a bit more before he set up a second meet. The most dangerous part of this was not the initial meeting, but rather the moment he chose to reveal the target. That was the point of no return. Once Abel told them the target was Rapp they would be locked in. Abel turned the page of his magazine and looked over the top of it at the intriguing woman he was to meet. Five more minutes, he told himself, and if she didn't get up to leave he would go over and proceed as planned.

He watched her look at her watch, and he wondered what she looked like naked. He doubted she would disappoint him. Abel let out a sigh of expectation, and just when he was ready to inhale he felt something pressed against his lower back and a warm breath on his neck.

A man's voice whispered in his ear, *"Elle est belle . . . n'est-ce pas?"* *She's beautiful, isn't she?*

Abel started to turn around, but was stopped by a gloved hand that clamped down on his neck with an alarming firmness. The man was so close he could smell the coffee on his breath. Abel started to bring his right arm up so he could strike a blow and pivot free.

"Don't." The grip tightened. "Not unless you'd like me to sever your spinal cord."

Abel felt the blade against the small of his back. He struggled to remain calm. The man's English was perfect. For a split second Abel was confronted with the horrible image that it was Mitch Rapp himself who was holding him at knifepoint. He managed to take another breath and in an embarrassingly unsteady voice said, "I don't know what you're talking about."

"Erich," the man grunted, "you are not dealing with amateurs. Don't play games with us, or I swear I'll bone you like a fish, and you'll spend the rest of your days with a limp prick."

Despite the cool autumn air sweat began forming on Abel's upper lip. *How in the hell do they know my name?* he thought to himself. "I am merely trying to be careful."

"I appreciate professionalism, but don't toy with us. I followed you here and have been watching you for the past hour. In case you doubt me, I saw you buy both the card and the pen."

Frown lines creased Abel's forehead. He'd taken the metro and two separate taxis to the meet. He had diligently checked to make sure he wasn't being tailed. How in the hell had this man followed him so closely?

"I think you've made her wait long enough." The man leaned in so his lips were just inches from the German's neck. He knew his warm breath would further unnerve his prospective business partner, which was his intent. Fear was the only thing that kept people honest in this business. "Get going . . . and don't even think of turning around. You'll be dead before you see my face. Do you understand?"

Fearing his voice would fail him, Abel decided to nod in reply. The pressure of the hand on his neck relaxed, and he was nudged toward the café. Abel's knees were weak, and he staggered a bit. It was three steps to the curb where he stopped and started to check for traffic. He abruptly checked himself, fearing that the man would think he was trying to turn around. Moving only his eyes, he looked in each direction like an accident victim wearing a neck brace. When it was clear, he stepped off the curb. His stride was almost robotic as he crossed the street. In his mind he started going over all his movements since he'd left his hotel. *The man knew he'd purchased the card and the pen, for Christ's sake, and his English was perfect.* Petrov had said the man and woman were French. Could there be a third person? Abel did not like to be so caught off guard. These two were either really good, or he was getting really sloppy.

13

He approached the table, his legs still unsteady. The attractive brunette looked up at him from behind her dark glasses, and asked, *"Ça t'amuse de faire attendre les gens?"* *Do you like to keep people waiting?*

Abel cleared his throat and tried to look relaxed. *"J'ai eu un contre-temps."* *Something came up.*

"Really," she said in a doubting tone. "Like standing across the street pretending to read a magazine?"

"I was merely trying to be cautious." Abel wondered how in the hell they knew what he looked like.

"Not cautious enough." She tilted her head. "I noticed you met my business associate."

Abel glanced back at the newsstand. The corner wasn't crowded, but neither was it empty. People were coming and going in all four directions, but no one was standing there looking back at them. Abel was still a bit off kilter, and all he could manage to say was, "So that was your partner."

"Yes." She smiled. "He's a rather resourceful man. Not the type of person you want to upset."

Abel recalled the man's hot breath on his neck, and he suppressed a shiver. He composed himself and gestured toward the chair with the umbrella on it. "May I sit?"

"By all means." She grabbed the umbrella and hooked it to her arm rest. She did not bother to introduce herself. If they agreed to proceed to the next step she would provide him with an alias.

In an effort to lighten the mood, and get beyond his own professional embarrassment, Abel said, "I apologize for making you wait, but I am always a bit jumpy during these initial meetings."

"You do this type of thing often?"

The dark sunglasses made it impossible to get a complete idea of the woman's face, which he supposed was intended. "Often enough, but I have a short list of contractors that I usually use."

"If you have other skilled people, why are you talking to me?"

The waiter approached before he could answer. Abel ordered a cup of coffee and when the waiter was gone he said, "My services have been retained by someone who would like a problem to go away. A very interesting problem. One that I'm not sure I'm comfortable using any of my ordinary contacts on."

She studied him from behind her one-way glasses. "If things don't go as planned, you don't want anyone tracing the job back to you?"

She was a smart woman. Abel conceded the point saying, "That is part of it."

"And the other part?"

Abel put on a humble face. "Some jobs require nothing more than brute force. I have many people who fit this profile, and to be honest, I do not enjoy doing business with any of them. Other jobs require a bit of cunning and deceit." Abel shrugged. "I have a few people who aren't so rough around the edges and are competent enough. Still other jobs require a true professional. Someone who is creative with solutions and adept with follow-through. I have maybe one man who I would put in this category."

"So why not use him?"

The waiter appeared with the fresh cup of coffee. Abel held his answer until they were alone again. "I considered it, but in the end I decided there was one limitation that might prevent him from succeeding."

"What, may I ask, is that?"

There was a line that Abel had predetermined he would not cross. This bit of information fell just shy of that line. "We are nearing a juncture in our conversation that I like to refer to as 'the point of no return.' "

She nodded, but offered nothing more.

"I will answer this one question, and then it is my turn to do some asking."

"You may ask all you'd like." She pushed her chair back slightly and recrossed her legs.

"Some jobs require that nothing is left to chance. This is one of those jobs, and whoever takes it must be fluent in English. My man is not, and I feel that this could be a potential problem either before or after the job."

"Is your target British or American?"

Abel ignored her question, and instead asked, "Can your partner speak in both the British and American dialects?"

"Yes."

"Good. Now I would like to go over your résumé."

She put her hand up to stop him. "Before you go any further, I need to lay down a few rules. First, no heads of state. We don't care how much money you're willing to pay. We have no desire to spend the rest of our lives living under a rock. Second, we will set the terms and conditions. You will have nothing to say, operationally speaking. The only thing we will allow you to do is set a deadline."

"And pay you, of course." Abel smiled.

She smiled back. "Of course."

Abel was struck by how beautiful her smile was. He desperately wanted to reach out and take her sunglasses off so he could complete the picture. "Now, on to your résumé."

"I forgot the last point, and I doubt you will like it." She folded her arms across her chest. "We reserve the right to back out at any time prior to the deadline. You will of course receive a full refund with the exception of the hundred-thousand-dollar retainer that you have already paid."

Abel kept his cool even though his German temper was bubbling up just beneath the surface. "I have never heard of such a preposterous thing."

"I'm afraid those are our conditions."

"You cannot conduct business this way." Abel pushed his cup and saucer away. "I have proceeded in very good faith. I have paid an obscene retainer for which I have received nothing in return other than a list of your conditions. I need to be protected just as badly as you do, and I must tell you that if you insist on being so one-sided in this negotiation I will be forced to look elsewhere."

"Herr Abel," she began, "you can look all you want, but if you need something done in Britain or America, you need to look no further." She opened her purse and fished out a cigarette. "We are not in the business of sharing secrets. We are a fee-for-hire service and our reputation is everything." She lit the cigarette and pointed it at him. "Things come up in this line of work. Unexpected things that we cannot control. A true professional knows when to walk away. I can guarantee that we will do everything possible to fulfill the contract, but in the end, if we decide to walk away, that will be the end of it. You will get your money back, and we will take your secret to our graves."

Nothing was going as he'd planned. These two had done their homework. They had allowed him to think he was the smarter man and then they had knocked him off balance and set the entire tone. He was the one supposed to be doing the interviewing, not them. As much as he wanted to stay and continue chatting with this lovely woman he needed to show at least one sign of strength.

Abel pushed his chair back and stood. "I am sorry we have wasted each other's time. The fee you stood to earn was extremely large." He extended his hand more in hopes that he could touch her skin than as a courtesy. She did the same, and he held her hand delicately. "If you decide to be more flexible in your negotiations, I will reconsider doing business with you." He gave her a curt bow and left.

A BLOCK AWAY a man stood leaning against his motorbike pretending to read a copy of *Rolling Stone.* Gnarled dreadlocks cascaded down to his shoulders. He had a messenger bag slung over his shoulder and his helmet was hooked onto one of the handlebars. Clipped to the strap of the messenger bag was a two-way radio. A wireless earpiece was linked to the radio via Bluetooth technology. For the last fifteen seconds there'd been nothing but the background noise of the city.

Finally, her voice asked, *"As-tu tout compris?"* Did you get all of that?

"Yep."

"You don't sound very concerned."

"Nope." He glanced sideways at his rearview mirror and just as he expected he saw the German walking in his direction.

"What are we going to do?"

"Give him a little private audition, I think."

She sighed. "Why do you always insist on taking risks?"

He began tapping his foot and singing a Peter Tosh song replete with Jamaican accent. Once the German had passed he said, "We're in the risk business, my darling. I'll see you back at the place. Give me a ten-minute start." He closed the magazine and shoved it in his saddlebag. After strapping on his helmet, he started the bike and raced out into traffic.

14

R app pulled into the parking lot, shut off the car, and got out. He walked to the asphalt curb and looked out across the playing fields. His mood began to change almost immediately. It had been more than fifteen years since he'd been back, but the place was more familiar to him than perhaps any in the world. It was pretty much as he'd remembered it. Some of the trees were bigger, some were gone, and there were a few new ones planted near the parking lot, but other than that, it was the same old place—the place of his youth.

The view, the smell, the weather, all brought back a deluge of memories—most of them good, but not all. This was where he'd broken his arm at the age of seven. He'd gone running home bawling, only to have his father enforce his "no blood, no tears" rule. After a brief check, his father, who was fond of the phrase "Suck it up," told Mitch it was just a sprain. When young Mitchell awoke in the middle of the night soaked in sweat, and his arm twice its normal size, his mother intervened and Mr. Suck It Up was ordered to take his son to the emergency room. It was not their first trip to get x-rays, but it was their last. The next year his father died of a massive heart attack and left behind a relatively young wife and two kids: Mitch and his younger brother, Steven.

Rapp didn't think of his dad often, other than the brief periods when he lamented the fact that they never really got to know each other. They'd been together for just eight years, the first four of which Mitch had no real recollection, and the next four which were pretty vague. His dad, like most dads back in the seventies, wasn't around much. He was a lawyer and worked long hours. He played golf on Saturday mornings, rain or shine, so Sundays were really the only time they spent together as a family. What he did remember about his dad was that he was a firm but decent and fair man. His mother, a deeply religious and eternally optimistic person, made it very clear to her boys just how responsible their father had been both alive and from beyond. Like the good attorney that he was, everything had been in order when his heart stopped pumping. The estate planning was all up to date and their father had purchased more than enough life insurance to take care of them. The mortgage was paid off and money put aside for college. Financially speaking, his mom never had to worry.

Mitch never heard his father raise his voice other than the few times that he or Steven had done something really bad—like the time Steven almost burned the house down or the time Mitch got the ladder out of the garage and got up on the roof with Steven. Mitch jumped and landed in a pile of leaves and Steven, who was only a year and a half younger but considerably smaller, didn't quite make it. Little Stevey, as he was known by the entire neighborhood, landed instead on the sidewalk and ended up in the emergency room with two broken legs.

Mitch actually got slapped upside the head and spanked for that one. It was the only time he ever remembered his dad laying a hand on him, and even all these years later he still felt like shit about it. Not because his dad had hit him, but because he'd let his father down. Steven was the miracle baby. Born five weeks early, he'd spent the first three months of his life in the hospital, clinging to life. Mentally, Rapp's kid brother was a phenom, but on the athletic fields of their youth, Steven was a runt. He was extremely small for his age, and to draw further attention to himself, he was topped with a shock of blond, almost white hair. He and Mitch could not have looked more different. Where Mitch had black hair and olive skin, Steven had light hair and fair skin that would turn pink inside fifteen minutes if a liberal coating of sunscreen wasn't applied. Mitch spent summers in swim trunks or shorts, and Steven spent them covered with light-colored clothes or in the shade. Mitch took after his dad and Steven took after their blond-haired, blue-eyed mother.

Rapp looked over at the baseball diamond and remembered how Steven used to bellow out the pitch count, number of outs, and runs after every pitch. For a little kid he had an unusually deep voice, and he used it to great effect. Even back then the little genius had a thing for numbers. Because nobody wanted him on their team, he was designated permanent catcher and scorekeeper. In addition to his ability to never lose track of the score, he was also perfect for the job because he was incapable of telling a lie. There was no favoritism when he was behind the plate.

It was also decided at Mitch's urging that Stevey didn't need to tag the runner. All he had to do was catch the ball and touch the plate. This way there would be no collisions with kids twice his little brother's size. Everything had gone fine that summer until Bert Duser, the fat neighborhood bully, decided to steamroll the minute and neutral catcher. Mitch had caught a fly ball on the run in shallow center field and one-hopped it on a line to home plate. Duser was on third and tried to tag. In direct relation to his size Duser was very slow. Knowing he was out with a good ten feet to go Duser brought up his elbows and nailed little Stevey. Rapp remembered his little brother's black athletic glasses flying up in the air and the tiny white-haired catcher going ass over teakettle into the backstop.

What happened next became the stuff of neighborhood legend. Mitch was ten, Duser was twelve. Duser was half a head taller and at least twenty pounds heavier, and no one ever challenged him, but on this sunny summer day none of that mattered. After his father's death, Mitch took his oath to protect his little brother very seriously. Overcome with rage, he broke into a full sprint. Somewhere between second base and home plate he threw his glove to the ground. He didn't remember this, but it was recounted to him in great detail later. He also didn't remember screaming like an Indian on the warpath, but that's what his friends told him. He did remember leaving his feet and hitting Duser like a human missile. After that there was a flurry of punches thrown, all by Mitch, and then there was a lot of blood, all of it Duser's.

It ended with Duser running home in tears, and Mitch getting grounded when Mrs. Duser showed up on their doorstep with her bloodied son. Mitch didn't argue with his mother much, but he remembered saying some pretty mean things that day—most of it having to do with how his dad would have handled Mrs. Duser if he'd still been around. Not Mom, though, she was a Jesus-loving, turn-the-other-cheek Lutheran. Dad, on the other hand, had been an eye-for-an-eye God-fearing Catholic. Mom was New Testament, and Dad was Old Testament. Mitch was decidedly more in his father's camp than his mother's, and rather than suffer an unjust punishment he ran away from home. The next morning a Fairfax County deputy found him sleeping in Turkey Run Park and brought him home. When he saw what he'd put his mother through, he was sufficiently shamed to stay put until he graduated from high school.

Rapp shook his head. That day had been the start of it all—his first fight, and the first time he ever truly challenged authority. He wondered briefly if Duser turned out all right, or if he was still a prick. Rapp looked over at the practice fields, where he'd learned to play football and lacrosse, and where he'd first laid eyes on Maureen "the Dream" Eliot. He fell for her hard, and she ended up being the real reason why he decided to take a lacrosse scholarship at Syracuse rather than the one offered by the University of North Carolina. Maureen wanted to get into broadcasting, and Syracuse was the best. Looking back on it now, it seemed foolish, but the two of them believed with all their hearts that they would get married one day. Rapp honestly believed they would have, but unfortunately, they never got the chance because on December 21, 1988, Pan Am Flight 103 was blown from the sky on its way back to America with 259 passengers on board. Maureen had been one of thirty-five Syracuse students returning from a semester abroad. What Rapp didn't know at the time was just how deeply that terrorist act would change his life.

Maybe it had changed before that, when he was fifteen and he saw Maureen for the first time, maybe it had changed when he felt the undeniable satisfaction of pounding the crap out of a bully. It was strange standing here looking back on his youth and the decisions he'd made at such a young age—decisions that eventually led him to where he was today. It made him wonder how things would have been if he'd never met Maureen and fallen in love with her. In the wake of the catastrophe he'd asked God a thousand times, "Why couldn't she have missed that plane?" He'd analyzed all of the choices she'd made. If only she'd stayed at Syracuse instead of spending a semester overseas. If only they'd gone somewhere else to school. He'd done the same things people always do when they are visited with such unexpected tragedy. He asked why, and wondered endlessly how things could have been different.

It wasn't until almost a year after the tragedy that he was approached by someone who got him to look at the disaster in an entirely different way. A woman from Washington came to visit him and after a lengthy discussion she had asked him, "What if someone could have prevented the attack in the first place?" That was the first carrot that had been dangled in front of him. The first trip was followed by a second, where an even more enticing question had been asked. "How would you like to track down the people who did this and kill them?" Rapp had the talent and the drive, and the CIA wanted him.

Only twenty-one at the time, and awash in a sea of self-pity and despair, he found the idea of retribution powerful. Desperate people need a cause, and this was a cause that spoke to him. The week after graduation he threw himself into the dark world of counterterrorism and clandestine operations. The CIA did not run him through their standard training program at The Farm, outside Williamsburg, VA. They had other plans for Rapp. For a year straight he was shuttled from one location to the next, sometimes spending a week, sometimes a month. The bulk of the training was handled by Special Forces instructors who taught him how to shoot, stab, blow things up, and yes, kill with his bare hands. Endurance was stressed. There were long swims and even longer runs. He'd always been in good shape, but these sadists had turned him into a machine. Between all of the heavy lifting, they worked on his foreign language skills. He had been an international business major at Syracuse and had minored in French. Within a month at the CIA he was fluent, and then it was on to Arabic and Farsi.

They taught him how to operate independently, how to blend into foreign environments, and how to cross international borders without being noticed. But most importantly they taught him how to kill. Rapp remembered a conversation he'd had with one of his Special Forces instructors. The man's name was Mike. Mitch had asked him one time if he'd ever killed a man. Mike grinned and asked him, "What do you think?"

The question had come up while they were having beers at a dive near Fort Bragg. Mike had spent the entire day teaching Rapp how to kill people with everything from a pen to a stick to a knife. Mike had more intimate knowledge of the human anatomy than most doctors, and he knew the body's weakest points. The last move they'd worked on involved grabbing a man from behind and shoving the knife up through the base of the skull at the point where the spinal column connects to the brain. As with everything Rapp did, Mike insisted he master the move with both hands. This particular move was punctuated with a quick twist of the wrist once the knife was all the way in. Mike informed Rapp that most people referred to this move as scrambling the brain, but he called it pulling the plug. He then described in great detail what the victim would be experiencing at this point. Yes, Mike had most definitely killed men before.

Rapp asked Mike if it ever bothered him. If he ever regretted the killing. Mike looked into his beer for a long time and then said, "Listen, we're all wired differently. Some people aren't cut out for this, but I was born for it, and I can tell you were too. Maybe we were warriors in a previous life. . . . I don't know, but there's a general rule out there. Don't kill kids and don't kill women and you'll be fine. Kill a man who wants to kill you, and it's the most healthy primal feeling you'll ever experience."

Rapp asked him, "If you could do it over again would you choose a different line of work?"

Mike laughed and said, "Hell no. This is the best damn job in the world. Your government gives you the consent to go out and kill terrorists. For guys like us, it doesn't get any better than that."

15

Dinner was lonely. Normally Abel didn't mind eating by himself, but tonight he felt restless. He was staying at Hotel Balzac, a small, luxurious establishment only a short walk from the Arc de Triomphe. He had decided to dine early in the hotel's restaurant and miss the rush. He was given a small but satisfactory table, and he was immersed in the menu when a couple about his age were seated within perfect view. He watched as they held hands and spoke intently. They appeared to be in love. About the time his main course arrived another couple was seated. They were a little younger than Abel, and it was soon obvious that they were also in love. She reminded him of the woman with the large black sunglasses who he had met earlier in the day. She looked roughly the same age and had a similar hairstyle.

Abel was haunted by the mysterious woman from the café. She exuded a quiet confidence more powerful than any aphrodisiac he could imagine. She had dealt with him from a position of strength from the moment he'd sat down. She'd known he'd been watching her from across the street. He cringed to remember how smug he had been. She'd even learned his identity in advance and God only knew what else. The entire experience was very unnerving for Abel. He was the one who was used to negotiating from a position of strength. He was supposed to be the unflappable professional who saw all and gave away nothing in return.

Having lost his appetite, he decided to go for a walk. After retrieving his black trench coat and new cashmere scarf from his room he left the hotel and began walking south toward the Seine. There was a chill in the evening air, but Abel didn't mind. It felt good to get out and stretch his legs, and the bite of the air seemed to help clear his mind. Something told him this strange couple Petrov had recommended were the perfect people for the job, but he needed to make sure. Abel had stopped at a pay phone after the meeting and called his old Russian master. Hours later he was still replaying the conversation in his mind.

After some brief banter he had casually asked Petrov, "Did you give this couple my name?"

"They called to make sure we knew each other," Petrov admitted. "I told them we did, and that you were someone who could be trusted."

"Nothing else?" Abel asked.

"Not a thing. What is wrong? You sound troubled."

"They tailed me to the meet," Abel admitted uncomfortably.

"What else?"

"They knew my name."

"I told you they were good." Petrov laughed loudly. "Hire them and be done with it. They will not disappoint you."

Abel got the distinct impression that Petrov was enjoying his discomfort. "They are a bit inflexible in their demands."

"Sounds like a certain German I know."

"Yes, well, I'm the one doing the hiring."

"And they will be the ones risking their hides. I'm telling you . . . hire them and get out of their way."

Abel considered telling him about the man, and how he'd threatened to sever his spine, and then thought better of it. Petrov would only laugh at him. "What can you tell me about the woman?"

"Did you meet her?"

"Yes."

"Ha," Petrov bellowed. "I have heard she is beautiful. Very mysterious. Do you agree?"

"She is an attractive woman," Abel admitted while trying not to sound too interested. "What do you know about her?"

"Get her out of your mind. I have heard that they are more than just business partners, and trust me . . . this man is not someone you want to upset."

"I gathered that. Where does he come from?"

"I do not know, and I do not care. I'm telling you for the last time, hire them and be done with it." The Russian hung up on him.

Abel did not like feeling like a fool, but that was exactly the way he felt as he walked the streets of this old city. By the time he reached the river he realized he would probably hire these two, but not yet. Petrov was getting old and the vodka had softened his normally keen intellect. There was too much at stake to simply hire them without having a say in how things would proceed. It was tempting, though. There was another ten million waiting for him as soon as Rapp was dead. Twenty million on the table minus the fee he would have to pay the killers. Abel had a number in his head. There were many variables to consider, but typically the going rate for killing an intelligence officer was in the low-to-mid six figures. This wasn't just any intelligence officer, however, this was Mitch Rapp, a spy's spy, who had the very nasty habit of biting back. They would have to track him. If they got lucky, they might catch him traveling. Getting him off American soil would help greatly. Very few contract killers liked working in America, because of the increased security with facial recognition systems at virtually every port of entry and the fingerprinting of certain visitors. The cost of doing business in America would more than likely double the fee.

He turned east and began walking toward the Louvre, racking his brain to come up with his best contacts in France. He needed to send these two a message that they were dealing with a professional, not someone who they could toy around with and scare like an amateur. Unfortunately, he didn't trust the people he knew in France enough to get them involved in this. On the other hand there were some Hungarians he knew who were excellent at surveillance work, and they were cheap. It was a whole family for the price of one—grandparents, parents, children, even some uncles. When he got back to the hotel he would call and see if he could get them here first thing in the morning. He would wait a day to see if the woman contacted him, and if not he would e-mail and request another meeting. He hoped it wouldn't come to that. He did not want to look desperate.

He left the river and started back to the hotel. When he turned on to the Champs-Elysées he was faced with a cold breeze. Abel turned up his collar and quickened his pace. He decided that by ending the meeting himself, and getting up and walking away, he may have saved enough face to get them to come back to him. They were businesspeople after all, and he had been very clear that there was a large fee to be earned. When they called he would be prepared. He would have the Hungarians in place. They would get photographs for sure and possibly a thumbprint from her coffee cup if they met at a café again. The Hungarians could trail her back to an address that would provide more information. The man would be about, undoubtedly, and maybe they would spot him. All he needed was a single thread, and then from there he could begin unraveling. He would learn everything there was to know about the two and then he would shock them into dealing with him from a position of mutual respect.

Abel arrived back at the hotel refreshed and invigorated. He had a plan, and he was hopeful that they would call him back and renew negotiations. He took the elevator up to his suite and after taking off his coat and scarf he went into the bedroom to open the safe and get his PDA. He turned on a table lamp near the closet and punched in his four-digit code. He listened to the whirl of the locking mechanism retracting, and then opened the small, heavy door. The safe was empty.

Abel reached in and felt around to make sure, and then placed his hands on his hips. He was certain he had put the small handheld computer in the safe before he'd gone to dinner, but with the way the day had gone, he was already second-guessing himself. Maybe he'd left it in his briefcase. He turned to head back into the living room, and out of the corner of his eye he thought he saw something in the shadows. Abel froze when he zeroed in on a pair of shoes that he immediately knew were not his. He followed the legs up to the dark, barely discernable outline of a man sitting in a chair. For some inexplicable reason his mind jumped to the conclusion that it was Mitch Rapp himself who had broken into his hotel room. It was the second time in a day that Abel had been surprised and overcome with this dreadful portentous feeling.

"*C'est ça que tu cherches?*" *Are you looking for this?* asked a low voice.

A gloved hand emerged from the shadows. In it was Abel's PDA. Abel looked past the hand at the man. His eyes had adjusted just enough that he could see his visitor was wearing something to cover his face. The voice, unfortunately, was familiar and it made Abel think of coffee and warm breath on the back of his neck.

Straining to appear calm, Abel said, "I see you have lowered yourself to thievery."

The gloved hand reappeared and flicked the PDA across the room. It spun through the air and landed in the center of the king-size bed. "I have stolen nothing. A man in your line of work should know better than to trust hotel safes."

Abel listened to the man's words and decided he must be American, but he couldn't quite place the dialect. "You have a nasty habit of sneaking up on people . . . maybe I can return the favor someday."

The man scoffed, "That would be stupid."

"And why is that?" Abel was proud of himself for not sounding too nervous.

"If I returned to my hotel room and found a man sitting in the dark, I would put a bullet in his head."

Abel had been around some very unsettling individuals, but this man was in a league of his own. He was beginning to give Abel a feeling of inadequacy. "What if you didn't have a gun?"

"I always have a gun."

"But if you didn't?"

"I would still kill the man. It just might take a split second longer."

"So what do you think I should do?" asked Abel. "I have just returned to my very expensive hotel and have discovered a burglar in my room. Should I kill him?"

The man laughed in a very low, almost snickering way. "Impossible."

"Please tell me why." Abel folded his arms across his chest.

"For starters . . . you do not have a gun, and I do."

"How do you know I don't have a gun?"

"I watched you eat dinner. You looked very lonely, by the way," the man added. "I watched you put on your coat before you left for your walk. I can tell if a man has a gun on him. You do not."

Abel conceded the point with a nod. "Continue."

"I am a trained assassin and you are not, Herr Abel. While I know you are not a stranger to violence, you do not strike me as the type of person who gets his hands dirty."

"Don't be so certain." Abel held his ground. "Any other reasons I might be missing?"

"Yes, as a matter of fact. One very obvious operational detail. You have registered under your real name and put the room on your credit card. If you were to succeed in killing me . . . which you wouldn't . . . you would have a mess to deal with."

"I have many contacts . . ." Abel paused in search of a name. "What should I call you?"

"We'll get to that later." The man crossed his legs and placed both hands on his knee. "You were saying?"

Abel noticed for the first time that the man was holding a silenced pistol in his other hand. "I have many contacts. I could easily make a phone call and have your body disposed of in a very discreet manner."

The man did not answer right away. "I suppose you could, but I do not see you as that type of a risk taker. It would be too impulsive. You are a man who must analyze every detail before you are moved to action."

"And you?" asked Abel.

"I am a killer. That is what I do for a living, and I live in such a way that the decision to kill or not to kill can be made instantaneously, without having to worry about how it will affect my life."

Abel was starting to enjoy this. With a slight smile he asked, "And how does one live their life in such a way as to be able to make such decisions instantaneously?"

"By any reasonable standard I am a wealthy man, but unlike you I own nothing. I am tied to nothing. You, on the other hand, own significant real estate in both Switzerland and Austria. If you have to run, those assets will be seized . . . bank accounts will be frozen. You have too many roots to kill a man, where I have none. I am like the wind. Here one moment and gone the next."

"I have taken certain precautions," Abel said with a tight voice.

"I have no doubt that you have, but the vast majority of your net worth is tied up in hard assets that are owned under your name. You are also a very meticulous and prudent man. You will not throw away the fruits of your labor so lightly."

Abel hated being wrong. He conceded the last point with another nod and announced, "I need a drink." He turned for the other room. Over his shoulder he asked, "May I get you one?"

The man followed him. "No, thank you. I never drink when I'm on the job."

Abel opened the minibar. "That's a very American sentiment. Are you American?"

"I am American, I am British, I am Canadian, I am French, I am German, I am Russian . . . I am whatever I need to be."

Abel grabbed a bottle of Remy Martin VSOP. "How about German?"

Abel poured the cognac into a snifter while he listened to the man talk about the weather in absolutely perfect German spoken with a slight Rhineland dialect. He picked up his glass and turned around. It was the first time he'd actually gotten a look at the man and unfortunately, there wasn't much to see. His head was covered in a black hood with slits for his eyes, nose, and mouth. He guessed him to be about five ten, but couldn't be sure since the man was already sitting on the armrest of the salon's couch.

"How about Russian?"

This time he broke into a scathing rebuke of Lenin and Stalin. He spoke so rapidly that Abel had a hard time keeping up. He was so pleased, however, that the man shared his hatred for two of the last century's biggest thugs and mass murderers that he actually flashed an approving smile. Abel held up his snifter. "I will drink to that."

He went over to the other couch and sat. "I assume I won't be able to talk you into taking that mask off."

The man shook his head. "Trust me . . . it is as much for your safety as mine."

Fine, Abel thought to himself. *I will know what you look like sooner or later.* "What should I call you?"

"What would you like to call me?"

Abel was beginning to relax. "Come now, you must have an alias that you use?"

"Never more than once. Pick a name."

Abel smelled the cognac and tried to come up with something significant. He decided to toy with him. "How about Hector?"

The man thought about it for a second. "Bad name. He was killed by Achilles."

"How about Achilles, then?" Abel smiled, proud of himself for trapping the man.

The man shook his head. "Nothing Greek. Far too much tragedy with the Greeks. Let's start over. Who is the target?"

Abel shook his head vigorously. "I need to know more about you before we get to that."

"Fine. I will be satisfied with his or her nationality, and city or country in which I will be operating."

Abel set his glass down. "As I said, I need to know more about you before I start getting into details."

The man hesitated before answering. "I am in the business of killing. Have I ever turned down a job before?" he asked himself. "Yes, but not because I had a moral dilemma over ending an individual's life. I have turned down jobs because I did not feel the person with whom I was dealing was being honest with me."

"How long have you been doing this?"

"Long enough."

"This will not work for me," Abel said as he shook his head. "I need to know more about you. This is a seven-figure contract we are talking about. I will not simply hire someone without knowing their history."

The man sighed and said, "Listen, I know this is hard for you to understand. You are a German. You are organized, you are anal-retentive, you worked for the Stasi for ten years, and you like to keep records, but trust me when I tell you . . . this is as much for your own good as it is for mine."

Abel made a sour face. "I don't see how knowing nothing about you benefits me."

The man raised the silenced pistol and pointed it at Abel. "This interview will conclude shortly, and I must stress one thing above all. If you try to find out who I am, if you try to follow my business associate, I will kill you. This is your first and only warning, and don't let your thirst for details get the best of you. Think of it as a simple mathematical equation. A plus B equals C. A is your curiosity, B is me, and C is you lying on the ground staring up at the sky, knowing for only the briefest of seconds that I have just ended your life." He lowered the weapon. "Two plus three equals five, and you trying to find out who I am equals death. They are both mathematical certainties."

Abel picked up his glass and took a sip of cognac. His hand was shaking slightly, so he lowered the glass and clasped it in both hands hoping his visitor didn't notice. After clearing his throat, Abel asked, "How am I to trust you if I know nothing about you?"

"You shouldn't trust me," he said flatly. "I am a contract killer . . . an assassin. You act as if you are dealing with someone who should be virtuous."

"Still, before we come to an agreement on the terms, we must reach some level of trust."

"Don't take it personally, but I do not trust you. I never trust the people who hire me, and I never lose sight of the reason why you are hiring me. You want someone killed. I don't ask why. I just do it. But at the same time, I am very aware of the kind of person who pays for this type of work. A few are practical, but many have serious psychological problems. They are often sociopaths who must have their way in everything they do in life. They like all the loose ends tied up and everything tucked away neatly in a box. And for some of them that means getting rid of the man who pulled the trigger." He pointed the gun at himself and said, "That would be me."

Abel could not disagree with a single thing the man had just said. "So there is no trust?"

"None. Just professionalism. You watch your back, and I'll watch mine."

He held up his glass. "I can drink to that."

"Good. Now I will give you my terms. You tell me the target, and I will tell you my fee. If you agree, you will wire half of the money as a deposit and the other half upon completion of the contract."

"What if you turn down the job after I have given you the name?"

The man waved Abel off. "As long as you agree to my fee, I will not turn down the job."

"But your associate earlier today told me no heads of state."

"As a general rule, yes." He shrugged. "But for the right price I will kill anyone."

Abel thought that sounded promising. It was the moment to decide. If he had one flaw he knew it was overanalyzing. He had not gotten what he wanted from this man, but it was hard to argue with his logic. Abel thought of the other ten million that was waiting for him, and then thought of starting over and trying to find someone as talented as the unidentified man sitting across from him. It was time to jump in with both feet.

Abel drained the rest of the cognac and bit down hard as the liquid burned his throat. He held up the drained glass, exhaled, and asked, "Have you ever heard of an American named Mitch Rapp?"

The man did not answer for several long seconds. "Yes," he said, finally, in a tone that was anything but enthusiastic.

Abel was overcome with a horrible feeling that the two men knew each other. "Please, tell me you don't know him?"

"No . . . only of him." The man's voice had taken on a brooding tone.

"Will you take the job?"

The man appeared to be studying Abel through the two openings in his mask. After what seemed like an eternity he said, "That depends on how much you are willing to pay."

Abel relaxed a bit. "The fee is substantial."

"I'll be the judge of that. How much?"

Abel had gone over this a hundred times already. The trick was to start off the negotiations at the low end, but not so low as to insult the other person. "One and a half million U.S. dollars."

"Don't insult me."

Abel looked at his watch. "I do not consider a million and a half dollars an insult."

"I have no doubt you could find someone who would take the job for a million and a half, and I also have no doubt that Monsieur Rapp would kill that man before he got anywhere near him."

"There are plenty of good people out there who would jump at this chance."

The man laughed at him. "You are going to send a good killer to dispatch a man with Mitch Rapp's skills? Do you know anything about Rapp? Are you a fool?"

Abel felt uncomfortable. "This is a negotiation. A million and a half is a starting point. Tell me what you think the job is worth."

"Who wants him dead?"

Abel shook his head vigorously. "You know I will not tell you that."

"Fine," said the masked man, fully expecting Abel to refuse. "I know how the business end of these things works. I am guessing that you are taking a fee off the top of anywhere between ten and thirty-three percent. Knowing you are a greedy man who likes the finer things in life I will grant you a third of the contract, but not a penny more. Have you already negotiated the contract?"

"No," Abel lied.

"Have you been given a budget?"

"In a manner of speaking, yes."

The man thought about it for a while. He knew of Abel's connections and could hazard a pretty good guess at who had hired him. He decided to shoot for the stars. "The price is ten million, and since I like round numbers you will cut your fee to a flat thirty percent."

The number was at the high end, but within what he thought would be asked. "I will have to check and see if they are willing to pay that much."

The man got off the couch and started for the small balcony. "E-mail my associate in the morning with your answer." The man opened the French door.

They were on the eighth floor, and Abel was about to ask him how he was going to leave, but decided not to. The man made him curious, though. He was different. "Tell me . . . Why did you get into this line of work?"

He looked over his shoulder and said, "Because I am very good at it."

With that, the man was gone. Abel stared blankly at the closed door for almost a full minute, resisting the urge to go look. During that time he was left in a strange state of limbo wondering if he'd just made the best or worst decision of his life. He decided he needed another drink. Abel refilled his snifter and let the smooth cognac envelop his tongue before swallowing it. The man was talented, he had to grant him that, and he was correct that Abel could not simply send one of his regular people to take care of this. In the end he would just have to take some comfort in the knowledge that he was about to make thirteen million dollars for what would likely be less than a week's work. Abel smiled and held up his glass in a toast to the man who had just disappeared into the night.

"To the death of Mitch Rapp, and thirteen million dollars." Abel threw back the rest of the cognac and went to bed.

16

A big Ford Excursion rolled into the parking lot and parked one spot over from Rapp's car. Scott Coleman got out. He was wearing a blue polo shirt that was a little on the tight side, a pair of jeans, and black boots. The blond-haired former Navy SEAL looked more like a construction worker than the head of a private security firm that was now billing the federal government more than twenty million dollars a year. Rapp didn't see a gun on him, but he had no doubt there was one within reach of the driver's seat and probably an entire arsenal in the back cargo area.

"What's with all the cloak-and-dagger shit?" Coleman asked. He sounded irritated. "I thought we had friends in high places these days."

"Yeah, well, we also have enemies in high places."

"Fuck 'em."

Rapp scanned the parking lot. "You sure you weren't followed?"

"No." He looked at his vehicle. "You think you'd have a hard time putting a tail on this thing?"

Rapp looked at the nine-passenger truck. "You get married and have a bunch of kids I don't know about?"

"No, I've got a lot of shit I have to haul around," the former SEAL replied a bit defensively.

"The environmentalists must love you. What's that thing get . . . about two miles to the gallon?"

"The environmentalists can go fuck themselves," growled Coleman. "There isn't a bigger group of brainwashed dipshits on the planet."

"Come on, Scott, tell me how you really feel about them."

"The same way you do," snarled Coleman. "Now, I didn't drive all the way across town to meet you in some high school parking lot so you could give me shit about my truck."

Rapp held up his hands. Coleman was normally a pretty cool customer. "Calm down. What in the hell is wrong with you?"

"I haven't killed anyone in a while. What's wrong with you?"

"God," Rapp moaned, "you SEALs are a weird bunch."

"Oh . . . and you're the picture of mental health."

"Good point," Rapp laughed, "but seriously . . . what's up? You just find out you have testicular cancer or something?"

"Worse . . . the fucking IRS called me this morning. They want to see all my records . . . personal and business."

Rapp didn't like the sound of this. He got noticeably more serious. "Have you ever had any problems with them before?"

"Hell no. I was an officer in the Navy for almost twenty years. We don't make enough money for them to mess around with."

"And now that you're getting all of these government contracts . . ."

"Shit, I suppose. I mean, Mitch, we're billing seven-plus figures every month. I've had to hire five people just to handle all the paperwork."

"How are your records?"

"How the fuck would I know . . . I'm not an accountant."

Rapp stared at him with his hawklike eyes. "Do you have anything to hide?"

Coleman looked down and kicked a rock. "I don't know. Like I said, I'm not an accountant."

"Scott, it's me . . . Mitch. If I'm going to help you out here, you have to be straight with me."

"Can you make this go away?" Coleman asked hopefully.

"As long as you haven't fucked up too bad . . . yeah."

Coleman kicked another rock. "As far as I know all the domestic stuff is in order, but I've got an offshore company that I run most of the foreign contracts through."

"And you keep the money offshore."

"Yeah." He looked up at Rapp uncomfortably.

Rapp nodded. "Don't worry. You're not alone. Anything else happen in the last few days?"

"Like what?"

"Anyone poking around asking questions? Anyone from your past try to contact you? Any new unexpected business come in?"

Coleman thought about it for a moment. "No." He studied Rapp. "Why?"

Rapp leaned against his car and put his hands in his pockets. "I got a call from a source over at the DOD this morning." By DOD, Rapp meant Department of Defense.

"You mean a mole?"

"I wouldn't call the chairman of the Joint Chiefs a mole."

"General Flood called you?"

"Yes."

"What'd he want?" asked Coleman.

"He didn't want anything. It was a courtesy call. It appears someone in Washington has a real hard-on for you this week."

Coleman closed his eyes. "Please tell me the IRS didn't call the Pentagon and ask to review my contracts."

"No. Someone else called and asked for a copy of your personnel file."

"They can look all they want. That file is clean."

"They called back and asked for your classified file. They wanted to know how many times you've been sheep-dipped by the CIA, and if you've ever worked with yours truly before." Rapp pointed to himself.

"They asked General Flood this?"

"No . . . they tried to browbeat someone much further down the totem pole. It got kicked up to the Joint Special Operations Command, who in turn called Flood."

"So who's asking?"

"Someone who works for the director of National Intelligence."

"Why would they give a rat's ass about me?"

"That's what I'm trying to figure out. I think it has something to do with our meeting the other day."

"In Irene's office."

"Yeah . . . that was a mistake."

"Hold on a minute. We haven't done anything wrong."

"You're kidding . . . right?" Rapp looked at him like he'd lost his mind.

"Well . . . nothing recently. I mean for Christ's sake we're on the same team. Aren't we?"

"That doesn't always matter with these pricks." Rapp shook his head. "It was stupid to meet at the CIA the other day."

"You're telling me that's what this is all about? Mark Ross didn't like my smart-ass attitude, so he's going to have the IRS bend me over and give me an exam?"

"Scott, we're in the middle of the biggest power grab this town has seen in fifty years. Mark Ross is trying to exert his new authority over the CIA and the rest of the intelligence community, and the billions of dollars that goes along with their budgets, and I'm guessing he wants full disclosure by everyone under his command."

"And what does that have to do with me?"

"He's not stupid. He wants to know what we were talking about with Irene. He called her the next day and asked her to brief him."

"What'd she tell him?" asked Coleman.

"We're looking at using your firm for some of our overseas security needs."

"Well, you are."

"And we're also thinking about using you to do a few other things."

"Yeah, but he can't know that."

"He suspects something, and I'd say based on your audit and the request for your jacket at the DOD, he's not satisfied with the answer Irene gave him."

"Fucker." Coleman's fists were clutched so tight the veins on his forearms were bulging.

"Don't worry . . . I'll figure out a way to make this go away."

"How?"

"I'm not sure, but I'll figure something out."

"The IRS is coming by tomorrow."

"I know a lawyer." Rapp smiled. "A real bastard. He specializes in this stuff. They hate him at the IRS. I'll have him call you. He'll have no problem putting them off until I can call off the dogs from the other end. In the meantime, keep working on what we talked about. I don't want this to slow us down one bit. I'll have you all freed up by next week, and then we can get moving."

Coleman nodded. "Anything else?"

"Yeah. Anything else unusual happens I want you to call me right away."

The former SEAL nodded.

17

The assassin had been wandering the streets in a seemingly aimless pattern for over two hours, which was about how long it had taken him to sort things out. He could be an exceedingly patient man when the situation called for it, and this was one of those times. The first thing he had to do was dump the motorcycle. It had been waiting for him two blocks from the hotel. He would miss the agile, high-powered Ducati, but scooters and motorcycles in Paris were like beautiful women; they were everywhere. He would find another motorcycle in the morning, and he was done chasing beautiful women.

He no longer considered himself a Frenchman. He was a man without a country, but he supposed if there was any place that he had to call home it would be France. He knew Paris very well and had a network of motorcycle and scooter garages that specialized in servicing the underbelly of Paris. They sold new machines, but always had plenty of used bikes, and preferred to deal in cash, which suited him perfectly. When he was actively engaged in new business, like now, he sometimes changed bikes daily, and even resorted to stealing them himself. Among his many skills, he was a mechanic. He knew how to take a pile of junk and turn it into a dependable machine in a matter of hours. If it had an engine and two wheels, he could fix it.

He drove all the way out to the Grand Arch, turning sporadically, doubling back, and in truth, not paying too much attention to whether or not he was being followed. That would come later. If they'd found the bike while he was in the hotel they could have concealed a transmitter.

These types of devices kept shrinking in size and increasing in sophistication. He did not have the wherewithal to keep up with such things, so he had to take other countermeasures. As he drove through the city he was in no rush to finish the first act. There would be many tonight. It would all depend on what his very acute sixth sense told him. For this leg of the journey he went through the motions and thought more about the contract he'd been offered than the real or imagined people who might or might not be following him.

He parked the bike near the Victor Hugo metro stop in the Chaillot Quarter and left the keys in the ignition. It would be stolen within thirty minutes. He took the blue line clear across town. From there the assassin found his way up the steep steps, took in a few breaths of the cool night air, and lit a cigarette. He was a handsome man in a very masculine way. He was of average height and build, standing one inch shy of six feet and weighing 172 pounds. His longish dark hair was the color of his black leather motorcycle jacket, and was tucked behind his ears. He hadn't shaved in two days and his face was covered with a thick dark stubble. He had the uncanny ability to blend into a crowd when he wanted to, which was strange when one considered the fact that he was quite striking.

He finished the cigarette, flicked it end over end, and then ground it into the sidewalk with his boot. While he did this he looked around, noting any parked cars and people who seemed to be standing about. As soon as he had a complete picture in his mind he went back down into the metro. It was now that he went on full alert. The subterranean tunnels were not very crowded at this time of night so it was relatively easy to catalogue the various faces. He timed it just right and at the last second jumped onto a departing train. Five minutes later he got off at the St. Ambroise Station, where he took a casual five-block walk to the St. Paul Station and descended once again. And so it went for nearly an hour. After that, he walked awhile, stopping at a few off-the-beaten-path taverns where he had a beer and thought about the turn his life had just taken, and how she would react when she heard the name. He had a pretty good idea. He knew her well enough. As the clock struck midnight he decided he couldn't put it off any longer. He was confident he had not been followed, so he drained his glass and went to the apartment.

She was up waiting, as she always was. Beneath her calm demeanor she was as taut as a wire. She knew he wasn't reckless, although he walked a fine line. It was just that they did not lead an average life. She cast her book and afghan to the side, revealing a silenced Glock pistol. She was in tactical mode just like he had taught her. They had been through this drill so many times it had become second nature. At this late hour she should have been in bed or at least in her pajamas, but she wasn't. She was dressed in a pair of jeans and a tight black sweater. Two backpacks, loaded with only essentials, sat ready to go by the door. They always had to be prepared to run at a moment's notice.

She stood and walked over to him, raising her arms and enveloping him in an embrace. In French she whispered in his ear, "Louie, why must you always make me wait?" She rested her head against his shoulder and breathed a sigh of relief.

He had many names, but the one given to him at birth was Louis-Philippe Gould. That part of his life seemed like ancient history now. She was the only person who ever used his given name. He gently placed one hand on the back of her head while his other hand found the familiar exposed skin of her bare hip. His groin began to swell almost immediately. He had been with many women—so many in fact he had lost count, but she topped them all.

"How did it go?" she whispered.

He kissed the top of her head and smelled her freshly washed hair. "I think we need to open a bottle of wine." The sex would come later.

She lifted her head and took a step back. "That bad?"

He shrugged. "I wouldn't say bad . . . just . . ." He didn't bother to finish the sentence.

Taking him by the hand, she led him into the tiny kitchen. She was a good listener. "I'll get the glasses. You get the bottle."

The one-bedroom apartment came furnished, and they'd paid for the first six months in cash. They'd only been there eight days, and they would leave in the morning. The chances of them returning were slim. There was some cheap art on the walls, a couch, a chair, and a color TV that didn't work. The bedroom consisted of a bed barely big enough for the two of them, and a rickety dresser. The kitchen hadn't been remodeled in thirty years, but none of this bothered them. They were used to living a life void of material possessions. They had traveled the world together, staying in cockroach-infested hostels and war-ravaged villages. Hot water and indoor plumbing were luxuries. The rest of the stuff was mere distraction. He was thirty-two and she was twenty-nine. They were still young. Someday they'd spoil themselves with the finer things in life, but not yet. Luxury softened the primal instincts, and they needed every last ounce of those instincts to do their job.

She sat on the couch while he opened the bottle of red. The path that led Louie to his current profession was unusual, but he doubted no more unusual than the road taken by his colleagues. One did not simply wake up one morning and decide to become a paid assassin. His father had come from old money that had been derived from old connections and knowing how to curry favor among France's often changing ruling groups. The Goulds were professional diplomats who could trace their service all the way back to the coup d'état by Louis Napoleon in 1851. Five generations of Gould men had attended L'École Polytechnique, France's premier technical university that specialized in preparing young French citizens for a life of civil service or military duty. With three daughters and only one boy, all his parents' hopes of continuing the tradition were on young Louie's shoulders and, indeed, he looked forward to following in his father's footsteps.

More than half of Louie's youth had been spent overseas while his father rose through the ranks of the French Foreign Service. There had been postings in French Guiana, New York, London, Berlin, and Washington, DC, where his father served as France's ambassador to the United States of America. It was a life filled with excitement and privilege. Louie enjoyed every minute of it, embracing the language and culture wherever the family went. He himself could think of nothing he'd rather do than become a career diplomat.

That was right up to the point where he learned of his father's rampant infidelity. At seventeen he lashed out at the man he had spent an entire life idolizing. When Louie found out about his father's inability to stay faithful to his mother, he surreptitiously applied for and received a scholarship to L'École Speciale Militaire, or as it was more commonly known, Saint Cyr. The institution was France's equivalent of West Point. On the surface it may not have seemed much of a protest, but the Goulds had a long history of contempt for the French Army. Professional diplomats to the core, they believed most, if not all, of France's great failures of the last two centuries to be the fault of the Army.

When his father found out he nearly lost his mind, but with his youngest child now legally of age, there was nothing he could do. After Louie left for Saint Cyr, things worsened between his mother and father. The secret out of the bag, his father became more brazen in his philandering, and his mother, a proud and deeply religious woman, retreated within the walls of the family's estate in the South of France. During his final year at Saint Cyr, Louie's mother took her life, and the heart and soul of the entire family was ripped from them. Devastated, Louie blamed it all on his father and decided to never speak to the man again.

She held her glass while he poured. "Did they try to follow you?"

"No."

She frowned. "What took you so long?"

"Just being careful." He poured his own glass and sat next to her on the tattered sofa.

"Herr Abel . . . did he wet himself when he discovered you in his room?"

"He was calmer than I would have expected." Louie held up his glass. "To what just might be our last job."

She wasn't sure she liked the sound of this, and did not raise her glass right away. She stared at him with her piercing eyes. He prodded her by extending his glass farther and after a moment she relented.

They had met when Claudia Morrell was just eighteen. He was a twenty-one-year-old second lieutenant in the French Foreign Legion when he'd laid eyes on her in the village of Aubagne. He fell for her almost immediately, and over a two-month period their romance intensified. Then one day in early July he was called in to see his commanding officer. It turned out Claudia was the daughter of a certain Colonel Morrell, a highly decorated Legionnaire. The colonel had just returned from a six-month deployment in Bosnia and had been promoted to brigadier general. It appeared that the general was rather upset that someone new under his command was attempting to deflower his precious daughter.

Gould's transfer to the island of Corsica and the 2nd Foreign Parachute Regiment set a record for expedited paperwork. He was literally gone that very morning on the first transport out, with nothing more than a rucksack and a change of uniform to his name. There had been no chance to say good-bye to Claudia. The transfer was bittersweet. The bitter part was leaving the lovely Claudia. The sweet part was getting a transfer to the Foreign Parachute Regiment—the elite of the French Foreign Legion.

Once he arrived on Corsica, there was little time to feel sorry for himself. Word had been passed down from on high that this particular Legionnaire was to be worked to the bone. For months on end he rappelled down cliffs, shot everything in the Legion's arsenal, went on grueling hikes in the hot summer sun wearing a fifty-pound pack, jumped out of planes, and swam for miles in the Bay of Calvi. The paratroopers bought into Nietzsche's creed—what doesn't kill you makes you stronger. He looked back on it now and knew that the time he spent with the paratroopers had turned him into the man that he was today.

Several months into his banishment on Corsica, he found out that the general's decision to have him abruptly transferred had come back to bite him in the ass. His very beautiful, but very stubborn daughter was making him suffer for his insensitivity to her emotions. She wrote to Louie under a pseudonym, and explained that she had moved to Paris and was refusing to speak to her "dictator of a father." On the rare occasion that he received a leave of more than two days Louie began visiting her.

Gould, however, had found a home with the paratroopers, and as much as he missed Claudia, there was no abandoning this elite band of warriors. Over the next four years he traveled the globe, going from one hot spot to the next honing his skills and discovering that he was exceptionally good at killing other men. He and Claudia remained in contact, but as she entered university life they began to drift apart. Her new friends, a bunch of socialists, had great disdain for the military and he, like all soldiers, found it very difficult to be around people who had no concept of the sacrifice made by a professional soldier. He was not asking for gratitude, but he was not about to tolerate outright contempt.

So after one long weekend in Paris that involved far too much drinking and not enough sex, all hell broke loose. The signs that her deep love for him was beginning to wane were clear. Her appearance had changed, and she'd gotten involved with a particularly rabid clique of antiestablishment types. The male leader of this tribe was hell bent on inserting his pompous ass between Claudia and Louie every chance he got.

The last straw was when he draped his arm around Claudia, and with a glass of wine and clove cigarette in the other hand, asked Louie, "Is it true that homosexuality runs rampant amongst you Legionnaires?"

He probably would not have let the comment pass, but when Claudia began laughing, that sealed the deal. The punch wasn't too vicious, nothing more really than a snap of the fist, but it was well placed. It broke the twit's nose and sent a deluge of blood cascading over his upper lip and past his blabbering mouth. It could have ended there. He had nothing more to say to Claudia. Just being in her presence now disgusted him. He was turning to leave, and then some fool jumped on his back. Like most bar brawls, what happened next was a little confusing, but it didn't change the end result. Elbows snapped, fingers were bent in directions they weren't meant to go, and noses were flattened and bloodied. Louie ended up in jail and five of Claudia's male friends ended up in the emergency room.

In the aftermath, she told him she never wanted to see him again. He asked her if that was a promise. That set her loose on a diatribe against the French Foreign Legion. He listened passively, and when she was done he calmly told her he wished that someday she could put aside her pettiness and recognize the fact that her father loved her. It would be years before their paths crossed again, and it would not be under the best of circumstances.

"What makes you think this will be our last job?" she asked.

"Because the payday is huge."

She looked into his eyes and said, "You are making me nervous."

Wait until you hear the name of the target, he thought. Without really believing it this time he said, "You worry too much."

"You," she said with an edge, "do not worry enough."

"That is why we are the perfect team." He leaned in and kissed her.

She pushed him away. "Do not try to distract me. Why do you think this will be our last job?"

"Because the contract is worth seven million dollars."

"Seven million dollars," she repeated with a little gasp. Claudia liked the independence wealth offered, but any job worth that much money had to be exceedingly dangerous.

"The dollar amount impresses you?" Louie asked with a raised eyebrow.

"It scares me, and it should scare you too."

He shrugged. "It's just another job."

"For seven million dollars . . . I doubt it. Who does he want you to kill?"

Louie took a gulp of wine and then said, "An American."

She crossed her legs. "Please tell me we do not have to travel there. You know I do not like working in America."

" 'Don't,' " he corrected her. "Remember, Americans don't say 'do not'; they say 'don't.' "

Her nostrils flared ever so slightly. "This is not a time for you to lecture me about syntax or idioms or whatever it is you call these things. Answer my question."

"We will more than likely have to work in America."

She closed her eyes and shook her head. "Who is the target? And don't say the president."

"No, it is not the president." He laughed.

She was running out of patience. "Name! I want a name!"

"Shhhhh . . ." He tried to place a hand on her knee but she slapped it away.

"Tell me right now!"

"Mitch Rapp."

She blinked once and then twice and then slowly set down her glass. She stood and walked to the window. She checked the street, and then came back and in a voice barely above a whisper asked, "Why?"

"I didn't ask him why. It is not my place."

She folded her arms across her chest and said, "I thought you admired this man Rapp."

"I do."

"Then why do you want the job?"

"You don't think seven million dollars is a good enough reason?"

"You have to be alive to enjoy seven million dollars."

"I am not going to get killed."

"You do not know that. This isn't some banker, like the other day in London. This is Mitch Rapp. He bites back."

"He will never see me coming."

She walked from one end of the tiny apartment and back. "Who wants him dead?"

"Abel was not about to tell me."

"I bet it's the Saudis."

"He didn't say."

"I'm not asking," she snapped. "Abel has been doing dirty work for them for some time." She blew a loose strand of hair from her face and said, "I'm not crazy about the idea of working for them. Mitch Rapp happens to be on the side I believe in. As you like to say, he's one of the 'good guys.' "

"I've told you I don't know how many times . . . leave politics out of this, but as long as you're on the subject, I find it interesting that you would label Rapp 'one of the good guys.' I can think of about a billion Muslims who would disagree with you."

Her face flushed and she pointed her finger at him. "Don't start this with me. You hate the Catholic Church because of your father. 'It's a religious war,' she mocked him, 'that goes back thousands of years and the Catholic Church has been wrong more than it has been right.' "

"And I still stand by that."

"You are naïve, Louie, just like I was when I grew to hate my own father. We are in the here and now. Not a thousand years ago. The Catholic Church has nothing to do with this. This is about a bunch of racist, bigoted, sexist, small-minded men trying to hold on to their arcane way of living as the world passes them by." She pointed to herself. "And I for one have no desire to help them."

He almost told her to relax, but then thought better of it. That would only upset her further. "I wouldn't argue with a thing you just said."

"Good. Then we are going to tell the German no."

"I did not say that."

"I thought you agreed with me."

"I do, but there is a lot more to it than what you just said."

"Like what?" She began tapping her foot.

"Like settling down and having a baby." He could see the mere mention of offspring stopped her in her tracks.

He was right but for the wrong reasons. Claudia desperately wanted to talk about this, but now was not the time. Not while they were angry. "How do I have your baby if you are dead?"

He stepped around the table and grabbed her hands. "I know this isn't easy for you, but I promise I will be careful. If it takes six months, I will wait. He does not know I'm coming. The German has no idea who we are. Rapp will never see me. I will kill him, and we will be done."

She was tempted, but something told her they should run from this job as fast as possible. "I don't know."

"That's fine. Sleep on it. Think about finally being done with looking over our shoulders, moving every month . . . finally settling down. Think about a house on the beach filled with little kids." He took her in his arms and held her tight. "I promise you, nothing bad will happen. I will be extra careful."

She looked up at him. "You really think you can walk away from this lifestyle?" It was a subject they had visited on more than one occasion.

He smiled and said, "Yes," even though he wasn't sure he meant it.

She looked into his eyes. They were intelligent, caring eyes, but she knew what lurked just beneath. She had seen him kill, and it had shocked her how little it affected her. It was even beautiful to watch. He was so skilled and effortless in his actions. She rationalized her feelings by hanging her conscience on the fact that the men he killed were guilty of some crime or transgression against humanity. But Mitch Rapp was a different matter. He was someone she admired. This one would be hard to rationalize. In the end, though, it was the promise of walking away from it all, once and for all, that tempted her forward. Things were coming to a head whether Louie wanted them to or not. Their life was moving ahead and it was time for them to put all of this behind them.

18

Traffic was light, but Rapp nonetheless drove aggressively. It was a little after six in the morning and they were making good time. There was no reason to rush, but Anna wasn't about to tell him to slow down. They'd been down that road before, and he had been characteristically inflexible. Whenever possible Mitch liked to drive her to work. The thirty-minute commute without traffic was a nice way for them to spend time together and since they were both headed in the same direction, it made sense. They had settled into a routine. Mitch drove fast, his head on a swivel, checking his mirrors constantly, noting the faces of drivers as he passed them, and trying as much as possible to vary the route they took. It was all second nature to him, ingrained from years of living in hostile environments.

Anna, for her part, kept her face buried in the *New York Times* and the *Washington Post*. Her job required a heavy dose of reading. As a White House correspondent she had to not just follow the goings-on at 1600 Pennsylvania Avenue, but keep an eye on all things Executive Branch. In addition to that she had to at a bare minimum be aware of what the president's opposition was up to. There was a lot to keep up with and the dirty secret of most TV journalists in DC was that they relied heavily on print reporters to do their work for them. The *Post* and the *Times* were a must. Read both, encapsulate, and take to the air with a thirty-second blurb about whatever scandal was brewing at the White House. In theory, if there was time, and if you could get anyone at the White House to talk to you, you would ask a few questions. In reality, however, the "stay on message" attitude of the White House and time constraints meant that more often than not you encapsulated and regurgitated. So while her husband drove like a bank robber fleeing the feds, she tried her best to ignore everything that was going on outside the armored vehicle that was their family sedan.

The customized silver Audi A8 weighed approximately thirty percent more than the factory model. Almost all of the increase in weight came from the bulletproof Kevlar fabric that lined the doors, floor, and ceiling of the vehicle. The bulletproof windows added a bit as did the run-flat tires, but it was the bullet-stopping density of the double layer of Kevlar that added an additional fourteen hundred pounds to the vehicle's gross weight. The sedan had more than enough horsepower to handle the extra weight. The only noticeable difference was in the gas mileage.

"There's a good article in the *Post* about your new boss," she said without looking up. "You should check it out."

With a frown on his face Rapp accelerated and changed lanes. "What are you talking about?"

"Ross . . . the new director of National Intelligence."

"I wouldn't call him my boss."

Anna glanced over at the speedometer and resisted the impulse to look beyond the dashboard. They were on Highway 50 and to be honest she didn't know if the speed limit was fifty, fifty-five, or sixty-five, but she knew it wasn't eighty, which was what the speedometer read. Such was life with Mitchell Rapp. It had taken some time, but she was finally learning to sit back, trust, and relax.

"According to the article he's your boss," she said.

Rapp hadn't thought of it that way, but he supposed if he ever bothered to pay attention to those worthless organizational charts that came across his desk from time to time they would indicate that Ross probably was his boss. "He's a paper pusher, honey. Just another layer of bureaucracy to add to the top of the inverted pyramid."

This time she looked up at him with her stunning green eyes, smiled, and said, "And you're Atlas, right, honey?" She reached out to put her hand on the back of his neck. He blinked, but didn't flinch, which was good. It had taken many months to get him to trust her. Like a dog that was beaten as a puppy, Mitch did not like people touching him.

"Why are you trying to be hurtful?" This was his new ploy with her. Throw the PC mantra back in her face and act like a victim. "I thought we were on the same team."

She rubbed his neck. "We are, honey. I just like teasing you. So have you met him yet?"

"Who?"

"Ross."

Rapp was paranoid for a variety of reasons, but he tried to limit it to his professional life. There were times, though, when his very nosy wife liked to blur the line between their personal life and their jobs. He glanced over at his Anna to see if she knew more than she was letting on. "I've met him a few times."

"And?"

"And what?"

"What's your impression of the guy?"

"I don't know." Rapp shrugged unconvincingly.

"Do I sense dissension in the ranks?" Her index finger had found a curl and she began wrapping it around her finger.

"Easy, Lois Lane."

"Do tell," she pressed. "The article makes it sound like everybody likes the guy. Republicans and Democrats alike."

"And you believe everything you read in the paper?"

"Until I have proof otherwise . . . yes." She turned a little more in her seat so she could face him. "Are you mad because Irene didn't get the new top job?"

"No." He frowned. "I like Irene right where she is. She keeps people off my back and makes sure I get what I need. Besides . . . it remains to be seen how much of the new job is just window dressing."

Anna raised one of her thin eyebrows. "Is Irene going to be able to keep Ross off your back?"

Rapp glanced over at his wife and smiled. "Not bad for a talking head. I'm very proud of you."

They passed the National Arboretum on their left and entered a run-down part of the city. Anna gave his hair a quick yank. "Why did I ever marry you?"

Rapp kept his eyes fixed on the road. "Because you have serious control issues and you like a challenge. I'm your Mount Everest and you want to summit me." He smiled to himself and looked mischievously at his wife. "I like the sound of that. How would you like to summit me tonight?"

"Not with that line."

"Honey, I think our love is a beautiful thing, and when I express that love I'd appreciate a little reciprocation. You know . . . I have feelings too."

"You're unbelievable." She laughed. "I have no doubt that I have a few issues, but you saying that I have control issues is like Donald Trump telling someone they have a big ego."

"Darling," Rapp's voice took on a softer, decidedly NPR-esque tone, "remember, any comment that isn't a positive comment is a cry for help." He reached over and patted her knee. "When you're ready to talk, I'm here for you."

Anna had three brothers and she was no wilting flower. She wound up and punched him on the shoulder.

Rapp began laughing uncontrollably. "Spousal abuse . . . help!"

She hit him twice more in the arm and was about to hit him for a fourth time when she had a flashback to playing slug bug with her brothers when they were kids. She was in her early thirties, for Christ's sake. "Oh . . . Mitchell, why do I let you get to me?"

Rapp was still laughing. "Because you love me."

"I swear sometimes I think I'm married to a child." She sat back in her seat and folded her arms stubbornly across her chest.

He was still laughing, and reached over to place his right hand on her thigh. "I'm sorry, honey." Even as he said this, though, he was planning to torment her further. He slid his hand down to her knee, where she was deathly ticklish, and clamped down hard enough to send her through the roof.

She slapped his hand twice and then began clawing at his fingers, while alternating between cries of laughter and pain. Her husband finally relented and she sat there in her seat giggling, her shoulder length, auburn hair covering her face. After a good ten seconds she sat up and flung her hair over her shoulder. "I'm going to get you. You know that . . . don't you?"

Rapp nodded. "I'm sure you will."

Just when he was congratulating himself for getting her off a subject that he didn't want to talk about, she said, "And don't think I don't know what you were doing back there."

"Back where?"

"When you decided you didn't want to talk about your new boss, so you turned everything back onto me. Would you like to tell me why you don't like him, or should I spend the day on the phone asking other people why they think you don't like him?"

"See . . . there you go again."

They were nearing the White House. "Slow down, and don't change the subject. You know I'll spend the whole day working the phones if you don't answer me honestly."

He knew she was dead serious. "Fine, you big bully. I'm not sure how I feel about the guy. I don't know a lot about him, but I have some reservations."

"Like what?"

"I think he's screwing around with someone I know." Rapp was thinking of Coleman's IRS troubles.

"How so?"

He looked at her. "I'll know more by the end of the day . . . I hope."

They pulled up to the northwest vehicle checkpoint a block away from the White House. Rapp put the car in park.

She leaned over, her emerald eyes locking onto his dark brown ones. "You'll fill me in tonight."

Rapp pointed to himself. "Right after you summit me."

She tried not to smile, but couldn't help it. "Maybe."

He leaned in and kissed her. "I love you, honey."

"I love you too." Anna got out of the car with her purse and shoulder bag. She walked around the front of the car and gave him a final wave and the million-dollar smile that made her so perfect for TV.

Rapp rolled down his window. "Be safe."

"I will. You too." She waved to the uniformed Secret Service officer behind the greenish bulletproof Plexiglas. She would have to show her credentials at the next checkpoint.

Rapp sat there, one hand on the gearshift, the other on the steering wheel, admiring the view of his wife's slender yet curvaceous figure. She turned around and gave him one more smile. Rapp waved and yanked the gearshift into drive. He pulled away with a smile of absolute contentment on his face. Things just kept getting better between them. They were hitting their stride, and to be honest he'd never been happier.

19

Abel stepped from the terminal and paused to take in a full breath of the hot dry air. He had mixed feelings about coming back to the Kingdom so soon and hoped the prince would not require more than a few days of his time. He understood, however, that the delicate nature of this business meant talking on the phone, no matter how secure they might think the line, was not wise. As much as he didn't want to leave the Alps, he knew he must.

The fall colors would be blazing near his mountain retreat, and the air would grow crisper with each day. This was the best time of the year to hike. The summer months were still a bit too humid for his asthma, and heavy exercise could be a problem. Now that everything had been set in motion he had a second reason to long for his tiny Alpine village. His survival instincts were kicking in. Sequestered in his mountain retreat he could think clearly and plan for the proper contingencies should things go wrong. So, he would as politely as possible tell Prince Muhammad that he had pressing business to attend to in Zurich, and with any luck, the sociopath would grant him leave.

Prince Muhammad bin Rashid had sent his minions to whisk the German through customs. A white limousine was waiting for him just outside the door with a security detail of two. Another man was placing his carry-on bag in the trunk as if it was a fine piece of art. The fourth and final man was holding the door open for him, gesturing with an up-turned palm for him to enter the air-conditioned chamber. For a fleeting moment Abel had the ominous feeling he was being invited to his own funeral. He hesitated briefly and then got in the vehicle.

Why he didn't turn around and take the first plane back to Europe he did not know. It was not because he trusted Prince Muhammad. He did not. It probably had more to do with the difficulties that would have been caused by not getting in the car. It was quite possible he would have been forcibly removed from the airport. And there were also the inherent risks, occupational hazards if you will, that came with the territory. Things he had grown callous to after two decades of deceit, subterfuge, and murder. He doubted Rashid would kill him, but it was not out of the question. In Abel's astute opinion the man was a narcissistic sociopath. He lived literally behind fortress walls, surrounded by bodyguards and the opulent wealth that his billions provided. His contact with the real world was severely limited. The royal family had a schism running through its heart. One side looked to the future while the other clung to the past. It was pitting brother against brother and before it was over there would be a bloodletting.

Rashid was a thorough man. A man who liked to cover his tracks. What was it that the assassin had said to Abel in Paris?

I am very aware of the kind of person who pays for this type of work. A few are practical, but many have serious psychological problems. They are often sociopaths who must have their way in everything they do in life. They like all the loose ends tied up and everything tucked away neatly in a box. And for some of them that means getting rid of the man who pulled the trigger.

That pretty much summed up Prince Muhammad. The assassin was a smart man. He still had been given no name by which to call him, but the woman had told him to call her Marie. She had done that right before she told him they were backing out of the deal unless he raised the fee from seven to an even ten million. Abel had begun to argue and she hung up on him without bothering to reply. He waited frantically for the next three hours for her to call back. When she finally did, he was forced to use every ounce of restraint he could muster to keep his cool. He'd never dealt with anyone like these two before. They were like a beautiful woman who told you no and slapped you in the face. For some inexplicable reason he kept coming back for more.

Rather than start the search over, he acquiesced to the new number, and just like that, three million dollars was yanked from his pocket. They had kept him off balance every step of the way and in the process had proven to him that they were more than up to the task. Now he just had to sit back, and let them do the heavy lifting. That was of course unless Rashid planned on having him killed. Abel looked out the heavily tinted window and decided he would have to subtly indicate to the prince that his death would be a mutually disastrous event.

The palace was massive and looked strikingly similar to a five-star resort Abel had once visited in Arizona. It occupied 225 acres and contained thoroughbred stables, six outdoor pools, three indoor pools, a nine-hole golf course, and a small amusement park. All four of Rashid's wives lived on the property, in separate mansions, as well as many of his twenty-one children and his quickly growing brood of grandchildren. The large metal gate opened and the limousine rolled up the palm tree–lined cobblestone path past a colossal fountain and pulled under the huge portico of the main palace. It wasn't always easy keeping Rashid's dwellings straight. There was the one in Mecca, one in Jeddah on the Red Sea, a home in Zurich, and an amazing villa outside Granada, Spain.

The prince did not like to travel abroad very much, but his villa in Spain was his pride. It was one of his stated goals to see Islam once again take its rightful place on the shores of Spain. Abel was often amused by this. Spain was an overwhelmingly Catholic country, and Islam's reign in the southern part of the country was very short lived by historical standards. Prince Muhammad and his cabal saw no inconsistency in their position on Spain and their desire that Israel be wiped off the map. Abel, being German, felt he was in a unique position to understand the Zionist movement and the desire of the Jewish people to have a state in their historic homeland. By any fair historical standard the Jews had a far better case in their quest for a secure homeland than the crazy Wahhabis had in their desire to reimport Islam to Spain. For obvious reasons, Abel chose to keep his mouth shut rather than point out this flawed line of thinking to Rashid.

PRINCE MUHAMMAD WAS waiting for him near his main pool which was built in the shape of a camel. Every time Abel came here he got the feeling that the place had been decorated by a ten-year-old boy. The prince was situated under a large khaki-colored tent dressed in full tribal regalia, which was his custom. Two of his ever present bodyguards hovered nearby.

Abel stepped under the tent and bent slightly at the waist. "Good afternoon, Prince Muhammad. How may I be of service to you?"

"Come sit, Erich. We have much to discuss. I hope you are hungry."

"Yes, I am."

A servant stepped forward and held a chair for Abel. The German noted the chair was situated right next to the prince, which was unusual. Rashid must be in an extraconspiratorial mood. They made small talk while they drank—Rashid coffee and Abel iced tea. After about five minutes the prince dismissed his bodyguards, and Abel immediately relaxed. If Rashid had any thought of killing him, he would never dismiss the two bookends.

Rashid offered his visitor a bowl of fruit. "How are things going with my old friend?"

Abel assumed he was talking about Saeed Ahmed Abdullah. "I met with him, as you asked, and I am in the process of helping him solve his problem."

The prince nodded thoughtfully. "You understand he is not well?"

"In what way is he ill?"

"His heart aches for his son, and I'm afraid it has made him crazy."

Abel nodded that he understood.

"My friend is not stable, but he is someone to whom I owe a great deal."

Abel was at a loss for words.

"I appreciate you helping him with his problem," continued Rashid. "I do not know who he wants killed, but I have my suspicions."

"You know I will tell you if you'd like, Prince Muhammad."

Rashid held up his hand and shook his head slowly. "No. I do not want to know such things."

"I would agree that it is very important that as few people as possible know about this. I instructed your friend to speak to no one."

"I stressed the same point with him, but still I worry." The prince fingered a grape and regarded it while he tried to decide what to say next. "The man Abdullah wants you to kill . . . if it is who I am thinking of, you must be extremely careful. He is not just any man. If you fail, he will come after you, and he won't stop until he has your head on a spit."

Abel had considered this. "The person I have hired is exceptionally good."

"You have seen him in action?"

"In a manner of speaking, yes. He is very capable, and I suspect the perfect man for the job."

The prince popped a grape into his mouth. "How well do you know this person?"

Abel regarded the question cautiously. "In my line of work, we try not to get to know each other too well."

The prince stared off in the distance for a moment. "There is much at stake here. I cannot be associated with any of this, and neither can you. You are far too valuable to me."

"What do you have in mind?"

"I would like you to make sure there is no way you can be linked to any of this. If this man you have hired succeeds, there will be some very upset, very powerful people . . . and they will want to find out who was behind it."

Abel considered himself an expert at risk assessment. "The man who your friend wants killed . . . he has many enemies. Without any hard evidence the U.S. will have a very hard time tracking down who was behind this."

"And if they get evidence, if this man you have hired makes a mistake, or even worse, if he fails and gets captured . . ."

"There are no guarantees, Prince Muhammad. All of that is possible, but unlikely. The man I have hired is very good. The odds are in our favor that he will succeed, and no one will ever link him to us." Abel noticed the doubtful look in Rashid's eyes. In an effort to further assure him he said, "I have covered my tracks. Even if my man fails it would be exceptionally difficult for them to trace it back to me."

"I do not share your confidence."

Abel exhaled a tired sigh. He did not know what else to say.

"If the man you have hired is captured, the U.S. authorities will find out it was you who hired him."

"The man has no idea who I am, other than a vague description of me and an alias I used." Abel could tell where this was going and felt it necessary to lie to the prince.

"The U.S. has gotten much better with their interrogation techniques. I assume this man has a way of contacting you."

Abel nodded.

"All they need is a phone number, an e-mail address. You have paid the man, undoubtedly through electronic transfer?"

"Yes."

"They will get it out of him and they will trace the money all the way back to Abdullah."

Abel disagreed. "I used a network of banks that are known for honoring the confidentiality of their clients. Even with the new terrorist banking laws I am protected."

A cynical smile formed on Rashid's lips. "I have heard rumors. The U.S. no longer bothers going through the Swiss courts. They simply hack into the banking networks and get the information they need. They come and go with impunity and the banks never even know they are there."

"With all due respect, Prince Muhammad, those rumors are grossly exaggerated."

"You have your sources, and I have mine," the prince said with a mischievous smile.

They were at a stalemate. Abel did not know what else he could say to assuage the prince's concerns so he gave in to the inevitable. "What would you like me to do?"

"I want you to cover your tracks."

"I told you . . . I have already done that."

Prince Muhammad looked at the German with the stern look of a wise father who had grown tired of debating a point. "I will say this only once more. I want you to make sure there is no possible way for the Americans to trace any of this back to you or Abdullah."

Abel looked away from the prince and let his eyes settle on the shimmering surface of the ridiculous camel-shaped pool. He knew all too well that Prince Muhammad really meant he didn't want the Americans tracing any of this back to him. Abel was in a tough position. If he continued to resist the prince on this issue he might find himself at the bottom of the camel-shaped pool staring up at the surface with a couple of lungs filled with heavily chlorinated water. There was no other option at the moment other than submitting. Once out of Saudi Arabia he would have to sort things out. For now he would have to make the best of a bad situation.

He looked back at the prince. "It can be done, but it will not be cheap."

"How much?"

The truth was, he was not so sure it could be done, but Rashid would not be satisfied with that answer. He had no idea who the man was, and there was so little to go on where the girl was concerned. Add to that the explicit warning from the assassin that he would kill him in a second if he caught him trying to find out who they were. Maybe Petrov knew more about them. Maybe he could bribe the old communist into setting them up. Abel thought about what that would take and said, "Five million . . . maybe more."

Rashid looked at him with his best poker face. Unlike Abdullah, whose judgment was clouded by the murder of his son, Rashid was not going to simply open the vault and hand him over a mound of cash. "Do you take me for a fool?"

"No."

"Five million is far too much."

"With all due respect, Prince Muhammad, it might not be enough. I will need to hire a small army to go after this man, and I will have to bribe many officials to get the information I need to find him. Five million is the minimum."

Rashid did not speak for a long time. His brown, almost black eyes stayed locked on the German. Abel for his part held his ground. He did not look directly at the prince, for that would have only provoked him, but he kept his mouth shut, which was the number one rule of negotiating.

After a full minute Rashid relented. "Not a penny more."

"I will do my best," replied Abel in a voice void of any sign of victory.

"Yes, you will." Rashid fingered another grape. "You always do."

"I expect you wish me to get started on this immediately."

"Yes. I have a plane waiting to take you wherever you need to go."

Abel thought about it for a second and then said to the prince, "Moscow."

The prince smiled cynically. "So you are working with your old friends the Russians? That is good. They will do anything for money. They are like whores that way."

Abel decided not to comment. He wondered if Prince Muhammad had any idea how the Russians felt about the Saudis. It was tempting to tell him, but then again he had no desire to end up in the pool. He stood and gave the prince a curt bow. "Thank you for your hospitality, Prince Muhammad. I will keep you informed of my progress."

"I will have your money waiting for you on the plane. No more wire transfers."

"However you wish to handle it."

A member of the prince's vast staff appeared as if out of nowhere and gestured for Abel to follow him. As soon as the two were out of sight, a stern man dressed in white robes stepped from behind a curtain and joined Prince Muhammad. He remained standing with his arms folded across his broad chest.

"What do you think?" asked the prince.

The man sneered and said, "I do not trust him. I have never trusted him."

The prince smiled. Colonel Nawaf Tayyib had served under Muhammad when he'd been the secretary of the interior. Tayyib worked for the Saudi Intelligence Service, and had been one of the prince's most trusted officers. He was an extremely efficient man who was not afraid to use force to get results.

"What should I do with him?" asked Muhammad.

"I think you should let me deal with him."

Muhammad nodded. This was the answer he had expected. "Keep a discreet eye on him. When the time is right you will know."

20

Rapp pulled into the underground parking garage beneath the Old Headquarters building at Langley, and parked next to Kennedy's armored Lincoln Town Car. The spaces in this relatively small underground garage were highly prized. One of the misfits in the Counterterrorism Center had informed Rapp of this a few years ago. Apparently there was some recently promoted deputy director over in Science and Technology who was furious that Rapp was using his executive parking spot. Rapp couldn't care less—about the parking space or the upset bureaucrat for that matter. He did care, however, about the private elevator that allowed him to bypass the main lobby and people who might want to bend his ear. That was one of the first things Rapp had noticed when he was brought in from the field. People worked at a different pace at headquarters. They had a lot of time to talk, attend meetings, and surf the Internet. Rapp's loner attitude was directly at odds with anything that involved socializing. He prided himself on spending as little time as possible at headquarters and when he was there he did his best to avoid conversation.

The private elevator that went directly from the garage to the director's office suite helped significantly. Rapp got in and slid his ID into the card reader. No buttons needed to be pressed. The elevator either went all the way up to the seventh floor or all the way back down to the garage. The elevator started to move, and Rapp looked up at the tiny camera mounted in the corner. He held his right hand up in front of his face and flipped the bird. Just before the elevator stopped, Rapp stepped to one side and grabbed the butt of his shoulder-holstered pistol. The doors slid open and Rapp was confronted with a mirror image of what he might look like in another fifteen years. The man was even standing like him with one hand resting on his own holstered pistol. His name was Vince Delgado. He was the head of Kennedy's security detail, and he and Rapp loved to give each other crap.

"Good morning, Vanessa," Rapp said crisply.

"Good morning, Michelle."

"Is she in her office?"

"No, she's up on the roof having tea and crumpets, ya dumb ass."

"Cranky this morning, you old codger? Still not getting any?"

The fifty-two-year-old Italian American from Philadelphia laughed loudly. "Now that's not true, Mitch." He stepped closer to Rapp, and after looking over both shoulders said, "You should have seen me last night. There's this new gal I met at the club. I was like a rock star. I'm amazed I can walk this morning, because I'll tell you right now she's in traction." He looked once again toward Kennedy's office door and stepped even closer to Rapp. "Listen to this."

Rapp's arm shot out like a traffic cop. "Stop." He closed his eyes and shook his head in an attempt to erase the picture big hairy Vince Delgado was attempting to scar him with.

Rapp walked toward Kennedy's door and then knocked on it.

"Hey, are we still shooting this afternoon?" Delgado was a former Recon Marine and phenomenal shot, which was in part how he and Rapp had got to know each other so well.

"Yep," answered Rapp. "I'll see you there at two."

Rapp entered Kennedy's office and found her sitting at her desk focusing intently on an opened red file. "Morning."

"Good morning," Kennedy answered without taking her eyes off the top secret document.

"How's Tommy?" Rapp was referring to Kennedy's eight-year-old son.

"He's busy, but he misses you, of course. He just asked about you last night."

"Does he have a game Saturday?" Tommy was playing his first year of tackle.

"Yes. Eleven a.m."

"I'll be there."

"Good." Kennedy took off her reading glasses. "Make sure you bring Anna with. He likes to show her off."

"Oh . . . he's getting to that age now." Rapp raised an eyebrow.

"I don't think he's been the same since he saw her in a swimsuit last summer."

"I don't think I've been the same either."

Kennedy slid her chair away from her desk. "He's definitely changing. Very brand-conscious all of a sudden. He has to have his hair a certain way . . . this shirt is cool, this one is lame and on top of all that . . . he's gotten quite mouthy."

With a straight face he asked, "Did you ever think maybe it's your management style?"

"You're a very funny man."

Rapp shrugged. "All kids go through phases."

"Apparently. What's your excuse?" Kennedy looked at Rapp and thought, not for the first time, how nice it would be to have a man at home to help. Not Rapp of course. They were more like brother and sister. But it was impossible to miss the way Tommy was drawn to him, or the tone Mitch would use when Tommy was out of line and the way her young son would instantly react. Her prospects, however, were not good. Working sixty plus hours a week did not leave much time to date, and the fact that she was the director of the CIA tended to intimidate men a bit.

"Now you're the comedian," Rapp said.

Kennedy nodded. She was wearing a stylish yet conservative brown jacket with matching pants. She crossed her left leg over her right and asked, "What's on your mind?"

Rapp plopped down in one of the side chairs. "I need you to talk me off the ledge."

"Oh no . . . what now?"

"Ross."

Kennedy closed the file on her desk. Conflict was a part of her job, especially post 9/11. A power grab was afoot, and she needed to be very careful. She had high hopes for a smooth relationship with the new director of National Intelligence. She respected Rapp, but his insolent attitude, and bull-in-a-china-shop demeanor, could easily put her and Ross at odds. "I would think he hasn't been at the job long enough to cross you."

"Well, you're wrong."

"What did he do?"

"For starters he had one of his people call over to the Pentagon and request Scott Coleman's personnel file."

"And?"

"The Pentagon sent over the sanitized version, and Ross didn't buy it. He or one of his deputies called back and tried to browbeat some captain into handing over the full file, especially anything involving any work he may have done for the CIA. The captain directed them to the Joint Special Operations Command, who in turn kicked it all the way up to General Flood."

"Did Flood give them what they wanted?"

"Are you kidding me? The only people who are more pissed than us about National Intelligence is the Pentagon. Flood told them, in a not so polite way, that unless he got a phone call from the president telling him to release the file they could go to you know where."

Kennedy in fact did. General Flood was in his final months as chairman of the Joint Chiefs and he seemed to be taking great pleasure in telling certain people exactly how he felt about them. "Did they go to the president?"

"Not that I know of, and I doubt they'll bother."

"Why would Ross be so interested in Coleman?" Kennedy set her reading glasses down on her desk. "Has he been up to anything that I don't know about?"

"No. He's clean."

"The timing of this is not good."

"I agree, and there's one more problem. The IRS showed up on Coleman's doorstep yesterday. They want to see all of his books."

Kennedy brought her hands together and formed a pyramid under her chin. The frown lines on her forehead deepened. "What in the hell is he up to?"

"He's either picked up some intel that we're reconstituting the Orion Team or he's on a fishing expedition."

Kennedy's mind ran through a half dozen possibilities. She wondered if Ross would be so bold as to have her office bugged. As paranoid as it sounded, it wouldn't be the first time that an intelligence overlord had decided to spy on the home team. Ross had been on the job less than a month. She doubted he could move that fast, but she still made a note to have Delgado's group sweep the office.

"My gut," she said, "tells me a fishing expedition."

"What if we're being set up?"

"By whom?"

"Senator Hartsburg."

Kennedy shook her head. "No. If Hartsburg wanted to fry us he wouldn't go through Ross. I think it's a fishing expedition."

"Why?"

She thought about it for a while and said, "Mark Ross is a good man. He's not out to destroy us, or Coleman for that fact."

"You'll excuse me if I don't share your confidence."

"I think he has a natural distrust for the operations side of the business. He comes from the intel side, and guys like you and Coleman make him nervous."

Rapp frowned. "Why?"

"If I had to guess, I'd say he thinks you're going to embarrass him. He's the new guy in charge, and a lot of people are hoping he falls flat on his face."

"Again, what in the hell does that have to do with me?"

Kennedy sighed. Rapp was very good at his job, but he was a complete neophyte when it came to the politics of Washington. "Thank God much of what you've done is classified. You've had an amazing track record, but one of these times, I fear, you're going to have an operation head south and you're going to land all of us in the middle of a monumental scandal."

"Thanks for the vote of confidence."

She shook her head. "You know you have my confidence."

Rapp nodded. "Well, if you want to win, you have to play the game. We can't just sit on the sidelines and hope they start liking us."

"I agree." She reached out and grabbed a pink message slip from her desk. "I'll figure out a strategy for Ross, in the meantime we'd better put your project on hold."

This was not what Rapp wanted to hear. "For how long?"

"I don't know. Give me at least until the end of the week."

Rapp had no intention of slowing down. He would just have to be a little more careful. "What about the IRS?"

"I'll see what I can do, but once these audits are started things can get tricky."

Rapp leaned forward, placing both elbows on his knees. "I want the IRS off Scott Coleman's back by tomorrow morning, or I am going to make someone's life miserable. Every time we've needed him to handle some shitty job he's been there for us, and he hasn't complained once."

She knew Rapp was serious and she knew better than to argue with him. "I'll do my best." She held up the pink slip of paper. "Onto another subject. I got a call from your old friend Sayyid." Kennedy was referring to Ali Kyer, the head of the Jordanian Intelligence Service.

Rapp immediately wondered what he had done wrong. Sayyid knew how to get hold of him directly. If he was going over his head to Kennedy, there was a good chance he'd pissed someone off. "And how is my old friend?" Rapp asked cautiously.

"He's fine. He sends his regards. He says you are no fun now that you are married." Kennedy's left eyebrow arched in a curious expression. "What is that supposed to mean?"

"It means now that I'm married I'm no fun anymore."

"Lovely. It's good to hear you've settled down. Anyway . . . Sayyid wanted to pass on a bit of intel. Apparently you're still very popular in Saudi Arabia."

"Good. Are they planning a parade for me?"

"Not quite. The opposite is more like it . . . a price has been placed on your head."

Rapp leaned back and crossed his legs. "By who?"

"We don't know. Sayyid is looking into it."

"Is that all?"

"For the moment."

Rapp thought about it for a few seconds while Kennedy observed him. This wasn't the first time he'd been on someone's hit list, and he doubted it would be the last. He looked at his watch. "I'd better get over to the CTC for the morning briefing."

Kennedy tilted her head and regarded him. "Doesn't this news worry you?"

Rapp shrugged. "Irene, there's always going to be some crazy fucker out there who wants to kill me. This is nothing new."

Kennedy nodded. "Just promise me you'll be careful."

"I always am," Rapp replied. "I always am."

"And promise me you won't hesitate to ask for security if you notice anything out of the ordinary."

Rapp stood and buttoned his suit coat. "Absolutely." He started for the door and then thought of something else. He stopped and asked, "Irene, would you do me a favor?"

"Of course."

"Would you let the Secret Service know about this? I'd appreciate it if they'd keep an eye on Anna as she's coming and going from the White House."

She was already planning on it. "I'll call Jack Warch right away."

"Thank you." Rapp left the director's office . . . his mind already jumping ahead . . . going into tactical mode. He'd feel much better when the new house was finished. The damn thing was going to be more secure than Fort Knox. The crazies could come after him all they wanted once he moved into the place. Unless they brought some heavy explosives, there was no way they were getting in, and if they did, well . . . he'd have a few surprises waiting for them.

21

He had made almost no effort to talk her into taking the job, knowing any such attempt had the potential to drive her further away. That night he simply stopped talking and let her begin to sort it out in her mind. They'd made love, forgetting about Mitch Rapp and killing for a while. When they were done, there was no mention of the German or Rapp or anything else, for that matter. They'd simply fallen asleep in each other's arms. The next morning they sat through a pot of coffee and some fresh fruit without a mention of it. They read the paper, smoked a cigarette, and literally didn't say a word. He recognized it for what it was. Claudia was not playing a game with him. She was not waiting for him to make the first move. She was simply thinking it through in a very thorough manner.

That was Claudia Morrell. She was the general, the field marshal, the tactician. Louie was good at the hunt and the kill. He was gifted beyond measure with the instinct to know when to press forward and when to retreat. He had a sense of the overall picture, but his attitude was inevitably one of invincibility. Claudia's strength was in the details. She was better at analyzing the risk whereas Louie thought anything could be overcome with the right amount of skill and determination. She knew when to walk away, while he was sometimes driven by the challenge. A dark, mad part of him had actually hoped the German would ask him to kill the American president. He had no feelings about the president one way or another, it was simply a challenge, a test of his skill, something that would be discussed for hundreds of years and maybe longer. To kill the most protected man in the world and get away with it, that would be the ultimate test. He'd dreamt of it. He was an old man giving a deathbed confession. Giving details that only he would know. Maybe even telling them where he'd hid the rifle. That was the only way to kill a man so heavily protected, that or a bomb, but bombs were clumsy and ended up killing too many innocent people. They were the easy way out, not the way of a talented assassin.

Rapp, however, was an entirely different matter. Despite Claudia's worries, Louie knew he had a huge advantage, and there was nothing cocky about recognizing this. Surprise was on his side. He knew if the roles were reversed he probably wouldn't stand a chance against a man of Rapp's talents and significant resources. Any disadvantage he was dealt by having to operate in Rapp's backyard was negated by the fact that he had gone to high school in Washington while his father had been ambassador. Louie's Americanized English was flawless. Despite Claudia's reservations, he was very optimistic about pulling off this job and simply fading away into early retirement. Well, he was a little less optimistic about the fading away part, but he hadn't shared that with Claudia.

After she'd finished two cups of coffee she closed the paper and said, "Do you want to know what I think?"

"I've been waiting all morning."

"The German is working for the Saudis. That's where his contacts are. I don't like the Saudis, but I like the idea of settling down." She paused and fixed him with a very serious look. "But I'm not so sure you do."

"That's not true."

"What are you going to do? Lie in the sun every day and drink beer . . ." She shook her head. "I don't think so."

"Claudia, we are going to be extremely wealthy. I will do whatever I want."

She studied him with open skepticism. "I want you to really think about this. I want children, and I want to put all of this behind us. Killing people was not what I wanted to do with my life."

She extended her arms and motioned toward the dirty walls of the run-down apartment. "No more assignments, no more moving from place to place. I want to stop."

"So do I." Louie knew the important thing was to keep agreeing. Like an alcoholic, he had the desire to stop. The benefit was undeniable, but he just didn't know if he would be able to resist the call of the hunt.

His answer, and her need to believe in the possibility of a different life, was enough for her. "Here is what we are going to do. I don't trust the German. He would throw us overboard in a second, and as far as the money goes he is a shyster. We know he's acting on behalf of the Saudis, and it's my guess that he is not working for the government but rather some individual or group. Either way," she shrugged, "they have deep pockets."

"I would agree."

"Good. I am going to call Herr Abel and tell him our fee is ten million."

Louie didn't like changing the deal. "But I already told him seven."

"I know you did, but Saudis are not rational when it comes to money. They are impulsive. If they are willing to pay seven they are willing to pay ten . . . trust me."

"Why not ask for fifteen, then?"

"That's too big of a jump." She reached out and patted his hand. "You're good, darling, but not that good. If we demand fifteen million, Abel will go find someone else."

"All right. Ten million is the number. What if they say no?"

"They won't."

She was right. Louie sat there at the kitchen table and watched Claudia turn on her phone and call Abel. It didn't go well at first. Louie could hear the German's voice bellowing from the tiny speaker of the mobile phone. They had a deal. Seven million was the agreed-upon sum. He said he would find someone else. Claudia wished him luck, pressed the end button, and turned her phone off. Fifteen minutes later she turned her phone back on and there were three messages from the German. She played them back and listened to Abel negotiate with himself. The first message he agreed to go to eight, during the second call he went to nine, and finally on the third call he agreed to ten million but not a dollar more. Claudia called him back and told him she would e-mail him the wiring instructions. As soon as the five-million-dollar deposit was in their hands they would start.

By midafternoon of that same day they received verification that one million dollars had been deposited in each of the five separate banks that Claudia had requested. The German appeared eager for them to get the job done, and they were more than happy to oblige. Staying in Paris, with the German there, was not a good idea. Abel was too sloppy to be trusted, and if an intelligence agency was tracking him, they were only one step away from Louie and Claudia, so the first order of business was to sanitize, dismantle, and ditch both Claudia's phone and his since they had made enough calls to each other that it would be easy to link the two. After the phones were disposed of, they collected their meager belongings and left the rented apartment, never to return. Claudia called the landlady from a pay phone and told her there was a family emergency and they would not be returning. With any luck the woman would have the place rented within the week.

They then took the metro, zigzagging across the city until they arrived in the Montmartre neighborhood where they had met the German only a day earlier. Six blocks north of the famous Roman Byzantine Basilica of Sacré-Coeur they separated. Claudia stopped at a small café for an espresso while Louie started his sweep. After ten minutes of walking the narrow streets and making a single phone call, he deemed it safe to enter the apartment. The two-bedroom apartment was located on the top floor of a five-story Belle Epoque era building. Louie had purchased the apartment through an offshore corporation three years earlier. He skipped the elevator and used the stairs, taking them two at a time.

Once in the apartment he turned off the alarm and went straight to the kitchen. He placed a gloved hand on each side of the refrigerator and slid it away from the wall. White subway tile covered the wall down to the height of the countertop. Beneath that was plaster. Making a fist with his right hand, Louie hit the wall in just the right spot and the plaster section popped out about an inch on the left side. Louie grabbed the corner and swung open the hinged door. Inside were three eighteen-inch-deep shelves. A single black duffel bag sat on each wooden plank. Louie grabbed the top bag, closed the door, and pushed the refrigerator back up against the wall. Emblazoned on the side of the duffel bag was the name of Peugeot, the French car manufacturer.

Gould had a mind that was uniquely suited to breaking rules and not getting caught. He'd first noticed it during childhood. He had a friend who seemed to have a nose for trouble, both at home and at school. No matter how many times the boy was told not to do something, he did it. No matter how harsh the punishment, he persisted. The boy was oblivious to his surroundings, unlike Gould, who seemed to always know what was going on around him. Even at an early age he instinctively knew the key was to understand the rules first, and then find a way to avoid detection while breaking them.

There were a variety of ways to circumvent the ban against bringing weapons across international borders. Prior to the terrorist attacks against America in September 2001 everything was much easier. A man of Gould's profession could even be brazen enough to carry the tools of the trade concealed beneath his own clothes or in a suitcase, but those days were long gone. That left two options. The first was to acquire the weapons once you arrived in the country where you would be operating. Again this had grown more difficult since 9/11, but it was still doable, especially in the old Eastern Bloc countries of Europe. He'd also done it once in America, but for this job, Gould wanted to be absolutely certain he minimized his exposure as much as possible. He had yet to decide how he would kill Rapp, but he would more than likely end up using either a silenced rifle or pistol. For that he wanted to use weapons that he himself had already field tested and zeroed in.

Each of the three bags concealed in the wall behind the refrigerator contained a TTR-700 tactical sniping rifle that was designed with a collapsible butt stock, bipod and quick release scope, silencer, and barrel. Each bag also contained a Glock 17 pistol with silencer, and a complete set of ID including passport, credit cards, driver's license, and cash. Due to the new wave of screening machines that sniffed for explosives, the bags did not contain ammunition.

Gould left the apartment with one of the bags and called Claudia, telling her he was clearing the area. They would meet at a predetermined location in two hours. He hailed a taxi, and directed the driver to the Gare du Nord train station. From there he took the metro clear across town. He was being more careful than normal, but it would be criminal to have come so far and get caught right on the verge of the biggest job of his career. His next stop was at a packaging store where he purchased a three-by-three-foot cardboard box. He put a layer of Styrofoam packaging peanuts on the bottom, placed the black duffel bag in the box, and then filled the rest with the white peanuts. After taping the box shut, he walked two blocks to a FedEx office and filled out an international air bill. He showed the woman behind the counter a fake ID that matched the name on the air bill and explained that he was mailing sales samples to Canada for a convention he would be attending. It was a common practice, and the woman didn't even bat an eye.

22

The old bar was on Pennsylvania Avenue just a few blocks from one of the world's most well-known buildings—the United States Capitol. The neoclassical seat of democracy was bracketed to the south by Independence Avenue and to the north by Constitution Avenue. The House offices ran along Independence Avenue, and the Senate offices ran along Constitution Avenue. As a general rule, representatives quenched their thirst at establishments located south of East Capitol Street, and senators dined at more upscale restaurants to the north. Certain representatives were fond of migrating north in hopes of someday joining the infinitely more exclusive club of the U.S. Senate, but rarely did a senator travel south. It was simply beneath them.

None of this would have been known to Rapp, but then again he tried to spend as little time as possible thinking about politics and politicians. His source for tracking down this particular senator, however, was a political junkie who had found all these cultural tidbits extremely interesting. The source, who also happened to be his wife, couldn't get over the fact that a senator would go to the Hawk and Dove in the middle of the afternoon to be by himself, but that's what the senator's chief of staff had told her. Always inquisitive, Anna wanted to know why it was so urgent that he track down this particular senator. He almost told her he couldn't talk about it, but that would have likely ended in her refusing to help him. He was learning to trust her. She had an insatiable curiosity, but she had also proved to him that she could keep a secret when he demanded it. Rapp told her he didn't want to talk about it on the phone, and that he'd fill her in over dinner.

So, for the second time in a week Rapp found himself plugging a meter in a part of town he rarely visited. Automatically, he did a quick search of the area, locked his car, and reached around to the small of his back to give his H&K P2000 a quick check. The air felt heavy and Rapp tilted his head skyward. It was overcast and it looked like it might rain at any moment. It matched his mood perfectly.

The bar was hard to miss. The Hawk and Dove was a Capitol Hill institution. Rapp had been there a few times during college, but hadn't been back in years. He stepped into the tiny entry and looked down the length of the bar. The place had a patina about it that could only be attained through lots of spilled beer, deep fried food, and the residue left from a steady haze of cigarette smoke. The brick floor was chipped and uneven, and the once white grout was now as dark as asphalt. It was a real bar, not some cookie-cutter chain where the servers wore obnoxiously colorful outfits and sat down with you to take your order.

It was a few minutes before three in the afternoon and the place was nearly empty. At the far end of the bar, Rapp found his man. He was instantly recognizable by his ridiculous comb-over hairdo and oversized ears. Rapp was not surprised to see that he was sitting with his back to the door. Rapp walked the length of the old wood bar and nodded to the bartender who was watching him intently.

The senator was perched on the last stool reading a book. Rapp stopped and delivered the rickety stool a good kick.

Senator Hartsburg grabbed the bar to steady himself and turned with anger in his eyes and a french fry dangling from his mouth. "What in the hell is wrong with you? Are you trying to give me a heart attack?"

Not a bad idea, Rapp thought to himself. "We need to talk."

Hartsburg's perpetual scowl deepened. "Call my office and set up an appointment." He turned his back to Rapp.

Rapp considered flicking one of the man's large ears, but thought better of it. "That's not going to happen. We need to talk now." Rapp was not a patient man. That was why he had come all the way across town. Kennedy did not seem too excited about locking horns with her new boss, and Rapp had a feeling if they didn't get the IRS off Coleman's back pronto they might be camped out on his doorstep for the next year. It was time to get something back from his new associate.

The bartender showed up. "Is everything all right, Carl?"

Before Hartsburg could reply, Rapp said, "I'll take a beer."

The bartender checked with the senator to see if this was okay. Hartsburg mumbled something under his breath and returned to his book.

"A Guinness, please?" Rapp said with a forced smile.

The bartender hesitated for a second and then left to pour the beer. Rapp peered over Hartsburg's shoulder and asked, "What're you reading?"

"None of your business."

Rapp glimpsed the title across the top of the page. *"Nineteen Eighty-Four* . . . George Orwell." He couldn't have been more surprised. "I'm impressed."

"Don't be," growled Hartsburg. "I'm reading it again so I can better understand how your type thinks."

Rapp laughed. "Well, when you're done be sure to pick up *Animal Farm,* so you can better understand how your type thinks."

The senator closed the book. "Would you mind? I'm here so I can eat, have a drink, and be alone. If you want to talk, call my office."

Rapp grabbed the next stool. "Relax, Carl." He figured if the bartender could call him by his first name, so could he. "Trust me . . . you don't want me calling your office." Rapp unclipped his BlackBerry, punched a series of buttons, and set it on the bar.

The device seemed to get the senator's attention. Hartsburg pushed his plate away and said, "Why did you come here? I really don't want to be seen with you in public, and how in the hell did you find me, anyway?"

Rapp lowered his chin. "You're kidding me . . . right?" He wasn't about to tell him it was his wife who had tracked him down. It was better to leave him thinking he'd employed the vast resources of the CIA to find him.

Hartsburg took a drink, and looked up at the TV. He was more uncomfortable with this encounter than Rapp had expected.

"Senator," Rapp leaned in, "you're the one who wanted to have our little off-the-record meeting. You're the one who proposed this new agreement. If you'd like to back out, I'll walk out of here right now, and believe me I'll be a happy man if I never have to lay eyes on you again."

An uncomfortable silence passed and then Hartsburg said, "Just please, not here. Don't bother me when I'm here. This is where I come to get away from everything."

There was something oddly melancholy in the senator's tone. He began to nod slowly and said, "All right."

The bartender showed up with the beer. "Put it on his tab," Rapp said as he reached for his wallet. "Just kidding." Rapp threw a twenty on the bar. "Take it out of that, and get the senator another one."

Hartsburg nodded his consent and the bartender left. After looking at his book for a moment he asked, "What's so important?"

Rapp took a sip of his dark beer and asked, "Have you told anyone about our new arrangement?"

"Are you out of your mind?"

"You're sure?" Rapp took another sip. He doubted that Hartsburg had, but he wanted to get the man on his heels.

The crotchety senator from New Jersey turned and faced Rapp. "I don't like repeating myself."

Rapp watched him intently. "What about Senator Walsh?"

Hartsburg's face twisted like he'd just bit into a lemon. "No. Bill's a vault. He keeps secrets better than anyone on the Hill. That's why he's chairman of the Intelligence Committee."

"Neither of you consulted anyone further up the chain of command?"

"Whose chain of command?"

"Mine," said Rapp.

"Dr. Kennedy, of course."

"No one else?" asked Rapp. The bartender came back with Hartsburg's drink. From the color of it, Rapp guessed it was probably scotch.

Hartsburg, like most senators, was a lawyer by training and he did not like to be on the receiving end of questions. "Stop pussyfooting around, and tell me what's on your damn mind."

Rapp admired the man's tenacity. "Mark Ross is on my mind."

"The new director of National Intelligence." The senator had a frown on his face. "Why?"

"He's taken a sudden interest in a colleague of mine."

"I'm not following."

"There's someone who we use from time to time to handle delicate matters. We'll call him a consultant. The other day this consultant came out to Langley to sit down with Dr. Kennedy and myself so we could discuss our new venture." Rapp pointed to Hartsburg and then himself. He wanted the senator to take ownership. "Right in the middle of the damn meeting Mark Ross comes barging in unannounced. He introduces himself to the consultant, he leaves, and the next thing you know, Ross's people are calling up the Pentagon asking for this consultant's personnel file. Then the next day the IRS shows up on this guy's doorstep, bends him over, and starts to give him an anal cavity search."

A pleased smile formed on Hartsburg's face and he got a faraway look in his eyes. After a moment he said, "That's why I put him there."

The answer surprised Rapp. "What in the hell is that supposed to mean?"

"Ross is a detail guy. He's extremely controlling and curious. That's why I pushed him on the president."

Rapp was missing something. "And why is this good . . ."

"The whole idea behind creating the new cabinet position of director of National Intelligence is to consolidate all of these far-flung agencies. We need someone who will get into the minutiae and reform from the top down."

Rapp shook his head and set his beer down. "Listen, for the most part, I could give a rat's ass what this guy does. Just keep him away from me, and the people I deal with."

"I don't see how I can help you here."

A disbelieving expression formed on Rapp's face. "The whole reason why I agreed to sit down with you and Walsh was that you guys were willing to offer me some serious funding, and that you'd keep people off my back. I've got enough enemies out there without having to worry about people who are supposed to be on my own team. If you can't rein in a clown like Ross, we might as well end this right here and now."

Hartsburg was smiling. He waved to the bartender. "Charlie, another beer for my friend."

My friend, Rapp thought. *I wouldn't go that far.*

Hartsburg made Rapp retell, in detail, what had happened when Ross popped into Kennedy's office unannounced. By the time Rapp's second beer arrived he'd told the senator the entire story.

"I assume you've seen the movie *Patton,*" said Hartsburg.

"Of course."

"Remember the scene where they're celebrating and the Russian general gives a toast and Patton refuses to drink."

"Yeah."

"And then the Russian calls him a bastard and Patton laughs and says, 'All right, from one bastard to another . . . I'll drink to that.' "

Rapp took a swig of the dark brown Guinness. "It's one of the best scenes in the whole movie."

"Well," Hartsburg held up his glass, "you're one of the biggest bastards in a town filled with bastards. So . . . from one bastard to another."

The two men clanged glasses and drank. "Just so we're clear," said Rapp, "I'm Patton and you're the commie."

Hartsburg laughed. "That is my point exactly. You are Patton. You are this politically incorrect warrior who is good at only one thing and that is fighting terrorism. You've saved the president's life on one occasion, and you had a very big hand in making sure this city wasn't nuked. I have never agreed with your tactics, but that close call last Memorial Day woke a lot of us up. These are drastic times and they call for drastic measures. We need to isolate these radicals, and we need to turn their own people against them. It needs to be done covertly and it needs to be off the books. You," the senator pointed to Rapp, "are the perfect man for the job."

"You still haven't solved my problem."

"Maybe we need to bring Ross in on this?"

Rapp shook his head. "No way. Too many people are already involved."

"Then that leaves only one option."

"What's that?"

"You act like Patton."

Rapp frowned.

"Let me explain what makes Mark Ross tick, and then let me tell you how to handle him."

23

Gould took the overnight flight from Paris to Montreal and arrived early morning. He was traveling with a French passport under the name of Marcel Moliere. His stated purpose was business—pharmaceutical sales, to be more precise. He hailed a taxi at the airport and headed for the Hyatt downtown. A haven for international businessmen who visited the largest French-speaking city outside of France, the Hyatt suited his needs perfectly. It was upscale, with over 300 rooms and a very well staffed business center. Claudia was several thousand miles away en route to the island of Nevis to make sure their fee was secure from the army of snoops and hackers now employed by the U.S. government.

Louie Gould had many secrets, and one of them was that he had worked briefly for France's Direction Génerale de la Securité Exterieure or DGSE. The DGSE was France's main intelligence arm for industrial and economic espionage and for penetrating terrorist organizations. Gould had done his time in the Legion and had been looking for new challenges. As an officer, and a citizen of France, he was a priority recruit for DGSE. What sealed the deal was the fact that his diplomat father detested the spy agency and everything it stood for.

During Gould's one year with the spy agency, he worked almost exclusively on industrial espionage and had absolutely nothing to do with terrorism. It was during his year with the DGSE that he realized two important things—freelancers got paid far better than government employees, and they had to put up with a fraction of the bullshit. And Gould was sick of putting up with bullshit. As romantic as the French Foreign Legion may have been portrayed in the old movies it was anything but. The pay was atrocious, the facilities were run-down, and the duty was often grueling. What made it all bearable was the esprit de corps, the brotherhood, and the pride that went along with training at such a high level. After one complete tour, however, Gould was done. He wanted something that he had grown accustomed to in his youth, and that was money. Too prideful to ever go back to his father, he saw the DGSE as a way to make double what he was making in the Legion and still stay in the action. He knew from the day he took the job, though, that it was merely a stepping stone.

Gould knew fellow Legionnaires who were making big bucks working corporate security. While the money sounded great, he knew the job would bore him to death. He needed something that would both pay well and test his skill. He found it one day when they discovered that one of their DGSE informants was playing both sides of the fence. Due to this informant's duplicity a fellow DGSE agent had been picked up by the Syrian secret police and had gone missing. There was little doubt within DGSE headquarters that the agent was sitting in a Syrian jail getting beaten with rubber hoses. Gould wanted to kill the informer himself, but his superior, who also happened to be a former paratrooper, told him that was not how they handled things.

What he saw next opened his eyes to a whole new world. His boss called a contract agent and in less than two minutes arranged to have the informant disposed of. Gould's job was to deliver the cash to the contract agent. On his way to the dead drop he pulled over and counted the money. The attaché was filled with twenty thousand francs, more than half of what he earned in a single year. All for killing some worthless, self-serving asshole.

Looking back on it now, the decision had been relatively easy. He drove straight past the dead drop and called his boss's office. It was past eight in the evening and Gould knew he would not be there. He left him a message, telling him he was changing careers, and that he'd fax him his resignation. His first stop was a bar where the informant liked to hang out. Gould walked in, the bar was crowded, but he found the man with little difficulty. They had met face-to-face a dozen times, usually in this smoky dive. Gould made eye contact and nodded for the man to follow him.

They met near the back door and Gould said, "They are onto you. I need to get you out of here now." Gould stepped into the narrow, dark alley and the idiot followed him without hesitation. After walking only a few steps, Gould put an arm out like he was going to usher the man along and then in a flash he grabbed the man by the back of the neck with his right and brought his left hand up with blinding speed. The four-inch blade of his knife plunged into the man's chest and the two men stood clutching each other, eye to eye, for what seemed like a minute. Gould felt no shame, even as the man began to release his grip and slide to the dirty ground. He wanted him to die, he wanted him to feel the pain and see the look of hatred in his killer's eyes.

Gould looked back on it now and shook his head in embarrassment. What he had done that night was very stupid—very impulsive. Things could have gone awry at any moment. There could have been surveillance, someone could have recognized him, or worst of all, the man could have shot him in the back as they entered the alley. It seemed like it was all ages ago, and in terms of his skill level, it was. Back then he wouldn't have had a prayer against a man like Mitch Rapp, but now their skills were more even, and with surprise on Gould's side, the deck was stacked in his favor.

THE CAB PULLED underneath the car park in front of the Hyatt in downtown Montreal and Gould got out. It was 9:36 in the morning. He subtly began to inventory the surrounding area while the driver handed the bellman his suitcase. Gould paid the driver, tipped the bellman, and then casually followed him into the lobby. The attractive woman behind the reception desk informed him that she would have a room ready for him in thirty minutes. She directed him to the restaurant. Gould picked a table with a nice view of the lobby and asked the waitress if she could get him a copy of the *Washington Post*. They did not carry the *Post,* but they did have the *New York Times.* He told her that would be fine.

She returned a few minutes later with a pot of coffee and the paper. Gould ordered an omelet with a side of fruit and started in on the paper. From time to time he looked up to see who was coming through the door. He also noted the other patrons in the restaurant and those in the lobby. No one stood out. They all fit the profile of countless business travelers going through their morning rituals the world over. Eat, read, and get ready for whatever the day might bring.

Gould was on his second cup of coffee when the omelet arrived. Not long after that the receptionist came over and handed him a small envelope containing his room number and cardkey. She informed him that his luggage would be sent up momentarily. Gould thanked her and she went back behind the reception desk. Midway through the meal he moved onto the sports page. He quickly found out that Washington was at home this weekend. Gould wondered if Rapp was a Redskins fan. If he was, it might present an opportunity. He'd finished the omelet and was picking at his fruit when the FedEx man entered the lobby with a two-wheeler. Gould immediately recognized his box sitting on the bottom with a stack of smaller boxes and air letters balanced on top of it. This was all a good sign. The box was to be delivered by 10:00 a.m. With such a tight schedule there was very little time for customs to screen the package and set up any type of a sting. The more likely scenario was that they would have seized the box at the airport.

The FedEx man stopped at the concierge desk and wiggled the two-wheeler out from underneath the stack. The concierge signed for packages and the FedEx man left in a hurry. Everything appeared to be business as usual. Gould kept his eyes on the concierge as he pecked away at a keyboard behind his station. The waitress brought his bill and he signed for his breakfast. Gould continued to appear as if he was reading the paper when in fact he was keeping an eye on the front of the hotel watching for any unusual activity.

Satisfied thus far, he proceeded to the next phase and retrieved a mobile phone from his pocket. He'd purchased it this morning with a dummy credit card upon landing in Montreal. The phone was disposable and had 250 minutes of air time. He punched in the number for the hotel and held the folded newspaper in front of his face. A woman answered in French and then English and asked how to direct the call.

In English, Gould said, "I'm going to be checking into the hotel this morning, and I want to make sure a package has arrived for me."

"Just one moment, sir. I will transfer you to the concierge."

Gould peeked over the top of the newspaper and listened as the line began ringing. He watched the concierge reach for the phone and heard him say, "Good morning. How may I help you?"

"Hello," Gould said with an American accent. "I'm checking into the hotel this morning and I'm expecting an important FedEx package to be delivered. Could you tell me if it has arrived?"

"Certainly, sir. What is the name?"

"Johnson . . . Mike Johnson. It should be a big cardboard box."

"One moment."

Gould watched him set the phone down and lift the other boxes off the large one on the bottom. The man bent over to read the air bill and then returned to the phone. "I have it right here, sir."

"Wonderful. Would you please have that sent up to my room, and give yourself a ten-dollar tip. Put it on my bill."

"Absolutely, sir . . . thank you. I'll have it taken care of right away."

"Thanks." Gould pressed the end button on the phone and watched the concierge walk over to the reception desk. From where he was sitting he could only hear pieces of the conversation. He heard the woman say something about not having checked in yet, then she went to work checking her computer. After a few seconds she gave the concierge a room number. He wrote it down on a sheet of paper and went back to his station.

Gould put his newspaper back in order and stood. He strode casually across the lobby and approached the concierge. In French he said, "Excuse me. Do you have a forecast for the rest of the week?"

"Absolutely, sir." The concierge grabbed his computer mouse and clicked it several times. The whir of a printer was heard somewhere beneath his station. As he reached under the work surface to grab the freshly printed sheet, Gould looked down and noted the room number written on the sheet of paper.

The concierge handed him the sheet. "Here you are, sir."

"Thank you." Gould turned for the elevator bank and heard the concierge call for a bellman. He took the elevator to the sixth floor and noted Mr. Johnson's room as he walked past it to reach his. What may have seemed like luck, actually wasn't. Early check-ins at hotels were dictated by what rooms were cleaned first, and since the staff usually cleaned in teams, one entire floor was usually cleaned before they moved on to the next.

Gould entered his room. His suitcase was waiting for him at the foot of the king-size bed. He opened his briefcase and pulled out a Palm Pilot, a short ribbon cable, and a magnetic card. He pieced the three together and waited by the door to hear the bellman come and go. He heard the man enter and then leave only a few seconds later. Gould opened his room door and watched the hotel employee walk down the hall and turn for the elevators. When he heard the chime of the elevator arriving he darted across the hall and down a few doors. He slid the magnetized card into its slot and waited a second for the light to turn green. He grabbed the box and brought it back to his room.

With his pen pressed down hard, he ran it across the seam on the packing tape. He yanked the top open and reached into the sea of packing peanuts until he found the duffel bag. As he pulled it out, quite a few of the peanuts spilled onto the floor. Gould unzipped the duffel bag and gave it a quick check to make sure everything was in order. He then grabbed a garbage bag from his suitcase and put all the Styrofoam peanuts in it. After that he broke down the box, tore off the air bill, and brought both the box and the garbage bag down to the service room and placed them where the other bags of garbage were.

Back in his room, Gould took a shower, shaved, and laid everything out on the bed. His old identity was on the left, his new identity was on the right, and twenty-five thousand dollars in cash was in the middle. He double checked to make sure he'd accounted for everything that said he was Moliere and placed it all in a brown bag. His first order of business was to burn the bag before he reached the border. Gould methodically repacked his belongings and put everything by the door. After messing the bed up to make it look like it had been slept in, he left his room key on the dresser and left the hotel through the side door. Unless he ran into some unforeseen problem, he would be in America by mid-afternoon.

24

The offices for the director of National Intelligence were temporary for a variety of reasons. Like any new department in Washington, it was evolving. Which in Beltway speak meant it was growing. The original plan called for a staff of approximately twenty-five to help support the new director. The idea was that the organization would act as a clearinghouse. A filter between the various intelligence assets and the president, designed to both coordinate and streamline the process. Within six months the organization doubled in size, then tripled, and then doubled again. At last count it had shot past the two-hundred-person mark, and had no sign of slowing. It was a fledgling little bureaucracy, growing in size and scope and each day becoming a little less efficient. It was quickly becoming exactly what its detractors had feared.

Until the new organization was on its feet the Secret Service had been given the job of protecting the director. This was good for Rapp. He had friends at the Secret Service who were more than willing to do him a favor. Rapp called Jack Warch, the Special Agent in Charge of the Presidential Protective Detail, and asked him if he knew the guy running Ross's detail. Warch did. The Secret Service was a tight group. Rapp told Warch what he needed, and the man in charge of guarding the president's life knew Rapp well enough to not ask any questions.

Rapp had to park on a ramp a half block away and across the street. The place was only a stone's throw from the White House. Rapp entered the main door of the building and flashed his credentials to the uniformed Secret Service officer manning the desk. He asked for Agent

Travis Small and then walked over to the corner of the lobby to wait. He stood near a large potted plant with his back to the wall, hoping to remain as inconspicuous as possible. He didn't want Ross to know he was in the building. He wanted to return last week's favor.

Rapp didn't have to wait long. Travis Small was anything but. He looked like a power forward for the Washington Wizards. Rapp liked the team better when they were named the Bullets. It was more honest that way. More representative of the murder capital of America.

Small half-walked, half-shuffled across the terrazzo floor of the sunny lobby. He was six foot six and had to go at least 250. He had probably played basketball or football or both. His knees were undoubtedly less than perfect. He had short black hair and skin the shade of burnished walnut. Rapp guessed he was in his early forties. His eyes swept the lobby as he approached. He was an imposing man. All business. You'd have to be one spectacular badass to want to take this guy on. Either that, or crazy. Small was just the type of guy the Secret Service liked. Surround the president with a half dozen guys like Travis Small and he'd be pretty damn safe.

The big man drew close and extended his hand.

"Mitch . . . Travis Small. Real honor to meet you."

Rapp took his hand. It was dwarfed by Small's. "Likewise, Travis."

"No." Small flashed a perfect set of teeth and a surprisingly warm smile. "I mean it. I was on the president's detail back when they hit the White House. I was on the evening shift, so I wasn't there when it went down."

Small was referring to a terrorist attack on the White House. The president had narrowly escaped capture, and would have probably died if it hadn't been for Rapp.

"Sorry about that," said Rapp. "You must have lost some close friends."

"Yeah." Small got quiet for a second. "But I would have lost more friends that day if you hadn't put your ass on the line like that."

Rapp wasn't real good at stuff like this, so he just nodded his head a few times and looked around. He felt like a midget standing next to this mountain of a man.

"So how do you like working for Ross?"

Small eyed Rapp and carefully considered his answer. "I try not to have opinions about the people I'm charged with protecting."

Rapp grinned. "Bullshit."

Small shifted his girth from one foot to the other. "He's probably a little on the high-maintenance side."

"I bet. He strikes me as the type of guy who might not be so nice to the hired help."

"No . . . it's not that really. He's nice enough. Remembers all of our names. Asks about our kids and stuff, but he's a politician." This was one man who carried a gun talking to another man who carried a gun. There were certain things they could communicate without speaking.

"He asks the questions, but doesn't listen to the answers."

"Yeah. He's on the move. Bigger and better things to tackle. The way I see it, he was a senator who wanted to be president. Senators don't become presidents. It's rare. The road to the Oval Office goes through the state governorships or the vice presidency. So Ross knew he needed to either go run for governor back in New Jersey, or get on the president's cabinet and starting angling for a VP slot. Senators don't like going home and running for governor. It's more work, less national notoriety . . . unless you're talking New York or California. Definitely not New Jersey. So he takes the appointment from the president, and before he's a year into this job he'll be looking to move on to State or Defense. His résumé will be spectacular at that point and he'll be a shoo-in for the VP slot on his party's next ticket. Hell . . . he might even run for president."

Made sense to Rapp. "What about the little guy who works for him?"

"Jonathan Gordon."

"Yeah."

"He's a sharp one. He kind of balances the director out. Ross has a bit of a temper, but he keeps it real close. He blows up around Gordon and that's about it. Gordon is real good at taking it, and then pointing out why it might be a bad idea to do whatever it is that the director wants him to do."

"So Ross has a temper?"

Small nodded. "Real bad. Never loses it in public, though. Always behind closed doors."

"Where is he now?"

"Up in his office with Gordon."

"All right. Let's go."

The two men walked across the lobby. Small gestured for Rapp to pass through the metal detector first. Both of them set off the alarm, and they both ignored it. They stepped into the elevator and started up.

Rapp looked up at Small and said, "You want a little career advice?"
"Sure."

"Ross is not going to like the fact that I just walked in here like this unannounced."

"I've thought about that."

"Tell him the truth. Tell him Warch called you, and said I had something important to discuss with the director. I wanted to keep it real quiet. If Ross flips his lid, he can call Jack. Jack and the president are tight. He'll be fine, and let's just say if Ross wants to take it all the way to the president, I'll be happy to lock horns with him."

"Sounds good to me."

The elevator lurched to a stop and the doors opened. Two men, who were slightly smaller versions of Small, were standing post to the right. Small nodded to both men; they'd already been told what was up. Small led Rapp through a reception area and into an outer office where two administrative assistants were manning the phones and pecking away at keyboards. Small peeled off to address one of them and Rapp just kept going straight for the door. The older of the two women started to come out of her chair.

"Excuse me, the director is in a meeting."

"That's all right," Rapp said without turning. He could hear Small telling the woman that Rapp was from the CIA. "We're old friends," Rapp half shouted as he grabbed the door handle, twisted, and pushed. He stepped into the office and closed the door quickly.

Director Ross sat at the head of an oval conference table immediately to Rapp's left, opposite a massive oak desk. The office was not very big. Maybe a fifth the size of Kennedy's. Not very plush. He was sure that pissed off the new director of National Intelligence.

Ross looked up at Rapp, his head turned slightly. His expression froze and his brow furrowed. He was in a white dress shirt with French cuffs, replete with fancy links, and a really bold red power tie. He looked very important. The other three people at the table were all wearing their suit coats.

Rapp walked right over. It was only three quick steps.

"Don't get up." He intentionally used the same line Ross had used when he barged into Kennedy's office earlier in the week. "I was just in the neighborhood and thought I'd stop by."

Ross slid his chair back and stood. He was the type of guy who preferred to meet someone eye to eye. There was a slight smile on his face, but it was obvious he was irritated by the unannounced interruption.

Rapp stuck his right hand out and grabbed the director's with a firm grip and an over-the-top enthusiasm. Instead of looking Ross in the eye, he glanced across the table at Gordon and placed his left hand on the shoulder of whoever it was he was standing behind. Rapp was dead set on mimicking Ross's unannounced intrusion into Kennedy's office.

"Jonathan . . . good to see you again." Rapp released Ross's hand and looked down at the other two individuals who he did not know. Before he had the chance to introduce himself, something on the surface of the conference table caught his eye. Rapp stopped and stared at the grainy black-and-white photo on the table. His blood pressure started to rise almost instantly. His lips parted. Nobody moved.

"You've got to be shitting me." Rapp reached down and grabbed the photograph.

It was a surveillance photo of a warehouse. Rapp had been there many times. Parked in front was a large Ford Excursion and standing next to it was a man with blond hair. The man was Scott Coleman. Rapp's face was now flushed with anger. The man sitting beneath his hand started packing up the contents that were laid out on the table. Rapp grabbed the guy between the collarbone and clavicle. His fingers dug in.

"Don't touch a thing." Rapp reached over and placed the photo on the table. He released the man's neck and put both hands on the back of his chair. He stepped to the side and wheeled the chair with the man in it away from the table. These people were anonymous. Underlings of some sort. They did not need to be involved in this. Looking at the other person who he had not met, Rapp said, "Would you two please excuse us for a minute?"

The men got up and left without a word. The solid door closed with a dull thud. Gordon stayed seated and to his credit remained calm. Director Ross on the other hand did not.

"Just what in the hell do you think you're doing?" he asked furiously.

"Saving you from stepping in it your first month on the job." Rapp didn't bother looking up. He was leafing through the files on the table. Coleman's service jacket from the Pentagon was there, his last five years of personal and corporate tax returns and a nifty little surveillance file that looked to have been compiled over the last few days. Rapp held up the surveillance file.

"Are you out of your *fucking* mind?" He looked Ross right in the eye and resisted the urge to reach out and whack him across the head with the file.

Ross began to shake, he was so angry. "Get the hell out of my office right now!" He pointed at the door for good measure.

Rapp grabbed Ross's finger like he was snatching a fly out of mid-air. He bent the index finger back and forced the director down in his chair. Men like Ross were always shocked by physical contact. Most of them had never been in a fight, or if they had, it had been a long time ago.

"What kind of a control freak are you?" asked Rapp. "You have over a hundred thousand people spread over I don't even know how many agencies. Your job is to make these agencies work better together. That's it. It's not to run operations or investigate people, but you meet Scott Coleman for all of two minutes and you don't like the way he answers you, so you start trying to dig up dirt on him."

Ross's face was twisted with anger. "You wait until I talk to the president. You have finally gone too far. You have no right barging in here like this."

Rapp grabbed his cell phone from his hip. "Let's call him right now. I've got his private line right here on speed dial." Rapp thrust his phone in front of the director's face. "You didn't even know he had a private line, did you?"

The look on Ross's face betrayed the truth.

"We can tell him," said Rapp, "how good a job you're doing of micromanaging the various intelligence agencies. We can tell him how you called up one of your lackeys over at the IRS, and told them to audit Scott Coleman . . . who the president knows and likes by the way. A decorated veteran. The president will be furious. While we're at it, why don't we call a few of your old buddies on the Hill and tell them how you're using your staff to spy on private citizens?" He waved the file in front of Ross's face. "That's what this is by the way. It's spying on a private citizen, you *fricken* hypocrite. And you spent twelve years up on that fucking hill pissing and moaning about the CIA. Grandstanding in front of the cameras and saying that we'd better not be spying on American citizens . . . suspected terrorist or not."

The file was arranged with thumb tabs. One of the tabs was labeled Phone Records. Rapp opened it and started looking at the calls. "You have a subpoena for these records? Did you go to a judge? I didn't know you had investigative powers. I don't think the press knows you were given investigative powers. I'm sure they'd love to write about it. Get you all bogged down and ineffective before you even had a chance to make any reforms."

Ross was indignant. He yelled, "I demand to know what the two of you are up to, and I demand to know right now! Neither of you are private citizens! You work for me!"

This time Rapp couldn't resist. His anger got the best of him. The file was about an inch thick. He cracked Ross across the left side of his head with it. Ross's perfectly combed hair went askew, with a clump falling across his forehead, partly obscuring his left eye.

Rapp grabbed him by the front of the shirt. "Listen, you idiot. I don't answer to you. I answer to the president. I hunt terrorists for a living, and the last thing I need is some hack like you, who doesn't know jack shit about what we're up against, looking over my shoulder and telling me what to do." Rapp released his shirt and shoved a shocked Ross back into his chair.

Rapp took a step back. "Don't think I don't know the game here. This is your stepping stone to bigger things. That's your plan, isn't it, Ross? You want to be president someday."

Ross was too angry to speak. Rapp glanced over at Gordon, who was still cool as a cucumber. "I heard you're the reasonable one. Talk some sense into him, because I promise you this . . . I can't make him president," Rapp pointed at Ross, "but I'll guarantee you I can make sure this is the last government job he ever holds."

Rapp grabbed the other files and stuffed them under his arm. He didn't even bother to address Ross. He looked at Gordon. "Call the IRS off by noon, or I'll see you two in the Oval Office, and I promise it'll make this look like a fucking picnic."

Gordon didn't answer. He just nodded.

Rapp left with the files and slammed the door shut behind him.

Gordon waited a few seconds and then heaved a huge sigh. He slowly began shaking his head. He looked over at his boss, and said, "I told you . . ."

"Don't say it," snapped Ross. "I know you told me this was a bad idea. I know you told me Rapp was the wrong guy to mess with. I know! I know! I know!" Ross sprang out of his chair. He walked over to his desk and looked out the window and down the street toward the White House. After fifteen seconds of silence, he said, "I think I should talk to the president about this."

Gordon just looked at him. "Are you out of your mind?" There was no malice in his tone. It was more clinical. Like a shrink. "Did you hear anything he just said? That was Mitch Rapp, Mark. He kills people for a living. He penetrates terrorist cells. He ran I don't know how many deep-cover ops. He's on a first-name basis with the president. Get him out of your mind. Get Coleman out of your mind. We have more than enough stuff to tackle."

Gordon watched his boss. He knew how the man thought. He knew how large the man's ego was. He knew how hard it would be for him to walk away from something like this. "Mark, this isn't worth it. It's beneath you. You're going to be president someday and when that happens, you can do whatever you want. Right now, though, we need to just walk away from it."

Ross ground his teeth and kept staring at the White House. He'd never been more humiliated in his entire life. He didn't give a crap who Mitch Rapp was. He could outmaneuver anyone in this town. Ross told himself to get control of his anger. He would regroup. Be more careful next time. Hire better people. As much as he hated to admit it, Gordon was right. It was good advice. At least for now. But if an opportunity presented itself, he would crush Mitch Rapp and make that Neanderthal pay dearly. Rapp needed to be taught his place in the natural order of things. He needed to be brought to heel at the boot of the elected officials. Ross nodded slowly, and a sly smile crept over his face. He would get even. No, he would get more than even. When the time was right he would destroy Mitch Rapp.

25

It had taken Gould the better part of the day to drive down from Montreal. The border crossing had been a joke. He put on a suit and tie. He bought a big travel mug, the kind you can purchase at any gas station in North America, and filled it with bad coffee. He put his brief-case on the front passenger seat and hung a garment bag in the back driver's side window of his rented Ford Taurus. He was just another sales rep hitting the road. He timed it so he made the crossing during the morning rush. Cars were lined up in both directions for a hundred plus meters. The customs agent at the border didn't even ask him where he was going. The woman took his Canadian passport, opened it to the first available page, hammered it with a stamp and handed it back. If she had asked, he was going to tell her he was headed to Boston for the rest of the week and would be returning on Friday. But she hadn't asked. She had a line of cars to deal with and Gould was just another calm, bored business-man doing his job.

The drive took twelve hours with a few stops along the way. He started out on Interstate 87 going south through upstate New York. It was beautiful country. The road skirted the west side of Lake Champlain. When Gould had lived in the States, he'd traveled a lot. He'd been down to Georgia and Texas. Had gone out to see Mount Rushmore and Yel-lowstone National Park with some of his classmates during one summer break. He'd traveled from Vancouver to San Diego and from Portland, Maine, to the Florida Keys. The one thing that always amazed him about America was its vastness, its never-ending, always-changing landscape.

Each part of it was different and each part beautiful in its own way. This slice of northern New York had been no different. The fall colors were in their glory, and the towns that dotted the landscape were quaint.

He took the interstate straight south to Albany and filled up on gas, a single pastry, and some water. He paid for it all with cash. The rental car had been paid for with a credit card belonging to Peter Smith. Gould was Peter Smith. At least he was to the bank teller in Montreal where he had set up the account more than a year ago. He'd gone into the bank and opened a corporate account into which he deposited $5,000. He listed a P.O. box as the business address. Pretty standard stuff. The teller had offered him a cash card and a credit card right there on the spot. Gould had received both within a week. The credit card bill was automatically deducted from his bank account. The cards fit very nicely with the passport and driver's license he'd had forged by a close friend from his Legion days. Neither card had been used before today, and neither would be used after today.

From Albany, he took Interstate 88 to Binghamton, New York. This part of the journey wasn't as nice as the first leg, but the road was in good shape and most of the traffic moved along at 80 mph. Gould moved in packs of cars. Tried not to be the lead vehicle or the last one. He went with the flow, and stayed in the right lane as much as possible. At Binghamton, he turned south and crossed the state line into Pennsylvania. He couldn't remember if Pennsylvania was a red state or a blue state, but he did know it was a hunting state. Gould kept alert for the right type of place and found it on the outskirts of Scranton.

He pulled into the massive parking lot and walked into the equally massive building. It was some type of retail Mecca for hunters, fishermen, and outdoorsmen. A big stuffed grizzly bear greeted him at the front door, its front paws up, claws extended, ready to strike. It was an impressive beast, and made him think of Mitch Rapp for a moment. He wondered how the beast had been slain. Probably a rifle shot from a good distance. It would be far too risky to get close to an animal like this. They had a great sense of smell and good hearing and they were surprisingly quick for their size. You'd need a heavy bullet with a lot of punch to take him down. If you didn't hit him in the brain, or the spine, he'd just keep coming. Even if you hit him in the heart, he might last another ten seconds, which would give him enough time to tear your head off with one of those big paws. What a shame to kill a beast like this without ever giving him a fighting chance.

He wondered if he'd give Mitch Rapp that chance, or if he'd simply conceal himself and shoot him in the head with a long rifle shot, like this hunter had undoubtedly done. Gould honestly didn't know. Part of him wanted to see who was better. Do it up close, just to prove he was the better warrior. But that was his ego talking, and he knew it. Rapp was like this grizzly. You'd have to be crazy to go toe-to-toe with him.

Gould shook his head and turned his attention away from the stuffed bear. Canoes, kayaks, and small aluminum fishing boats hung from the ceiling. At the far back of the store was a climbing wall, replete with colorful toe- and handholds. Bright colored ropes hung from the steel girders that supported the barrel roof. Gould grabbed a shopping cart and started off in the fitness department. He picked out some sweats, a shirt, and a pair of shorts. The women's stuff was right across the aisle and he loaded the cart with the same type of clothing for Claudia. Next he grabbed a pair of running shoes and socks for himself and then for Claudia. Gould had the beginnings of a plan. At least as far as the initial reconnaissance went.

He left the shoe department and found the hunting department. It took up half the store and it took him five minutes to get his bearings straight. He started off with the field glasses, and found a nice sturdy pair. He was about to move on, but spotted a night vision scope. It might come in handy. He smiled to himself and thought, only in America can you buy gear like this with such ease. He kept filling the shopping cart with the various things he might need. He had spent enough time on patrol to know what worked and what didn't. His last stop was the ammunition racks. He took his time finding the highest-grade ammunition available. The 9mm rounds for the pistol was no big deal. There was plenty of hollow-point steel jacket ammo to choose from. He grabbed two fifty-round boxes which was a lot of rounds considering he wasn't planning on firing more than five shots to make sure the sights on the Glock were as he had last left them. The rounds for the rifle took a little longer. He eventually settled on a box of Federal 168-grain HPBT bullets. It was amazing what you could buy off the shelf in America.

He finished up and went to the checkout line. Both sides of the line were merchandized with trinkets and other small items. Gould grabbed a few Power Bars and a pack of gum. He plopped everything down on the scanning counter and dug out a wad of hundred-dollar bills. The total came to just under a thousand dollars. He paid the polite woman and carried his four shopping bags out to his car. The bags were placed in the trunk and he was back on the road. From Scranton he continued on Interstate 81 south to Harrisburg and took 83 across the state line into Maryland. The sun was firmly in the west and daylight was fading by the time he reached Baltimore. Gould called the American Airlines toll-free number to check on Claudia's flight. It was on time and so was he. Just before the main entrance to Baltimore International Airport, Gould exited the highway and filled the car up. Claudia called while he was pumping gas. It was the first time his phone had rung since he'd purchased it two days earlier. It was good to hear her voice.

Gould topped off the tank, ran into the little shed, and paid for the gas. He pulled up to the American terminal just as she was exiting the building and fought the urge to jump out and kiss her. There were cameras everywhere. He kept the visors down and sat up straight. All Claudia had was a shoulder bag and a generic black carry-on bag. She put the carry-on in the backseat and got in the front with her shoulder bag. She leaned over and grabbed his face with both hands.

"I missed you." She kissed him on the lips.

Gould smiled and took his foot off the brake. "Are you hungry?"

"Famished."

"I know of a good place. I think you'll like it."

The operational rules had been set. They only spoke English. While Gould's was so good he seemed like a native, Claudia wasn't as proficient. Like him, she was traveling with a Canadian passport. At least for the remainder of the day. Tomorrow morning they would change identities yet again.

She nodded. "No problem crossing the border?"

"No," he said, "and you?"

"Landed in Miami and cleared customs without too much difficulty."

"Did they fingerprint you?"

"I'm afraid so."

Gould nodded. He thought they would, but at least the new system wasn't in sync yet. The airports had months of backlogged fingerprints that needed to be input and correlated. "The money?" he asked.

"No problem. It's safe." That's where Claudia had been. Making sure the five million dollars was sliced and diced, moved and shuffled and then put back together in the vault of a boutique financial institution on a beautiful island in a very warm and sunny part of the world. Claudia was very good at such things. She had been in the banking business before they had decided to strike out on their own. She kept up on all the laws, regulations, and most importantly, which banks knew how to guard their clients' privacy in the face of an overzealous war on terror.

"What's the plan?" she asked as the car picked up speed.

"Downtown."

She looked at him sideways with a confused expression.

"I thought they lived out on the Chesapeake Bay."

"They do, but we don't know exactly where, and it would be foolish to start poking around. If he hears that strangers are asking questions, he's likely to come looking for us."

The explanation made sense to her. "But why are we going downtown?"

"Because that is where she works. We'll check into our hotel. Have a nice meal. Make love and then sleep."

"Tomorrow?"

"We'll do a little sightseeing. Get rid of this car, and if all goes well . . . we'll follow her home."

26

WASHINGTON, DC

They were to meet at the Capitol Grill. It was one of their favorite restaurants. *Bulletproof,* Rapp liked to call it. The place had yet to let them down. Order anything on the menu and it was great. It came out hot or cold depending on how it was supposed to be served. They covered the surf and the turf equally well, which was important because she ate fish and he ate steak. He actually ate anything, but at these prices he preferred red meat.

Rapp was on time. She was late. This was nothing new, but it unnerved him to no end. They'd gone round and round over her lack of punctuality and had a few pretty big blowouts. Even under normal circumstances it would have bothered him, but their relationship was not normal. She was a TV correspondent who received at least one stalker letter a month. Nothing unusual really. At least not for women in her line of work. Middle-aged single men who undoubtedly had deep issues with their mothers. Voyeuristic sickos who got off on writing down their dirty thoughts. Every attractive woman at every TV station across the country had to deal with it to some degree or another. The good news was that ninety-nine percent of these perverts never graduated beyond the letter-writing stage. The remaining one percent gave Rapp cause for concern, but they were not the real source of his worries.

Rapp was a marked man with a price on his head. Fatwas, religious findings by Islamic clerics, had been handed down demanding that he be killed. This in part fed his desire to see men like Khalil resting in a pool of their own blood. They had entered the fray with their bellicose mouths and soft bodies. They were men who had never seen battle, and never would. Men who took perverse joy in inflaming the hearts of young Muslim boys, sending others to do work they had neither the skill nor the courage to perform. Those boys, and the ones who had grown into men, were the people Rapp worried about every time Anna was late.

Lovely Anna Rielly was a study in contrasts. Her delicate features and enchanting green eyes conveyed a sense of classic beauty. Just beneath the surface, though, lurked the tough street-smart daughter of a Chicago cop. Rielly had grown up with four brothers, three of whom had followed in their father's footsteps. The fourth brother became a lawyer. His choice of profession and Anna's created a bit of a divide among the siblings. The three brothers who donned the uniform referred to Anna and the lawyer sibling as *the enemy.* True to their Irish blood, the political debates were heated and shit was deep. As was their love for each other.

This colorful upbringing on Chicago's South Side added tenacity to her beauty and smarts. Anna did not like defeat, and she knew not how to retreat. It was a very potent mix for a reporter. Rapp sought to hone these natural instincts, and hopefully teach her to detect trouble before it was upon her. She teased him about the Dictaphone he bought her, but eventually came around to the wisdom of the device. "If you think someone is following you," he told her, "record the license plate and I'll run it." She'd seen Rapp do this himself at least once a week. He put her through a defensive driving course, and taught her how to shoot both pistols and shotguns.

She was pretty good with both. Since she'd never shot before, there were no bad habits to break. Unlike most guys she held the weapon without trying to choke it. She had a smooth steady trigger pull and didn't anticipate the shot. She just put the front site on the target and fired over and over. How good would she be if ever confronted with a real situation? It was hard to tell. The human body had automatic survival mechanisms. Chief among them was the release of adrenaline. At the first sign of danger the body released it before certain parts of the brain even knew what was going on. Adrenaline levels spiked in preparation for either of two choices—fight or flight. This is where it got tricky. It was where people came unglued, and it happened when they chose to do neither. They froze and were hit with the aftershock of the adrenaline hangover leaving them soggy and depleted. The only way to prepare someone for this was to practice over and over. Make all of the motions second nature. First work on the fundamentals, stance, grip, front sight, and trigger pull, and then work on marksmanship, and then after a solid foundation was built move on to situational training.

He had Anna practice drawing the gun from her purse and firing. They worked on both the left and the right hand. He taught her how to draw and fire at close range as if she were struggling with someone. How to reach out and punch the gun into the person's ribcage and let loose a round. He taught her to get in tune with her natural instincts. "If you're walking to your car at night and something doesn't seem right," he'd say to her, "unzip your purse and put your hand around the grip." Rapp got her a permit to carry and made sure every time she left the house she had the Smith and Wesson .38 AirLight revolver. It was light, had a short barrel and a relatively small hammer. It was very user friendly, and the ideal personal defense weapon for someone in Anna's position. He was obsessed with her well-being, and with giving her the edge that he himself possessed through years and years of training. He never worried about his own safety. Only hers.

Rapp was situated in the back of the restaurant in a corner booth. His drink arrived, and a short while after that the calamari was set on the table by one of the servers. It was the best calamari in town. Rapp did not wait for Anna. He was famished and surly, so he dug in. After devouring half the plate, he paused and took a sip of his whisky. He chased it with some water, looked toward the front door with his dark, almost black eyes, and shook his head in frustration. She was now twenty-five minutes late, and his mood was getting more rank by the minute. She was going to give him an ulcer.

Add to his wife's habitual tardiness his earlier meeting with the new director of National Intelligence, and it was no wonder he was in such a foul state. He'd been tempted earlier in the day to pay the president an unannounced visit and tell him to get rid of Ross before the man really stepped in it, but Rapp dismissed the idea almost immediately. It was naïve of him to think the president would do something so drastic based on one blunder. Gone, in Washington, were the days of people being shamed from public office and slinking out of town under cover of darkness. Now people hung on for weeks, sometimes months, while their media and publicity flacks tried to spin their way out of the problem. The media, especially the cable news outlets, loved this.

Rapp sincerely hoped Ross would heed his warning. For everyone's sake. Something told him, however, it was wishful thinking. He'd dealt with this type of man before. Washington was filled with them. They didn't like losing. Ross would be licking his wounds right now, and try-ing to figure out a way to get even, or more likely, bury him. Kennedy was the obvious target, but Ross would have to be careful. He would still be afraid of Rapp carrying through on his threat and rightly so. If the presi-dent caught Ross wasting his time and resources following Scott Cole-man he would be furious. It wasn't enough to get the man fired, but it would be enough to provoke some genuine anger.

Rapp would have to prepare contingencies, find some additional leverage on Ross, and he would have to tell Coleman to be extra careful. An easy move for Ross at this point would be to anonymously put the FBI onto Coleman's trail. Rapp should have covered that during their meeting. He'd have to call Ross's right-hand man, Gordon, and make it crystal clear what was at stake. Gordon at least seemed like someone he could deal with.

Kennedy was another problem. She would not be happy when she found out what he'd done. He'd put off telling her all day. His excuse to himself was that the timing was never right, but that was lame. He just didn't want to tell her. She was the one who would be dealing with Ross on a day-to-day basis, though. He'd do it in the morning.

He was reaching for his phone to call his wife when she entered the restaurant. A mini commotion ensued as the mass of men in the bar area turned to get a look. Several of them cut her off before she could get to the restaurant. Rapp was uttering profanities under his breath as he watched. Reporters, especially the TV variety, were celebrities in D.C.

She would have turned heads anyway, Rapp thought.

Anna Rielly was full of life. She had a smile that lit up the room, and a whole lot of confidence to boot. She carried herself like someone who knew exactly what she wanted and that was no front. Anna really did know what she wanted and she almost always got it.

Anna shook hands as she moved through the crowd quickly, but po-litely. She was good that way. She flashed her infectious smile, tossed her hair about, and laughed, but kept herself quartered at all times. She never let them fully engage her and suck her into a potentially lengthy conver-sation. She kept smiling and nodding and then pointed at her watch and then her husband located in the far corner of the restaurant.

"I'm sorry," she apologized as she finally strode up to the table. "I was walking out the door when Sam called." Sam was her producer in New York. "He wanted to go over tomorrow's live shot for the *Today* show, and then he just kept talking and talking." She made a puppetlike gesture with her hand, mimicking the chattering motion of a person's mouth.

Rapp stood and kissed her on the cheek. His anger was already melting away, but he couldn't let it go entirely. "It was nice of you to call."

"I know," she said in defense, "but by the time I got off the phone with Sam, Liz called me on my cell, so I just grabbed my bag and left."

Liz O'Rourke was Anna's best friend. He took her jacket and hung it on the hook at the end of the booth. Anna scooted in across the bench and he joined her on the same side. Rapp considered pointing out that she could have called Sam back on her mobile phone, but knew they'd simply end up in a fight. She'd just say he was the last person who should be complaining after all the nights she'd lain awake wondering if he was dead. It was better to just let it go.

"So," she said, "would you mind telling me what's going on?"

"What do you mean?" he asked. He had no idea what she was talking about.

"Well, when I was leaving work Jack Warch escorted me to my car." She looked at him with her unwavering green eyes.

Rapp tossed his head to the side as if to say *oh that,* but nonetheless tried to downplay it. "Irene got a phone call from one of our allies. Supposedly some crazy Wahhabi has been shooting his mouth off that he wants to kill me." Rapp said this with as much gravity as if he was announcing to her that they were out of her favorite Chardonnay.

"Lovely." She sat back and folded her arms.

The waiter appeared with a glass of wine that Rapp had already ordered for her.

As soon as the man was out of earshot Anna said, "You must be pretty worried if you called Jack."

Rapp considered this for a moment. He didn't want to alarm her, but at the same time he didn't want to make light of it. "I'm no more, or less, concerned than I normally would be. I had to talk to Jack about something else today, so I mentioned it to him. He's offered before, so I decided it was a good idea to take him up on it."

She looked at him with her reporter's eyes, trying to detect how forthright he was being.

"Honey, I'm serious. I don't want you to be alarmed, but at the same time I want you to be aware."

"Fair enough," she said after a few seconds.

The conversation turned to the more mundane topic of how their days had gone. Rapp neglected to mention his meeting with Ross. She ordered the sea bass, and Rapp ordered the New York Strip medium rare. He switched to red wine with his meal and Anna continued to nurse her glass of Chardonnay. The fish and the steak were perfect. She nearly finished hers, and he made it through half the juicy steak. Rapp had the other half boxed up for Shirley, their beloved mutt. The waiter approached with a dessert menu, and to Rapp's surprise Anna took it. She never ate dessert. After the waiter left he teased her about this, and she played coy. Rapp let it go for the moment and asked about the O'Rourkes, their friends. Anna beamed with pride over how cute their little baby boy was, her godson, little Gabriel Seamus O'Rourke.

"I had lunch with Liz and precious Gabe today." She closed her eyes and took in a deep breath through her nose. "I could just eat that little guy."

Rapp smiled. Liz O'Rourke and Anna had been journalism majors together at the University of Michigan. They were impossibly close. They talked every day, at least once, and giggled like grade schoolers when they got together. Anna inhaled little Gabe every chance she got. Rapp had just watched. It wasn't that he didn't like babies, it was simply that when they were really little, in that infant stage, they seemed so frail. He could tell, though, by watching his wife, that the siren of maternity was calling to her. Rapp had asked her if it was time and without hesitation she had replied, "Not yet. Soon, but not yet."

The dessert arrived. It was some triple chocolate mound of sin with a hunk of ice cream on top. It had to be over 2,000 calories. Rapp stared at it in awe as his wife dug in. After three bites she set her spoon down and said, "I have some big news."

Rapp cringed, and thought, *Please don't tell me you're getting promoted and they're moving you to New York.*

"Do you want to guess?"

"You got a promotion."

"No." She smiled. "I'm pregnant."

Rapp didn't move for several seconds. His mind was trying to cross the divide. As far as he knew, his wife was on the Pill.

"I know," she said reading his expression, "but I took the test twice, plus I'm late."

"But how?"

She shrugged. "It says right on the birth control package, 'Ninety-nine percent effective.' I guess we fall into the one percent."

They'd talked about having kids almost from the day they'd met. They both wanted at least two, but Anna was in no rush. There were certain things she wanted to do careerwise first. Rapp looked at her carefully. "Are you okay with this?"

"Of course I am! Are you kidding me?"

He breathed a sigh of relief.

"Are you okay with this?" she asked a bit tentatively.

Rapp looked at her angelic face. He could see now that she was worried about his reaction. He reached out with his hand and gently held the side of her face. "I couldn't be happier."

27

Abel sat quietly at his desk. His office was on the third floor of a building built just prior to the start of WWI. The building, like much of Vienna, was a work of art. The immaculate baroque structure was made out of stone and marble. The roof was a patina covered copper and the fifteen-foot-tall plaster ceilings were decorated in ornate relief. It was well ordered, occupied mostly by business professionals. From his window Abel looked out onto Parliament and its monument to Athena, the goddess of wisdom and warfare. *My, how mankind has changed in one century,* he thought. No society that he knew of today would associate wisdom with war, let alone erect a statue in homage to the goddess of the latter. Abel continued looking at the golden-leaf headdress of the Greek goddess. Where was it all headed? he wondered.

Great civilizations rose and fell as surely as the tides. The Egyptians, the Incas, the Mayans, the Greeks, the Persians, the Romans, the Mongol empire, the Ottoman empire all came and went. The Austro-Hungarian empire, the French, the British, the Russians, and the Nazis would someday merit only a footnote. Who knew what waited for the Americans? The other superpower, the Soviet Union, had lasted less than a hundred years with their grand experiment of communism. A blink as far as history was concerned. If Abel had to guess, America's preeminence on the world stage would last no more than another hundred years. The country had too many rights and too much wealth. Not enough sacrifice. Too much selfishness. The civilizations that had made their mark did so through brutality or great self-sacrifice by the populace, and often both.

The Chinese would become the next sole superpower. They were hungry for change. Such long-range forecasts were always interesting to him, but in the here and now he had more pressing issues.

There was a certain Saudi prince whom he no longer trusted. Abel drew his attention away from the statue of Athena and looked at the documents on his desk. They represented his complete financial picture. Based on the papers before him, the assassin had been right in his assessment. Abel was not liquid enough. His real estate holdings in Switzerland and Austria were worth approximately $3,000,000. He had an additional $1,200,000 in cash and securities that he could liquidate without too much difficulty. It was not enough to live on for very long if he was forced to run. At least not with the lifestyle he'd grown accustomed to. What the assassin did not know, however, was that Abel was pocketing a full half of the fee. To add to the $1,200,000 in securities he now had $5,000,000 in cash. With that type of money he could probably disappear for a while. If the assassin succeeded in killing Rapp he would get another $5,000,000. Now he was talking real money, but still the thought of leaving behind his current life was not appealing to him.

Abel was facing a real quandary. As things sat now he had to prepare for three possibilities. The first was that the assassin would succeed and the Americans would start beating the bushes in search of Rapp's killer. This was the best outcome. Abel felt confident that, short of capturing the assassin, there was no way the Americans could link him to any of this. He'd been very careful in covering his financial tracks. The second possibility, which he was not even confident that he could pull off, would be to kill the assassin after he completed the job. That approach could blow up in his face in a variety of ways, the worst of which would be the assassin not dying and hunting Abel down. So far the assassin had been ahead of him every step of the way. There was no logical reason for him to think that he could suddenly outwit this extremely capable man. The third contingency to prepare for was that he himself was already a target. It would be just like Prince Muhammad to have already hired someone to take care of him. Any feeling of loyalty he'd felt toward the prince, which was really nothing more than a professional obligation to perform the duties he was paid for in the best possible way, was now almost entirely gone. He had suspected it would someday come to this. From the very beginning he had known the score with the Saudis. Family and tribal members came first. It was time to part ways with Rashid. The trick would be to do it while still collecting the remainder of the fee and keeping his life. Beyond that he desperately wanted to hold on to his real estate possessions.

In the meantime he would have to plan for all three contingencies. First, he would see if he could get any more information from his old handler Dimitri. The former KGB spook had to know more about this assassin than simply a phone number and an e-mail address. If he could find out who the assassin was, matters would be greatly simplified. If the man succeeded in killing Rapp, he would be expecting another $5,000,000 for fulfilling the contract. Abel could probably get the Hungarians to kill him for $100,000, maybe $200,000 at the most. Abel could then pocket another $4,800,000 and sever his business relationship with Rashid in an amicable fashion. If he couldn't find out any more about the assassin he would simply have to tread very lightly until things blew over. He reached a conclusion about what he must do in the meantime.

Abel swiveled in his chair and tapped the space bar on his computer to get rid of the screen saver. His Internet browser popped to full color on his flat-panel monitor. His fingers remained poised above the keys for a second and then he began typing his message. He was well aware of the interception capabilities of the Americans, so he kept his prose businesslike and to the point. For now he would keep his options open, but he would be a fool if he didn't begin to take certain precautions. Once this e-mail was sent he would need to make himself scarce. Now was the perfect time to take a vacation.

28

WASHINGTON, DC

She woke up before he did, and started for the bathroom. As soon as she stood up she noticed something wasn't right. The room came in and out of focus, her steps were unsteady. She reached for the door frame to steady herself and then dashed for the toilet. She vomited once and then a second and third time. She sat there for a few seconds, leaning against the glass wall of the shower stall and holding her hair in a makeshift ponytail with her right hand. A thin layer of sweat covered her upper lip, but other than that she felt almost immediately better. *So this is what morning sickness is like,* she thought.

Claudia pulled herself off the floor and regarded her reflection in the mirror. She looked pasty white with a touch of gray. Not very flattering. When would she tell him? She had been so close, even last night, but at the last second something always came up. Now she was worried that she would distract him, and they could have none of that. He needed to stay focused and get this over with as quickly as possible. She looked at herself and struggled with what she should do. She turned on the faucet and doused her face with cold water repeatedly. She decided to wait until they were done with this job. Then she would tell him.

She brushed her teeth and took a shower. She felt almost normal despite the fact that she was famished. After wrapping herself in one of the plush white robes, Claudia opened the door and immediately registered the unmistakable aromas of sausage and cinnamon. She remembered that Louie had filled out the room service card for breakfast and left it on the door before they went to bed. He was now sitting on the couch in front of the TV with a large glass of orange juice in his hand. Claudia wasted no time parking herself next to him and grabbing the other glass of orange juice. She drank nearly half of it before she set it back down. The relief it brought was nearly instantaneous. She pulled the metal cover off of her breakfast and started slathering butter on her French toast. Next came the warm syrup and she dug in. Her focus on filling her stomach was so thorough she didn't notice that Louie was watching her.

The local NBC morning news was on the TV. Louie was also wearing one of the white robes provided by the hotel. His brown hair had that bed-head look, and the front page of the *Washington Post* sat folded on his lap. He'd stopped reading the paper and the TV was nothing more than background noise. His undivided and very discerning attention was focused entirely on the object of his affection. Claudia finally noticed that he was watching her. She set her fork down and wiped her mouth. After taking a drink of orange juice she turned and smiled. It seemed a bit forced.

His eyes narrowed and he said, "Are you pregnant?"

Claudia blinked. "What?"

Louie noted that her response was defensive. "It's not a difficult question."

She tugged at the neck of her robe and then crossed her legs, draping her left arm protectively across her abdomen.

He watched her every move, knowing the answer without having to hear it from her lips. Gould reached out and placed a gentle hand on her forearm. He pushed from his mind any thoughts of personal hurt that she hadn't told him and instead said, "If you are, it will make me the happiest man in the world."

Gould tilted his head and watched her intently. Her bottom lip trembled ever so slightly, and then her eyes filled with tears. "That is, if the child is mine," Gould added.

The tears spilled over and fell down the smooth skin of her cheeks. She let out a half laugh, half cry and swatted at him. "Yes . . . all those other men I sleep with. You'll all have to take blood tests so we can sort the whole mess out. Of course it's yours, you jerk."

Gould laughed and pulled her close. He kissed her forehead and rocked her like a baby. He was smiling from ear to ear. In a soft, almost apologetic voice he asked, "Why didn't you tell me?"

"I didn't want it to distract you. I want us to get through this and then we are done with this life once and for all." She tugged at the sleeve of her robe and wiped her tears. "How did you figure it out?"

He smiled. "There were a few telltale signs here and there."

"Like what?"

"Well . . . I noticed when we were having sex last night that your breasts looked . . ." He gestured with his hands and groped for the right word.

"Bigger," Claudia offered.

"Yes, that would be the right adjective." He smiled and then added, "When I picked you up yesterday at the airport you were literally glowing. I thought it was from your brief stop in the Caribbean, but that didn't make much sense. You weren't there long enough. The giveaway, though, was your dash to the bathroom. I haven't seen you throw up in years. And then you came out here and inhaled half of your breakfast before you even noticed I was sitting next to you."

"You saw all of that," she said in a surprised tone.

"Claudia, darling, that's what I do for a living. I watch people. I study them."

She looked toward the window and nodded. *And then you kill them,* she thought. She sat in silence for a moment and then turned her attention back to his eyes. How could those caring eyes belong to a man capable of such violence? She needed to purge that part of him. He hadn't always been that way. Surely at some point he had been a carefree sunny little boy. Even as an adult, as a hired assassin, there was a gentle side to him. His father unwittingly pushed him into the arms of the Legion, and they had turned him into a killer. It would be her job to eradicate those instincts, to turn him back into the man he should have been.

She touched his face. "Now do you understand why this must be our last job?"

He nodded and wrapped his arms around her. "Yes. I do." He held her tight and thought about the very fundamental ways in which his life would soon be changing. Almost immediately, though, his thoughts returned to the here and now. The baby could wait. Would have to wait. They had to keep their focus and see this last job through.

He looked at the clock and asked, "Can you be ready to go in twenty minutes?"

"Why?"

Gould pointed at the TV. "I want to walk over to the White House and get a look at Mrs. Rapp."

She regarded the TV for a moment and then Louie. Part of her simply wanted to take the money and run, but she knew such talk would only upset him. *We have the rest of our lives together,* she told herself. *Just get through this week and everything will be different.*

IT WAS A still morning. Not even the slightest breeze. The temperature was in the mid-fifties and rising with the climbing sun. Louie told Claudia to put on the workout clothes he'd purchased for her and he donned his new Nike pants and zippered top. They both wore baseball caps and Oakley sunglasses. They looked like Mr. and Mrs. American fitness. Before picking up Claudia at the airport he'd stopped on the outskirts of Baltimore at a Best Buy superstore and bought a Canon 10D digital camera and a 20 x 140 zoom lens. Louie looped the strap around his neck and brought his left arm up through the opening so that the camera lay snug against the left side of his back. They took the stairs rather than the elevator and exited the lobby onto Farragut Square. There was a Starbucks on K Street near the metro stop and they took their spot in the busy morning queue. Louie got a small black coffee and Claudia ordered some herbal decaffeinated tea.

With warm cups in hand they headed south for the short walk to the White House. It was October in DC, so there were nowhere near as many tourists as there would have been in the summer, though there were still a fair number. They came upon a group of Asians who were being led by a private tour guide. They were headed in the same direction as Louie and Claudia and took up most of the sidewalk. At the corner of 17th and I, they stopped to take photos of some building of interest across the street. Louie took the opportunity to find a way around them and kept moving. He did not want to be late. A block later they reached the northwest corner of Lafayette Square and passed the statue of Baron von Steuben. Steuben was a German officer who fought alongside George Washington during the Revolutionary War. The White House and the impressive neoclassical facade of the Treasury Building were now in full view. Louie checked his watch and slowed his pace.

"When I was a child my father used to bring us here for picnics on Sunday afternoons." Louie kept walking and looked around. "My father was very fond of this park."

Claudia was surprised by the disclosure. Louie rarely spoke of his father. "Why is that?"

"Lafayette . . . the famous Frenchman who fought with the Americans in their War of Independence. The park is named after him." Louie pointed to the southwest corner. "Over there is General Rochambeau, the French hero of the battle of New Orleans, and in the far corner is General Lafayette himself."

Claudia looked to the center of the park where there was a magnificent statue of a man on horseback. The horse was set atop a large block of granite, frozen in time, rearing back on its hind legs. The rider was holding on to the beast's reins with one hand and waving his hat in the air with the other. The base of the statue was encircled by four cannons. "Don't you mean that statue right there?"

Louie scoffed. "You would think so, but that is President Andrew Jackson. It infuriated my father to no end that in a park that was designed to honor those allies who stood by America's side at the fledgling country's most crucial hour, they erect in the center of that very park a statue of, not Lafayette himself, but instead an American president."

"If it bothered him so, why did he bring you here?"

"That is a good question." Louie did not answer right away. They walked hand in hand for a while. Finally, as they neared the south end of the park he said, "Maybe it was my mother who liked to come here. My sisters and I were little then. It was during my father's first posting at our embassy in Washington. TV was very big in America . . . even then. My mother did not like TV. My sisters and I did. There was no better way to master the American way of speaking English than watching TV."

Claudia nodded. Louie had told her this before. "So why the park?"

"Anything that got us outside and away from TV. Our Saturdays were filled with educational trips. We scoured every museum in town, every park, every statue and then on Sundays if the weather was nice we'd come here." That seemed to give Louie pause and then he added, "My father both loved and hated America. He was very fond of pointing out, though, that the American Dream would not have been possible if it hadn't been for French aid, French naval power, and men like Lafayette and Rochambeau."

"And if it wasn't for the American Revolution, we French would still be ruled by a monarch."

Louie laughed. "I said that same thing to him one day when I was in high school. He turned so red that I thought for a second he might hit me."

They reached the southern edge of the park. Pennsylvania Avenue was all that separated them from the White House. That and a heavy, black wrought-iron fence and gang of heavily armed men, only a few of whom were visible. Louie looked beyond the fence. Out in front of the West Wing, TV cameras were set up and people were milling about. Louie picked her out almost immediately. From this distance he couldn't tell it was her for certain, but he was pretty sure.

"Here." He handed Claudia his cup of coffee and grabbed the digital camera. The camera was high-end, with a lens that cost over a thousand dollars, but it was very user-friendly. Louie turned the selector switch to the automatic mode and removed the lens cap. He brought the camera up and pointed it at the White House. He took one shot and then another, just like hundreds, if not thousands of tourists do every day. He moved the camera over to the West Wing and snapped off a couple more. With his right hand he twisted the telephoto lens clockwise and zeroed in on the reporters and camera people. He found her with ease. She was talking on a cell phone and laughing. Louie snapped a photo and then looked at the viewscreen. It was her. He showed it to Claudia, who nodded.

"That's her. What do we do now?"

"We get a closer look. We watch her do the news, and then we see if she leaves to go anywhere."

Claudia looked to her right and then her left. At both ends of the street were guard booths. There was another one ahead and to the left where they were headed. "There are cameras everywhere as well as security people."

Louie glanced at the roof of the White House and spotted two Secret Service guys wearing blue coveralls. Probably snipers. "Don't worry, darling. We're not going to hang around long. We're going to act like tourists. Do a little sightseeing, maybe get some more coffee, check out a few parking garages."

"Parking garages?"

Louie took his coffee back and grabbed her hand. "Remember that credit report I had you run?"

"Yes."

"Did you learn anything from it?"

"She likes to shop."

"So do you." He couldn't see beyond her dark sunglasses, but he knew she was glaring at him.

"I don't spend anywhere near what she spends."

"That is true. But we'll see how you fare when we settle down."

"Are you done analyzing my shopping habits?"

"Yes. What else did you learn from the report?"

"She has no mortgage; she pays her credit card bills and her car lease in full every month."

"What kind of car?"

Claudia finally realized what he was getting at. "Oh . . . you are good."

"Thank you, darling." Louie grabbed her hand. "Let's go watch her do the news."

29

He didn't know how she'd found out, but she had, and she was as mad as he'd ever seen her. For the second time in a week Rapp felt like he'd been called to the principal's office. He stood on one side of his boss's desk, and she stood on the other. She wanted explanations, and he, for the moment, wasn't willing to give any. She was getting louder with each unanswered question, and he was getting more belligerent with each query. They were stuck at an impasse.

"I want to know how you found out," stated Rapp in a no-nonsense tone for at least the third time.

"How I found out is none of your concern."

"Tell me how you got your information, and I'll be happy to answer your questions." He widened his stance and held his ground.

"Listen," she pointed her finger at him. Her face was flushed with anger. "Contrary to what you think, you actually have a boss. I am that boss, and you have stepped over the line this time."

"Well, if you had gotten the IRS off of Coleman's back, like you said you were going to, I wouldn't have had to go to Ross's office and intercede."

Kennedy's fists balled up in anger. "And if you didn't have the patience of a hamster, you would have waited one more day and I would have taken care of it."

None of this made sense to Rapp. Kennedy had always been the most unflappable, professional person he'd ever dealt with, and now twice within the span of a week she was acting completely out of character. "Is everything all right?" Rapp regarded her for a moment. "Everything okay with Tommy . . . is your ex bugging you?"

Kennedy buried her face in both hands and shook her head. When she looked up she said, "You just don't get it, do you? You walk around in your own little Mitch Rapp world. All you care about is what you want. You have no regard whatsoever for those around you." She tapped her own forehead with her forefinger. "No clue of the chaos you leave in your wake. Chaos that I have to deal with. And you have no idea how bad it looks to have you go over my head like this."

"Oh . . . well, I'm sorry to have been such a burden. I hope no one around here got any paper cuts while I was out getting shot and stabbed." Rapp turned his head to the side and pointed at the thin scar that ran down the left side of his face.

"Don't," she yelled at him. "Don't play the martyr with me. I have always respected your sacrifice. That is not what this is about. It's about you being so bullheaded, and sure of yourself, that you just go and do whatever the hell you want whenever you want."

"I've managed to do just fine on my own."

"Yes, you have. But let me warn you, Mitchell, your luck is running out. You're starting to piss people off. The fervor that we need to wage this war on terror is already waning. It won't be long, another two to eight years, and the liberals on the Hill will be back in charge, and mark my words, they are going to launch a witch hunt like we haven't seen since the Church hearings. They are going to tear this place apart. That's what National Intelligence is all about. That was the deal they struck. They're going to use it to run roughshod over the Agency. To make sure cowboys like you are properly supervised and kept on a short leash."

"Well, then you'll be surprised to know that it was Senator Hartsburg who advised me to go pay Director Ross a little visit."

Kennedy regarded him warily.

"That's right," Rapp continued, "so while you're sitting here dithering about what's happening on the Hill, I've got one of the most liberal senators in this whole town telling me the best way to handle Ross is to go light him up face to face."

"You talked to Senator Hartsburg about this?"

"Yep."

"I don't believe you."

"Call him."

Kennedy glanced at her phone, hesitated a second, and then asked,

"Why in the world would you go to Hartsburg on something like this?"

"The man's seen the light. He's on our side. Ross was the junior senator from New Jersey. Hartsburg pushed him on the president, so I figured now that he and I are such close friends, I'd ask him to give Ross a nice yank on his leash and get him to back off Coleman."

"And?"

"He told me I should go pay him a visit and make him pee down his pants leg."

Kennedy frowned. "You're not serious."

"Damn straight. Those were his exact words. He told me to do exactly what I did. Said Ross was well aware of the fact that the president was in my corner, and he'd back off the second I confronted him with it."

"And how did Ross react?"

She was fishing for information. Which meant that whoever told her that he'd met with Ross did not give her the specifics of the meeting. Up until this point Rapp had been pretty sure it had been Ross himself who had called Kennedy. Rapp assumed he reamed Kennedy a good one. And if that was the case, Rapp was raring to go pay Ross a second visit. "He didn't tell you himself?"

Kennedy shook her head.

"Who told you?"

"I'd prefer not to say."

This was the problem with two career spies. Neither wanted to give an inch.

"If you want me to tell you how the meeting went, you're going to have to tell me who told you." Rapp crossed his arms and waited. He was prepared at this point to walk out of her office rather than give her any more information.

Kennedy thought about it long and hard and then finally said, "Jonathan Gordon called me this morning."

"Gordon?" Rapp said in a slightly surprised tone. He'd guessed wrong on him. "What did he tell you?"

"Only that he was sorry that the whole thing had to happen. When I asked him 'what thing' he realized I had no idea what you had been up to. I think that was actually the reason why he called. He wanted to figure out if I had sent you over or if you were acting on your own."

"What did you tell him?"

"I told him I had no idea that you'd had a meeting with them. He said he really wouldn't have called it a meeting. I asked him to elaborate, and he said it would be better if I got the story from you."

"Nothing else?" asked Rapp. "No mention of the Coleman thing?"

"Only that he'd told Director Ross he thought it was a bad idea to go poking around in the private business of private citizens."

Rapp was pleased. Maybe this Gordon would be a good influence on Ross.

"So tell me the story."

"Well," Rapp paused a moment to remember exactly how it had unfolded. "When I walked in it was Ross and Gordon and two other people. I started off real polite, and then things turned ugly pretty quick."

Kennedy closed her eyes and asked, "What happened?"

"I looked down on the conference table and saw a surveillance photo of Coleman's warehouse and I lost it. I realized they were talking about Coleman. I told the two people I didn't know to leave, and then I reamed Ross pretty good."

Kennedy still hadn't opened her eyes. "And how did he take that?"

"Not well."

"He got angry?"

"Yeah."

"Which means you got even more angry."

"Pretty much." Rapp cocked his head and chewed on his lower lip.

"Please tell me you didn't hit him or threaten him with bodily harm?"

"Ummm . . . I didn't really hit him. I kind of cuffed him across the head with Coleman's surveillance file. It was either his surveillance file or his tax returns . . . I don't remember which."

"Oh, Mitchell." She opened her eyes. "What in the hell are we going to do with you? The man is the director of National Intelligence. He is my boss. Doesn't any of this mean anything to you?"

"To be honest, Irene, no. It's all a distraction. His job is a distraction. His new agency is just another couple hundred suits doing exactly what is already being done by at least three other agencies. Scott Coleman is a good man who has put his ass on the line more times than you or I could count, and I'm not going to stand by while Ross fucks with him, just so he can send us a message that there's a new sheriff in town."

"I'm not going to disagree with you, but there were better ways to handle it."

"How?" asked Rapp indignantly. "How could it have been handled any better? The problem is solved, Ross has been sent a message, and Coleman and I can get back to targeting extremists."

"And if Ross didn't get the message? What if all you've done is make him angry?"

"I could care less if the guy likes me or not."

"You're too reckless, Mitchell." Kennedy shook her head. "Jonathan Ross is a man you might want on your side someday."

"I don't need men like Ross on my side. I just need them to get out of my way."

30

The day did not go exactly as planned. Right after Anna Rielly finished her first live shot, Claudia was hit with another wave of nausea. Louie barely got her across the street before her breakfast came back up, literally at the feet of the great Jean-Baptiste-Donatien de Vimeur Rochambeau. Gould's father would have been very disappointed that she had not made it to the statue of Andrew Jackson. Louie cared only that they got away from the myriad of surveillance cameras around the White House. When Claudia was done heaving, Louie helped her back to the hotel. She almost made it without having to stop but she was overcome again just a half a block from the hotel. Louie stood guard while she placed one hand on a light post and the other on a newspaper box. He rubbed her back and smiled sheepishly at concerned passersby. One older woman actually stopped. Louie explained that Claudia was pregnant, and she'd just been hit with a wave of nausea. The woman understood completely and went on to tell Louie how she'd had it something awful with all four of her kids. Every morning without exception she'd get hit with two or three waves of it. She would have had a fifth, but she couldn't bear the thought of going through the morning sickness again. She told Louie he needed to keep her in bed. Make sure she got plenty of rest. There was nothing the little darling could do but ride it out.

Louie thanked the older woman for her sage advice and helped Claudia up to the room. This time they took the elevator. She sat on the edge of the bed while he took off her shoes. She didn't bother with the rest of her clothes, electing instead to crawl under the covers and clutch the blanket around her neck. She began shivering and her normally beautiful skin had taken on a pasty pallor. Louie stood there helplessly, wondering what he should do. He did not want to seem insensitive, but there was a lot of work to be done and he honestly didn't know if she needed him to stay by her side. Almost as if she could read his mind Claudia told him to leave. She would be fine on her own. All she wanted was sleep.

Gould changed out of his walking clothes and put on a white shirt, tie, and dark gray suit. After unlocking his suitcase he carefully pried his fingers between the liner and the hard outer shell. Slowly, the layers began to separate. Gould retrieved a new set of credentials and put them in his breast pocket. A small clock radio sat on the desk. He flipped it upside down and removed the false bottom. Two items roughly the size of a pack of playing cards fell out, as well as a tiny circular object the size of two stacked nickels. All three items were black. He stuffed them in his pockets and checked on Claudia one more time before leaving. She was fast asleep. He took the stairs down to the lobby and donned his sunglasses as he stepped out into the bright sunlight. Gould walked west along the north edge of Farragut Square. At Connecticut he took a right and two blocks later he found what he was looking for. He perused the display window from the street and looked to see if any surveillance cameras were visible inside. There was one behind the clerk. Gould hesitated briefly. It was unlikely that he would find a store like this without cameras.

He cinched up his tie, adjusted his sunglasses, and entered.

The kid behind the counter looked up at him and smiled. "What's up?"

"I need to get a phone for my teenage daughter."

"All right. Do you have a preference . . . Motorola . . . Nokia . . ."

Gould shook his head.

"Does she need a camera?" the young man asked.

"I suppose."

"How many minutes a month are you willing to get her?"

Gould thought about it. He'd probably put five or ten minutes on the thing at the most, and then he'd chuck it. "It's mostly for emergencies, so probably one of the smaller plans."

"Are you already a customer?"

"No."

"Do you want to be? We've got some great friends and family plans."

Gould shook his head. "I'm under a government contract."

"Okay." The young man reached under the glass and grabbed one of the phones. "I'd put you into this one right here. It's got a two-mega pixel camera, she can download ringtones and . . ."

The clerk went on and on about the phone's features, but Gould had already stopped listening. He reached into his wallet and pulled out a credit card. "How much?"

"It's twenty-four ninety-five a month plus tax and fees, and if you sign a one-year contract, the phone is free."

"Can you bill it automatically to my credit card?"

"Absolutely."

"I'll take it."

Gould left the store with the phone in his pocket and a block later he chucked the bag and packaging in a garbage can. He turned down 18th Street and started working his way back to the White House. He had a good idea where to start his search. He'd studied a map and earlier in the morning, before Claudia got sick, he'd checked out the immediate area around the White House. The street that ran along the west side of the White House was West Executive Drive. It was blocked off at both ends by a heavy gate and manned by the Secret Service. There were a limited number of spaces, probably reserved for people who worked directly for the president. Gould checked the area anyway and did not see any BMWs. This did not deter him. Convenience and logic were on his side. Rapp's wife got to work early, which meant she would have her pick of garages and at the same time, she would not want to walk far.

The first ramp on his list was just off the corner of 17th and H. An attendant dressed in black pants and a red windbreaker stood at the top of the underground entrance next to a sign that announced how much it cost per hour and for the day. Gould walked right up to the guy and fished out his new credentials. He held them in his left hand to the side of his face like he did it countless times every week.

"I'm Agent Johnson with the IRS." Gould snapped shut the case and continued, "You guys park any blue BMWs this morning?"

The attendant shrugged and looked down the concrete ramp to one of his coworkers. The two spoke briefly in a language Gould did not understand. The other man hustled up the ramp.

"You are looking for a blue BMW?"

Gould guessed the man was probably Somalian. "Yeah. Series Five. Do you know which make that is?"

The man nodded. "I parked a silver one thirty minutes ago, but no blue ones." The man studied him warily. "What is this about?"

"I'm investigating a tax cheat who works in the area. We're looking to seize her vehicle." Gould had taken the story right from the IRS's Web site.

"Is there a reward?" the first man asked.

"Hundred bucks."

"How do we get ahold of you?"

"I'll be back by before lunch. Anyone else parking cars with you guys this morning?"

"No."

"Any chance you missed a blue BMW?"

Both men shook their heads confidently.

"All right. Thanks for your time. I'll see you later."

The next garage went pretty much the same except there were three attendants. One of them couldn't remember if he'd parked a blue or black BMW, but that it had been about an hour ago. Man or woman, Gould asked him. The attendant said it was a man. Gould thanked them for their time and told them he might be back later. The third garage was the one that he thought she'd probably used and he was right. This time he didn't ask about a specific car. He just flashed his credentials and told them he needed to look for a vehicle that might be involved in an investigation. They asked if they could help, and he politely told them no. Gould descended into the concrete cavern and found a blue BMW Series Five on the first level. He looked around, a bit surprised to see that there were no surveillance cameras until he realized customers weren't allowed down here. The attendants met people on the sidewalk and parked their cars for them. Gould knew luck was shining on him when he spied the keys in the ignition of the car.

He went and stood by another car in case one of the attendants showed up, and pulled out the new cell phone. From memory he punched in a number. Two rings later a woman answered.

"Comm Center."

"This is Detective Johnson from Five D," Gould said in a tired voice. "I need a 1028 on District plate echo, echo, foxtrot, one, eight, three."

Police departments were the same the world over. The woman sitting at the Communications Center for the Metropolitan Police Department was supposed to ask for his badge number, but she didn't because she was overworked and underpaid and the guy on the phone sounded like all of the other cops who called her hundreds of times each day to access the Washington Area Law Enforcement System. The database they all referred to as WALS.

"The vehicle is registered to an Anna Rielly."

"BMW Series Five?"

"Yep."

"Do you have a 1029 filed on the car?"

"Nope."

"Okay . . . thanks." Gould closed the phone and put it back in his pocket.

He walked slowly back to the ramp and checked on the attendants. Both men were standing at the top talking. As Gould hustled back to the car he put on a pair of latex gloves. He opened the driver's door and fished the smallest device from his pocket. There was a thin plastic film on the back of the miniature listening device. Gould peeled it off exposing a tacky adhesive surface. He stuck the device under the dashboard and hit the trunk release button. Gould slid a blanket and a shopping bag to the side and pulled the small lever that opened the compartment where the spare tire was kept. He checked to make sure both of the larger devices were working and then placed them in the well of the compartment. He closed the door carefully and put the shopping bag and blanket back where he'd found them, before closing the trunk. The gloves came off with a snap, and Gould dumped them in the garbage can right before he started up the ramp. He thanked the attendants for their time and started back to the hotel with a smile on his face. So far things were going exactly as planned.

31

The day was drawing to an end, and they were getting ready to pull out. Gould had returned the rental car he'd picked up in Montreal and grabbed a new one from a different company using yet another identity. The vehicle, a black Ford Explorer, was packed and parked on a ramp less than a block away. The transponder Gould had placed in Rapp's wife's car contained miniaturized GPS technology. Gould had checked every thirty minutes or so to see if the car had moved. It hadn't. Even if it had, he would have only been mildly interested. He doubted she was going to go home in the middle of the workday, and home was what he wanted. That was where Rapp would be most comfortable.

Claudia was feeling much better. She'd even managed to keep down a late lunch. While Gould was out switching cars she had gone online and checked out NBC's Web site. In addition to reporting up-to-the-minute news, the Web site promoted the evening news. It mentioned three key stories they would be covering, and one of them was a controversy brewing over the president's nominee for Secretary of Education. It was the same thing they'd watched Anna Rielly report on that morning. They were running on the assumption that she would do the evening news and then head home.

While online Claudia took care of some banking and checked their various e-mail accounts. There were really only two messages of any concern. The first was an offer for a job. She was tempted to reply that they were getting out of the business, but Claudia realized that might attract

undue attention. People would wonder why they had so suddenly decided to drop out. When the news broke of the great Mitch Rapp's
death, people would begin to speculate. It was better to tell former clients
that they were too busy to accept new contracts at the moment. The second e-mail of consequence was from the German. Abel was offering
them an additional million dollars if they could fulfill the contract in such
a way as to make it look natural. Like it was an accident. He didn't want
this to compromise the job, however. The priority was to make sure they
succeeded on the first order of business. If a readily available solution presented itself, however, it would be preferred. It did not have to be overly
convincing. Just leave the door open for interpretation.

Claudia had stared at the message for a long time. She wasn't sure she
should show it to Louie, but in the end she did. When he got back she let
him read the e-mail and then she asked him what he thought. Louie simply said, "We'll see." Later he surprised her by saying that he was already
considering doing just what the German had suggested. He reasoned that
the CIA would make it a top priority to catch the people responsible for
Rapp's murder. If they could make it look like an accident, they could retire without having to look over their shoulders for the rest of their lives.
The idea sounded great, but implementing it would be difficult. Gone
were the days of running people off the road at night, or hitting them in
a head-on collision. They were in America, where airbags were common. Gould told her to remain flexible. If an opportunity presented itself
they would discuss it. Otherwise, he would take him out at a safe distance
with the silenced rifle.

They ordered room service at 5:00. It arrived at 5:34. Louie devoured
a California burger with french fries. Claudia ate a light salad and bread.
She felt good but didn't want to push it. She drank water and he drank
water and coffee. He was worried about her but didn't say anything. He
hoped this morning sickness thing was a onetime occurrence, but he
doubted it. At 6:00 they watched the local news and sanitized the room,
wiping down common surfaces where they may have left prints. They
had absolutely no reason to think they were being followed, or that they
would be discovered once the job was complete, but that didn't matter.
They were professionals, and professionals were thorough. The room service cart was pushed out into the hallway and Claudia called for it to be
picked up. At 6:30 they sat on the edge of the bed and watched the start
of the *NBC Nightly News.*

Rapp's wife came on in the first five minutes. She was standing in the same spot she had been in the morning and wearing the same outfit. She spoke for maybe ten seconds and then they rolled some footage. When the footage was done, the anchor asked her a question, she answered it, and they went to a commercial. Gould stood and turned off the TV. They each grabbed a bag. All of the other stuff was already loaded in the new rental car. They were paid for one more night and depending on how things went they might need to come back here and sleep.

It took six minutes to leave the hotel and reach the car. By the time they pulled out of the ramp Claudia had the GPS device hooked up to her laptop. She waited a few seconds for the software to load and give her an overlay of the streets. Right now it was set for a two-square-mile overview, but she could narrow it down to a block-by-block look or bring it all the way back to an overview of North America. They had no idea where Rapp and his wife lived. The credit report listed a P.O. box in DC, and Rielly's last known address was an apartment in Georgetown.

Gould drove the Explorer over to 19th and H and waited. The parking ramp where he'd found her car was two blocks away. They didn't have to wait long. Claudia announced that the target was moving. Louie waited patiently while she relayed the direction the BMW was headed. Louie didn't need to look at the map on the computer screen. He had the map of downtown memorized. H was a one-way street heading east.

"The car is heading north on Seventeenth Street." Claudia stared intently at the screen. "She crossed H . . . no, forget that. She just turned east on H."

Louie pulled the gear lever out of park and took his foot off the brake. He hit the turn signal and eased out into traffic. They continued east on H until they hit New York Avenue. They missed the light and had to wait almost a minute. Claudia gave him constant updates. The car was on New York Avenue heading northeast. Louie was nowhere near panicking, but he did want to at least get a visual to make sure it was Rapp's wife who was in the car. Due to the lights, she maintained a one-mile lead until they were out of the District. Then New York Avenue opened up to a three-lane highway. Gould stepped on the gas and started passing cars. Nothing too crazy, but he was steadily gaining. At some point the road changed from New York Avenue to John Hansen Highway and U.S. Route 50. By the time they reached the Beltway they had a visual on the car. In the failing light they could barely make it out a hundred yards ahead. They passed under Interstate 495 and Gould closed the distance. At Lottsford Vista Road he eased up beside her. It was now past seven and the traffic was moderate. Both he and Claudia agreed it was her. She was talking on her cell phone so her face was partially obscured, but she gave them a glance like she was thinking about changing lanes.

Gould eased off the gas and fell back several cars. He retrieved an earpiece from his pocket and stuck it in his right ear. It was plugged into a small receiver that was tuned to the frequency of the miniature listening device he'd placed under the dashboard of the BMW. A voice came over the small speaker. There was a fair amount of background noise, but even so it was unmistakably her voice. Gould listened to the one-sided conversation with a critical ear, hoping to gain any information that might involve their schedule. They continued on U.S. Route 50 for another five minutes, then took U.S. Route 301 south for approximately six minutes and then started turning down a series of county roads. They were a decent ways from the city. Gould did not know what to think. Did they live way out here? Was she going to visit someone? Was she working on a story?

"How far are we from the Chesapeake Bay?" Gould asked.

Claudia pecked a few keys on the computer. "About four miles."

Gould nodded and watched his distance. He did not want her to notice she was being followed, but it was getting harder. Sooner rather than later they were going to run out of land. He was right. They ran out of land. Claudia told Gould that the car had just turned onto a dead end road. He pulled over and watched on the computer screen as the BMW inched closer and closer to the Chesapeake Bay. It finally stopped as if it had pulled right up to the water's edge. They waited several minutes to make sure the car didn't start moving again and then Gould continued on. He turned down the dead end road and set his speed five miles an hour above the posted speed. On the right were farm fields and woods and a few scattered houses. On the left were houses every couple of hundred feet. In the failing light he could glimpse the water of the big bay as they passed between houses.

"We're close," Claudia announced. "Less than a hundred meters."

Gould was already scanning ahead, looking for the car.

"Fifty meters."

He approached a white house and saw the car. There was a second car parked next to it. Gould tensed ever so slightly. "I see it."

"Try to get an address off the mailbox if you can."

Gould took his foot off the gas but did not hit the brakes. They were on a straight, narrow road. As they passed the house he read off the numbers on the mailbox. She checked the map to make sure they were still in Anne Arundel County. They were. She accessed the county's Web site and clicked on the property information tab. She punched in the address and five seconds later the corresponding information came up on the screen.

"The house was purchased in 1997 for two hundred and thirty-five thousand dollars by Bay View Shores LLC. No officer listed under the company."

"It's him." Gould looked back over his shoulder.

"How can you be so sure?"

"He would never put it under his own name."

"What if she is merely stopping by to visit a friend?"

"It's him." Gould gripped the steering wheel and then flexed his fingers. "I can feel it. He's in there right now."

32

ANNE ARUNDEL COUNTY, MARYLAND

Mitch Rapp ran along the gravel shoulder, pounding out each step. His mood was anything but upbeat. There was a day not long ago when he flew down this road at a clip that would have left all but a few of the world's best athletes gasping for breath and falling to their knees. Even so, Rapp was a realist. He knew it was impossible to maintain the peak performance he'd had in his twenties and early thirties, but that didn't mean he had to like the aging process. He'd dealt with pain his entire life. He knew how to taunt it, suppress it, or just laugh it off. In fact, pain was something he'd actually learned to embrace. It was a welcome ally that propelled him to the finish line while it forced others to quit. The mind controlled the body. It could tell muscles and joints to ignore all kinds of warning signals. The problem, though, was that those warning signs were there for a reason. If they were ignored for too long, the body eventually broke down.

On this warm fall morning, as Rapp took each lengthy stride, he began to wonder if there was something different about this pain. It was his damn left knee again. He'd been trying to work through it for the better part of a month, and he was finally coming to the conclusion that it wasn't going away. No matter how hard he tried to block it out or get past it, no matter how much ice or Advil he used, the pain only worsened. His body was telling him something. It was telling him to stop running.

Only thirty-seven and he was falling apart. It should not have come as a surprise to him, knowing the way he'd pushed and abused his body over the years, but Rapp was the type of man who thought any obstacle surmountable with enough will, determination, and talent. There were the broken bones and cuts from sports as a kid and then in college, there was the inevitable wear and tear that came with competing as a world-class triathlete, and then there were the scars, both mental and physical, of his trade. On the outside were four pucker marks left by bullets that were meant to kill him and two decent-sized scars left by knife blades. On the inside, most of the physical damage done by the bullets had been repaired, but the mental toll his work had left on him was something he simply tried not to think about. His wife liked to tell him his brain was like a basement filling up with years of junk. If you didn't clean it out every year, you were one day sure to be left with one hell of a mess to take care of.

Instinctively, he knew she was right, but the only person who could ever understand what he'd done was someone who had walked in his shoes. And Rapp doubted there was a therapist on the planet who had any practical experience as an assassin. One of Rapp's forms of self-therapy was to never deceive himself. He didn't sugarcoat what he was, even though other people did. In national security circles he was referred to as a counterterrorism operative. He knew it was a nice way of saying he was an assassin. This had never bothered him, but now that Anna was pregnant, it gave him cause to rethink his profession. His days of being self-sufficient, of thinking first and foremost of himself, were receding with each heartbeat of the little baby in his wife's womb. Rapp was not afraid of fatherhood in the least. He was surprised, though, by the feeling of melancholy that accompanied the news. At first he didn't know the source but it came to him soon enough. It was his own unfulfilled relationship with his father. Rapp did not want his child to go through the same agonizing pain of losing a parent that he had. He was suddenly looking at the risks he took on the job in a whole new light. He'd been fighting it since the day he'd fallen in love with Anna, but now there was no more putting it off. He owed it to both her and their unborn child. He would have to step out of the line. Let someone else take the risks.

Half a mile short of the end of his run, it happened. Rapp felt a spike of pain and shifted his weight to his good leg just as his left knee locked up like an engine throwing a rod—metal on metal, no more oil to aid the simple mechanical movement. Bone on bone, no more cartilage to reduce the friction. As he hopped to a stop he muttered a series of curses under his breath. He was the only person out on the road at this early hour, but even so, swearing at the top of his lungs wasn't his style. After a few excruciating steps, he realized how serious the injury was and blurted out a single four-letter curse.

Slowly and carefully, he began hobbling his way back to his house on the Chesapeake Bay. The birds were chirping, and the early morning sun cast long shadows across the dewy grass and bathed his face in warmth. All things considered it should have been a glorious morning, but it wasn't. He rounded a slight bend in the road and was surprised to find two people standing on the side of the gravel shoulder another fifty or so yards ahead. The man had his hand on the woman's back and she was bent over. Two mountain bikes lay on the ground next to them. It was not uncommon to encounter someone on this road, but it was almost always someone he knew. There was Mr. and Mrs. Grant, retirees who rose early and walked with their two chocolate Labs. There was Mrs. Randal, the Energizer Bunny, who did her shuffle jog for hours on end, and there were a handful of others who Rapp vaguely knew. He was always polite, but never stopped to talk.

He immediately crossed to the other side of the road placing as little weight as possible on his left leg. His hand reached for his fanny pack. Inside was a FN Five Seven pistol. The weapon carried twenty 5.7 x 28mm armor-piercing rounds. Rapp unzipped the fanny pack and kept his left hand near the opening. Every move was second nature, done almost completely without thought. He checked the couple again. She appeared to be sick, which could either be genuine, or a classic diversionary tactic. He looked at everything he encountered through this prism of primal pessimism.

Ambushes were typically set up in one of three ways. The first, and most common, was to lie in wait and spring the trap on the unsuspecting quarry. The second way was to lure the target in, as could be the case with this couple. Act like you need help and then when that target steps in to offer assistance you have them right where you want them. The third and final way is to distract the target. Get them focused on one thing, and then hit them from somewhere else. At the moment this was what Rapp was most worried about.

In all likelihood the couple was nothing more than a harmless husband and wife out for a bike ride, but Rapp couldn't risk that. He checked over his shoulder and then began looking further afield to his left and right. He knew every inch of this road. He drove on it, ran along its shoulder, and biked on it. His mind was trained to catch anything that was different. He finished his sweep. Everything looked normal. Rapp turned his attention back to the couple. He was close enough now to hear the woman gagging. If this was a trap she was doing a pretty convincing job.

The man glanced over his shoulder. He was wearing a bike helmet and a pair of Oakley sunglasses.

"Everything all right?" asked Rapp. He kept moving, doing his best to mask the fact that his knee was killing him. His left hand stayed poised right above the fold of his fanny pack. Rapp could instantly tell the man was in good shape.

"She's pregnant," the man offered. "Morning sickness."

Rapp gave a slight nod, but didn't respond. He wasn't out to make polite conversation. His eyes scanned the man from head to toe as well as the woman. The man was also wearing a fanny pack, but his was spun around so it sat at the small of his back. There was something about him. A certain lean athletic quality. Broad shoulders, thin waist, developed legs, all three parts in balance. Rapp had worked with guys like him before. His thoughts turned almost immediately to the warning that had been passed along by the Jordanians that there was a price on his head, but they then turned almost as quickly to the new director of National Intelligence, Mark Ross. Could the man be so foolish as to send a couple of his people out here to collect intel on him?

The thought of Ross deciding not to back down got his blood going. Rapp stopped almost directly across the street from the two. His left hand remained poised only an inch from his gun. The weapon was chambered and hot.

"You need any help?" Rapp asked in as friendly a tone as he could muster.

"No, thank you," the man said almost immediately. He glanced at Rapp and then returned his attention to the woman.

"Are you sure?" asked Rapp.

"Yeah. It'll pass in another minute."

"Do you live around here?" Rapp watched the man's every move. He wished he would take his glasses off so he could see his eyes.

"No," the man said. "Just visiting."

"I live nearby. I can get my car and give her a ride."

"No . . . no . . . thank you, she'll be fine."

"Where are you staying?"

The man hesitated and then offered, "Not far. A little bed and breakfast just up the way."

As if on cue, the woman stood up and wiped her mouth with the sleeve of her sweatshirt. She took a swig of water from her bottle and spit it out. She repeated the process three more times and then announced, "Oh, what we do for you men!"

Rapp smiled. He detected a slight French accent from the woman. If she was acting, she was doing a damn good job. Her skin was an awful pale shade of green. Rapp decided they didn't work for Ross.

"I hope you feel better." With that he started on his way again. His knee was getting worse with each step, and he wondered briefly if it wasn't he who would need a ride. He checked back over his shoulder and caught the man quickly looking away. He probably recognized him from some of the unwanted media attention he'd received a few years ago. The couple got back on their bikes and started off, while Rapp hobbled along the shoulder with increasing difficulty.

By the time he reached the front porch, he was no longer able to bend or straighten his knee out of its slightly crooked position. Rapp grabbed the house key from the fanny pack. He glanced over both shoulders and then stuck the key in the first of two deadbolt locks. When the two locks were opened he grabbed the door handle and pulled. Rapp had personally reversed the house's three door frames so they opened out instead of in. The front door, service door, and the frames were made out of steel and covered with a wood veneer. Anyone trying to break in would have to pack a lunch. All of the windows on the first floor were bulletproof. This was his first line of defense. It was what allowed him to decompress and sleep at night. It was a safe house in the literal sense of the word.

Rapp stepped into the foyer, and Shirley was right there with her tail wagging. He gave her a quick pat on the head before disarming the security system. After locking the door he turned the security system back on and limped into the kitchen where he found his wife sitting in her robe, reading the *Post* and sipping a cup of coffee.

Anna looked up at him, noticed the unusual pained expression on his face, and dropped the paper. "What's wrong?"

"Nothing." Rapp deflected her question with a shake of his head and continued to the sink.

"It sure the hell doesn't look like nothing," she said.

Rapp clutched the kitchen sink with one hand and poured himself a glass of water. "It's my knee. It's a little stiff . . . that's all."

Anna set her mug of coffee on the table. "A little stiff? Honey, re-member who you're talking to here. You look worse than when you were shot in the ass that time."

Rapp took several gulps of water and then went fishing in a drawer near the sink for some Advil. "Yeah . . . well, you saw me two days after the fact. You should have been there when I was rolling around in the mud screaming like a little girl."

Somehow she doubted he had acted anything less than manly. "Nice try. Tell me what's wrong with your knee."

"It's nothing." Rapp wrestled with the childproof cap and practically tore the bottle in half. "It's just a little stiff," he lied. "A couple of pills and some ice, and I'll be fine."

Anna folded her arms across her chest, offering Rapp an uninten-tional show of cleavage. She studied him for a moment and then asked, "What's on your schedule today?"

Rapp succeeded in separating the cap from the bottle and threw three of the pills in his mouth. He chased it with water and steadied him-self one more time. "Same old crap. I've got a few meetings at Langley and something I might have to do tonight . . . but I haven't decided on that yet." Knowing his wife's reporter instincts, he knew he had to ask her a question before she fired another one at him. "How about you? How's your day look?"

"I have a real slow morning." She tilted her head and studied him.

Rapp watched as she shook her shoulder-length auburn hair off to one side and lowered her cute little chin. She locked in on him with her seductive emerald eyes and smiled. The warning bells started to sound as she walked toward him loosening the belt of her robe. Rapp stood frozen while two conflicting parts of his brain wrestled with the whole pain-pleasure principle.

Anna pressed her body up against his and pinned him to the counter. She wrapped her arms around his neck and kissed his ear. "Why don't we go upstairs and have a little fun? I think being pregnant makes me frisky."

Rapp wavered for a second as the pleasure part of his brain scrambled to come up with a position that might work. The pain part of his brain screamed at him to ignore any such thought. The knee simply hurt too much so Rapp smiled awkwardly and gently pushed her away. "I don't think I have time. I've got to shower and get moving."

Anna took another step back and closed her robe. "You're a liar,

Mitchell." Flashing a fake smile, she asked, "Do you want me to call a doctor and make an appointment, or will you be man enough to do it yourself?"

He hesitated, trapped in his lie. "I'll take care of it," he offered weakly.

"No, you won't," she said as she finished tying her robe. "I'll call Liz. She and Michael know the best orthopedic surgeon in town." Anna grabbed the phone to call her best friend. "Morning or afternoon?"

Rapp looked down at his knee. It was starting to swell. "You'd better see if he can get me in this morning."

33

Gould took the front wheel off the mountain bike and lifted the back hatch of the Ford Explorer. The bike went in first and then the wheel. Claudia was sitting on a nearby park bench wrestling with another wave of nausea. Gould consulted his watch. It was 7:36 in the morning, and what had started off as a promising day was now an unmitigated disaster. He looked over at Claudia with an anger that he usually reserved for people who had threatened him. They were at the city park and there was no one around, but still this was not the place to have this conversation. Her illness had already brought them enough unwanted attention.

He yanked her bike off the ground and flipped the release for the front wheel. The bike was light but even so, Gould tossed it around like it was a kid's trike. He'd purchased both bikes the evening past at yet another massive sports superstore across the highway from the hotel they'd found in Bowie, a suburb of DC. There were a few motels and bed and breakfasts closer to Rapp's, but they didn't offer enough anonymity. Gould already imagined Rapp calling the handful of bed and breakfasts near his house to see if a couple fitting their description had checked in. He was just that type of man, Gould supposed. Very thorough. Gould was not one to come unnerved, but meeting Rapp had sent a chill down his spine that he hadn't felt since he'd been surrounded by an angry mob of machete-wielding Hutus in Rwanda while he was serving in the Foreign Legion.

The man had been less than a mile from his home, the one place where Gould expected to find him with his guard down, but he couldn't have been more wrong. Gould hadn't even noticed him at first. He was helping steady Claudia. She had started to feel queasy as they approached Rapp's house, but the first wave passed so they continued on. They had made it to his house and then turned around and were on their way back to town. That's all they had planned on doing—a simple drive-by. Gould wanted to get the lay of the land and confirm what his eyes could only guess in the dark of night. He also wanted to explore the possibility of making it look like an accident. The German was offering an extra million dollars, and while Gould wasn't crazy about the added risk, he would at least give it consideration. Claudia pulled over abruptly about a half mile past Rapp's house and began throwing up. At this point Gould was still calm. They had seen both cars in the driveway, and it was before 7:00 in the morning. Claudia would get this over with in a few minutes and they would move on, no one the wiser to their presence.

The last thing Gould had expected was to come face-to-face with his quarry. Then Gould heard something and looked over his shoulder, and there in the flesh was Mitch Rapp. He had gotten very close, too close, and had done so without intentionally stalking Gould. It was supposed to be the other way around. His only saving grace were the sunglasses that covered his eyes. Eyes were by far the most difficult feature to change. Behind the shield of tinted glass, Gould watched Rapp's every move with keen interest. He saw how the American's left hand remained poised just above the pack he wore around his waist. Gould had zero doubt what was concealed in the pack, and he also had zero doubt that Rapp could draw and fire the weapon in the time it would take most people to blink. He also knew it was almost a certainty that Rapp would hit his target.

While the chance encounter was not something that Gould would have preferred, everything up to this point was manageable. Rapp had seen him, but thanks to loose-fitting clothes, the helmet, and the sunglasses there really wasn't much to go on. Rapp asked him a question and Gould was forced to answer. Still, everything was fine. Gould spoke such flawless English that there was no way for Rapp to glean that he was French. Then Claudia decided to open her mouth and ruin everything.

They got in the truck and drove back to the hotel in silence. Claudia reclined her seat as far as it would go and covered her eyes. When they got to the hotel they entered through one of the side doors. Claudia dropped onto the bed with her workout clothes still on. She kicked off one shoe and then the other. She let out a moan and covered her head with one of the fluffy pillows.

"Close the curtains, please," she said from under the pillow.

He yanked the fabric shut with such force that he practically pulled the whole thing off its rails.

She cracked one eye and lifted the pillow. "What are you so upset about?"

He stopped his pacing and stared at her. "Why in the hell did you open your mouth back there?"

"Back where?"

"On the street. In front of Rapp."

She pulled the pillow down and muttered something.

"What in the hell were you thinking?"

"I was sick. I didn't even know it was him."

"Do you realize what the stakes are? Do you have any idea what you did by speaking back there?"

"You are overreacting," she groaned.

"The hell I am. If we fail, you don't think he's going to remember that couple he ran into one early morning? The woman with the French accent, and the man she was with?"

"He didn't see our faces."

"He didn't need to. All he needs to do is put out a general physical description of us and then stipulate that the woman was French. How many male/female teams do you think there are?" He stared at her waiting for an answer that he never got. "Not a lot to start with, but add the fact that he now knows the woman is French and he's narrowed the search down to only a few people."

"Then let's quit. Let's just walk away from it and keep the German's money."

Gould didn't speak for a second. He just gawked at her stupidity. "Have you lost your mind?"

"Then give the money back. I don't care . . . just leave me alone. Can't you see I'm not in the mood to argue with you right now?"

"You sure picked a hell of a time to get pregnant."

She lifted the corner of the pillow and looked out at him with an angry eye. "Believe me, you had something to do with it."

"Why now? We've been having sex for years and it's never happened before." He had wanted to ask this question, but until now had been too worried about how she might react. Now he simply didn't care.

"It happens," she replied with a tinge of anger in her voice.

"Bullshit," he growled. "You stopped taking the Pill, didn't you?"

"Va-t'en. Je ne me sens pas bien."

"Speak English," he snapped.

"Go away. I don't feel well, you bully."

Gould's jaw clenched in anger. He hesitated for a second, fighting the urge to press his point. He decided he needed to get away from her before he said something they would both regret. He marched across the room and grabbed one of the backpacks. He threw the pack over one shoulder and left without saying another word.

HE STOPPED AT a nearby gas station and filled the tank. He also got some coffee and a donut that he regretted buying soon after he'd wolfed it down. Before pulling out of the lot Gould checked the GPS tracking device he'd placed on Anna Rielly's car. The screen on the handheld device was only three inches by three inches and was not capable of the detail that Claudia's laptop provided, but for now it would do just fine. A quick check revealed that she was on her way back into the city. More than likely she was on her way to work. Gould had placed three devices in her car. The first, the one he stuck under the dashboard, was a simple bug. Anything she said while in the car would be relayed to a digital recorder and scanning device in the trunk. That small black box also randomly scanned the most common frequencies used by cordless phones. It had an effective range of up to 100 feet. It also contained a small digital phone so it could be accessed remotely. The third device was the GPS transponder itself, which allowed him to track the location of the vehicle.

Gould plugged an earpiece into his Palm Pilot and dialed the number to connect with the scanning device in Rielly's trunk. At the prompt he punched in the four-digit code and waited with the Palm Pilot's thin black stylus poised above the screen. He followed several more commands and then waited while the data was transferred from the scanner to the handheld computer. The code on the bottom of the file told him that he had sixteen minutes and eighteen seconds worth of conversation. As soon as it was done he erased the recordings on the scanner and ended the connection. The scanner in Rielly's trunk could hold up to five hours of digitized phone conversation, which for his purposes should be more than enough. Gould opened the audio file on his Palm Pilot and began replaying the time-stamped conversations. The first one was from the night before and was nothing more than Rielly listening to the radio on her way home from work. Gould fast forwarded through parts of it to make sure he didn't miss anything. Eight minutes and thirty-seven seconds into it she made a call to a girlfriend named Liz. She asked how her godson was doing and began talking about babies. Gould skipped ahead. He would go back and listen to every word later, but for now he wanted to hear if he had Rapp talking on the home phone.

Gould put the car in drive and pulled out onto Annapolis Road. A few blocks later her car took the Blue Star Memorial Highway south. His plan was to spend the rest of the morning familiarizing himself with the countryside. When he lived in the States he'd spent a little time in both Annapolis and Baltimore and had gone on two cruises of the Chesapeake. One was for school and the other was a private outing, a day of sailing that Gould remembered fondly. A friend of his father's had taken them. His sisters and mother were left at home. Gould remembered it well because they had entered a regatta and it had been thrilling. The weather was perfect; sunny, warm, and blustery.

He had spent zero time, however, in the area where Rapp lived just south of Annapolis. He wanted to make sure what the map showed actually existed, and was where it was supposed to be. In a country like America this was not usually a problem, but in some of the Third World hellholes where Gould had served, good maps were rare. No matter what, though, a map was still just a map. A flat representation of a real place. It helped with names and places, but still, to get a real sense of what was out there, you had to see it with your own eyes. Maps, unless they were extraordinarily good ones, did not show foot paths through the woods, they did not show clumps of bushes, and they did not tell you which way the wind blew. And then there was the change of seasons to consider. What might be a great place to lie in wait in the summer might be useless in the winter. All of these things needed to be experienced firsthand, but still one had to be very careful. Especially when dealing with a man like Rapp. Reconnaissance was only useful in a situation like this if your target remained oblivious to the fact that he was being watched. Reconnaissance was in many ways the most difficult aspect of Gould's job. Training and planning were important, but they were things that he could control in an almost lablike setting. Reconnaissance meant that he had to expose himself.

Gould continued south for approximately five minutes and then turned east. Most of the cars were headed west at this point so traffic was light. He continued to play the recordings as he went, half listening, half thinking about how quickly the ebb and flow of the operation had turned. Everything had gone so smoothly until this morning. They'd had no trouble entering the country, all of the money was safely transferred into untraceable accounts, and they had followed Rielly home without incident. And then they had come face to face with Rapp and Claudia had opened her mouth. This was exactly what Gould was thinking when a snippet of the recorded conversation caught his attention. He could scarcely believe what he was hearing. He was still in a surly mood, upset with Claudia and believing firmly that she had gotten pregnant intentionally. He was lamenting how quickly things had turned when lady luck came roaring back into his life via a simple phone call. The conversation had taken place between Anna Rielly and a friend barely an hour ago. That phone call was followed quickly by a second one where Rapp's wife was making an appointment for him to see a doctor. An orthopedic surgeon. The next conversation was the doctor calling for Rapp. He asked Rapp to explain the problem. The short version was that Rapp could barely bend his left knee. The doctor told him to try and stay off it and come in immediately. They would do an MRI and then decide if he needed surgery.

Gould pulled over to the side of the county road and checked his map. Now that he thought back on it Rapp had been walking with a slight limp when he'd seen him earlier in the morning. *Surgery,* he thought to himself. *Could I be so lucky?* If Rapp had to go under the knife, he'd be laid up for a while and Gould's job would be made significantly easier. Gould yanked the car back into drive and waited for a small tanker truck to pass. Gould was already plotting, exploring any possible way he could make Rapp's death look remotely like an accident. A car crash would be difficult with the type of vehicles they drove. As long as they were wearing their seat belts both the BMW and the Audi would protect them from any crash Gould could help orchestrate.

Several hundred yards ahead, Gould watched a truck turn off the road. At the moment he didn't think much of it, but as he slowed for a stop sign he looked to his left and noticed the truck parked in the driveway of someone's home. The driver was out of the cab and dragging a hose over to a silver tank next to the house. Gould read the stenciled lettering on the door. Chesapeake Bay Propane Co. Underneath was a phone number and address. Gould memorized both and continued on. He remembered some obscure fact that he'd picked up years ago. Where, he could not remember, but it had something to do with natural gas being odorless. He tried to picture Rapp's house, but couldn't be sure. It was a possibility, he supposed. How else would they heat their homes in this rural area? After he got to Rapp's house he would look into it. The extra million would come in handy, and if it was done right, there would be no reason for the CIA to come looking for him. They would of course suspect foul play, but without hard evidence, there would always be doubt.

34

ANDREWS AIR FORCE BASE

The Saudi delegation arrived on four massive 747 long-haul aircrafts. The planes were designed by Boeing to carry 400 plus passengers depending on how they were configured, but these were no ordinary planes. Each one was owned privately by a member of the Saudi royal family. Due to an almost endless source of petrodollars, and the Saudis' need to constantly trump one another, each plane was lavishly decorated in the most opulent manner possible. Marble showers with gold fixtures, king-size beds, and Jacuzzis were standard on each plane, as were workout facilities, steam rooms, and gaming rooms. Plasma TV screens were in great abundance as well as DVDs, CDs, and pretty much anything that had an ounce of entertainment value. Each wide-body plane carried a world class chef, masseuse, manicurist, and barber. The jumbo jets were the equivalent of flying private yachts. Not counting the flight crew and staff, fewer than fifty passengers flew on each plane.

Maintaining this lavish lifestyle was anything but easy. Two separate 747s loaded with security people, protocol officers, junior diplomats, and servants had arrived earlier in the week. Entire five-star hotels had been booked, the top floor in some cases reserved for just one person. Extra cigarettes were ordered in quantities befitting an army going into battle. The hotels stocked up on the most expensive cognac, the finest cigars, and the rarest of wines. Escort services flew in call girls from Chicago, Miami, New York, and L.A. When the Saudis came to town they provided a boost to the local economy that was akin to hosting a major sporting event. Instead of doing it with tens of thousands of people, though, they simply did it with a thousand or less.

The protocol officers had argued over every detail of the state visit. It started with lodging. When the president offered Blair House to the king, it looked like things were off to a good start, but it all went downhill from there. The foreign minister, minister of commerce, and minister for Islamic affairs all wanted to stay at the Saudi ambassador's estate outside the city. The estate was big, but not big enough to handle two, let alone three, of the ministers and their entourages. The foreign minister's people argued that he had the most important job. The minister of commerce's people argued that the ambassador was his full brother, and thus it was his right to use the estate, and the minister of Islamic affairs' people refused to give a reason other than the fact that it was what Prince Muhammad bin Rashid wanted. In the end this was reason enough. Rashid had the ear of the clerics, and his contacts ran deep in the state security agencies. In many ways he was the most feared man in Saudi Arabia. Only King Abdullah and a handful of young princes dared stand up to him.

In hindsight, they realized that they were fools for not having suggested that Prince Muhammad and his entourage stay at the estate in the first place. Prince Muhammad was one of the only truly pious members of the royal family, and he refused to partake in alcohol or tobacco even when traveling abroad. With Muhammad and his people sequestered at the estate, the rest of the delegation could relax and have fun without fear of being reported back to the clerics at home. The Saudi royals had a "What happens in Vegas, stays in Vegas" attitude. While in the Kingdom they at least kept up the appearance that they were following the Wahhabis' strict interpretation of Islam, but as soon as they left the country they went wild.

The remaining Saudis were left to fight over the Ritz Carlton in Georgetown and the Ritz in Foggy Bottom a mere eight blocks away. In the end the foreign minister got the Ritz in Foggy Bottom since the hotel had more rooms and his entourage was larger. They were not done arguing, though. There were still important issues to settle, such as the order in which the planes would land. It was a given that the king would land last, but the other three slots were up for grabs. Again, Prince Muhammad's people refused to negotiate. This infuriated the other two camps, but after much yelling and complaining they got nowhere. In the end the foreign minister secured the number-two spot, and the minister of commerce was forced to land first.

Security was a major issue, but the Americans were running the show where that was concerned. As the planes came in on final approach, the motorcades were readied and the military marching band stood poised to play. The king was going straight to the White House, Prince Muhammad and the foreign minister were going to the State Department, and the minister of commerce was going to the Kennedy Center where he would be hosted by the U.S. commerce secretary and important business leaders. The DC Metro Police were on hand to provide motorcycle escorts, and the Secret Service had pulled in agents from all over the East Coast to provide diplomatic protection. The king, as well as his three half brothers, had all brought their own armor-plated limousines, which had been flown over to America in advance of the visit.

Prince Muhammad had wondered more than once on the long journey just how close Abel's assassin was to getting the job done. It would be very interesting to watch the story reported from the American perspective if it happened during his visit. It would also be priceless to see the reaction on the faces of their government officials. Especially the director of the CIA. Muhammad knew the woman favored Rapp and that his death would hurt her. *This is what she deserves for meddling in the affairs of Saudi Arabia,* he thought.

After the attacks on the World Trade Center and Pentagon, Muhammad had learned that it had been that damnable woman who had advised the American president to press for his reassignment. Kennedy herself had visited with then Crown Prince Abdullah and provided evidence that Saudi Security Services were in some cases knowingly protecting al-Qaeda and its members. She stated that the president, along with the leaders in the House and Senate, did not feel Prince Muhammad bin Rashid was up to the job of running the Ministry of the Interior, which oversaw the security services. If he was not moved out of the position, and replaced with someone who was willing to go after al-Qaeda aggressively, Saudi–American relations would suffer greatly.

His half brother caved in to the demand, but in order to save face at home, and keep the tenuous balance between the bickering princes, he gave Muhammad the important position of minister of Islamic affairs, endowment, *dawa,* and guidance. In terms of sheer power, it paled in comparison to running the Ministry of the Interior, but in terms of influence, it was second to none. Oil was the blood of Saudi Arabia, but Islam was its heart. The royal family could not rule without the backing of the clerics in Mecca and Medina, and the clerics were growing increasingly leery of the king and his cozy relations with America. Muhammad knew he needed to show the religious men that he was a man of action. Someone who was willing to stand up to the Americans.

There would be great personal satisfaction in having a hand in the death of a foul nonbeliever like Rapp, but in the more strategic sense, Rapp's murder would eventually provide proof not just to the clerics, but to the other members of the royal family that Muhammad bin Rashid was a great defender of Islam, and not some pandering fool like the king. Revealing his hand in the matter would have to be handled very delicately and over a certain period of time. Prince Muhammad was fifty-nine and in good health. He could bide his time for another five years and slowly chip away at the king's support. When the time was right, the clerics would support him, that he knew for certain. They wanted Rapp dead more than he did, and they would be very grateful that a member of the House of Saud had finally picked up a sword and defended Islam. For now, though, he had to go through the motions and act as if he actually liked the Americans.

Prince Muhammad bin Rashid stepped from the plane into the late-afternoon sunlight. He was dressed in his white robes and he clutched them against the blowing wind. To the undiscerning eye it was difficult to tell him apart from his half brother, the king, especially when he was wearing sunglasses as he was at this moment. Both men stood six feet tall and had jet black mustaches and goatees. This sometimes caused a bit of confusion as it did now with the group of dignitaries and photographers who were waiting on the red carpet at the foot of the stairs. Prince Muhammad descended with a slight smile on his face as he watched one of the king's protocol officers pointing frantically at the last of the jumbo jets which was pulling to a stop just a little ways down the tarmac.

The air force general waiting to greet him held his ground. He was not about to slight the Saudi foreign minister by bolting. Enjoying the spectacle, Prince Muhammad took his time getting down the stairs. Upon meeting the base commander, he clutched the man's hand in both of his and became quite effusive in his praise for the military band. The whole time he kept one eye on the protocol officer and took great joy in seeing the man begin to tremble. Finally, the base commander broke free and with a hand on Prince Muhammad's back he sent him down the carpet toward his waiting limousine.

35

Kennedy stood in the corner of the John Quincy Adams State Drawing Room and nursed her glass of Chardonnay while two State Department undersecretaries tried to sell her on a new approach toward North Korea. They knew if she sided with their boss, the president would likely change course. That was not going to happen. Kennedy listened politely even though she disagreed with everything they were saying. The North Korean leader was mentally unstable, and nothing these two diplomats said would change that irrefutable medical fact. Single-party talks were a nonstarter and nothing more than an ego game by the North Korean premier. China, Japan, and South Korea had to be at the negotiating table. It was their backyard. Kennedy was tempted to tell the two Ivy Leaguers that she had been secretly counseling the president that it was time to give the Chinese an ultimatum; either rein in North Korea, or the United States would help Japan develop a nuclear weapons program. Kennedy was convinced the specter of a nuclear Japan would force China to bring North Korea to heel. There were others who understandably disagreed. China could counter by saying it would invade Taiwan and things could spin out of control rather quickly.

Telling these two doves any of this, however, would be foolish. She let them drone on and on about how it wouldn't be such a bad concession to conduct single-party talks. After all, they could always go back to six-party talks if it didn't work out. This conversation was a perfect example of why she had been reluctant to attend the reception for the Saudi foreign minister. Mixing with other departments in a social setting, especially State, often meant being trapped in these types of diametrically op-posed discussions. She looked around the room for her new boss. This had been his idea. A command performance. Had Kennedy been invited by the secretary of state herself, she would have still been ambivalent about attending the diplomatic reception, but Ross had ordered her to come, and had done so in a very condescending manner. He told her, as if he was giving her an employee review, that she needed to work more on relationship building with their allies. She took all of this in stride and bit her lip, but in the back of her mind she heard Rapp's warning—Ross is an idiot.

Kennedy wondered if this was about Rapp—if Ross was punishing her for what he'd done. She had not let on that she knew about their con-frontation, but it was safe to assume Ross thought she knew all the details. What had started off as a decent enough working relationship was sud-denly not looking so good. Whether this was exacerbated by Rapp or in-evitable she did not know, but she was beginning to seriously wonder if Ross was the wrong man for the job.

Kennedy had been tempted to force Rapp to accompany her as a form of punishment, but he had gotten out of it. He'd shown up at her office limping earlier in the day and told her he was going in to have his knee operated on in the morning. She asked how serious it was and he shrugged it off with a mumbled answer. After a few more questions she found out they were going to scope his knee and he'd be back at work in two days. That didn't sound like such a big deal, so she pressed him fur-ther and found out the procedure was only a short-term solution. The doctor told him within five years he'd need to undergo knee replacement surgery. Kennedy was surprised by her own lack of concern for his health. On the contrary, she was pleased to hear that he would finally have to slow down. With any luck, she could get him behind a desk soon and keep him there.

Ross entered the room in a manner befitting the president himself. He was followed by the ever-present Jonathan Gordon; two female staffers, whom Kennedy only vaguely recognized; and four immense Se-cret Service agents. Kennedy looked across the room at Secretary of State Berg and noted that not a single member of her security detail was in the room. They were in one of the most secure buildings in Washington, after all. There was no reason, other than hubris, to have the agents so close to their protectee.

Kennedy stood in the corner and continued to listen to the two State

Department officials. She was in no rush to talk to Ross so she waited for him to make his way over. Ross was shaking hands and slapping backs. Kennedy was amused to read the lips of a senator who asked Ross, "What are you doing here?"

Very good question, Kennedy thought to herself. She looked at her watch and noted that he had told her to be on time, and yet he had arrived thirty minutes late.

Ross made his way over to Secretary Berg and kissed her on the cheek. After a few minutes he spotted Kennedy and waved her over.

Kennedy excused herself and made her way through the crowd. "Secretary Berg." Kennedy extended her hand. "How are you?"

"Well, Irene, and you?"

"Just fine, thank you," answered Kennedy. She and the secretary of state were often at odds philosophically, but had a good working relationship.

"I didn't expect to see you here," Ross said, thinking he was funny.

"I thought I'd crash the party," Kennedy replied with a half smile.

"I'm glad you came," said the secretary of state quickly. She squeezed Kennedy's arm and gave her a reassuring nod.

Kennedy knew exactly what she meant. The Saudis had a way of making women feel very uncomfortable. To the old guard of Saudi men a woman's place was at home, taking care of the children and running the household. It was inappropriate to look a woman in the eye or address her directly. This made for some awkward moments when powerful women like Berg and Kennedy were placed in the same room with an all-male delegation of Saudis. In Kennedy's twenty plus years in the intelligence business things had gotten much better. The next generation of Saudis, the ones who had been educated at universities in Europe and America, were far more accepting of women, at least when dealing with foreign governments. Back in Saudi Arabia, though, the great divide between the sexes was still alive and flourishing.

One of Secretary Berg's assistants came up and informed her that the Saudi foreign minister had entered the building. Berg excused herself and left Ross and Kennedy to take up her position in the diplomatic receiving line. Ross grabbed Kennedy by the elbow and pointed toward the far corner of the room. They wove their way through the crowd with Ross's bodyguards shadowing them as they went. Kennedy thought the security must have looked ridiculous and was relieved when Ross finally gave the detail leader a signal to stand down.

Ross stood with his back to the room, facing Kennedy. Jonathan Gordon stepped from his shadow and took up position beside his boss. Ross smoothed his light-blue-and-silver-striped tie with the palm of his right hand and then adjusted his trousers before placing his hands on his lips. The director of National Intelligence looked at her, tilted his head slightly, as if he was going to say something, and then stopped.

Kennedy had a pretty good idea what was on his mind, so she said, "Mark, about you and Mitch, and what happened the other day . . ."

Ross cut her off. "You don't need to say a word. It's water under the bridge."

Kennedy glanced at Gordon, whose expression said different. "I just want you to know I don't operate that way," Kennedy said to Ross. "If one of my people has a problem with you they need to come to me first. Mitch went behind my back, and I'm not happy about it."

Ross considered his reply. "I know Mitch has sacrificed a great deal for this country, but a lot of people worry he's uncontrollable. That it's just a matter of time before he does something that really embarrasses the Agency. Neither of us want that to happen."

"No, we don't," Kennedy said honestly.

"Then I suggest you keep him on a short leash."

Kennedy nodded. She couldn't really tell him that there were as many or more people in Washington who wanted to simply let Rapp loose.

"And this Coleman guy. I wasn't born yesterday. That guy spells trouble."

Kennedy said nothing.

"I'm going to do my best," continued Ross, "to stay out of the day-to-day business of the Agency. I have a lot of faith in you, you've done a great job so far, but I worry that you have a blind spot where Rapp is concerned. I've already talked to the president about this and he shares my concerns."

Kennedy listened to the words without showing an ounce of emotion. Inside, however, her stomach started to churn.

"We've decided," said Ross, "to keep a close eye on the situation. If Rapp can't start following orders and respect the chain of command, some changes might have to be made."

"You talked to the president about this?" Kennedy wanted to be clear on this point. One of the classic power plays in Washington was to drop the president's name to bolster your position.

"Yes, and he's been worried for some time about it."

Kennedy looked Ross in the eye and wondered if he had bothered to tell the president what had caused Mitch to become so insolent. She doubted that Ross had told him about his investigation of Scott Coleman and his company. Scott Coleman, a man who had been the commander of SEAL Team 6 and who had won both the Silver Star and the Navy Cross. A man who after leaving the navy had conducted dozens of black ops, a handful that the president himself had authorized.

Where Rapp was quick to anger, Kennedy was the opposite. She didn't like any of this. She hated the fact that Ross was meddling in such delicate matters, and it really irked her that he had already begun politicking with the president. In spite of those emotions she remained calm.

She gave Ross a slight nod and said, "I'll have another talk with him." *And with the president,* she thought to herself.

"Good." Ross pivoted so he was standing next to her. Gordon moved into position on her left. The two men had her bracketed. Talking out of the side of his mouth Ross said, "You're probably wondering why I asked you to come to this reception."

"The thought has crossed my mind."

"The Saudis are the key."

Kennedy looked across the room to the diplomatic receiving line. The foreign minister and his lengthy entourage had just entered the room. Kennedy had noticed that Ross liked to make statements like "The Saudis are the key" and then add nothing more. His aim was to get you to ask him why, so that he could then dispense his wisdom. Kennedy, a professional spy from the old school, was very good at keeping her mouth shut and listening.

"Don't you care to know why they are the key?"

Kennedy spoke Arabic. She'd spent the majority of her youth moving around the Middle East, and understood the Saudi culture about as well as a foreign woman could hope. She had forgotten more about Saudi Arabia than Ross could ever hope to learn, but nonetheless, she was actually interested to hear where he would go with this.

"Why are they the key, and to what are they the key?"

"Very good qualification," Ross replied. "They are the key to solving this whole mess."

"Which mess?" asked Gordon in a slightly impatient tone.

"The whole mess . . . the Middle East, terrorism, the spread of radical Islam. They hold the key. If we can get them to trust us . . . to see that we mean them no harm, we will do more to secure this country from terrorist attacks than we could ever hope through use of force."

Kennedy was suddenly hopeful, not that Ross would offer her a realistic solution, but that she was about to get an invaluable look at how the man's mind operated. "And how do we go about doing this?"

Ross pointed. "The problem isn't with people like the foreign minister, or the king. They like us. They get it. They know we don't want to take over their country and their culture. The problem is with people like Prince Muhammad bin Rashid."

Kennedy spotted the minister of Islamic affairs. He was in line right behind the foreign minister. He was the problem all right. The man had softened his rhetoric as of late, but Kennedy didn't buy any of it.

"How well do you know him?" asked Ross.

Kennedy could write a lengthy briefing on the man. At the moment, though, she was more interested to hear what Ross thought of him. "I know a little. What's your take on him?"

"The road to peace lies through their religious leaders, and he is the way to get to those leaders. He is the key," Ross said emphatically. "I personally asked him to come on this trip. I told him I wanted to open an honest dialogue about how our two great nations can get to know each other better."

Kennedy nodded. The fact that Ross would use the word *great* to describe the United States and Saudi Arabia in the same sentence would have been business as usual if he had been from the State Department, but this was the director of National Intelligence talking, a man who was supposed to use his words very carefully, a man who was supposed to collect intelligence. It was not his job to conduct affairs of state with any foreign citizen he chose, let alone someone who had a history of sponsoring terrorists. Kennedy understood the need to interact with adversaries and allies alike. She also very much wanted to get to know Prince Muhammad bin Rashid better, but not the way Ross did. She wanted to study him the way an FBI profiler studies a serial killer.

The man was an incurable bigot, and for Ross to not already know this was a bit unsettling. He was, after all, the president's chief advisor on intelligence and the international terrorist threat. If their relationship had been better, she would have taken the time to explain to Ross why Muhammad bin Rashid could not be trusted, but at present it would be a waste of breath. Ross would not want to hear why his plan wouldn't work. He would have to spend some time with the prince and figure it out for himself. In the meantime, Kennedy would have to make sure he didn't reveal anything, or promise something that might screw up the delicate balance they fought to maintain with the Saudis.

"Irene," said Ross as he looked at Prince Muhammad, "he is in certain ways the most powerful man in Saudi Arabia."

"I suppose you're right," Kennedy reluctantly agreed. "And what a shame," she added under her breath. Ross was too busy looking above the crowd to hear her, but Jonathan Gordon laughed softly. Kennedy turned to look at him.

"Prince Muhammad does not strike me as someone who is very receptive to change."

Ross left them to go shake hands with someone.

"He's a dyed in-the-wool Wahhabi. Change is not in their lexicon."

"That's what I tried to tell him, but he thinks his personality can win anyone over."

Kennedy knew the type. The best politicians were all that way. They honestly believed in their personal power of persuasion. These were the men and women who never stopped campaigning. Every dry cleaner, bar, and café they stopped in, every golf outing and fund raiser they hit, they shook hands, smiled, remembered an amazing number of names and convinced people through nothing more than their personality that they were likable. These men and women excelled in politics. They were willing to make concessions and be flexible so others thought them reasonable. On the international stage, though, these types got taken to the cleaners. Neville Chamberlain, the British prime minister at the onset of WWII, was the classic modern example. He had met Hitler, looked him in the eye, made him laugh, and concluded that he was a decent chap despite the evidence to the contrary that had been provided by the British intelligence services. Hitler took Chamberlain for a fool and played him through the occupation of Austria, the invasion of Poland, and right on up to the invasion of France. Somehow Hitler had been able to resist the irresistible charm of Chamberlain.

Kennedy had dealt with Prince Muhammad in the wake of 9/11. Her station chief in Riyadh as well as her counterparts in Britain, Germany, France, Israel, and Jordan all came to the same conclusion about him. While they couldn't prove that he knowingly provided money to al-Qaeda and other terrorist organizations, they did know that he had given more than twenty million dollars to charities that were linked to terrorist organizations. Across the board the intelligence chiefs agreed that Muhammad was far too cozy with the religious extremists in Saudi Arabia to be trusted to run the Kingdom's intelligence services. The leaders of America, Britain, France, and Germany all convinced the king to move his half brother to a different position on his council of ministers. The official Saudi position was that Mohammad was quite chastened over the whole thing. Unofficially, Kennedy had heard that Mohammad did not go quietly.

Kennedy watched Ross work his way across the room. Prince Mohammad had decided to eschew the diplomatic receiving line, a major breach in protocol, and something that was sure to be noted by all. He instead went straight for Ross, who was roughly in the middle of the room. They met and clasped hands, Ross with more enthusiasm than the prince. They were roughly the same height; both a little over six feet tall. Ross wore an expensive handmade suit, and Prince Muhammad wore his robes and ornamental headdress. Kennedy looked on with great interest as the prince broke into laughter. His perfect set of white teeth contrasted against his black goatee. Prince Muhammad clasped Ross's shoulder with his free hand and continued to smile warmly. His gaze wandered and for an instant he looked straight at Kennedy.

"You don't seem too excited to meet him," said Gordon.

"Excited." Kennedy continued to observe the two men talking. "There aren't many people at CIA who would be excited to meet Prince Muhammad."

"You don't trust him?"

What a question, Kennedy thought to herself. "We're not in the trust business, Jonathan. We're in the business of espionage." She was well aware that whatever she said would be repeated to Ross so she chose her next words carefully. "Prince Muhammad is no ally of ours. He is a man who in his heart supports everything al-Qaeda stands for. Don't forget that, no matter how pro-America he acts on this trip." Kennedy looked at Gordon. "If your boss has any future political aspirations, I'd advise him to not get too cozy with Prince Muhammad."

36

Rapp sat on the edge of the exam table and looked down at the swathe of smooth skin that ran from the middle of his left thigh to the middle of his shin. He was proud of the fact that he'd managed to shave it without cutting himself. He knew they would have done it for him, but he wasn't all that crazy about people touching him with sharp objects. The reality that he was going to be put under for the procedure gave him enough anxiety as it was. As much as he hated it, though, he knew it had to be done. He'd put it off long enough.

Anna was in the room with him, but as usual she was talking on her cell phone. Sometimes Rapp wondered if the device was surgically attached to her head. He had no doubt, if the roles were reversed, and she was about to go under the knife and he was chatting away on his phone, she'd be shooting him daggers with her eyes. Rapp pointed at the sign on the wall above the small desk. There was a cell phone with a red circle and a line going through it. Anna frowned at him. Rapp pointed at the sign again. She stuck her tongue out and turned her back on him. Rapp laughed to himself.

According to his watch it was three minutes past seven in the morning and he was hungry as all hell. He was under strict orders, though. No food before surgery. They didn't want him puking on the operating table. Anna got off her phone and turned around.

"That was Phil. He says good luck."

"Who's Phil?"

"My boss, Mr. Smart-ass."

Rapp had never met the man even though his wife had worked with him for nearly a year. "Where's the love, honey?"

"It's right here." Anna rubbed her belly.

Rapp smiled and motioned for her to come closer. She was wearing a dark brown Juicy Couture sweat suit. He placed his hand on her stomach and asked, "How are you feeling?"

"A little constipated, but other than that, fine."

"Lovely." He made a face.

"You asked." She sat down next to him and leaned back. She tugged at the ties on his hospital gown. "I can see your butt crack."

Rapp shook his head. "Why in the hell do they make people wear these things?"

"You don't know?" she asked sounding a little surprised.

"No."

"It strips away the patient's identity so you'll be more docile and do what you're told."

"Where did you hear this?"

She shrugged. "I can't remember."

Rapp thought about it for a moment and said, "I'll bet you're right."

"I know I am. Think about it. What do you guys do when you interrogate a terrorist? You shave their head and beard and you take away all of their clothes." She tried to straighten the back of the gown, but it wouldn't cooperate. She let it hang loose and asked, "Seriously, how are you doing?"

"Fine. I just want to get it over with. I hate hospitals."

"At least you're not here to get a bullet taken out."

Rapp looked at her sideways. "Thanks for that happy thought."

She put her arm around him. "Honey, everything is going to be just fine. The doctor said it's pretty straightforward. An hour or two at the most in surgery, and then two more hours in recovery. We'll be home by one at the latest." She was genuinely worried about him and not for the reasons one would think. Most people going in for surgery feared the recovery and the pain that were to follow. Pain was not a problem for Mitch. She doubted he would take anything stronger than Tylenol Three for more than a day or two. The real issue was not being in charge. Mitch was such a lone wolf, he was so used to being in charge and doing things his own way, that the idea of putting himself in the hands of others was purely unnerving to him.

"I'm starving," Rapp blurted out.

Her husband was a big eater. She reached out and ran her fingers through his thick black hair. "We'll have to stop and get something on the way home."

The door opened and a petite nurse entered. She was wearing blue surgical scrubs and black clogs. She held a clipboard a few inches in front of her face. "Mr. Mitchell Rapp?"

"That's me."

She flipped through the chart. "We've got you scheduled for a vasectomy this morning."

Rapp stared back at the woman, speechless. Before he could form a sentence, the woman said, "Just kidding. My name is Deb, and I'm going to get you ready for surgery."

Anna laughed. Mitch didn't.

"You must be Mrs. Rapp." The nurse stuck out her hand.

"Anna. Nice to meet you."

"Where'd you find a big stud like this? Look at these shoulders." The nurse stepped back and sized him up like he was a piece of beef.

"It wasn't easy. I had to go through a lot of guys."

"I'll bet."

Rapp laughed.

"Okay," the nurse returned her attention to Rapp. "The right knee, right?"

"No." Rapp looked alarmed. "The left."

"I know, I know." She waved her hand at him. "I'm just kidding. Trying to get you to relax, you know? You look so tense. Here, sit all the way up on the table." She took out a big black marker and wrote NO on Rapp's right knee and YES on his left knee.

"Dr. Stone is the best. He did the vice president's knee last year."

"I've met the vice president. I'm not impressed."

"Me neither," she whispered and rolled her eyes. "Kind of an ass if you ask me. Anyway . . . Dr. Stone handles all the hockey players on the Capitals. Big strong guys like you." She grabbed him by the shoulders. "Come to think of it . . . you two look familiar. Are you someone important?"

"I'm nobody," answered Rapp, "but she's important."

The nurse put her hands on her little hips and looked at Anna.

"I'm the White House correspondent for NBC. Anna Rielly."

"That's right. My husband loves you."

"Doesn't everyone's," said Rapp dryly.

Anna delivered a backhand to his chest. "Pay no attention to him. He's a little crabby."

"Is he worried?" the nurse asked without looking at Rapp.

"I think so."

"I'm hungry," moaned Rapp.

"Well, then, we'd better get things moving. Anna, I'm going to take him into prep, and then he'll head straight into surgery. You can wait in the lobby and when we're done, I'll come get you and bring you to recovery."

They both stood. Anna grabbed his face and kissed him on the lips. "I love you, honey. Good luck."

"I love you too." Rapp turned and limped toward the door.

Anna followed him into the hall and watched the tiny nurse lead him away. She glimpsed his backside through the flapping gown and couldn't resist giving him a whistle. "Nice butt."

Rapp lowered his head and shook it at the same time. Anna stifled a laugh and cursed herself for not bringing the camera.

37

Gould had found the pickup truck the day before at a small used car lot on the outskirts of Annapolis. It was the type of place that preferred to deal in cash. The truck was black with a gray cloth interior. The asking price was $4,999.99. It had high miles, which he expected, and a few dents here and there, but otherwise it was in decent shape. He got the guy to come down to $4,500 on the price and paid him in hundreds. The only glitch came when the guy asked to see a proof of insurance. "Maryland state law," he told Gould. It was the one thing he hadn't thought of. Fortunately, the guy did not want to lose the sale, so he wrote down *Progressive* and told Gould to fax him the information when he had a chance.

Gould left the car lot and found a big auto center a few miles down the road. He dropped another twelve hundred bucks on new tires, belts, filters, an oil change, and a new battery. The car salesman had told him everything was in great shape, but Gould knew better than to trust him. With so much on the line it wasn't worth leaving the dependability of the vehicle to chance. The next stop was Home Depot, where he picked up an extension ladder, a chain and lock, a set of tools, an extension cord, two high-pressure hoses, five different types of tape, a roll of clear plastic, a utility knife, six five-gallon gas cans, two forty-gallon propane tanks, and a few other odds and ends. The final stop for the night was Radio Shack where he purchased a remote switch. Gould went back to the hotel, locked everything up in the truck, and chained the ladder to the truck bed.

He then went about briefing Claudia on the plan. Any anger he felt toward her over what had happened earlier that day was now mitigated by the news that Mitch Rapp would be going under the knife in the morning. Since Gould had first learned about the knee problem that morning things had only gotten better. Rapp's wife unwittingly gave Gould a constant stream of updates as she called friends and family and told them in detail that Rapp was going in for arthroscopic knee surgery in the morning. She had given away the entire timetable. When they were supposed to be at the hospital, and what time she expected to get back to the house. Gould had at minimum a seven-hour window to get things ready.

In almost all matters tactical, Claudia deferred to Louie. In this instance she made only one request—that he avoid killing the woman. She was not part of the contract. Gould had expected this, and it was one of the reasons that he had withheld from Claudia the fact that Rapp's wife was pregnant. He would make an effort to keep the woman out of it, but he would not let it compromise the mission. Rather than argue with her, though, he promised her that Rapp's wife would be fine.

Gould took the opportunity to lay down the law to Claudia. He didn't want her leaving the hotel until her new morning ritual was over. He couldn't have her out in public drawing attention to herself by throwing up every thirty minutes. Claudia agreed. She would stay back at the hotel and monitor the position of Anna's car and any new audio they might pick up. With the plan solidified they packed everything up. Gould would be leaving the hotel in the pickup truck before sunrise and Claudia would check out around noon as long as Anna's car stayed put at the hospital.

At 6:00 a.m. Gould left the hotel, and stopped at a gas station midway between the hotel and Rapp's house. He was wearing a pair of Carhartt blue jeans, brown work boots, a blue and gray flannel shirt, and a Washington Nationals baseball cap. He hadn't shaved in three days, and was already well on his way to having a full beard. Gould topped off the truck's tank and then filled all six gas cans. He grabbed a newspaper, paid for everything in cash, and left. At a separate gas station a few blocks away, he pulled in and had them fill the forty-pound propane tanks.

He'd picked out his spot the night before and pulled into the strip mall parking lot at exactly 6:22 in the morning. He checked the tracking device and noted that Rielly's car had not moved. He looked east and then west down the highway and wondered for the twentieth time what the odds were that they would take Rapp's car instead of hers. There wasn't much he could do at this point other than wait and see. Gould turned off the truck, went into the Starbucks and grabbed a black coffee. He came back out a few minutes later and settled in for what he hoped would be a short wait. He started reading the paper and tried to take his mind off what lay ahead. At 6:31 the device beeped, telling him that her car was moving. Gould breathed a sigh of relief. This was going to be much easier if they knew exactly where Rapp and his wife were.

Six minutes later, the blue BMW Series Five came flying past Gould. Rapp was in the passenger seat and his wife was driving. Gould watched with professional detachment. Rather than leave right away, he stayed put. Getting to the house too early might raise some suspicion, so he drank his coffee, read the paper, and kept on eye on the tracking device. At five minutes before seven Rielly's car stopped near George Washington University Hospital. Gould waited another fifteen minutes and then finished the last of the coffee. He backed out of the spot and headed for Rapp's house. A mile down the road he dialed Claudia's mobile phone. She answered on the fourth ring.

"*Allô.*"

Gould nearly bit his own tongue in an effort to stop himself from screaming at her for answering in French.

"How are you feeling?" he asked in a tense voice.

"Not good," she answered.

"Go back to sleep. I just wanted to tell you that everything looks good. I'm headed over. I'll call at ten to give you an update."

"Okay."

Gould ended the call and gripped the wheel tightly with both hands. Claudia was not herself. The sooner he got this over with the better. Gould considered how much of it was due to her being pregnant and how much of it was due to burnout. He'd noticed the first sign four months ago. She'd gotten drunk after an operation they'd run in Ukraine and asked him if he thought she would go to hell. A self-professed atheist, he told her there was no such thing as hell. She shook her head and told him he was wrong, and then she began to sob uncontrollably.

Gould looked back on it now and saw it all very clearly. Getting pregnant was her way out, and it was her hold on him. He had little doubt she had stopped taking the Pill. She wanted an excuse to walk away, and better yet, one that would make him walk away with her. Gould shared none of her guilt over what they had done, but he understood it. This one last job was all he wanted. Seven more hours tops was all he needed. Rapp was being handed to him on a silver platter. He'd be disoriented from surgery, his instincts and skills greatly diminished. He could never again hope to have such a chance. Six million dollars if he did it right. A total of eleven million dollars to kill one man. He must have really pissed someone off to get a price tag like that on his head. Gould smiled at the prospect of so much money. They would have true independence. Live wherever they wanted and do so lavishly. *A few more hours,* he told himself. *Keep it together and stay focused.*

When he reached the road that Rapp lived on, he put on his Oakley sunglasses and slowed down like he was looking for an address. From the county road turnoff it was 2.4 miles to Rapp's house. Gould passed an older couple walking their dogs, but that was it. He hoped it stayed this quiet all morning. He continued past Rapp's house to where the road dead-ended and then turned around and came back. Everything looked good. Rapp's car wasn't in the driveway so Gould assumed it was in the one-car garage.

He backed the pickup down the long driveway and came to a stop ten feet short of the garage. Gould hopped out and was putting on a pair of work gloves when a dog came bounding around the corner. For a split second he froze. The dog let out a bark, but it was not the kind of bark Gould was so familiar with, the type a dog gives right before it lunges for your throat. This was more playful. Gould took off one of his work gloves and squatted down. He held his hand out, palm up, and the dog approached tentatively. Once it got a good sniff of him the animal relaxed and Gould scratched its neck.

"Not much of a guard dog, are you?"

The dog, a collie mix of some sort, just wagged its tail and looked at Gould with its big brown eyes. Gould glanced around and wondered if the dog belonged to one of the neighbors. He couldn't imagine anything this docile was owned by Rapp. There was at least two hundred feet between houses on either side and there was a stand of trees and shrubs that delineated the property line. While the leaves had started to change color, none had yet fallen. Gould checked the dog's neck for a collar. It wasn't wearing one. *The important thing is to keep acting normal,* he told himself. If a neighbor came up he was here to do an estimate for new gutters.

Gould stood and unlocked the extension ladder. He lifted it out of the bed and carried it around to the side of the house where he set it on the ground. Six paces from the garage stood a big silver metallic propane tank. It was partially concealed on three sides by pyramidal arborvitae. Gould walked over and read the gauge. It was just over two thirds full. He nodded to himself and got to work. After standing the ladder up against the side of the house he went back to the truck and grabbed the roll of plastic, the knife, and tape. As he climbed onto the roof, the dog sat at the base of the ladder and watched him. Fortunately the fireplace and the two vents were all situated on the water side of the gable. Anyone driving down the road wouldn't see him on the roof except when he was working on the chimney. That's where Gould started. He tore off four long strips of duct tape and stuck them to the waist of his jeans. Next he cut out a large section of plastic and laid it over the top of the chimney. After all four sides were secured, he ran a strip of tape around the entire thing to make sure it was sealed. The vents took only a minute or two apiece.

Once off the roof he walked around to the back of the house. He stopped on the back deck for a moment and looked out at the bay. There were a couple of smaller boats not far from shore. He thought they were probably fishermen. Gould leaned over the railing. It was almost a straight drop down to the water. There were two boats tied up: a ski boat and a fishing boat with a deep v-hull. He walked up to the glass French doors and looked inside at the kitchen area. Going inside was a nonstarter. A guy like Rapp would have the place wired with every type of security device known.

Gould completed the circle of the house and ended up where he started. The air-conditioning unit was located between the propane tank and the house. Right next to where the cooling hose entered the house was the fresh air vent for the heating and cooling system. It was a six-by-six-inch galvanized cover that angled out from the house so that there was a three-by-six-inch opening at the bottom. Gould got down on one knee and with a needle-nose pliers removed the screen from the inside of the vent. He went back to the truck and got the extension cord and the remote receiving unit he'd picked up at Radio Shack. He plugged the remote receiving unit into an outdoor outlet, checked to make sure it was in the off position, and then walked to the end of the driveway. The dog followed him. He pointed the handheld remote at the garage, pressed the button once, and walked back. Gould was satisfied to see the remote receiving unit was now in the on position. He flipped it back to the off position and grabbed the extension cord.

The French Foreign Legion had taught him a lot of things, and one of them was how to make improvised explosive devices. Gould cut off the female end of the extension cord and stripped away the insulation. He twisted the two exposed wires together and then fed the cord into the fresh air vent on the side of the house. He figured eight feet was enough and plugged the male end into the remote receiving unit. Now things got a little tricky. Gould uncoiled the two high-pressure hoses, fed them into the vent with the extension cord, and then taped off the opening with plastic. There was only one thing left to do. He took the two forty-pound propane tanks from the truck, hooked them up to the high-pressure hoses, and opened the valves.

The dog came up and dropped a dirty tennis ball at his feet. Gould picked it up and threw it toward the road. The dog came roaring back and Gould gave the ball another good chuck. He checked his watch. It was ten after eight. He figured it would take about five more minutes to empty the tanks. Between throws of the tennis ball, he grabbed all but two of the gas cans and carried them over to the side of the house. Gould dropped down to one knee and listened to see if the propane was drained from the tanks. The hissing noise was gone, so he closed the valves and carefully extracted the high-pressure hoses from the side of the house. Gould quickly sealed the plastic with more duct tape, and then lined up the rectangular gas cans between the house and the large propane tank.

With a rubber-handled crescent wrench, he crawled under the big metallic tank and began to slowly loosen the gas line that ran from the bottom of the tank, underground, and into the house. With every half turn he'd stop and listen. He didn't want the connection too loose or the neighbors might smell it and call in a gas leak, or possibly Rapp and his wife. He wiggled the line a bit and gave it one more quarter turn. A soft hissing noise came from the connection and Gould caught a slight whiff of liquid propane. He remained there for a few minutes to see if it remained constant. It did, so he crawled out from under the tank and unscrewed the caps on each of the gas cans.

If all went according to plan, the gas cans would be knocked over by the initial explosion. The cascading fuel would reach the underside of the large tank almost immediately. The fireball from the house would ignite the gas which in turn would mix with the slow leak from the large tank. The secondary explosion would obliterate the extension cord, the remote receiving unit, the gas cans, and probably the entire house. With no evidence left, all fingers would be pointed at the Chesapeake Bay Propane Company.

38

Rapp came out of his drug-induced sleep feeling groggy and disoriented. After a moment he realized he was in a hospital room. He looked down the length of his body at his knee. His leg was there, but he couldn't feel anything. It was propped up in the air and covered with a blanket. Her touch was so gentle he didn't even notice at first that she was holding his hand. He slowly turned his head and looked into his wife's beautiful green eyes. Rapp blinked several times and looked around the room. The shades were drawn. He had no idea how long he'd been out. When he looked back at Anna, she smiled her perfect smile and asked him how he felt.

"Thirsty," he answered in a hoarse voice.

She raised the bed up a few degrees and gave him some water through a straw. "The doctor says you did great."

Rapp looked around the room again. "What time is it?"

"A little before eleven."

"In the morning?"

"Yes."

Rapp rubbed his eyes. "When can we get the hell out of here?"

She smiled. "I told them you wouldn't want to wait around."

"Can you open the shades?"

Rielly got up and pulled back the heavy gray plastic curtains.

Rapp squinted. He had the twisted look on his face that belongs to an extremely hungover man who is forced to endure the bright midday light without sunglasses. Anna knew there was no way they could keep him in bed for two more hours so she left to find his doctor. They came back a few minutes later and the doctor pulled back the sheet covering Rapp's legs. He carefully unwound the Ace bandage and removed the ice pack. Rapp looked at his knee. It was yellow from the betadine they'd used to sanitize it for surgery. Rapp was surprised that it wasn't more swollen and said so. The doctor explained that the surgery had gone very well. He'd cleaned out the cartilage and removed two bone spurs that were the likely cause of most of the discomfort.

"Can you feel anything, yet?" the doctor asked.

Rapp wondered which answer would get him home quicker. "A little bit."

"Does it hurt?"

Rapp shrugged.

The doctor nodded. "Since you've been running around on this thing for as long as you have, my guess is you have a pretty high tolerance for pain. Your wife said you'd like to get home as soon as possible."

"Yeah."

"How do you feel?" the doctor asked.

"Fine," Rapp lied. He had a splitting headache and was slightly nauseated.

"Your wife says you don't want to take anything stronger than Tylenol Three."

Rapp nodded.

"Good, but if you change your mind, call and we'll get you something better."

"The Tylenol will be fine."

"I'll get the nurse to give you a five-day supply. You're in great shape, so I think you're going to recover quickly."

Rapp sat up a little more. "When can I start running again?"

"I'd like to see you give it up altogether, but since I know that isn't going to happen, you should wait at least a month."

"A month?" Rapp asked, obviously not happy with the answer.

The truth was two weeks, but the doctor dealt with guys like this all the time. No matter what he told them, they'd divide by two. "You can do some light biking in four days, and you can try swimming as long as it doesn't hurt, but I really want you to lay off the running for at least four weeks. The first step though is to stay off it for the next forty-eight hours and you have to ice it every other hour." He looked at Anna. "When he goes to bed tonight, elevate the knee with a couple of pillows and put ice on it. Try to get up at least once and change the ice pack. Above all, though, make sure he stays off it and he keeps it elevated."

"When can I leave?" asked Rapp again.

"I'll get the paperwork started, and we'll get you out of here in no time."

Rapp's idea of no time was fifteen minutes. The doctor's was an hour, so it was 12:07 by the time they wheeled him out the front door. He was dressed in a pair of workout shorts and a blue Syracuse T-shirt. His knee was bandaged and he noticed for the first time someone had placed a powder blue booty on his left foot. Anna had the car pulled up to the curb and was standing by the open passenger door. Before the orderly could help, Rapp pushed himself out of the chair and put one hand on the open door and the other on the car's roof. He hopped into position and lowered himself into the seat. Anna helped him with the seatbelt and closed the door.

She got behind the wheel and pulled away from the hospital. "You must be starving."

Rapp dug through the glove box and found an old pair of sunglasses he kept in her car. Even though it was a slightly overcast day, the light was really bugging him. "Not really," he answered. "It must be the drugs."

"Straight home then?"

"Yeah."

They cruised through the light midday traffic and within ten minutes they were nearing the Beltway. Rapp was starting to feel better. Up ahead he spotted the golden arches and suddenly he was extremely hungry all over again.

"Let's stop at this McDonald's on the right."

"McDonald's?" she asked in a disapproving tone. Rielly was extremely health conscious.

"Honey, humor me. I'm starving."

"All right." She reluctantly hit the turn signal.

A few seconds later they were in the drive-through lane and Rapp was placing his order. When he was done he asked Anna if she wanted anything. She relented enough to order a Diet Coke and small fries.

Back on the road Rapp tore into his Big Mac with a fury. In between gulps of Coke and fistfuls of fries he finished the Big Mac in short order and moved on to a Quarter Pounder with cheese.

Anna sipped on her Diet Coke and frowned. "You might want to slow down, honey."

Rapp kept eating and she kept driving. He'd finished every last scrap of food and was working on his large Coke when they turned onto their street. Rapp leaned back and said, "That really tasted good, but why do I get the feeling I'm going to regret eating it?"

"Maybe because you just consumed an entire day's worth of calories, and enough fat, salt, and sugar to last you a week."

Rapp knew she was right, but he turned to her and said, "Oh, was it ever delicious though."

"You're definitely going to regret it."

Rapp looked down the road. Their house was coming up on the left. A sweat was forming on his forehead and upper lip. His stomach turned and he felt a little light-headed. He looked over at Anna and said, "I think I already am."

39

After leaving the house, Gould drove up to Annapolis and ditched the ladder in an alley. Out on Riva Road he wiped down the handles of the propane tanks and left them behind a gas station. The rest of the stuff, with the exception of the two remaining gas cans, was thrown into a garbage bag and tossed in a Dumpster behind a grocery store. It was 10:23 when he got back to the hotel, and he was relieved to find Claudia packed and ready to go. Gould changed into his biking clothes and helped her go over the room one last time to make sure they'd wiped away any fingerprints. When they were done he used the express checkout function on the TV and they left the hotel through a side door.

Gould opened the back hatch of the rented Ford Explorer and lifted out his mountain bike. He set it in the pickup bed and asked Claudia, "Any questions?"

She looked like she might say something for a moment and then she simply shook her head.

"Go to Galesville and do a little shopping. Get some lunch if you want, but make sure you've got a signal on your phone at all times. As soon as I'm in position I'll call."

Claudia reached out and grabbed his face. "I know you're worried about me, but you do not have to be. I want to be done with this more than you do."

This was exactly what Gould wanted to hear. He put his hands on Claudia's waist. "Good. Be ready to move in case I need you." He kissed her on the lips and then whispered in her ear, "Let's get through the next few hours, and then we'll put it all behind us."

She wrapped her arms around his neck and held on tight. "I love you."

"I love you too." Gould held her for a long moment and then opened her car door. "I'll see you in a few hours."

GOULD HAD MISSED the path that first night when they'd followed Rapp's wife home, but when he and Claudia took their bikes by the house the next morning it jumped right out at him. There were no posted signs. He didn't need to say anything to Claudia, she just followed him. As far as Gould could tell it wasn't maintained by anyone. It was simply a dirt path, worn by use and use alone. They followed it for just under a mile through the woods until it split. The trail to the left led to a small public beach and to the right it joined up with a dirt road that ran along the edge of a small grass landing strip. Gould followed the dirt road until it hooked up with a county road and noted the spot on the map. On the way back he noted a few places where he could leave a vehicle.

He was now on that road, and so far his luck was holding. There wasn't a soul around. Up ahead he spotted the big oak tree he'd seen the day before and he pulled the truck as far off the road as he could. Gould put on his backpack and helmet and took out the mountain bike. Right as he was about to get on the bike, the tracking device in his backpack beeped. Gould took the pack off and looked at the GPS locator. Rielly's car was on the move. He clipped the device to one of the backpack's shoulder straps with a carabiner and got on the bike. He wanted to be settled in well before they got there.

It took him only five minutes to bike through the woods, and then he continued past Rapp's house for a few hundred yards and came back. He was fairly confident that no one was about, so when he got back to Rapp's house he hopped off the bike and picked it up with his right hand. He stepped over the first bit of grass carefully and then had to duck under the leafy branches and twist around others. He did not have to go far to find decent concealment—maybe twenty feet. He set the bike down on its side and took off the backpack. He pulled out a camouflaged hunting poncho and the 9mm Glock. He screwed the silencer onto the end of the Glock and chambered a round. The underside of the backpack had a large pocket. Gould unzipped it and slid the pistol in, silencer first. He shouldered the backpack again and checked to make sure he could reach around and grab the weapon. It wasn't ideal, but it worked.

Gould opencd his phone and punched in Claudia's number. She answered on the first ring and he said, "They're on their way."

"Good. Is everything set?"

"Yes."

"If you need me let me know."

"Absolutely. I'll see you in a little bit." He hit the End button and switched the phone over to the silent mode.

Gould lay down flat and covered his upper body and most of the bike with the hunting poncho. Its muted green and brown pattern blended in perfectly with the surrounding foliage. The air felt heavy like it was going to rain, which would be welcome as long as it didn't come too early. He needed the fire to destroy the majority of the evidence. After that the rain would help destroy it even further.

Gould was keenly aware of the GPS tracker and followed the progress of the vehicle closely. When they were two miles away, Gould turned the device off and picked up the handheld remote for the switch. It was a small black device similar in looks and size to the keyless door remotes sold with cars. Gould was careful not to press the button. He held the device gently in his right hand and focused on his breathing.

A short while later he heard a car approaching. He closed his eyes and listened intently. It had to be them. The noise grew and he looked to his left to get a glimpse of the vehicle but the woods were too thick. Gould held his position and waited. Patience was an integral part of any ambush. It would all be over in a minute as long as he held still. Rapp would walk in the house and he would die. No American would ever know he'd been here, and although they might suspect foul play, there would be no way to prove it. Rapp's enemies were terrorists, men who were not known for their subtle skills. What terrorist would ever go to the effort to make Rapp's death look like an accident? The answer was none. If it was a terrorist group, they would have driven a car bomb right through the front door and then called every media outlet available and taken credit for the death of Mitch Rapp. As much as they would hate the fact that their great counterterrorist operative had been killed by a gas explosion, a mere accident, the Americans would have no choice but to believe it, no matter the suspicions they harbored.

The car approached from the left and was almost even with his position when he got his first glimpse of it. The BMW slowed and then

turned into the driveway. Gould caught a quick glimpse of Rapp's profile, and the hair on his arms rose. He forced himself to stay put for a little
longer. He watched the car as it came to a stop in front of the garage and
then rose up on one knee. Even though it was doubtful that Rapp would
ever look in this direction, Gould was careful to keep most of his body
behind a tree. The driver's side door opened first. Rapp's wife hopped out
and Gould watched her with complete detachment. He'd already rationalized it away. She was well aware of who her husband was. She was what
the Americans liked to call collateral damage. In the larger scope of the
mission she was an acceptable loss. Gould had no doubt that Rapp would
feel the same way if the roles were reversed.

Anna hurried around to the passenger side and opened the back
door. She bent in and came out with a pair of crutches. The front door
opened and a leg swung out. Gould tensed only slightly. Rapp grabbed
the door frame and pulled himself from the car. The dog that had followed Gould around earlier came running up. They appeared to be more
concerned with getting Rapp in the house than saying hello to the dog,
so Gould couldn't tell if the dog was theirs or the neighbors'. Gould
noted that Rapp didn't look very good. It was probably from the surgery.
Rapp hopped on one leg, got the crutches right, and then the two of
them started down the sidewalk. The dog followed them. They now had
their backs to his position. Gould got to his feet and kept the poncho over
his head and shoulders. He stayed in a crouch and began quietly working
his way to the road. There were no other noises. No cars, only a few birds
chirping.

He reached the edge of the woods as she slid the key into the door.
Gould dropped the poncho and extended the small black handheld remote. He was ready to sprint across the street if the distance was too great.
The door opened and she stepped in first. Rapp remained on the threshold for an excruciating second and then he followed her in. Gould
pressed the remote and there was nothing. He pressed it again, and began
walking across the road. He pointed the device toward the garage. Still
nothing happened. Gould had reached the start of their driveway and he
was about to press the button yet again when he realized they had left the
car door open. He paused for a split second and realized Rielly would
have to come back out and close the door. His thumb remained poised
above the button. He heard Claudia's words, asking him to not harm the
wife. Gould swore to himself.

Straight ahead there was no cover, only the openness of the driveway and their front lawn. To the left there were trees and a few bushes. Gould broke into a sprint and started counting. He knew the house door could remain open for easily a minute if not longer, but he wasn't going to wait anywhere near that long. He would give her ten seconds and that was all. When he reached the clump of light blue hydrangeas he was at five seconds and a good twenty feet closer to the house than where he'd tested it from this morning. It was then that Gould realized the weather had changed. The air was heavier. Instead of hiding behind the hydrangeas he started moving again and kept his eyes on the front door. At eight seconds he heard her voice from inside the house. His arm was still extended. When he finished his count he pressed the button. At exactly the same moment she appeared in the doorway. Gould swore that for the briefest of moments they made eye contact, and then the explosion tore through the still afternoon air. An orange fireball burst from the house, sending glass, splintered wood, and Rapp's wife flying.

Gould dropped to a knee and buried his head between his arms. He wasn't overly worried about the first explosion. It was the big propane tank that gave him the greatest concern, and he was right. The second explosion, far more violent than the first, let loose a concussive blast that hit Gould with a heat wave that knocked him from his crouched position to the ground. Debris rained down all around him and he struggled to get to his feet. His glasses and bike helmet were still on but knocked askew. He straightened them and noticed a stinging sensation on his left arm. He looked down to find the hair on his forearm gone and his skin turning a bright pink. His ears were ringing, and he felt a bit disoriented. He remembered there was one thing left that he had to do. He ignored the pain and took a step toward the BMW. He wanted to get the bug and tracking device from the vehicle. He didn't make it more than a step. The vehicle was on fire. He hesitated for a second and a voice told him to get the hell out of there.

Gould ran back into the woods, picking up the poncho and stuffing it in his backpack. He picked up the bike and hustled back to the road. Before coming out he looked both ways to see if anyone was coming. The street was still empty. He wheeled the bike up onto the road and looked at the house, or what little was left of it. The roof and most of the garage were gone. Trees were on fire, as was the BMW, and none of it showed any signs of slowing. Gould started pedaling. He swerved to miss a chunk of wood with shingles still attached. The entire lawn was littered with junk. Next to a tree about thirty feet from the front door Gould saw two legs sticking out beneath a pile of debris. She had been in the door-way when the blast occurred and that would have been about where she'd landed. Gould didn't give it much thought, but it was possible that she was still alive. The important thing now, though, was to get as far away from here as quickly as possible. The blast would have been heard for miles around and it was sure to attract people. Gould raised his butt off the seat, put his head down, and started pedaling as fast as he could.

40

Rapp's eyes fluttered and then opened. He looked up at the faint light and the acoustic ceiling tiles. *Where the hell am I?* he thought to himself. He tried to lift his head, but his body wouldn't cooperate with his brain. He lay there completely still for a long moment. Nothing made sense. Finally, with what seemed like a monumental effort he got his head to roll to the left. There was a window with the shades drawn. There was no light around the edges so he assumed it was nighttime. There was an empty chair and railing on the side of the bed. Things were looking vaguely familiar. He blinked and looked at his arm. An IV was inserted in the back of his hand. *I'm in a hospital.* He remembered his knee surgery and for a second everything made sense. Then an unsettling feeling of déjà vu rolled over his body. Things weren't adding up. He'd already left the hospital.

What in the hell am I doing back here?

He rolled his head to the other side and saw that his right arm was in a cast. His brow furrowed. Nothing was making sense. He looked up at the door and something clicked. He had left the hospital. He remembered driving home with his wife. He remembered coming in the house and not feeling well. He remembered being on crutches and going for the back door, feeling that a little fresh air might help. He'd just gotten the door open and hopped onto the deck when he . . . he couldn't remember anything after that. Rapp looked up at the ceiling again, and wondered if he'd blacked out. He tried to lift his right arm to scratch his face, but it didn't cooperate. He remembered the cast. For a split second he thought he was paralyzed, and then he was able to wiggle his fingers.

I must have blacked out. It's the only thing that makes sense.

Rapp had never done well with drugs before. He went back to his last memory of standing on the deck, leaning against the railing and taking some gulps of air. There was no denying it; the fast food he had devoured was not helpful. Rapp thought of the steep stairs that led down to the dock and the crutches.

I must have lost my balance and fallen. That's how I broke my arm.

There was movement near the door, and Rapp turned his head to see who it was. Just that small effort sent pain screaming up his neck to his forehead. Rapp winced as his head began to throb. That pain led to the realization that more than just his head hurt. He took a deep breath and suddenly felt as if someone was sticking a knife into his side. A figure came through the door, but his eyes couldn't focus. He thought it was his wife for a second, but as the form stepped from the shadows into the faint circle of light that surrounded the bed, he realized it was Irene Kennedy. As she came closer, Rapp realized she'd been crying. It occurred to him that his injuries must be pretty serious.

She placed a hand on his cheek and said, "You had us worried there for a while."

"Where am I?" Rapp whispered.

"You're at Johns Hopkins."

A second person entered the room. It was a man Rapp did not recognize. "Where is Anna?"

Kennedy started to say something and then stopped. Her eyes filled with tears, and she said, "Mitch, there was an explosion."

"Where's Anna?" he asked in a much louder voice. Suddenly two more people entered the room. They were big guys wearing surgical scrubs. Rapp looked at Kennedy, panic in his eyes. The tears were now rolling down her cheeks and her bottom lip was trembling.

"Dammit!" he yelled. "Where is Anna?"

Kennedy lowered her eyes and said, "She was killed in the explosion."

Rapp's entire body tensed as he let loose an agonizing scream. With anger, shock, fear, and misery coursing through his body, he somehow managed to jerk himself halfway out of the bed before the two large orderlies and the doctor could wrestle him back down.

Kennedy had warned the doctor there was a good chance Rapp

would need to be restrained when he came to. The doctor listed off the injuries: two broken ribs, a broken right arm, a deep contusion on the right thigh, a left knee that had just been operated on, and swelling on the back of the brain. He assured Kennedy that the patient wouldn't be going anywhere for some time.

As the orderlies held him down, the doctor jabbed a needle in his thigh and hit the plunger. After about ten seconds the fight was out of Rapp. The orderlies released him and took a step back. Rapp lay there motionless, staring up at the ceiling, a single tear moving slowly from the corner of his right eye and tracing a path down his cheek.

THERE WASN'T MUCH left of the house other than the reinforced steel door frames, the chimney, a small section of the staircase, and a few charred studs that jutted up from the smoking hulk of the first floor. The entire scene was illuminated with portable floodlights. Gas-powered electric generators hummed in the night air while firefighters picked through the rubble with axes and long crowbars. Skip McMahon surveyed the scene from the end of the driveway. He was a big man, over six feet tall and closer to 250 pounds than he was to 200. He'd been with the FBI thirty-five years and this one hit close to home. He knew both Rapp and his wife and liked them. Kennedy had called McMahon and asked him to treat the house as a potential crime scene even though the sheriff for Anne Arundel County was calling it an accidental explosion.

Normally the FBI would have no jurisdiction over something like this, but Rapp was a federal agent, and if it turned out the explosion was intentional, they would take over the investigation. For now, though, McMahon and the agents he'd brought from the Washington Field Office were there to watch and try not to upset the apple cart. The Anne Arundel sheriff's department was well funded and professional. McMahon had worked with local law enforcement enough over the years to know that coming in and acting like you were hot shit did nothing but aggravate an already difficult situation.

McMahon leaned against his government-issue sedan and took a swig of lukewarm coffee. The sheriff approached and stopped a few paces away. He knew the Anne Arundel County sheriff from the DC-Baltimore Joint Terrorism Task Force. The man started talking, and despite the fact that McMahon disagreed with him he listened patiently.

"I'm telling you, Skip, I know it's hard to believe, but we get one of these explosions every year or so. Usually no one's home, but it happens."

McMahon looked at the smoking pile of debris that was once Rapp's house. "Pat, I'm only going to say it one more time. Guys like Mitch Rapp don't get blown up by accident."

"And terrorists don't fake explosions. You said it yourself. They like machine guns, they like suicide bombers, they like headlines. They don't kill people and try to make it look like an accident."

McMahon had to admit he was having a hard time squaring this one glaring inconsistency. The sheriff was right; terrorists liked big explosions. That's what got them news coverage. McMahon didn't know a lot about the forensics of bombs, but so far the local experts were saying all evidence pointed to a propane explosion. McMahon wanted to be sure, so he'd put a call into headquarters and asked for them to send the bureau's forensic bomb people out here. They were the best in the world, and if they couldn't find anything, he doubted they could prove it wasn't an accident. If that was the case the FBI would pack up its bags and head back to DC. The only thing left to take care of would be the insurance.

"Has anyone taken credit for the explosion?" the sheriff asked.

McMahon shook his head. The agents back at the Joint Counterterrorism Center were monitoring all news outlets for mention of the attack. McMahon had been tempted to pass on what Kennedy had told him about the threat on Rapp's life that had come in the week before, but for now he decided to withhold the information. Investigations were always tricky when they involved multiple jurisdictions, but they were never more complicated than when they involved the CIA. For good reason, the CIA didn't like sharing its sources and methods. Especially when judges ordered them to hand such information over to lawyers who represented suspected terrorists.

The sheriff was hammering his point home to McMahon when one of his deputies came up. Two men in street clothes were following him.

"Boss," the deputy said to the sheriff, "these two guys say they're here to see a Special Agent McMahon."

The sheriff jerked his thumb toward McMahon. "Here he is."

"There's also a news van at the checkpoint."

"Crap," said the sheriff.

"It's the NBC affiliate from Baltimore," the deputy offered. "They know the wife died. They said the network sent them down to get some footage for a tribute they're going to run in the morning."

"What do you think?" the sheriff asked McMahon.

One of the men who had come up with the deputy looked at

McMahon and shook his head. McMahon was not surprised that the man did not want cameras around. He looked over at the smoking house and turned to the deputy. "Tell them we're checking for gas leaks. It'll be about another hour."

The sheriff nodded his consent and the deputy left.

"Sheriff," said McMahon, "if you'll excuse me for a minute, I need to talk to these gentlemen."

"I'll go make sure the TV crew doesn't weasel their way in here."

"Good idea." When the sheriff was gone, McMahon looked at the two men. He knew the blond-haired man, but had never met the other guy. He could tell a great deal, though, by taking a quick inventory of him. He was wearing jeans, hiking boots, and a black Mountain Hardwear fleece jacket. He had a large black rubber dive watch on his right wrist, his hair was dark and shaggy, and although he was a good seventy-five pounds lighter than the FBI agent, McMahon had no doubt the little scrapper could kill him without breaking a sweat. The guy was Special Forces from head to toe.

All of this was easy to surmise since he already knew for a fact that the other man had indeed been Special Forces. McMahon turned his attention back to the taller of the two. "Scott Coleman," he said, "I was about to say you're the last person I expected to see, but now that I think about it I should have expected you."

"Irene called me." The former SEAL was all business. "She wanted us to take a look around."

McMahon thought about that for a second. He wasn't so sure he agreed with the director of the CIA. "Who's your friend?"

Coleman started to answer, and then McMahon put his hand out and cut him off. "Never mind," the agent said. "I don't want to know. Do I?"

Coleman shrugged. "It wasn't like I was going to give you his real name."

McMahon shook his head and turned toward the house. "You ever been here before?"

Coleman nodded.

"I suppose you and Mitch are pretty tight."

"Yeah." Coleman looked at the other man he'd come with and made a slight gesture with his head. "You know what to look for."

The man looked each way down the road, nodded, and was gone.

"They're saying it's a gas explosion."

McMahon nodded. "Propane."

"Who?"

"The sheriff and the fire chief."

"Can I talk to the fire chief?"

"Sure, follow me." They walked roughly halfway down the driveway and found the county fire chief nudging a piece of debris with his boot. The man had gotten rid of his jacket, but he was still wearing his heavy boots, helmet, and fire-resistant overalls. McMahon made a quick introduction, telling the chief Coleman's first name and nothing more.

The fire chief started by pointing back toward the left side of the charred house. "We found some traces of an accelerant over there where the garage used to be and near where the propane tank used to sit."

McMahon gave the fire chief a quick "See, I told you so" look and said, "So it isn't an accident after all."

"I wouldn't say that."

"I thought you said you found traces of an accelerant."

"I did, but it's not unusual to find traces like that in and around the garage. I see he has a couple of boats, it's a pretty big yard to mow . . . I'm sure he stored gas in the garage. He may have even had one of those gas caddies with a long hose. They're real popular around here. You save about fifty cents a gallon if you buy it at a gas station rather than filling up at the marinas."

Coleman nodded.

"A gas caddie?" asked McMahon.

"Yeah . . . they're a cross between a two-wheeler and big gas can." The chief gestured with his hands to show McMahon the approximate size. "They usually hold between twenty-five and fifty gallons. They're red, they have a hand pump, a hose, and a nozzle. You can wheel them around, but you'd never want to take it down stairs like the ones going down to the dock here. You'd just walk the hose down, leave the caddie up at the top, and fill the boats."

McMahon got the picture. "Can you tell if the accelerant was gas?"

"Pretty sure."

"How sure?"

"Ninety percent," answered the chief.

"Can you tell how much was used?"

"I'm not sure any was used," the fire chief said cautiously. "I'm just telling you it's pretty common for people to keep gas in their garage, especially around here, and when there's an explosion like this one, the gas goes up just like everything else."

"Can you show me where you found the traces?" Coleman asked.

"Follow me." The chief led them past the charred hulk of a burned-out car and pointed at the ground. "This is where the outer wall of the garage used to sit. You can see here where the slab starts." The chief kicked at the ground with his boot.

"Where did you find the traces of accelerant?"

The chief stepped over some debris and said, "It was concentrated in this area right here. From the outer wall of the garage to roughly over here."

Coleman remembered where the propane tank used to sit.

"My guess is," the chief pointed at the ground, "he had a small utility shed right there where he kept the gas. We think this might have been a two-banger. The first explosion came from the gas that had leaked into the house, and then the second explosion was the tank itself touching off a short while later."

"Any other hot spots?"

"We got a couple reads in the garage, but relatively small compared to this one."

The former SEAL nodded and said, "Thanks, Chief." He took McMahon by the elbow and led him back toward the road. When they were far enough away he said, "Mitch never had one of those gas caddies. At least not that I ever saw, and I can guarantee you, he didn't keep gas stored in a shed outside the garage a few feet from his propane tank."

"You know that for a fact."

"I know how the man thinks. He was very careful. There was no way in hell he would have stored gas in an outdoor shed, let alone that close to a propane tank."

"So what are you telling me?"

"I'm telling you Mitch didn't leave any gas outside his garage. You can figure the rest out on your own."

When they reached the street, Coleman looked back toward the house and beyond. He could see a few navigation lights out on the bay. "Irene tells me a fisherman pulled Mitch from the water."

"Yeah." McMahon pulled a small notebook from his suit coat pocket. "A local guy from Shady Side. Harold S. Cox." McMahon pointed north. "He was only a couple hundred yards away when the explosion happened. He says he literally saw Mitch flying through the air. He saw him hit the dock and then roll into the water. If the guy hadn't been there Mitch probably would have drowned."

Coleman was putting himself in the shoes of whoever it was who had tried to kill his friend. As a former SEAL he was drawn to the water. "Any other boats?"

"Two. They both called nine-one-one and helped Mr. Cox give CPR."

"Have they been thoroughly checked?"

"We're working on it right now."

"Did any of them see anything out of the ordinary?"

"Nothing came up during the initial interview that was handled by the sheriff's department."

Coleman's companion emerged from the woods. He held up his forefinger and said, "One guy. He had a bike, and he wasn't here long."

McMahon was completely dumbfounded. "Where? Show me?"

The guy walked over to the edge of the road and pressed his thumb down on the end of his tactical flashlight. The tiny device was extremely powerful. "See how the tall grass is pushed toward the street in that single line? Those are bike tires. The markings on the right are footprints. The tire track curves this way." The man pointed south. "The street dead-ends down there, but there's a trail that cuts through the woods." He looked at Coleman. "I've run it with Mitch before. After about a mile the trail forks—east to a beach and west, where it hooks up with a dirt road that runs along the edge of a small airstrip back out to one of the county roads."

"Back up a minute," said McMahon. "There were a fair amount of people running around here after the explosion. When I arrived on the scene I remember at least one person with a bike and who knows how many had already come and gone. How do we know it wasn't some neighbor who made that track?"

"Can you give me one good reason why a neighbor would carry their bike twenty feet into the woods, lay it down on the ground, and then lie down next to it?"

"Not off the top of my head."

The man looked back at Coleman. "I'm going to take a look at the path and see what I can find." He held up a Nextel two-way mobile phone. "I'll check in with you in fifteen."

"You want me to come with?"

The guy shook his head. "This tango is long gone." Without another word, the man took off jogging down the street.

"Who the hell is he?" asked McMahon.

"He's the best sniper I've ever seen. He can track anything."

"He works for you now?"

"Yep."

"Lovely. God, I hope you don't end up with the FBI on your doorstep someday."

"You and I both."

The sheriff returned, mumbling something under his breath. It was obvious things hadn't gone so well at the roadblock. "This TV crew is getting really pushy. They know we're stonewalling them. I spoke to their news director myself and he says we have five minutes until he gets a lawyer and judge involved. They're demanding to know the status of the husband, and they said they don't care if he worked for the CIA and neither will the judge."

Before McMahon could answer, Coleman said, "Sheriff, will you give us just a minute?"

The sheriff appeared hesitant at first and then consented. Coleman pulled McMahon a few feet away. "Can you take your FBI hat off for a second?"

"Do you really have to ask me that?" McMahon had proven to Coleman in the past that he was willing to look the other way.

"Throw the TV crew a bone. Have the deputy tell them Mitch is dead."

"Why in the hell would I want to do that?"

Coleman stared at him with a look that said, Do I really have to explain this to you? He would have preferred to not have this conversation with a law enforcement officer, but there wasn't a lot of time. "This was not an accident. It was a contract kill. One guy, maybe two."

"You're sure?"

"Yes."

"So why do you want us to leak to the press that Mitch is dead?"

"Theoretically speaking, in this line of work you get paid anywhere from a third to half of the fee as a down payment, and then when you complete the job you get the rest of the fee. If you don't complete the job, you don't get the rest of the money."

"And your point is?"

"If the media reports that Mitch is dead, this person will get the rest of the fee. Money will have to change hands. Probably a lot of it. That creates a trail."

"What if they get paid cash?"

"No trail, but my guess is a professional contract on Mitch would run at least four million dollars, maybe double that."

"And your point?"

"That's a lot of cash. Not the type of thing you want to try and get through customs. When you start talking that kind of money you're better off setting up dummy offshore corporations and transferring it electronically. The amount of money that's moved around every day is astronomical. It's like the old needle in the haystack."

"Then how in the hell are we going to find it?"

Coleman grinned. "We wait a few days . . . maybe more, and then we let it be known that Mitch is still alive. Whoever ordered the hit is going to be pissed. They're going to demand that this guy finish the job or give the money back." Coleman shrugged his shoulders. "Maybe we get lucky and they simply reverse the wire transfer. Same banks . . . same amount. The original transfer will be made tomorrow or the day after, and the refund will be made within a day or two from when it's announced that he's still alive. We could trace it."

"And if these guys decided they'd rather finish the job than give the money back?"

Coleman's face took on a wolfish smile. "Well, now that'd be even better, wouldn't it?"

McMahon got real uncomfortable. "Scott, you guys need to sit this one out and let us handle it."

Coleman let loose an ominous laugh. "Yeah, right. I talked to Irene on the way over here. He's awake." The former SEAL stopped and looked at McMahon for a long moment. "He knows she's dead. When he gets out of that hospital what do you think he's going to do? Sit on the sidelines like a good little Boy Scout while you guys push your subpoenas through the courts and try to get foreign governments to cooperate? Best-case scenario your investigation will take two years." Coleman shook his head. "It ain't gonna fuckin' happen. I'm telling you right now he's going to kill every last motherfucker who had anything to do with this, and there is nothing any of you can do to stop him."

McMahon ran a hand over his face and sighed. He knew Coleman was right. "Jesus, this is going to get ugly."

"You're damn right, and I've got a word of advice for you. Skip. Just get out of the way and tell anyone you care about to do the same."

41

Gould awoke to the sound of the TV and Claudia crying. It took him a moment to even remember where he was and he looked at the TV and saw a photo of Anna Rielly. They'd first heard the news on the radio the night before, driving through Columbus, Ohio. Claudia cried for the better part of an hour. Fortunately, he had told her the truth, which was that he didn't know if the woman had survived. He had waited as long as he could before triggering the explosion and when he left the scene she was in the front yard.

When they reached the hotel in Indianapolis, Claudia cried herself to sleep and now here she was in the morning shedding yet more tears. This pregnancy thing was really screwing with her emotions, and Gould didn't know how much more he could take. He'd tried to console her with words, he'd tried to comfort her by holding her, but nothing was working. This was not the first time he'd killed someone other than the primary target, and she had never so much as had a sniffle before.

Gould rolled out of bed and went into the bathroom. After relieving himself he stood in front of the mirror staring at his reflection. He looked the same. Same hazel eyes, same wavy brown hair, same broken nose. Nothing had changed, inside or out, for him, but something had fundamentally changed for Claudia. As they were falling asleep in the hotel room, Gould reached out and placed his hand on her shoulder. It was a gesture he'd made countless times. It was silent in nature, but it communicated the simple message that he was there for her. He did not expect his touch to cause her to shudder and whimper with even greater intensity.

Although her reaction hurt his feelings, he was too tired to pursue something that he knew words could not solve. This was going to take time.

Gould was still tired. After leaving Rapp's house he'd thrown the bike
in the back of the pickup truck and whipped a quick U-turn. Back on
the paved roads he made his way over to U.S. Route 301 and took it
south across the Potomac River and into Virginia. He'd located Caledon
State Park on a map, and it looked to be the perfect place to dump the
truck. It was only a few miles across the river into Virginia. Gould drove
past the main entrance and continued down Virginia State Route 218
until he found a secondary road that led into the park. A half mile into
the park, with no one else in sight, he put the truck into four-wheel drive
and turned onto an overgrown trail. Once he'd made it far enough in that
he could no longer see the road through his rearview mirror he shut the
engine off and grabbed his backpack and helmet. Gould took the license
plates off, shoved a hand towel from the hotel into the gas tank, and then
doused the cab and the rest of the vehicle in gasoline. The forest looked
pretty dry so he took a few steps back before lighting the match and then
let it fly.

He took off on the mountain bike and was near the town of Osso
when the fire trucks passed him heading in the other direction. Thirty-
four minutes later he pulled up in front of the James Monroe Museum
and left the bike unlocked in a bike stand. He then walked three blocks
and found Claudia waiting behind the wheel of a white Town and
Country minivan. Gould got in the front passenger seat, kissed her, and
they were on their way. Once they were a few miles outside of town
Gould had her pull over and he took over driving duties. He set the
cruise control five miles an hour over the posted limit and told Claudia to
e-mail the German and tell him it was done. That was when she'd asked
about Rapp's wife.

They'd driven through the late afternoon and well into the night.
Gould wanted to get as far away from Washington as possible. They were
now on their third rental car in as many days, all of them acquired under
a new license and credit card. There was no trail for anyone to follow.
They were going to disappear into America's heartland for a month if
need be and then make their move. At least that had been the plan, but
now Claudia was acting so strange, Gould wondered if it wouldn't be
better to turn south and get her out of the country.

He looked at his watch. It was 8:06 in the morning, and he was
horny. He stared at his reflection in the mirror and told himself to get any

thought of sex out of his head. He told himself it was the pregnancy. Once she got her hormones under control she'd be fine. She'd be back to her old self. Maybe she'd even miss the thrill of the hunt. He knew he would.

Gould came out of the bathroom. Claudia was propped up in bed, a box of tissues on her lap, her normally beautiful almond-shaped brown eyes looking very tired and puffy. Gould turned off the TV and said, "Stop torturing yourself. What's done is done."

She shook her head and refused to look at him. "How did it ever come to this?" *"Comment en est-on arrivé à un tel point?"*

Considering her current fragile state he didn't even bother to reprimand her, but he did note that her operational discipline was shot. It might not be wise to take her anywhere. "Darling, we have been through a lot together. The important thing is that we are putting all of it behind us. Do I wish things could have ended differently? Of course, but I have told you before . . . she knew who she was married to. Mitch Rapp was responsible for hundreds, maybe thousands of deaths. How many innocent women and children do you think were sacrificed so he could kill someone the United States deemed a terrorist?"

"I don't know." She raised her chin in defiance. "And neither do you. I think the Americans practice great restraint in this awful war."

"The Americans, with their arrogance, have brought this on themselves."

"You better be careful." Claudia raised her voice. "You're beginning to sound like some of my old university friends who you despise so much."

The mere mention of her socialist deadbeat friends sent Gould's temper flaring. The last thing they needed was a shouting match that ended with the hotel calling the police, so he checked his temper and in as calm a voice as he could muster said, "Everybody is killing each other. Each side tries to take the righteous high ground, and all we've done is sit in the middle and profit."

"It's a hell of a way to make a profit." She looked out the window and shook her head.

It was obvious she was disgusted, but Gould couldn't tell if it was with him or herself. "Claudia, I'm sorry." Part of him wanted to scream at her to go turn herself in if it bothered her so fucking much, but that wouldn't solve a thing. He lowered his head, and even though he didn't mean it, he said, "I'm sorry, I let you down."

With that he put on a pair of jeans and a sweatshirt and picked up the car keys sitting on the desk.

"Where are you going?" Claudia asked.

"I'm not sure." He grabbed a Chicago Cubs baseball cap he'd purchased at a truck stop yesterday evening and slid into his tennis shoes.

"I thought you wanted to get on the road."

He detected a bit of nervousness in her voice, which was what he wanted to hear. "I get the feeling you'd rather not be around me right now." Gould grabbed the door handle and said, "I'll be back in time to check out. If you decide you'd like us to go our separate ways I'll understand." Before she could say anything Gould opened the door and was gone. Pregnancy or not, he felt he had to do something to snap her out of her current emotional state. Yelling at her would only make things worse. Passive-aggressive was the better path to take. A subtle threat to leave would force her to look at more than just the last twenty-four hours. She knew he loved her, but she also knew he had the lone wolf gene in him. A little solitude and the thought of raising their child all on her own would get her thinking rationally again.

42

Irene Kennedy was emotionally drained. She'd gone straight from the hospital to CIA headquarters with the knowledge that she needed to put things in motion before meeting with the president and several of his cabinet members in the morning. From the moment the doctor told her Anna was dead, she knew where they were headed. There would be no stopping him. Under normal circumstances he was difficult enough to manage, but now in the wake of his own personal hell, it was foolish to think that anyone could control him. There would be those in Washington, however, who would think otherwise—powerful people who were used to having their orders followed to the letter.

Where the president would fall in this regard, Kennedy was unsure, but she had little doubt where her new boss would come down on the issue. Support from the other members of the National Security Council was sure to be sparse. Some of them would be deeply concerned that the rule of law be followed, and others would be terrified over the thought of a vengeful American on the loose undermining their diplomatic efforts. One or two of the members might support Rapp, but they would never do so publicly. For all of its bellicose underpinnings, Washington was a town that prided itself on civility. These people would blanch at the idea of a government employee on the loose seeking vengeance for the murder of his wife.

If they wanted to avoid the inevitable they had just two options. The first would be to incarcerate him, but Kennedy had already taken the precaution of having Rapp transferred from Johns Hopkins to a CIA safe house in rural Virginia. Even if they somehow managed to jail him it would only be a temporary solution. They could not hold him forever. The other, more permanent, solution would be to have him killed. The problem here was that the only people with the temerity to do so, the quiet warriors like Coleman, were already lining up to support him. Kennedy knew that in a month or a year many of these civilian leaders would have wished that they had thought of killing him, but none of them had the stomach to issue such an order. For now, though, they would delude themselves into believing they could actually order him to stand down.

During the night Kennedy had talked to the head of the Jordanian Intelligence Service three separate times. They now had a name to go with the bounty that had been placed on Rapp's head: Saeed Ahmed Abdullah, a Saudi billionaire. Kennedy had not made the connection at first, but one of her counterterrorism analysts did shortly after the information was dispersed. Saeed Ahmed Abdullah was the father of Waheed Ahmed Abdullah, a terrorist who had been involved in a plot to detonate nuclear bombs in both New York and Washington. U.S. Special Forces had apprehended the man in the border region between Afghanistan and Pakistan, just days before the attack was to take place. With the clock ticking, Rapp was left with little alternative other than to torture Waheed into revealing the details of the plot. The information Rapp got from the terrorist helped intercept one of the bombs before it could be brought into the country.

How the father had learned of Rapp's role in his son's downfall was unclear, but Kennedy had her suspicions. For now, she'd ordered the Counterterrorism Center to collect every scrap of information on Saeed Ahmed Abdullah, and keep it within the family. She'd already made the risky decision that the CIA would not be passing everything they learned onto their sister agencies—agencies that were hamstrung by the rule of law. They would give the appearance of full cooperation, and reams of information would be handed over to the FBI, but almost all of it would be useless. The valuable intel would be used to stay out in front of the actual investigation.

Kennedy arrived fifteen minutes early for the meeting, as was her habit when meeting with the president. She was escorted to the Oval Office by one of the White House staffers where she waited by herself until 9:05, when she was joined by the president's national security advisor, Michael Haik. The two possessed similar temperaments and had a very good working relationship. Haik unbuttoned his suit coat and sat next to Kennedy on the couch.

"How are you holding up?"

"Fine."

"I know you are, but how are you holding up?" It was a question from one friend to another.

"I've been better," Kennedy answered honestly.

"How's Mitch?"

"He's pretty beat up, but the worst of it is behind him . . . at least physically."

Haik was the steady type of thinker every president needed—pragmatic, disciplined, and cautious. There wasn't much that ruffled his feathers. "How did he take the news of his wife?"

Kennedy kept it together. She'd already cried and she would cry more, but not here, not in the Oval Office. "He had to be sedated."

Haik nodded as if he'd anticipated the answer and then he leaned back and draped an arm over the back of the couch. It was clear that he wanted to say something, but that he was trying to figure out where to start. "Irene, we've always been straight with each other, so let me tell you what's going on here this morning. Right now the president is in his private dining room finishing up a meeting with the vice president, Secretary of State Berg, Attorney General Stokes, and Director Ross."

Even though she was surprised Kennedy nodded as if she'd already known this.

"To put it bluntly, they are deeply concerned over what Mitch might do when he recovers."

"So am I."

"I mean they are really concerned. They don't think you can control him and a few of them think you won't even try."

Kennedy showed no emotion. Her breathing stayed steady and shallow. She obviously wasn't the only person who had spent the night strategizing. "Why?"

"They think you have a conflict of interest. That your loyalty to Mitch will cloud your judgment and put you at odds with what is best for the country."

What was best for the country was debatable, but Kennedy wasn't here to argue. "I can assure you there is no conflict."

Haik wasn't sure if he believed her, but it didn't matter; he wasn't the one raising the stink. "I sneaked out early because I wanted to give you some friendly advice. They're going to come filing in here any minute and you're not going to like what they have to say." Haik paused for a second and picked a piece of lint off his trouser leg. "Do yourself a favor and go along with what they want."

"I get the sense you're trying to help me, Mike, but your advice seems off the mark."

"What I'm trying to tell you is that a deal has already been struck. Three cabinet members are in there right now telling the president what has to happen and they say they have more members on board. They've got him buttoned up with no room to maneuver. Officially he has no choice but to follow their recommendation."

Kennedy felt a sickening feeling in her stomach, and she chastised herself for not getting to the president before them. "I'm not sure I can sit here and play nice on this one."

"You know what a riptide is?"

"Of course."

"You don't survive by fighting it. You conserve your energy, you go with the flow, and when the moment is right, you swim parallel to shore."

"So you want me to just sit here and go with the flow this morning?"

"Not entirely. I think the president would be disappointed if you didn't state the obvious, but in the end let them have their way."

"And what will I get in return?"

The door handle to the president's private dining room started to turn and voices could be heard on the other side. "When this meeting is over go down to the Situation Room. The president would like to speak to you in private."

The president entered the room first. Kennedy and Haik both stood. President Hayes was six foot one and his salt-and-pepper hair was mostly all salt after three years in office. He came straight across the room and opened his arms. He hugged Kennedy and said, "Irene, I'm so sorry. I know you were very close to them."

Kennedy stayed stoic. "Thank you, Mr. President."

The president released her and said, "How's Mitch doing?"

"He's resting."

The president stared at her for a long moment as he tried to imagine what must be going through Rapp's mind. "This is such a tragedy." He shook his head and motioned for everyone to take a seat. Haik and Kennedy sat on one couch while Secretary of State Berg, Attorney General Stokes, and Director of National Intelligence Ross sat on the couch across from them. There were two chairs in front of the fireplace. The president took the one on the left, and the vice president took the other one. President Hayes clasped his hands and asked Kennedy, "Have you learned anything since we talked yesterday?"

"Not really, sir."

"Is it still your opinion that this was a professional hit?"

"Yes it is, sir."

"Irene." Director Ross sat forward and addressed Kennedy in a gentle voice. "I'm going to get this out in the open for everyone's sake. I know this is very difficult for you. You have a personal relationship with Rapp and his wife and this is a horrible tragedy, but while we respect your opinion," Ross winced as if he was trying to be gentle and then added, "we do not share your conclusion that this was a contract kill."

Her brown eyes stared straight through him. Everything had changed in less than twenty-four hours. A day ago she had been willing to ignore the man's mounting flaws, but now she felt genuine hatred coursing through her veins. It took great restraint not to blurt out the obvious—which was that Ross had almost no experience in his current position.

"We were briefed by the FBI this morning," Ross continued, "and we feel that there is not enough evidence to support the theory."

Kennedy nodded. "You spoke to Special Agent McMahon?"

Ross looked at Attorney General Stokes.

Stokes answered Kennedy by saying, "No, as you know, Director Roach is out of the country so we were briefed by Deputy Director Finn."

"And has Mr. Finn been to the crime scene?"

"No," Stokes answered flatly.

"Irene," Ross said, "how did the press get the idea Mitch was dead?"

Both DC morning papers ran stories that Rapp and his wife had been killed in a propane explosion at their Maryland home and all of the TV outlets were reporting the story. With no guilt whatsoever, Kennedy looked Ross in the eye and said, "I have no idea."

"Where is he now?"

"He's at a secure location recovering."

"Where?" Ross persisted.

"One of our safe houses in Virginia."

"Which one?"

Kennedy tilted her head slightly. "Why are you so concerned about Mitch's location?"

Ross glanced at the others and then said, "Mitch has a bit of a reputation as a maverick. We think it would be best if the FBI kept an eye on him until things cool down."

"Oh . . . I wouldn't worry about that," Kennedy said in a sarcastic voice. "I'm sure if the three of you explain to Mitch that the explosion was an accident, he'll drop the entire matter."

It was obvious Ross did not like Kennedy's tone. He sat up straight and asked, "Who were the two men you sent to Rapp's house last night?"

"I'm not sure I know what you're talking about."

"I spoke with the Anne Arundel sheriff this morning and he told me that two men showed up last night and said that you sent them out there to poke around." Ross folded his arms across his chest. "Apparently they caused quite a stink."

"Really?"

"Yes. Who were they?"

"Professional assassins."

Ross's face flushed with anger. "I don't think this is the time for humor."

"No humor." Kennedy shook her head. "They were a couple of black-bag guys who specialize in killing people and making it look like an accident."

Ross's nostrils were flared in anger. "What were their names?"

Kennedy shook her head. "I can't tell you."

"Why not?"

"You don't have the security clearance."

"I'm your boss," he said in a voice on the verge of outright rage.

"That does not mean you have clearance," Kennedy insisted. The mood in the room got very tense. "Mark, I'm surprised that you seem more concerned about who they were than what they had to say."

"Who they were is a genuine concern," stated Attorney General Stokes. "If this was in fact a crime, my people will have to build a case, and it will not look good in court to have a couple of professional assassins poking around a fresh crime scene tampering with evidence."

"And, Irene," said Ross, "this so-called evidence they found is incredibly thin. A few trampled blades of grass and a tire track." Ross shook his head and frowned. "Balance that against the fire chief's report that it was an accident, and this thing will never get off the ground."

"So what would you propose we do? Ignore the warning we received from the Jordanians last week that a bounty had been placed on Rapp's head? Ignore the findings of two highly trained, and highly decorated, Special Forces veterans who know more about this kind of thing than all of us combined?"

"We're not saying that at all," answered Ross.

"Then why are you so hell bent on trying to write this thing off as an accident?"

The room got very quiet. The three cabinet members looked to the president as if this was the moment where he should step in, but the president wasn't biting. The vice president for his part stayed quiet.

Secretary of State Berg cleared her throat and said, "Irene, there's a right way to handle this and a wrong way."

Isn't there always, Kennedy thought to herself.

"The right way is to let the FBI handle the investigation."

"And the wrong way?"

"The wrong way," interjected the attorney general, "is to have CIA black-ops people poking around a potential crime scene."

Kennedy noted that Stokes had used the word *potential* and momentarily thought of explaining to the nation's top lawyer that if it weren't for Coleman and Wicker none of this evidence would have been discovered, but she knew it would be a waste of breath. Their minds were already made up. They were afraid of a vengeful Mitch Rapp, or more to the point, they were afraid of what he would do in the name of the U.S. government. The embarrassment he could bring to them and their organizations was immense.

"I can assure you," Attorney General Stokes continued, "if a crime was committed, we will make sure the perpetrators are brought to justice. It might take some time, but we will do it. In the meantime you need to explain to Rapp that he is in no way involved in this investigation, and if he *decides* to get involved, he's going to find himself in some serious legal trouble."

If the situation wasn't so serious, Kennedy would have found the attorney general's warning laughable. She turned to the president to see if he was actually buying into this nonsense. She found him looking at his watch and trying to avoid eye contact. She remembered Haik's warning, and turned back to the attorney general. "I'm sure Mitch will be sufficiently intimidated by your threat of legal trouble. Maybe you'd like to deliver the message yourself."

Stokes did not like the comment and turned to Berg and Ross for support. The director of National Intelligence spoke first. "The last thing we need is an employee of the Central Intelligence Agency acting as a judge, jury, and executioner."

"I would actually say the last thing we need is someone getting away with trying to assassinate an employee of the CIA."

"If someone tried to kill Rapp, we'll find them, and they'll be punished."

Kennedy nodded in a way that said she wasn't buying any of it, and then asked, "How do you plan to stop Mitch from pursuing this on his own?"

"As his boss I expect you to control him," Ross said flatly.

"And if he quits?"

Ross turned to Secretary of State Berg. She hesitated briefly and then said, "We've revoked Mr. Rapp's passport. He's forbidden to leave the country."

Now this truly was funny. The trivial precaution caused Kennedy to laugh out loud. Three stone-faced cabinet members stared back at her. "And you think that's going to stop him?" asked Kennedy. "Mitch Rapp . . . a man we trained as a deep cover operative? A man who speaks five languages, has I don't even know how many aliases, and has at one time or another crept in and out of virtually every country in Europe and the Middle East? You think revoking his passport is going to stop him?"

They ignored the question and Stokes said, "For his own good we're placing him under protective custody."

Kennedy shook her head and replied in a sarcastic tone, "That's kind of you to offer, but we'll pass."

"Irene, it's for the good of the country," said Ross.

"That's debatable, but in the meantime, he's safe and in no need of further protection."

"Irene," said Stokes, "if I need to, I'll get a court order."

"On what grounds, Marty?" Kennedy's temper flared for the first time. "You think you're the only person in this town who has a judge in his back pocket?" She let him think about the implied threat for a second and then added, "Trust me . . . you'll lose on this one, and it won't be pretty."

Ross held his hand up, signaling for them both to stop. "Let's all take a deep breath and calm down. I'm sure the CIA is more than capable of keeping an eye on Mitch until he's recovered. In the meantime, Irene, we're going to have to grant access to the FBI so they can interview him."

Kennedy hesitated and then said, "Have Special Agent McMahon call me, and I'll set it up."

"I would also like to talk to him," said Ross.

"I doubt he's up for visitors at the moment, but . . ."

"When he's ready," the president said, directing his comment at Ross and not Kennedy.

There was a brief pause and the president's national security advisor took the opportunity to end the meeting. He stood and said, "The president is on a tight schedule this morning, so if you'll excuse us." Haik pointed at Ross and asked, "Do you have fifteen minutes?"

"Of course."

Haik pulled the director of National Intelligence aside and began speaking in hushed tones. The president was gone before anyone noticed, ducking out through the door that led to his personal secretary's office. Kennedy took one last look at Secretary Berg, Attorney General Stokes, and Vice President Baxter and then left the room in disgust.

43

Kennedy went straight for the situation room. In her twenty plus years at the CIA she had never sat through a bigger cover-your-ass meeting. It was not her boss or the attorney general or the secretary of state who she was upset with, though. She had expected them to protect their fiefdoms, just not so soon. Her ire was directed at the president. She'd never seen him so ineffectual before and especially on an issue where she thought he would be every bit as upset as she was. None of it made sense.

She reached the outer door to the situation room and punched her code into the cipher lock. She opened the heavy door and ignored the duty officer who was sitting behind a desk a few paces ahead. Kennedy turned to her left and entered the soundproof conference room, where she was surprised to see two individuals sitting at the far end of the long, shiny, wood table. Before she had a chance to address them, the president entered the room and closed the door. The two men attempted to stand, but the president told them not to bother.

Kennedy assumed Senators Walsh and Hartsburg had been asked by the president to come to this meeting. As to why, she hadn't a clue. Instead of sitting in his normal chair at the head of the table nearest the door, Hayes walked to the other end of the room and grabbed the chair next to Senator Hartsburg, "Irene, have a seat."

Kennedy took her place and the president walked around the table and sat next to Senator Walsh. Hayes leaned forward and placed his forearms on the table. "Irene, I'm sorry you had to sit through that."

Kennedy was rarely caught off guard, and she rarely allowed anger to get the best of her, but today was a day of firsts. "Mr. President, would you mind telling me just what in the hell is going on?"

"Irene, there isn't a proverbial snowball's chance in hell that the explosion was an accident. You know it, I know it, and they know it."

"Then why are you allowing them to put Mitch on ice and cut the CIA out of this?"

"I'm not."

"That's not what I just heard upstairs."

"Irene, what do you think Mitch is going to do when he's well enough to get out of bed?" the president asked.

Kennedy knew the answer, but was reluctant to respond to the question.

Senator Hartsburg coughed and said, "He's going to kill anyone who had anything to do with his wife's death."

"That's right," said the president, "and I can't say I blame him."

"Then what's this nonsense about revoking his passport and putting him under protective custody?"

"Not my idea." Hayes shook his head. "And what does it really matter? You and I both know there's no stopping him. Passport or not . . . he's going to leave the country and go wherever he damn well pleases."

"Mr. President, I'm confused. Mitch has sacrificed a great deal for this country. I think there is a better way to handle this than treating him like a criminal." Kennedy shook her head in disgust. "To be honest, sir, after all Mitch has done for you, I would have expected you to stand by him when he needs you most. Not cave into the demands of a few cabinet members."

Hayes took the rebuke surprisingly well. He sat back and looked at his two former colleagues from the Senate and then slowly returned his gaze to Kennedy. "I'm going to let you in on something that only a handful of people know, but first I need your word that you will not discuss this with anyone."

Kennedy looked at him intently. "Of course."

"I've decided not to seek reelection."

Kennedy's eyes opened a bit wider upon hearing the shocking news. With a little more than a year left in his first term, and a solid approval rating, there wasn't a person in town who had even mentioned the possibility of Hayes not seeking a second term. "Do you mind my asking why, sir?"

"I have some health issues that I think preclude me from serving as president."

Kennedy wanted to ask what those health issues were, but knew it could be personal. "I'm sorry, Mr. President."

Hayes glanced up at the clocks on the far wall and then said, "Parkinson's. It runs in my family. My mother's side."

"But I haven't noticed any signs."

"They're there. Trust me. I've been taking medication for five months. At first the results were good, but over the last few weeks things have gotten worse. My doctor tells me I should have no problem serving out my first term, but any hope of a second term would be purely selfish."

"But Parkinson's . . ."

Hayes shook his head. He'd studied every side of it. He'd discussed it with his wife until they had beaten the subject to death. Was there a chance he could stay on top of his game for four more years? The answer was maybe, and maybe wasn't good enough. And then there was the other issue of his physical appearance. That was the thing that really decided it for him. Hayes smiled and said to Kennedy, "The man in charge of the word's most potent nuclear arsenal cannot be seen standing at a podium with shaky hands."

Kennedy blinked slowly and glanced at the other two men. They all knew he was right, and admired him for making the difficult decision. There were others who would not have relinquished the mantle of power so easily. "Mr. President, I'm very sorry."

"Don't be. This office is bigger than any single person. It's been my honor to serve." Hayes regarded his two old friends from the Senate. Walsh smiled, Hartsburg frowned, and they both nodded. The two career politicians would have gladly settled for one term. Not one to feel sorry for himself, Hayes changed the subject. "Irene, let me lay things out for you. I have a vice president who is in over his head, I have a deeply flawed attorney general, a secretary of state who is more concerned with appeasing foreign governments than protecting our own long-term national security, and I have a new director of National Intelligence who will probably throw a party when he learns that I have Parkinson's." Hayes gave Hartsburg a sideways glance. It was Hartsburg who had recommended Ross for the top intelligence job.

The gruff senator said, "Bob, he's an ambitious fellow, but I wouldn't go so far as to say he's going to celebrate your misfortune."

"Okay, he'll celebrate his own opportunity."

"He's off to a bit of a rocky start," Hartsburg conceded and then looked to Kennedy. "Don't worry. We'll have a talk with him and get him settled down."

"The point is, Irene," the president said, "that I don't plan on spending my last year in office refereeing battles between my cabinet members. They sprang this one on me this morning," Hayes shook his head, "I should have seen it coming, but I didn't have a lot of time to prepare for it. As it is, I don't agree with them, but I do see their point."

"I'm afraid I don't, sir."

"We are a civilized country ruled by laws. We are constantly preaching to other countries about free speech, due process, and fair and just courts. It is one of the most important missions of the State Department. Here at home, our Justice Department and the courts are tasked with keeping things fair. A crime has been committed on American soil. Yes, it was perpetrated against an employee of the CIA, but the jurisdiction still falls squarely in the lap of Justice, and there is nothing any of us can do about that."

"Irene," said Senator Walsh, "there's another angle to consider. Mitch's wife was a fairly well-known reporter. The press is going to follow this story closely. The Justice Department would much rather announce that this was an accident, that way they won't have to set the bar too high for themselves. They'll quietly continue to investigate, but my guess is they will not classify it as a crime unless they have a suspect they can pin it on."

"That explosion was not an accident."

"We all know that," answered Hayes.

"Then what are we going to do about it?"

"Let me be very clear about this." Hayes placed his forearms on the table and clasped his hands. "I want whoever did this brought to justice, and I want it to happen quickly. I don't want an investigation that goes on for years, and I don't want to see a single person dragged in front of a court unless there is absolutely no other alternative."

"What about the Justice Department?"

"Let them run their official investigation." Hayes waved his hand as if the massive Justice Department were some inconsequential nuisance. "You and Special Agent McMahon have a good working relationship. Anything he finds I want him to pass on to you, but to be honest, I expect you to be way out in front of him on this."

"Why is that, sir?"

"Because you don't have to play by the rules, Irene, and they do."

"What about Ross?" Kennedy turned to Senator Hartsburg.

"Mark will be fine."

Kennedy shook her head. "I don't think so." She looked to the president expecting him to back her up. Ross had after all told the president about Rapp's insubordination and thuggish behavior.

Instead of giving her a knowing nod, Hayes's face twisted into a frown of confusion.

Kennedy realized at that moment that Ross had lied to her. "Mr. President, I don't think Director Ross has been as forthright with you as he's led me to believe."

"What has he led you to believe?"

"He told me that he briefed you on a problem he'd had with Mitch recently."

Hayes shook his head. "He hasn't said a word to me about Mitch since he got the job."

"Last week I was having a meeting in my office with Mitch and Scott Coleman." Kennedy spoke directly to the president. "Director Ross showed up at Langley unannounced and barged in on the meeting." Kennedy went on to explain how the IRS showed up on Scott Coleman's doorstep the next day and that Ross had his people call the Pentagon and request Coleman's service record. She ended the recap by explaining that Rapp had decided to pay Ross a visit at his office and when he walked in, Ross was having a meeting with several investigators and the topic of conversation was Scott Coleman. Rapp picked up a dossier containing Coleman's tax returns and slapped Ross across the face with it."

Hartsburg looked a little stricken, while Walsh and the president sat in stunned silence until finally Senator Walsh said, "I told both of you he was the wrong man for the job."

"He'll be fine," said a defensive Hartsburg. "I'll have a talk with him."

"He's done listening to you," grumbled Walsh. "I told you, he's a damn power-hungry peacock."

"I'll talk to him," the president said quietly.

"I don't want you to have to do that, Mr. President." Hartsburg had pushed Ross on the president and he felt obliged to straighten out the mess. "Let me have one more shot at him."

"Fine." Hayes turned his attention back to Kennedy. "We'll keep Ross off your back. You just stay out in front of Justice and the FBI."

"What about Mitch?"

The president leaned back and gave the matter some thought. After a lengthy pause he said, "Officially . . . I want him involved in the CIA's international aspect of this investigation. Please take special note of the word *international*." Hayes paused for effect. "Unofficially . . . he has my consent to kill anyone who had a direct hand in this."

44

The cruise ship turned into the Canale di San Marco, churning up a muddy wake as it slipped slowly through the water. The vessel seemed ridiculously large to be entering such a narrow body of water, but Abel reasoned they knew what they were doing. Tourism was after all Italy's biggest industry and it wouldn't do to have one of these steel behemoths ramming its prow through the intricate façade of the Palazzo Ducale. This was the third such ship this afternoon and by far the largest. Abel was lounging on the terrace of his $2,000-a-night penthouse that overlooked the confluence of the Grand Canal and the San Marco Canal. During the peak summer season the room ran $5,000 a night, but only a fool would come to Venice in the summer. The city was overrun with tourists. Heat and humidity combined with sweat to give off a sour odor that could be exceedingly unpleasant. Prices were obnoxiously high and service was shoddy. Fall or spring, though, was a different matter. The temperature was mild and with the humidity gone the ripe summer smell of the canals was gone. The narrow streets were passable, and the service was good.

The ship let loose three quick bursts from its horn. Abel glanced up at the passengers who seemed to be on top of him. They lined the railings of all four decks, towering over him, taking photos, waving, and gawking. If there was one common denominator among them it was that they in general seemed unconcerned with physical fitness. While he perched atop his penthouse sundeck, they looked down on him like plump birds in search of a morsel of food. His initial awe over the engineering it took to assemble such a ship and then maneuver it through the tight channel was now gone, replaced by a sense of irritation that these commoners were intruding on his privacy. Abel did his best to ignore them and read the screen of his laptop.

It had been an interesting day. He had risen from a sound night's sleep at 7:00 a.m. and showered and shaved. Breakfast in the grand ballroom was followed by a long walk around the city. He'd crossed over the Grand Canal to San Paolo and then Santa Croce with no intent other than to observe how the unique floating city prepared itself for another day. Garbage barges came and went. Water taxis and ferries brought people from the mainland and the surrounding islands to work. Food, office products, mail, wine, merchandise, and everything else it takes to keep a city functioning was brought in by water and off-loaded by young, strong men wielding carts of varying shapes and sizes. It was a way of commerce that was unique to Venice.

Abel returned to the hotel before 10:00 and checked his e-mail. He was both pleased and shocked to find a message that Mitch Rapp was dead. And not only was he dead, but the assassin had managed to make it look like an accident. Abel was absolutely floored by the speed and apparent ease with which the contract had been carried out. Saeed Ahmed Abdullah would be a very happy man. It was no surprise that the assassins were demanding payment immediately. As tempting as it was for Abel to call Abdullah and give him the good news, he knew that he should confirm the story from an independent source. With the time difference between Venice and Washington, DC, it took a while. For fear of raising unwanted attention he did not want to call any of his contacts in the international intelligence community. At 2:00 in the afternoon he was finally able to track down the story on the *Washington Post*'s Web site. Abel read the words with his heart in his throat. A quarter of the way into it he began dancing around the room. He had just made an additional six million dollars without having to lift a finger. Abel was not a dancer, and he was not someone accustomed to spontaneous celebration, but this was an exception.

After finishing the article he called Abdullah directly via an encrypted satellite phone and told him the news. The father began sobbing. In between sniffles he praised Allah and thanked Abel profusely for giving him his just retribution. Not wanting the call to last too long Abel brought up the issue of payment. Abdullah said it would be taken care of before the close of business today and thanked Abel over and over for helping him. Abel demurred, and then ended the call by warning the billionaire to be very careful. Even though the American press was calling it an accidental explosion, there would surely be people at the CIA who would never believe it for a second.

Now the close of business was approaching, and Abel was nervously waiting for confirmation from the various banks that the funds had been received. Twelve million dollars in total. After Prince Muhammad bin Rashid requested that Abel make the murder look like an accident, the German had ignored the request to shoulder the cost himself and had taken the matter to Saeed Ahmed Abdullah. The billionaire seemed entirely unconcerned by any investigation that might take place after Rapp's death. Abel tried to impress him with the potential gravity of the aftermath, but Abdullah cared not how Rapp was killed—only that he was killed. Abel pressed him further until the billionaire finally agreed to foot the bill.

Twelve million dollars total, and it had taken less than two weeks. Abel thought that it must be a record in his line of work. It was going to be difficult not to brag about his payday, but there was an obvious disincentive. If the assassins found out they would likely kill him, and if the Americans found out they would torture him and *then* kill him. He would keep his mouth shut for some time. Maybe in twenty years, when he finally slowed down, he could write his memoirs and take credit for killing America's top counterterrorism operative. He knew where the real risk lay, and unfortunately there was nothing he could do about it. The father would want to brag. He would want to take credit for killing the mighty Mitch Rapp.

A thought occurred to Abel as he stared at his in-box waiting for confirmation. He was surprised he hadn't thought of it sooner. Why not use some of his newfound fortune to take out a contract on the father? He decided he'd have to explore the option. An e-mail landed in his in-box with a chime. Abel opened it and smiled as he read the confirmation that two million dollars had arrived in his account, and as per his instructions, one million of it was immediately wired to the designated bank in the Bahamas. Five more e-mails arrived in short order, all basically saying the same thing. Abel picked up the phone and asked for a bottle of 1989 Pichon Longueville Baron to be sent up. He looked out at the bulbous domes of Santa Maria della Salute across the canal and thanked God for the efficiency of the Swiss.

45

Rapp woke up, once again hoping it was all a dream, but one look at the unfamiliar surroundings told him it wasn't. His own personal nightmare was upon him. His wife and unborn child were gone. Those horrible memories that had haunted him after his girlfriend had been blown out of the sky over Lockerbie, Scotland, came flooding back, only this time they were worse. He'd spent years getting over her tragic death. The passage of time and taxing nature of his work combined to slowly mend him. And then Anna came along, and all was perfect again. The painful wound was healed, and he was left with a small scar that was the fleeting memory of a woman who had died more than a decade ago. Now in a flash Anna was gone and with her all his hopes and aspirations. The old wound had been torn asunder and it ached with a pain that was white-hot compared to the previous one. The love of his youth seemed utterly naïve in comparison to the absolute devotion and adoration he felt toward his wife. The pain gripped him in a writhing agony that he knew would have no end.

Rapp fought back the tears and forced himself to assess the situation. He had vague memories of being moved in the night. He could tell by his splitting headache, foggy vision, and general lethargy that he had been given a sedative. He lifted his head just enough to confirm what he'd already guessed—that his arms and legs were tied down with straps. He didn't like this one bit and immediately began to test how secure the bonds were. After a brief struggle he gave up. The room was dark, but there was enough light for him to realize that he was not in a hospital. It was more like a hotel room, or a bedroom in someone's house.

His only vivid memory of his time in the hospital was hearing Kennedy telling him Anna was dead and then having to be restrained by some very large men. After that there was a vague recollection of an ambulance ride. Kennedy must have moved him to a more secure location. Rapp went over a brief list of possibilities, and then whispered to himself, "How in the hell did this happen?"

He sensed movement somewhere in the building—like a heavy door had been shut. Now he could hear footsteps. He rolled his head toward the door and watched as the brass knob began to turn. It occurred to him that he was probably being monitored by a low-light camera. The door opened with barely a sound and a dark figure stepped into the room. Rapp couldn't make out his face, but there was something familiar in the way he moved. The man approached the bed cautiously, and Rapp wondered for an instant if he was in danger.

"How are you feeling, buddy?"

It was Scott Coleman. Rapp relaxed a notch and asked, "Where am I?"

"Agency safe house."

Rapp surveyed the former Special Forces operator. "Which one?"

"Near Leesburg." Coleman walked around to the other side of the bed and opened the blinds.

Light filled the room and Rapp turned away. "What time is it?" he asked with squinted eyes.

"Almost noon."

Rapp was bothered by the simple fact that he couldn't bring his hand up to shield his eyes. "Untie me."

Coleman hesitated. He weighed the alternatives. Kennedy had left orders that she wanted him to be kept sedated and tied until she had a chance to further assess his attitude. Coleman didn't like seeing him tied up as if he was some prisoner, and given all that he'd been through he didn't feel right ignoring him. He reached down and grabbed one of the canvas straps that held his wrist to the bed frame. "Don't do anything stupid, Mitch. You've got a broken arm, two broken ribs, a deep thigh bruise, and your knee is still swollen from surgery." The former SEAL finished with the straps and gently placed a couple of pillows behind Rapp so he was propped up.

Rapp guessed from the view that he was on the second floor.

The slight greenish hue of the glass also told him the window was bullet-proof. He had been here before but had never ventured to the second floor. To the average unsuspecting person, the place looked no different from all the other horse farms and corporate retreats that dotted the rural Virginia landscape. It was very charming on the surface, but the subterranean levels beneath the main building held a secret the CIA guarded very closely. The place was so covert, it didn't even have a name. To the handful of people who knew of its existence, it was referred to as *The Facility.*

It was off the books, not even listed in the black intelligence budget submitted in secret to Congress every year. The Facility was a place where they could clinically drain information from people. In decades past the subjects were usually traitors or spies, almost all of them atheists or agnostics. More recently the guests were decidedly more fervent in their religious beliefs. The place was located near Leesburg, Virginia, and was situated on sixty-two beautiful rolling acres which had been purchased by the Agency in the early fifties. The Facility was a necessary evil in the sometimes brutal high-stakes game of espionage.

Rapp was about to ask Coleman about Anna, but he choked on his words. After he got control of his emotions he asked, "What happened?"

"Do you remember the explosion?"

Rapp shook his head.

"As near as I've been able to piece it together, you came home after your knee surgery and the house blew up. Somehow you ended up in the bay. A nearby fisherman pulled you out of the drink and you were medevacked up to Johns Hopkins."

"Anna?"

Coleman shifted his weight uncomfortably from one foot to the other. "She ended up in the front yard. The EMS people said they think she hit a tree as she was blown out of the house. Massive trauma to the head. They operated," Coleman shook his head sadly, "but she never had a chance."

Rapp looked away from his friend and stared out the window. He was trying desperately to keep it together. To keep his mind focused on what had happened, and not on what had been lost. "Who did it?"

"We don't know yet, but we have some leads."

"Bring me up to speed," Rapp ordered with clinical detachment.

"I got to your house last night around ten. Skip McMahon was there with some other feds, but they were letting the locals run the show."

Coleman paused and then said blandly, "The fire chief says it was an accidental propane explosion, and so far the feds concur."

Rapp frowned.

"Don't worry, we're not buying into it for a second. Let me finish with the official version, and then I'll fill you in on the rest. The fire department found traces of an accelerant. They're pretty sure it's gasoline."

"Where?"

"Between the garage and the propane tank. They figure you kept your gas for the boats on the side of the garage."

"I fill my boats at the marina."

"I thought so. Besides, I told them there was no way in hell you'd leave gas stored that close to a propane tank."

"You're right. What else?"

"This is where it gets tricky, Mitch." Coleman folded his arms across his chest and widened his stance as if he was preparing himself for stormy seas. "You know how people like us tend to make the feds real nervous."

Rapp nodded.

"I brought Wicker with me last night and we found some stuff they overlooked."

Rapp knew Charlie Wicker well. They'd worked together many times, and occasionally they trained together. There was no better shot with a long barrel in the world. "Like what?"

"Someone was in the woods yesterday across the street from your house." Coleman studied Rapp for a reaction.

"Go on."

"Irene sent us out there because she knew we'd know what to look for. When we got there the feds and the locals were focused on the house. You know how good Charlie is . . . it took him all of two minutes to pick up the scent. We think one tango was in the woods when you got home. He had a bicycle with him. Wicker thinks the guy was careful enough to carry the bike into the woods, but then in the excitement after the explosion he wheeled it out, leaving a clear trail through the tall grass on the side of the road." Coleman made a curved gesture with his right hand. "The guy headed south where your street dead-ends. Charlie knew there were paths down there, so he took off with his flashlight and followed this guy's trail to the dirt road that runs along a landing strip a few miles from your house."

Rapp was proceeding along the trail in his mind. He'd covered it hundreds of times on both foot and bike.

"Charlie found a fresh set of tire tracks on the edge of the dirt road about where the bike tracks ended. We think the guy threw the bike in the back of a truck, pulled a U-turn, and vanished."

"Why do you say truck?"

"Fortunately, Skip is running the show for the feds so he ordered his people to take molds of the tracks. Apparently the tires were new, and they left very clear marks. The FBI says the tire is made by BFGoodrich and is used on a lot of the Chevy pickups, Tahoes, and Suburbans."

Rapp thought about what Wicker and Coleman had discovered and asked, "So why are the feds calling the explosion an accident?"

"Not all of them are. Skip knows this was no accident, but there're others who would prefer it if this investigation was closed by the end of the week."

"Why?"

"Do you have to ask?"

"Why?" Rapp asked again in an angry tone. He knew the answer, but he didn't care. He wanted to hear Coleman say it.

"You make people nervous, Mitch. They're afraid of what you're going to do when you get out of here, and they don't like people like us rubbing shoulders with their law-and-order types." Coleman walked over to the window. "Skip told me the attorney general went nuts this morning when he found out that Wicker and I were at the crime scene poking around. He says this evidence we discovered is trivial at best, but since it was discovered by a couple of spooks, it's now tainted and worthless."

Rapp had never cared for the attorney general, but now he felt an intense hatred toward the man. Rapp told himself that was fine. People needed to decide which team they were on. "Let's be clear about two things, Scott. First of all, when I'm well enough to walk . . . I'm out of here, and no one is going to stop me. Second, no one is going to be put on trial for this."

Coleman looked out the window and slowly nodded his head. None of this was a revelation. "Whatever you need . . . just let me know."

46

Prince Muhammad bin Rashid finished his morning prayer and went downstairs to greet his guests. The sun was shining, the air was a bit cold for his tastes, but it could have been snowing and it wouldn't have spoiled his mood. Mitch Rapp was dead, and that was all that mattered. Rashid had spent the previous day following the story as it unfolded on MSNBC. Throughout the day so-called experts debated whether or not the explosion was an accident and then finally in the early evening the local authorities held a press conference and announced their findings. A gas leak and accidental propane explosion had killed the husband and wife. Several of the experts, former government types, refused to believe what they called rushed findings and protested that there were ways to trigger these types of explosions and make it look like a mishap. The debate raged into the night, with conspiracy theorists who refused to believe anything the government said, a cabal of former Special Forces types who said the local authorities were in over their heads, and the reporters for the most part buying into the official story.

Rashid was tempted to call Abel and congratulate him, but he thought it unwise to make such a move when the chances were very good that the Americans were monitoring his communications. His old friend Saeed Ahmed Abdullah had phoned him, however. In between praising Allah and crying over his son, Abdullah thanked Rashid profusely. Rashid, fearing that Abdullah was speaking a bit too freely, admonished his friend and told him they would continue their conversation when he returned to the Kingdom.

The success of the operation was giving Rashid pause. He wondered if he hadn't been too hasty in ordering the removal of the German. It was rare for him to second-guess one of his own orders. Rashid admired men with a cunning personality and a decisive will. These two traits more than any others were the most important to his cause. Reversing his decision could be seen as weak and indecisive—traits that did not play well with Arab men. But still the German had succeeded in short order where Rashid had thought it was likely he would fail. And he had made it look like an accident. Maybe he would have to reconsider killing him. The man was very useful after all.

Rashid descended the grand plantation staircase, his lustrous brown riding boots showing from beneath a black robe with gold trim. A black kaffiyeh was fastened to his head by a matching gold braid, and his black goatee and mustache were perfectly groomed. He was an impressive man. A ride was planned for the morning and he was not about to eschew his Arab heritage simply because he was in America. A cortege of servants dressed in crisp white tunics and black pants awaited him. Rashid's personal secretary, who was dressed in a white robe and kaffiyeh, kept his eyes on the floor and stepped forward.

"Prince Muhammad, Colonel Tayyib is in the library. Would you like me to bring you coffee?"

"Yes." Rashid walked past the phalanx of men and continued down the long cross hall and through the double doors to the oak paneled library. Old leather-bound volumes filled the bookshelves, and there was a smattering of expensive oil paintings that were decidedly Anglo. Rashid decided he would have to register a complaint with his half brother that there wasn't a single painting that honored Arabia. Such an oversight was unforgivable. Maybe he would purchase several for him and send them as gifts. He needed to be careful to keep the right people on his side.

Colonel Tayyib was dressed in a black suit, with a blue shirt and tie. Anyone else would have received a rebuke from the prince for breaking with custom, but Tayyib had a job to do and it was better if he did not draw attention to himself. The man bowed his head and said in an unusually exuberant tone, "Good morning, Prince Muhammad."

Rashid smiled just enough to show his teeth. "Yes, it is."

Tayyib looked up and was unable to restrain his joy as he smiled at Rashid.

The two men silently communicated their happiness over Rapp's death for a moment. Servants entered quietly with a serving tray of Arab coffee and separate tray of fresh pastries. They poured coffee for two and left, closing the doors behind them.

Rashid took a sip of coffee and said with great satisfaction, "The American is finally out of our way."

"Yes. Finally," Tayyib agreed.

"Have you discovered more details?"

"None, but I expect you will learn more when Director Ross arrives."

"Yes," Rashid said, "but I will have to be careful not to seem too eager."

"You are never too eager, my prince, and besides, I told you that Ross and Rapp did not get along."

Rashid remembered. The two men had fought over something recently. But still, he would have to be careful not to gloat. "What have you found out about our German friend?"

"Nothing, I am sorry to report. He is not answering any of his phones, and his secretary will not tell us where he is."

Rashid wondered if he had come to America to monitor the business with Rapp.

"We have both his office and his apartment in Vienna under surveillance. He will show up sooner or later, and I will make sure it is taken care of."

The prince walked over to the large French doors that looked out onto the paddock area. A magnificent shiny, black Arabian thoroughbred was being led out to the track for some exercise. "Colonel, do you feel I have been too hasty in my decision to eliminate the German?"

Tayyib was an athletic man with broad shoulders and sturdy legs. He was six feet tall and did not have the outward appearance of a thinker. In truth he was an exceptionally good tactician when it came to operational matters. He attributed this ability to survey the battlefield and properly assess the situation to his years as a standout defensemen on the Saudi national soccer team. He was, of course, a devout Wahhabi, which was an absolute prerequisite for working so closely with the prince.

"It is not my position to question you, Prince Muhammad."

Rashid continued to look out the window and smiled. He prized loyalty and obedience above all. "For today let us make an exception."

Tayyib stroked his mustache and said, "I am not sure I trust the German, but he has proven himself very useful."

"Why is it that you don't trust him?"

"I don't know."

"Is it because he is a foreigner?"

"Probably."

Rashid nodded. "I have never trusted him completely for that very reason myself, but he has performed brilliantly."

"That is true. Maybe we should look at the problem in a different way."

Rashid turned around. "Continue."

"Do we have anyone else who can do for us what he does?"

The prince shook his head. He had already thought of this. "No."

"The decision to have him removed was a sound precaution at the time based on a realistic expectation that we would need to cover our tracks. It appears that the German may have done such a good job we no longer have to worry."

Rashid looked beyond Tayyib, through the French doors at the other end of the room, which opened onto the front yard of the estate. A motorcade of black vehicles was coming up the drive. It would be Director Ross. He was very much looking forward to this breakfast. The prince said, "Let the German live for now."

Tayyib accepted the order with a bow of his head.

"I think Director Ross is here. It might be a good idea if you make yourself scarce."

Tayyib left the room and a few minutes later Director Ross was escorted into the library. He was wearing a pair of blue jeans, cowboy boots, flannel shirt, and jean jacket. The prince thought he was trying a bit too hard to flaunt his American cowboy bravado. His attire in itself was a minor nuisance, compared to the faux pas he'd committed by dragging four of his people into the room with him. Rashid looked at Ross and then gave the other Americans a scornful glance. It was not Ross, or any of the other Americans with their ingrained egalitarian sense, who picked up on Rashid's irritation, but his personal secretary. The man gently touched each of the four on the elbow and gestured toward the door.

It seemed to finally dawn on Ross that he was in the presence of royalty and the prince did not enjoy the company of people beneath him. Rather than draw attention to the screwup he decided to lay it on. "Prince Muhammad, I can't thank you enough for taking the time to see me. I'm really looking forward to our morning together."

"So am I," Rashid said in a kind voice. "And I thank you for your invitation. I had not thought of coming with the delegation."

"Well, that's too bad. You are always welcome in America."

Rashid supposed this would have been a good time to tell him he was always welcome in Saudi Arabia, but the truth was that he wasn't. "You are very kind."

"I would just like to say, Prince Rashid, that I do not underestimate how important you are to Saudi Arabia." Ross paused and then offered, "The king may be the heart of Saudi Arabia, but you are its soul." Ross was very pleased with himself. He had worked on this line over and over to give it the perfect dramatic flair.

Rashid was momentarily stunned. For the first time in his life he felt genuinely flattered, not patronized, by an American. Although he completely agreed with Ross, Rashid had never shared this comparison between himself and his half brother with anyone. When he was alone in his thoughts, though, a day did not pass where he didn't think of himself as the soul and bedrock of the Saudi people. Maybe the reports on this new director of National Intelligence were wrong.

Servants entered the room with fresh coffee and pastries, taking away the others even though they had not been touched. Rashid walked over to where Ross was standing and gestured for him to sit. The servants silently poured two cups of coffee without having to be asked and then took the prince's barely used cup and left efficiently and most important, silently.

Rashid grabbed the folds of his robe, lifted it, and sat on the couch directly across from the American. Ross added some cream and sugar to his coffee and then took a sip.

"Oh . . . you Arabs make the best coffee in the world."

Rashid smiled and thought to himself, *That is true, but why do you ruin it by adding cream and sugar?* Instead he simply said, "Thank you."

"May I be frank with you, Prince Muhammad?"

"By all means." Rashid leaned back.

"Nine-eleven was a very unfortunate event for both of our countries. In its aftermath there was a rush to judgment. A lot of decisions were made." Ross hesitated and then added, "Some of those decisions were, to put it bluntly, wrong and unfair."

Rashid was not a talkative person under normal circumstances, but when dealing with foreign dignitaries he was practically a mute.

"The decision by my government to force your removal as minister of the Interior was wrong, and I would like to apologize for it."

Rashid was once again caught off guard. His relationship with the

American government had been so contentious since the glorious attacks of 9/11 he did not think for a second that he would be receiving an apology. He slowly took a drink of his black coffee and said, "Your words are very kind, Director Ross."

"They are long overdue in my opinion, and I have told the president so."

Rashid's demeanor remained placid, but inside he was scrambling to figure out what this American was up to. Even Rashid, as self-righteous as he was, knew that the last thing he deserved from the Americans was an apology.

"For our two countries to get along we must understand and respect our differences . . . especially when it comes to religion."

Rashid nodded, and continued to listen as Ross expanded on his thoughts. The man was beguiling. A charismatic speaker who had a way with words. He reminded himself that Ross had been a senator, and politicians were never to be trusted. After a few moments, Rashid told Ross what he wanted to hear. That America was Saudi Arabia's greatest ally and that the two countries must continue to work together to fight the scourge of terrorism. Ross offered a few ideas, most of them trivial, but there was one point he made that again shocked Rashid. Ross told him that it was his sincere opinion that America should set up a one-year timetable for the withdrawal of all U.S. military personnel from the Kingdom.

The prince was awash in a sea of elation as the servants announced that breakfast was ready. As the two men walked from the library to the dining room Rashid reached out and held the American's hand, saying, "You are a good ally. You have a better understanding of what it will take to defuse these terrorists than anyone else I have spoken with in your government."

Ross took the compliment and then proceeded to expand on what he'd already told the prince. By the time they sat down at the table, Rashid was so thoroughly pleased with how things were going he decided he might have to stay an extra day in America and get to know the director of National Intelligence better. Ross continued to do most of the talking as the exquisite breakfast was served. He commented effusively on the food, the service, the prince's robes. They were almost done with their meal when Rashid looked across the table and in a very respectful tone said, "I am sorry to hear that the famed Mr. Rapp was killed in an explosion."

Rashid had planned on bringing this up for two reasons. The first was that he wanted to see if he could discover more details, and the second was to deflect any suspicion from himself by making it seem that he cared about Rapp's demise. After Rashid had delivered his condolences, he noticed that Ross's demeanor had changed. In fact, he face looked as if he had bitten into a ripe grapefruit. Sensing something was amiss, Rashid asked, "What is wrong?"

Ross was hesitant to reply at first. He took another bite of his salmon and then slowly wiped the corners of his mouth with his napkin. He looked at Rashid, tossed the napkin down on the table, and said, "I might as well tell you. You'll know soon enough. Mitch Rapp is not dead."

47

Rashid remained surprisingly calm. His eyes narrowed slightly, but other than that, he showed no outward signs of his inner distress. He stared stone-faced across the table at Mark Ross and asked, "What are you saying?"

"He's not dead. His wife was killed in the explosion, but he survived."

"But the papers and the TV," Rashid said with a disbelieving look on his face, "both yesterday and today have reported him dead."

"And they are wrong." Ross leaned in and pointed emphatically toward the window. "He's at a CIA safe house not far from here right now. He was severely injured but he is very much alive."

"Why hasn't your government corrected the press?"

"It's a complicated thing, Prince Muhammad." Ross sat back and let out a deep breath. "Let's just say there are a few people who think the explosion was not an accident."

"Someone tried to kill him?"

"It looks that way," Ross said without much enthusiasm.

"You do not sound convinced."

Ross rolled his eyes. "The man has a lot of enemies. It's not hard to imagine someone trying to kill him."

Rashid was shocked that Rapp was still alive and also that Ross seemed distressed by his survival. He decided to take a gamble. "Mark, you are worried by this Mitch Rapp business."

"Absolutely."

"May I ask why?"

Ross thought it over briefly. He was here to build a relationship and that wouldn't happen unless he opened up. "Mitch Rapp is a very dangerous man. Under the best of circumstances he is extremely difficult to manage. Now, I'm afraid he will be impossible."

"You think he will want revenge against whoever killed his wife."

Ross nodded. "I can't say I blame him, but we can't have him running around executing people. It would look very bad for the United States."

Rashid nodded his agreement. "Is there any evidence?"

"There is one small bit of intel that points to one of your countrymen." Ross arched his right brow. "But the evidence is so thin I can't even remember his name."

Rashid was trying desperately to stay calm. "What did this man do?"

"Apparently he placed a bounty on Rapp's head. I doubt he's the first person to do that."

"Bounty," Rashid repeated the word. "Was it a bounty or a fatwa?" Rashid knew several Islamic clerics who had laid down fatwas demanding Rapp's death. He had no idea if Ross understood the difference.

"A bounty. The man is very wealthy."

Rashid's stomach tightened. "Why would a wealthy Saudi want Mitch Rapp killed?"

"Apparently Rapp killed his son last spring in Afghanistan during a counterterrorism operation."

The entire room went out of focus for a second. Rashid regained his composure a moment later and told Ross, "Get me the person's name and I will see what I can find out." Rashid did not need the man's name because he already knew it, but appearances must be kept up. "It is not good for anyone to have these loose cannons causing us such problems."

"No, it isn't."

Rashid set his napkin down and pushed his chair back. He stood and Ross followed suit. The two men walked along the opposite end of the table and met by the door. Rashid reached out and touched Ross's elbow. "This killing must stop. It is very bad for our two countries."

"I agree."

"I promise you, I will get to the bottom of this. If any Saudi had a hand in this, they will be punished." Rashid stopped and faced the director of National Intelligence. "I warn you, though, that Mitch Rapp must not meddle in the affairs of Saudi Arabia."

"I understand this and have already spoken to the president."

"Good."

The two men continued into the large entrance hall where Ross's people were waiting. Rashid turned to Ross and said, "We have many beautiful horses for you to choose from. If you'll excuse me for a few minutes I must freshen up and then I will join you in the paddock."

The prince's personal assistant came forward and gestured for the group to follow. When they were gone, Rashid walked quickly to the library. His calm, austere façade had vanished. His perfect morning had turned disastrous in a matter of minutes. Mitch Rapp would no sooner stay out of Saudi Arabia's business than the sun would fail to set. His wife was dead and he was alive. Things could not have gone any worse. Rashid sprang through the library doors and slammed them shut behind him. Tayyib was pacing behind the desk, his arms folded and his chin down. A set of headphones lay on the desk next to an open briefcase. The curtains at both ends of the room were drawn.

"Did you hear everything?" Rashid asked.

"Yes."

"Is it possible it is a trap? To see if I had a hand in this?"

"Possible, yes, but doubtful."

"What course do you advise?"

"The German must die immediately."

"Make it so."

"And I regret to suggest that Saeed Ahmed Abdullah should meet an untimely end."

This was Rashid's oldest, closest friend. A devout Wahhabi and a good man. He could never abandon him. "No. You heard Ross. What evidence they have is thin. If the Americans want to persecute every man who has wished Mitch Rapp dead, they will have a list numbering in the millions."

"But they just happen to be right in this case."

"I will return to the Kingdom tonight and take care of Saeed. He will be fine. The Americans will never be able to prove a thing."

"Mitch Rapp will not need proof," Tayyib said in an ominous voice. "He will start killing and torturing until he finds out who was behind this."

"Ross said the president has ordered him to stay out of this."

"Rapp has never been one to follow orders. With his wife dead, the Americans have no hope of controlling him."

"Then he must die," Rashid snapped.

Tayyib nodded. "I know of two CIA safe houses in Virginia. One is very close. I helped interrogate several prisoners there after 9/11. They are fortified facilities but not heavily guarded."

"I want him dead," snarled Rashid.

Tayyib thought about this for a moment and then said, "It will cost a lot of money and it will be very messy."

"I don't care. Just so long as Rapp is killed and none of it is linked to us."

"I will take care of it."

48

The news of Rapp's resurrection was for the most part lost on the general public. It appeared at first on news crawls—those obnoxious streams of words that flowed across the bottom of the twenty-four-hour cable news channels. Intelligence agencies weren't proud of it, but they got a lot of their information from cable news, and the people whose job it was to monitor these channels stood up and took note that Mitch Rapp was alive. Phone lines burned, and e-mails flew back and forth between secretive buildings and across borders. The international espionage community was a loose affiliation of spies, analysts, and operatives who were bound by the unique nature of their careers. The mission of each organization was to collect and disseminate information, and not just within their own government, but to allies as well. Rapp was an icon in their world, admired by friend and foe alike. He was a man who had worked in the field and come up through the ranks—something they could all respect.

The news that he had been killed had been met with mixed reaction. Some thought his demise inevitable—no man could so aggressively wage a war against religious fanatics and remain unscathed. Those few who were ideologically opposed to Rapp's stance and methods applauded his death, but most were saddened by the news. He was one of them, and his death was a reminder of how dangerous their jobs were. There was another element to the story, though, that gnawed at a great number of them. Rapp's wife had been caught in the crossfire, and there was an unwritten rule in their line of work that families were off limits. Whoever had gone after Rapp had gone too far, so when news broke that Rapp was still alive, the vast majority of these men and women were secretly, and some not so secretly, hoping that Rapp would make the killers pay.

As a former Stasi officer and current freelancer Erich Abel was still connected to the fraternity, and it was safe to say that he was more surprised than anyone to hear that Rapp was alive. His day had started well enough. He'd gone for another long walk, this time through the Castello neighborhood of Venice, stopping in the Campo Santa Maria Formosa for breakfast and then continuing on his meandering walk through the narrow streets and alleys. He found two small galleries that showed promise. They were far enough off the main path that he knew he could negotiate a reasonable price for individual pieces. Abel was already spending his money. He would buy a small villa in the South of France and keep his place in Zurich. The place in Vienna, he decided, would be put on the market and his office closed. There were too many Saudis in Vienna, and it was time to sever that relationship. It had been profitable, but he no longer trusted Rashid. The man was on a jihad and everybody was expendable except himself.

He'd decided all of this before he'd been blindsided by the news that Rapp was still alive. Abel had been on his way back to his hotel after a late afternoon tour of more art galleries when he turned on his phone to check messages. For reasons of security and serenity, he'd been leaving the phone off but turning it on only a few times a day. He instantly knew something was wrong when the screen on the phone told him he had eleven new voice-mail messages and sixteen new e-mails. The first four were from his secretary in Vienna reciting a list of people who were trying to get ahold of him—almost all of them Saudis. The fifth message was from Saeed Ahmed Abdullah, and it was not pretty. In his thickly accented English he demanded that the job be finished or all twenty-two million dollars be refunded. Apparently the man did not remember the part where Abel had told him half of the money was a nonrefundable deposit. The sixth call was from Prince Muhammad bin Rashid's personal assistant and then after that it was a jumble of people. The e-mails were pretty much the same. By the time Abel reached his penthouse he'd come to the reluctant conclusion that Mitch Rapp was in fact alive. How they had missed him, Abel didn't know, nor did he care. The reality was the man was breathing and Abel's entire world was in shambles.

Abdullah, in one of his messages, proclaimed that the job must be finished. Abel considered the feasibility of this only briefly. Going after

Rapp when he didn't expect it was one thing, but now that he was alert it was out of the question. Even before this disastrous news, Abel had felt he could no longer trust Prince Rashid. That was why he was in Venice, staying in a five-star hotel under an assumed name and paying for everything in cash. Now that the job had been botched, Rashid would want him silenced. Abel began packing his suitcase and pondering how quickly the Saudis could move on him. Their intelligence services were good within the Kingdom but they were anemic abroad. Rashid would have to hire someone like Abel, which would take time.

Abel closed the suitcase and zipped it shut. He walked over to the large window in time to see another cruise ship passing through the Canale di San Marco. Row after row of faceless people lined the starboard decks snapping photos, waving, and watching. The ship was massive. Abel considered how easy it would be to disappear on one of those ships. He would be lost in the myriad of tourists from around the world. A divorced man looking to take his mind off a disastrous marriage. He'd used it as cover before and in fact he was using it right now. That was the excuse he'd used to pay for the room in cash and use an alias. Abel had explained to the manager that he was going through a messy divorce and had decided to tour Europe in style rather than give the wretched woman a penny. Her lawyers, though, were right on his heels and if he had any hope of holding them off he needed to be discreet.

Abel stared at his phone for a minute and then turned it on. He dialed his personal assistant's mobile number and waited for her to answer. After the eighth ring he got her voice mail. "Greta, it's Erich. Remember that thing we talked about? Well, I've decided to take a sabbatical. If you need to get ahold of me, you know how to reach me. Good-bye." *Sabbatical* was a prearranged code word that was a warning to Greta. She was supposed to stay away from the office until he told her it was safe to go back to work. In the meantime she would be paid for six months of work. After that she should assume something had happened to him and look for other employment.

He checked his e-mail quickly and then decided to send a message. He pulled up the address for the assassins and began typing. It read: *You failed. Finish the job, or return the money.* He didn't bother attaching a name.

Abel scratched out a quick note and stuffed it in an envelope along with a thousand euros. He grabbed his bag and wheeled it to the elevator. When he reached the front desk, he asked to see the manager. A moment later Nico appeared from the back office and stepped out from behind the counter. He took one look at the suitcase and held his hands out in surprise.

"You are leaving us so soon?"

Abel adjusted his glasses and said in a low voice, "I'm afraid the lawyers are hot on my trail." He handed the envelope to the manager and said, "I may try to make my way back in a few weeks. I left a number along with a generous tip for your judiciousness."

The man clutched the envelope to his chest. "You are too kind."

Abel leaned in a bit closer and said, "Call me if anyone comes looking for me."

The manager winked. "I will."

Abel wheeled the medium-size black suitcase out the front door and turned left to catch a water taxi. A valet from the hotel was there to assist him and Abel tipped him generously.

"Marco Polo Airport," Abel said in a voice that was loud enough for both the driver and the valet to hear. The German sat on one of the long white vinyl seats and began mulling over his options. He would go to the airport, but he would not be getting on a plane. He would go to the terminal and then take a cab to the port where he would book passage on one of the floating buffets. And then he would try to fit in among the large people.

49

MONTERREY, MEXICO

The drive from Indianapolis to the Mexican border took nineteen hours with a stop for dinner and a quick nap near Lake Texoma in Oklahoma. Along the way the gun, the rifle, and the ammunition were all disposed of piece by piece. Neither weapon had been used to kill anyone, and there was no way of tracing them back to Gould, but they weren't worth the trouble of trying to take across the border. Gould drove the entire time and despite feeling unsympathetic to Claudia's depressed state he continued to apologize and at least act like he was sorry about the woman. In truth, though, he could have cared less about Rapp's wife. He knew it sounded harsh, and there were many, including the woman who was carrying his child, who would think him a monster for such a callous attitude, but it was the nature of his business.

To survive, much less succeed, his work had to be approached with an analytical detachment that focused on maximizing success and minimizing failure. At first it had been relatively easy. The men he killed were not on the road to sainthood. Their corrupt, and sometimes vile, behavior made it easy, but as larger contracts came in, the ethical waters became murky. Who was to say which side was right and which side was wrong? Gould came to accept the fact that the players had all willingly entered the arena with a full understanding of the risks. This rationalization started him down a path of moral ambiguity. Rapp knew full well the risks his job involved and by association so did his wife.

The secondary figures in these operations, the bodyguards and spouses, for example, had signed on knowing who they were getting involved with, or they should have. Would it have been better if Rapp's wife had survived? Yes, but Gould felt he'd made an honest effort to spare her. In the end, however, it wasn't meant to be. As much as Gould wanted to engage Claudia in this debate, he knew that in her current state it would be foolish. He had always worried that she would not be able to handle the messy end of the business, and he'd done everything possible to shield her from it. She had seen him kill only one person, and that was in self-defense.

It was during the mid-nineties after the Soviet Union had collapsed and the tycoons and robber barons were dividing up the spoils and killing whoever got in their way. Politicians, journalists, competitors all were fair game. This had been Gould's proving ground and where he had made a name for himself. The work was steady and the money was exceptional. Gould had just popped a man in his hotel suite and was leaving the lobby when the warning bells were sounded. The crazy Russian bodyguards drew their guns and tried to shut the place down. Gould had to shoot his way out, and when he got on the street, there was one last Russian waiting. Fortunately for Gould the man was a bad shot. He squeezed off a long burst from an Uzi submachine gun. He was off balance, though, and shooting at an upward angle as Gould came down the steps. The bullets whistled high past his head. Gould took only one shot with his silenced pistol, striking the man in the face, dropping him to the ground right in front of Claudia, who was waiting behind the wheel of the getaway car.

Claudia had understood the need for him to kill or be killed. They'd even had passionate sex that night, but this was all different. Gould suspected she saw herself in Rapp's wife and wondered if she saw him in Rapp, if she was making some twisted Freudian parallel between the two couples. Nineteen hours of mostly silence in a car gives the imagination ample opportunity to run riot.

They approached the border during the peak of morning rush hour and had no trouble making it through customs. They were a man and a woman in a minivan headed to Mexico. If they had been trying to cross from Mexico into America they might have faced more scrutiny, but going south was easy. Gould relaxed almost immediately and Claudia smiled for the first time in days. They rolled down the windows, held hands, and cranked the radio. The drive along the toll road from the border to Monterrey was easy. Gould followed the signs to the airport and they parked the van in the crowded lot. He left the driver's window down and the keys in the ignition. They grabbed their backpacks and entered the airport. Gould purchased two tickets at the Mexicana counter from Monterrey to Mexico City and then on to Zihuatanejo. They had a little more than two hours to kill before the flight left. After passing through security, they found a café with wireless Internet service. Gould finally felt like they could relax and ordered a margarita while Claudia turned on her laptop and began checking e-mail.

There was some strange game show on the television that was holding the attention of both the bartender and the waitress. Gould had to wave his arm to order a second drink. Claudia asked for a bottle of water. It wasn't quite noon and no one, including the other travelers, seemed to be in a hurry. Gould was starting to feel the buzz from the tequila when he realized something was wrong. He glanced over and Claudia had her face buried in her hands and was shaking her head.

"What's wrong?"

"I can't believe it," she mumbled, her hands still covering her face.

"What?"

She turned the laptop toward him so he could read the e-mail. "It's from the German."

Gould read it, his face contorted in disbelief. "This is bullshit. 'Finish the job or send the money back.' What in the hell is he talking about?"

"I'd say it's pretty obvious."

Gould kept his voice down but was intense. "The job is finished."

Claudia spun the laptop toward her and her fingers began dancing over the keys. Within seconds she was scanning the home page of the *Washington Post*. It didn't take her long to find what she was looking for. She turned the computer back to Gould and pointed at the headline that read RAPP STILL ALIVE.

Gould read it and said, "I don't believe it. It's a trick. See if you can find another source."

Claudia pulled up one newspaper after another. They were all running the same story. She suggested Louie call and check their messages. There were three. The first was from his father mumbling something about a family gathering. Gould skipped it and erased it. The next one was from the German. His voice was calm, but he was adamant as to what must be done. The third and final message was from Petrov, who said that he had been put in a very difficult situation. He had recommended them to the German and it was his reputation that was on the line. He ended by telling Gould he knew how he thought, and this was not some trick by the Americans. Rapp was very much alive and if Gould wanted to stay alive too he'd better do the right thing.

Gould turned off the phone and stood. His entire body was tense with frustration. He ran his hands through his hair and took a step to the left and then the right. "How the hell did this happen," he mumbled to himself. He looked at Claudia. "I was there. I saw the house blow up. I know he was inside."

Claudia pointed at the screen. "It says here he suffered a broken arm and several broken ribs. The explosion blew him into the water, where he was picked up by a fisherman who saw the whole thing."

"Damn it." He spun around and looked at the exit. "I can't believe this. Grab your stuff. Let's get out of here."

Claudia didn't budge. She looked at him with an icy stare and said, "Sit down."

Gould's head snapped around. "What?"

"You heard me. Sit down right now."

Gould placed a hand on the back of his chair, but refused to sit.

"Where do you want to go?" Claudia asked.

"Back," he said as if she was a moron. "We have to go back and finish this."

"No, we don't. We are done. We have the money and we are retiring."

"No." He shook his head emphatically. "We go back and finish the job."

"Why?"

"Because it's the right thing to do."

"The right thing to do," she mocked him. "Don't you think it's a little late for that?"

"What in the hell is that supposed to mean?"

"You killed an innocent woman, and now you're talking about doing the right thing." Her brow furrowed and she began shaking her head. "Have you really become so sick that you believe yourself noble . . . that right or wrong has anything to do with this?" She lowered her voice and through tight lips said, "We kill people."

"I know what we do, but we have a code we have to follow."

"We used to. We're done. How does this change anything? We are retiring. You promised me. We are going to raise a family."

"They will come looking for us."

She laughed. "They would not even know where to begin. They know nothing about us, and we know everything about them." She pointed at her computer. "A single message telling them to leave us alone or we will kill them will solve the problem."

Gould shook his head. "You don't know what you're talking about."

Claudia tilted her head and looked at him as if she was searching for some clue deep in his mind. "Fine. We'll do the right thing. Let's send the money back."

"No . . . we're going to finish the job."

"It's about him, isn't it?"

"Who?"

"Rapp. You want to prove you are better than him."

"Pack up your stuff. Let's go."

"You were never going to retire, were you?" She was too angry to cry. "Go." She pointed toward the door. "At least you won't have me or your child to slow you down."

Gould shouldered his backpack and stared at her with angry eyes. "I'm going to finish this, and then I'll come find you."

"Don't bother. I don't think I want to see you ever again."

Her words hurt and they gave him a split second of pause. "What about the baby?"

"I think the baby would be better off without you."

Gould had never been more hurt by anything in his life, but he was too proud to let Claudia know. He simply turned and walked away.

50

The car, a black Infiniti Q35, belonged to a friend of one of the embassy employees. It was a little small for Tayyib's six-foot-three-inch frame, but given his mission he figured it suited him well enough. The car had been waiting for him in a parking ramp several blocks from the movie theater. Tayyib and three other embassy employees had pulled up to the theater fifteen minutes before the start of their movie and stood in line for tickets, popcorn, and refreshments. Thirty minutes into the show, the keys and a slip of paper were handed to Tayyib. He got up as if he was going to the bathroom and never came back.

The U.S. and Saudi governments had an unofficial understanding that they were not supposed to spy on each other. Tayyib, and every other serious intelligence officer, knew this agreement was a sham. He ordered his own people to keep a close eye on American intelligence officials when they visited Saudi Arabia, and he assumed the Americans would potentially do the same—although Tayyib knew from experience the Americans were far more worried about offending the Saudi royal family than the Saudis were about offending Americans.

Too much was riding on this operation to take any shortcuts, so Tayyib drove around for more than an hour to make sure he wasn't being followed. Finally at 9:47 he headed for the meet. Tayyib had dealt with this individual on only one other occasion, and the man had performed exactly what had been asked of him. At that time, a crisis had caused the Saudi intelligence officer to seek the man's aid. A Saudi citizen had been arrested in Virginia and was charged with importing ten million dollars' worth of heroin. He was in federal custody awaiting trial when word got back to Tayyib that the man was trying to strike a deal with federal prosecutors. In exchange for a reduced sentence, the man would provide proof that the Saudi Intelligence Service offered direct aid and training to al-Qaeda in preparation for the 9/11 attacks. Accusations made by a man who dealt in illegal drug trafficking would normally carry little weight, but this particular man had in fact been one of Tayyib's officers. He knew far too much and would do great damage if he was allowed to speak to the Americans. When Tayyib informed Prince Muhammad bin Rashid of the problem, the prince made it clear what needed to be done.

Tayyib's greatest asset had always been his resourcefulness. He had not grown up a violent person. Other than the occasional fight with his brothers and cousins, he'd never so much as raised his voice in anger. He had an excessively calm personality. Even on the soccer field where his size and speed would have allowed him to bully others he held back. He'd grown up in Riyadh, a city of some three million people where crime was as rare as rain. It wasn't until Rashid had gone to work for the Intelligence Service that he began to see why Saudis were so law-abiding. The legal system in Saudi Arabia was unbelievably harsh. Police beat confessions out of suspects, judges rarely offered leniency, and the prisons were wicked.

The prisons in Saudi Arabia and America were both very dangerous places, but for different reasons. In Saudi Arabia it was the guards the prisoners had to fear, whereas in America, it was the other inmates. Tayyib had an acute understanding of this because he had been involved in a top secret program regarding American inmates. For years Muslim charities had been providing funds, materials, and guidance to help convert American inmates to Islam during their stay behind bars. What most people didn't know was that Saudi intelligence officials had been keeping track of these new converts with the hopes that if need be these non-Arab men would join their fight. These men were tracked as they were released from jail and steered toward mosques where they could continue to get the proper Wahhabi indoctrination into Islam.

It was during a meeting with one of the Muslim charity workers that Tayyib learned of a group called Mara Salvatrucha or MS-13. The fastest-growing segment of the American prison system were Hispanic men. Tayyib could not understand why it was that they had not a single Hispanic recruit in the two years he'd been involved with the program. The man explained to him that the Hispanic prison population was overwhelmingly Catholic and that they were very organized and extremely violent. He cited two cases where African-American Muslims had been beaten to death for trying to convert MS-13 gang members. Tayyib did some research into the group and found out that the FBI now considered them to be the number one organized crime threat in America. The group had started in El Salvador and had spread across America like a cancer. Outside of New York City, the group's strongest presence was in the Washington, DC, metropolitan area.

The most difficult part had been making contact with the group. Like most street gangs they had an unofficial uniform. They gravitated toward pro sports jerseys. Their group colors were blue and white, the same as the Salvadoran flag, and they liked the numbers 13, 67, and 76. Tattoos of MS-13 were big, and they kept their hair buzzed short. Tayyib found out they had a strong presence in Alexandria and Fairfax, Virginia. With little time to spare, he was forced to take some risks. He drove to a particularly bad part of Alexandria in broad daylight and found two young men standing outside an auto repair shop. One was wearing a North Carolina tank top and the other a University of Michigan one. The numbers on the jerseys matched the profile as did the short hair and the tattoos. Tayyib pulled up to the two men and did not get out of the car. He handed them an envelope. It contained $10,000, a note, and a phone number. Tayyib told the men to give the package to their boss. Within the hour he received a phone call and met face to face with the local gang leader. More money exchanged hands, a deal was struck, and Tayyib's former employee was found dead in his cell the next day. When Tayyib met the man to pay him the rest of the money, he made it clear that he might again need his services and asked for the best way to get ahold of him. The man came right out and gave him a name and a number.

Tayyib was now back in that same part of town on his way to meet Anibal Castillo. When Tayyib had called him earlier in the day, Castillo had taken his number and called him back from a different phone. Tayyib pulled into the parking lot of the body shop and got out. An old backseat from a vehicle was leaned up against the front of the building. Two men were sitting on the backseat and two were standing, one on each side. The building was covered with bright blue, white, and silver paint. Despite the cool evening air the boys were all in baggy shorts and tank tops—their arms and necks covered in tattoos. Tayyib was armed, but he had no illusion as to what would happen if things turned violent. He was here all on his own. He grabbed the briefcase from the trunk and walked into the building without acknowledging the four men.

The small waiting room was occupied by four more men—larger versions of the boys who had been outside. These guys all had big guns stuffed in the waistband of their pants and one of them had a sawed-off shotgun resting on his shoulder. The air smelled sour—body odor and cigarettes. Tayyib paused for half a step. He was wearing jeans, a white dress shirt, and a blue blazer. His .45-caliber pistol was in a holster on his right hip. One of the men looked at it and stuck out his hand palm up. Tayyib handed the weapon over. There was no sense in trying to keep it. Another man came up behind him and began patting him down. A man with MS-13 in gothic letters emblazoned across his forehead took the briefcase and nodded for Tayyib to follow. They continued through the shop. There were bays, and all of them were occupied. Even at this relatively late hour cars were being worked on.

Near the back of the garage, there was a short hallway that led to a bathroom and the back door. Tayyib spotted a fat man standing guard at the back door. Gripped in his beefy tattoo-covered fingers was a black submachine gun. They stopped in front of a steel-plated door and the escort clanged away with Tayyib's .45-caliber pistol. Metal could be heard scraping on metal and a second later the door opened. Tayyib followed the man into the room. A fifty-inch plasma TV dominated the nearest wall. Two men sat in recliner chairs playing video games. Behind the only desk a man had his back to them and was talking on the phone in Spanish. He slowly turned the chair around and Tayyib recognized the man as Anibal Castillo.

"My old friend," Castillo said, "you are back again." He made no effort to stand.

"Yes," Tayyib said. He had a serious expression on his face.

"What can I do for you?"

Tayyib looked around the room. "Would it be possible for us to talk in private?"

The man who had escorted the Saudi back to the office placed the briefcase on his boss's desk. Castillo looked at it. "Is it locked?"

"Yes," Tayyib said.

Castillo motioned for it to be opened. Tayyib spun the case toward him and went to work with his thumbs. When all six dials were in the right position he pushed the clasps and lifted the lid. Inside was a letter-size manila envelope and neatly stacked packets of $100 bills and a cell phone. Castillo moved the envelope out of the way and focused on the cash. His brow furrowed as he estimated the amount of money in the case. After a long moment he looked up and jerked his head toward the door. The other men left in silence. Castillo pointed to a chair and Tayyib sat.

"A hundred thousand?"

Tayyib nodded.

"You must really want someone dead this time."

"Yes."

"Who?"

The Saudi grabbed the envelope and extracted a photograph of Rapp. "Have you ever seen this man before?" Castillo shook his head and Tayyib silently thanked Allah. "He is in federal custody at a house not far from here."

"And you want me to kill him?"

"Yes."

"What did he do?"

Tayyib shook his head.

Castillo grinned, and responded, "Fine . . . it will cost you more."

"Before we get that far, I need to know something." The Saudi thought about what he'd seen so far. "How well are your men armed?"

Castillo laughed. "Better than the police. I will tell you that."

"Explosives?"

The Salvadoran nodded.

"What kind?"

"Some C-4, a lot of hand grenades . . . hell, we even have a few an-tipersonnel mines."

"Rocket-propelled grenades?" Tayyib asked.

"RPGs . . . sure. We have plenty."

Tayyib was pleased. "I assume you have no problem killing federal agents?"

"No problem. But that will drive the price up a lot." Castillo placed his hand on the briefcase. "I'm not sure this will even cover the down payment."

"I only brought the money to show you I am serious."

"Well, you have my attention."

"Good. Let me show you the plan, and then we will discuss the price."

Both men stood and Tayyib extracted several satellite photos from the envelope as well as a map of the area. Tayyib pointed to the fence and explained in detail the perimeter security of the property.

"How many people outside?" Castillo asked.

"Usually four."

"Inside?"

"I don't know. I assume at least two plus the man I want you to kill. The difficult part will be getting in the house."

"Four guards are nothing."

"It's not the guards I'm worried about. The house itself has an extra layer of security . . . reinforced doors . . . bulletproof glass . . . you'll have to blast your way in. You'll have to hit them with everything you've got. Start with the RPGs, and if that doesn't work use the C-4. Burn the whole house down . . . I don't care."

Castillo smiled. "What about the police? This is going to make a lot of noise."

Tayyib had anticipated this. "I will keep the police busy. You take care of the house. I don't care how many people you kill . . . just make sure this man is dead." Tayyib picked up the photo of Rapp and held it up in front of the Salvadoran.

Castillo smiled and said, "For the right price I will kill him myself."

51

Physical injury and mental anguish brought with them uniquely different problems. Individually, each can cripple. A physical injury immobilizes a person, whereas psychological trauma incapacitates by inflicting fear or taking away an individual's desire to live. Separately, they are bad enough, but together they are almost always devastating. The last two days had been the worst of Rapp's life. His mind bounced back and forth between overwhelming despair and vengeful rage. As much as he wanted to leave the house and begin the hunt he was unsure of himself. Physically, he needed to recuperate, mentally he was a basket case. Having spent years in the field operating by himself, Rapp was a master at self-assessment. The searing hatred that he felt toward whoever was responsible for Anna's death would drive him to do whatever it took to find the culprits, and while Rapp understood the importance of motivation, he also understood the danger of being overly zealous. It caused people to take foolish risks that did not match the rewards. He would have to be smart about this. There would be times when extreme violence would be needed, but there would also be moments when he would need to be careful and judicious.

His body would heal soon enough. It had before and from worse injuries, but it was his mind that was the chief concern. Never before had he been so frightened to be alone with his thoughts. The black bottomless hole that his life had become was terrifying. He had done and seen terrible things, but nothing had so thoroughly unhinged him as the murder of his wife. It had gotten so bad that he actually asked to be given sedatives. It was the only way to turn off his mind and escape the horror of her death and the unending what-ifs.

But when he awoke it all came flooding back. The emotions had raged back and forth between hatred and complete despair. One moment he was swearing to himself that nothing would stop him from avenging her death and making the bastards pay, and the next moment he was curled up in a ball longing to touch her face one more time. And then came the inevitable—he blamed himself for her death. It was this lack of emotional steadiness, the ability to remove himself from the situation and think about the dilemma logically, that gave him great concern. If he couldn't get control of his emotions, he would fail.

Failure was unacceptable. The thought of them getting away with it, the knowledge that the longer he stayed cooped up in this room, the more likely it was that the killers would simply disappear, was what stopped his descent into darkness and depression. Ultimately, though, it was the thought of how pathetic he must look, curled up in a ball sobbing, that forced him to throw back the blankets, ignore the aches and pains, and swing his feet onto the floor.

As soon as he was upright a stabbing pain hit him in the temple and he realized it was the sedatives. It was time to take a complete physical inventory. He was wearing a pair of pajama shorts. He briefly wondered where they'd come from and then it occurred to him that he no longer had any clothes. The house, the car, all of his possessions, they were gone. He assumed even Shirley, his dog, had gone up in the explosion. Compared to the loss of Anna it was all trivial. He looked down at his leg and examined the deep purple bruise on his right thigh and then the small surgical marks on his left knee. The thigh looked far worse than the knee. His broken right arm felt fine, but his ribs were tender. He pushed himself off the bed and stood. The first step was more of a shuffle. His left knee was stronger than he would have thought. There was a robe on the back of the door and he hobbled over and grabbed it.

He made his way downstairs slowly, and in the process realized that his right leg was definitely in worse shape than his left. He paused near the front door and looked out the side window. The sky was gray and there wasn't a person in sight. There was a mirror on the wall and he stopped to look at his reflection. His thick black hair was unkempt, and his face was covered with stubble. The entire house felt unusually quiet. Rapp, so used to being alone, suddenly felt the need to be around people. He wanted information. He wanted to know what was going on. He shuffled his way down the hall to the kitchen. His legs were beginning to work better. The smell of coffee caught his attention. The clock on the microwave told him it was 9:53 in the morning. He found a mug in the cupboard and poured himself a cup.

Out of the corner of his eye, Rapp caught some movement. He shuffled over to the sink and looked out the window. Two people were sitting at a table on the patio. It was Irene Kennedy and her eight-year-old boy, Tommy. Tommy was slouched in his chair looking bored, kicking his leg up and down. Irene was talking on her phone. Rapp took in a deep breath and slowly let it out. Tommy was like a nephew to him. The boy adored Anna. Rapp suddenly felt both foolish and selfish for thinking only of himself. Anna would be missed by a lot of people.

Rapp set his coffee down and made his way over to the door. He twisted the handle and pulled. The door didn't budge. Rapp remembered he was in a secure CIA facility. Just like his house, the door jambs were reinforced and reversed so they only opened out. He pushed the door open and stepped carefully onto the brick patio. He pulled at the knot on his robe and slowly made his way over to them. Tommy noticed him and stopped fidgeting. He sat up straight and appeared hesitant. Kennedy turned around and told whoever she was talking to that she had to go. Rapp noticed movement on both his right and left and turned in each direction. Two of Kennedy's bodyguards were standing post. Rapp made it to the table and little Tommy stood. His eyes were already welling with tears. Rapp opened his arms and the boy buried his face in Rapp's stomach.

Tommy began sobbing uncontrollably. In between quick gasps of air he choked out the words "I'm sorry."

Rapp fell into a chair and held him as tightly as his ribs could take. The sight of someone he cared so much for, someone he knew adored his wife, melted what little resolve he'd managed to muster and the tears flowed once more.

They sat underneath the umbrella like that for a long time. He tried to tell Tommy everything would be all right, but even he could hear the uncertainty in his voice. Everything wasn't going to be all right. The one person he loved more than anything in the world was gone, and he found himself teetering on the verge of complete despair. How did his life get to this awful place?

Rapp heard a dog bark and he looked up to see Shirley, his collie mutt, running toward him. The unexpected surprise put a smile on his face. Rapp let go of Tommy and held out his arms for Shirley. The dog jumped up, placing its paws on Rapp's lap. Rapp scratched her neck and said, "I thought you were gone."

"One of your neighbors took her in after the explosion," Kennedy said. "Tommy thought it would be a good idea to bring her with." Kennedy smiled at her son. "He said a person came to school this year and told them dogs helped people recuperate after they've been in an accident."

Rapp scratched Shirley's neck some more and looked at Tommy. "Thanks, buddy."

"You're welcome." Tommy reached out and petted the dog. "If you need me to, I can take care of her."

"That'd be nice."

"I also brought my Game Cube."

Rapp nodded, touched that the little boy was so concerned.

"Maybe we could play later." He started kicking his leg. "I thought it might help."

Rapp wanted to cry all over again, but managed to keep it together. "Thanks, Tommy."

Kennedy wiped away a tear of her own and asked Rapp, "Are you hungry?"

"Starved."

The three of them went back into the house and Kennedy made pancakes. She managed to keep the conversation off the explosion by handing Rapp a newspaper and sending Tommy into the other room to set up his Game Cube. As he read the paper, Kennedy informed him that his brother Steven had called. He was on his way down from New York. Kennedy offered to bring him to the house for dinner. Rapp simply nodded. Both Rapp's mother and father were gone. He and his brother were not close in the sense that they spent a lot of time together, but they shared a deep bond. It would be good to see him.

The hard part came when she brought up Anna's parents. They'd arrived the day after the explosion and were waiting to talk to him. Funeral arrangements needed to be made, and they wanted his input. It was obvious Rapp was dreading the confrontation. They would blame him for their daughter's death. Why wouldn't they? He blamed himself, after all.

They ate breakfast outside next to the pool. Rapp devoured four pancakes and three sausage links. Tommy tried to keep up with him, but only managed two of each. They were just finishing when Scott Coleman showed up. He entered the backyard through a side gate. He was wearing jeans, hiking boots, a blue T-shirt, and a baseball cap. A large black nylon bag was slung over his shoulder. He stopped next to Rapp and dropped the bag.

"I picked up a few things at some stores. I assume you're still wearing extra small."

Rapp ignored the barb and slowly leaned over to unzip the bag. His ribs were giving him some difficulty. There were several North Face T-shirts, a fleece vest and jacket, sunglasses, hiking boots, pants, underwear, socks. The colors ran decidedly toward muted greens and light browns. At the bottom of the bag he found a brand-new Glock 17 pistol complete with silencer and hollow-point ammunition.

Coleman rubbed Tommy's short hair and asked, "How are you doing?"

"Fine."

"Do you think I could have a minute alone with your mom and Mitch?"

Tommy looked at his mother and then said, "Sure." He stood. "I'm gonna go look at the horses."

"Be careful," Kennedy said as Tommy took off at a trot. The boy called for Shirley to follow and she sprang after him.

When he was far enough away Rapp pulled the pistol from the bag and held it up to the sunlight for a better inspection. He grabbed the back of the slide between the meaty part of his palm and his fingers and yanked it back. He moved the weapon around and checked out the chamber and barrel. The piece was well oiled and clean.

"What in the world are you doing bringing him a gun?" Kennedy was not happy.

Coleman ignored her. "I added the night sights and had them shorten the trigger pull."

Rapp pointed the gun toward the ground and squeezed the trigger. He nodded. "Thanks." Rapp set the 100-round box of ammunition on the table and began loading all three clips.

"Did you bring him a razor?" Kennedy asked.

Rapp scratched his thick stubble.

"You're not going to want to shave that just yet," said Coleman.

"Why?"

The former commander of SEAL Team 6 looked at Kennedy. She

turned her soft gaze back to Rapp. "We've made some progress. The man who placed the bounty on your head was Saeed Ahmed Abdullah."

Rapp's dark eyes narrowed. "Waheed's father?"

"Yes."

"How solid is the intel?"

"For obvious reasons the Jordanians are not revealing their source, but they say the man has never let them down before."

"What else do we have?"

"Yesterday the NSA picked up a phone call made by Abdullah. We don't know who he was calling, but he was extremely upset. He told the person to finish the job or refund his twenty-two million dollars."

"Twenty-two million," Coleman said in disbelief.

Even Rapp was shocked by the number. "What did the other guy say?"

"We don't know. Abdullah was leaving the person a voice mail."

"Any luck with the phone number?"

Kennedy shook her head. "We don't have it. They only picked up Abdullah's voice from his end."

"Shit."

"We're working some other angles," Kennedy offered. "The vastness of his wealth is making it difficult, but we're looking for any transactions in the last month that might add up to twenty-two million dollars."

Rapp stared off toward the stables for a long moment.

"What are you thinking?" Kennedy asked.

"On Monday morning I'm going to need your G-5."

Rapp was referring to Kennedy's executive jet. "Just where are you planning on taking it?"

"Afghanistan."

Coleman started laughing. He looked at Kennedy and said, "You haven't told him yet."

"No."

"Told me what?"

"Your passport has been revoked, and I have promised the National Security Council that I will keep you under protective custody."

"Why?" asked Rapp in an angry voice.

"The vice president, secretary of state, attorney general, and the director of National Intelligence all convinced the president that you should be kept out of the investigation."

"What little investigation there is," Coleman interjected.

Kennedy gave him a look that said, You're not helping things.

"What's going on with the investigation?" Rapp asked.

"We'll get into that later. Let me first tell you what the president had to say to me in private. First of all, he is very sorry about Anna. You know he liked her very much."

Rapp didn't want to hear condolences right now and the expression on his face made it clear that Kennedy better get to the meat of the discussion quickly or Rapp's lid would blow.

"Officially, he doesn't want you anywhere near this investigation. Unofficially, he says you have his consent to kill whoever was behind this."

Rapp's rising rage subsided immediately. "So I take it I can't use your G-5 on Monday."

Kennedy shook her head. "I can help you, but you're going to have to run this thing in the dark. No official ties to the Agency."

Rapp turned to Coleman.

The former SEAL grinned and said, "I have a G-3. Not as nice as the G-5 but it'll get us from point A to point B. I also know a few guys who are itching to make a trip to Afghanistan."

"Monday morning," Rapp said.

"I think that's rushing it a bit," Kennedy said in a concerned voice. "You need more time to recover."

Rapp shook his head. "Monday morning. The longer we wait the harder it'll be to find them." He glanced back to Coleman. "I expect to be billed."

"Right after you kiss my ass," Coleman said stone faced.

"I'm serious."

"So am I."

"Scott, it doesn't feel right. If you and your guys are going to put it on the line you have to be paid."

Coleman knew Rapp well enough to know that he wouldn't stop on something like this unless he got his way. "I'll tell you what we'll do. When we catch these rat bastards, we'll split the twenty-two million."

"It's all yours. Just make sure everything is ready to go Monday morning."

"Don't worry, the boys are raring to go."

52

A nibal Castillo looked down at a map of Loudoun County and traced his finger along a road. He nodded to himself and then stepped out into the garage to check on the progress. Three identical black Chevy Suburbans were parked in the stalls. His men were busy getting them ready. For an illiterate thug who had not a single year of formal education and had been raised in the harsh poverty of a war-torn Third World country, Anibal Castillo was anything but stupid. At thirty-four he had never known peace. The first seven years of his life were spent with his parents and four siblings in the unforgiving ghettos of San Salvador where they were often forced to beg for food. In 1979 his native El Salvador was plunged into a brutal civil war and Anibal's father did his best to keep the family out of the fray. The next year Archbishop Romero was assassinated. The Catholic priest was idolized by both of Anibal's parents. Romero had been an advocate for the poor against a corrupt government and his brutal murder motivated many silent peasants to join the leftist guerrilla forces of the Farabundo Martí National Liberation Front or FMNL. Anibal's father moved the family to the central highlands and he joined the fight against the forces of the Duarte regime.

Anibal started off as a courier for the rebel forces and then when he was big enough to handle a rifle he became a soldier. Like most civil wars there were atrocities committed by both sides. Anibal's mother and two sisters were raped, one of his brothers had been captured, tortured, and shot by the government, and his father had been blown in half by a land mine. By the end of the war Anibal knew only violence. In 1995 he immigrated to America with his mother and two sisters. His surviving brother stayed behind and got involved in the drug trade. Anibal's family was sponsored by a group of Christian missionaries and ended up in the Washington area. Anibal never tried to find a job. Through his service with the FMNL rebels he was almost a de facto member of MS-13. Those first seven years in Washington had been easy. MS-13 was still under the radar of the FBI, and the DEA hadn't quite figured out how pervasive the gang was. The local cops thought they were just another Hispanic gang involved in drugs and car theft.

With fellow gang members either being killed or sent to jail, Anibal moved up the ranks quickly. At thirty-four he was now in charge of all of Prince William County and the majority of Fairfax County. Like Cosa Nostra before them, MS-13 expanded its operations into gambling and prostitution. If they had stopped there, they may have been able to continue unnoticed for quite some time, but they made two crucial mistakes. The first was that they got into extortion and kidnapping—two activities that tended to get the attention of the FBI. Their second mistake was to allow their gang-on-gang violence to spill onto the evening news and the morning papers. Law-abiding citizens, the ones who vote, didn't care too much when thugs killed one another, but when innocent people started getting caught in the cross fire they became incensed. Their outrage was then directed at the politicians, and the politicians, who tend to have acute survival instincts, came down hard on law enforcement.

The end result was that MS-13 was being squeezed by the local cops and the feds. Drugs became harder to move, and extortion and kidnappings were a good way to end up behind bars. Castillo was forced to focus on stolen cars, which was chump change compared to the other stuff. This mysterious man who he had dealt with only once before had shown up at the perfect time. His posse was getting restless. They needed some real action. Stealing cars was fine for the teenagers, but many of his men considered it beneath them. They needed to spill some blood and this was the perfect opportunity.

Castillo approached the first black truck and asked one of his men, "How much longer?"

The man peeked out from under the hood, a wiring harness in one hand and a screwdriver in the other. "Ten minutes."

Castillo checked his digital watch. It was 6:23. The man with the strange accent should be here any minute. "How are the other two trucks?"

"They're ready."

Castillo walked over to the next Suburban. All three had been stolen in the last five hours. The license plates were switched out, and police emergency flashers added to the front grilles and back windows.

"Hey, boss." One of Castillo's men walked up holding a pair of blue coveralls and a baseball cap. "Do we really have to wear these?"

Castillo didn't bother to speak. He just looked at the man sideways like he was thinking about killing him right then and there.

The guy was wearing a white wife-beater T-shirt and a pair of super-baggy shorts. He looked down at the blue FBI hat and shook his head.

"You want to go to jail, you fucking moron?" Castillo stared at the man, half hoping he would give him an excuse to beat him to death. It might be a good lesson for the others.

"No, boss." The man was smart enough to keep from looking Castillo in the eyes.

"Well, how the fuck do you think we're gonna drive all the way out to Leesburg, kill a bunch of feds, and then get all the way the fuck back here without getting stopped? Huh?" Castillo slapped the man across the side of his head and then yelled, "Maybe you want to drive your pimped-out ghetto ride and see how far you get, you stupid bastard?"

The other gang members had stopped what they were doing to see what would happen next. Castillo did a half circle and yelled, "Does anyone else have any stupid questions?"

The gang members scrambled like cockroaches. Castillo was about to walk back into his office when his new friend entered the garage—this time with an even larger briefcase. Castillo jerked his head toward the office and the man followed. The Salvadoran closed the door so they could have some privacy.

Tayyib stood stiffly with the briefcase clutched firmly in his hand. In a cautious voice he asked, "Is everything all right?"

Castillo rolled his eyes. "That was nothing. My men will be ready."

Tayyib remained frozen for a moment, thinking of his options, which were extremely limited. "The trucks?"

Castillo nodded.

"Are they part of your plan?"

"Yes. I figure even with your diversion it might be difficult to get back into the city."

The Saudi agreed. He took it as a good sign that the man could be creative. "The car I asked for?"

"It's ready."

"I will have no problem with the law?"

"As long as you don't get pulled over you should be fine."

"What does that mean?"

"Exactly what I said," Castillo said sharply. "It's a stolen car. We changed the plates but if you get pulled over and they ask for the registration and proof of insurance you're in trouble."

Tayyib supposed it was the best they could do on such short notice. He hoisted the briefcase onto the Salvadoran's desk. "Four hundred thousand dollars." He was tempted to add that he would find him and kill him if he didn't finish the job, but considering his limited resources, and the fact that the comment might get him shot right here and now, he decided to keep his mouth shut.

Castillo opened the case and looked inside. He smiled and asked, "Your diversion you told me about?"

"I need to borrow a few things from you."

"Like what?"

"Can you spare an RPG and a few grenades?"

Castillo thought about it and then nodded.

"Good." Tayyib checked his watch. "Be in position by nine-thirty and I'll make sure the police have their hands full." The Saudi started for the door and then stopped. Looking over his shoulder he added, "Just make sure you kill everyone."

Castillo smiled and said, "Absolutely."

53

The black Lincoln Town Car pulled up to the heavy gate. Rapp stood in the living room and watched. The sun was falling in the east, shooting golden streaks of light and shadows across the fields. Rapp assumed Kennedy was in the backseat of the luxury sedan but he couldn't be sure. Lincoln Town Cars were a dime a dozen in Washington. It was 7:20, and his boss had been due to arrive at 7:00 with his brother. Steven had never been big on punctuality. Rapp had not seen his brother in almost two months. There was no strain in their relationship, it was just that they were both extremely busy. There was also the fact that the only thing they had in common was that they'd come from the same parents. At first glance, though, even that bond appeared debatable.

The car came to a stop in the circle by the front door. Out of habit Rapp watched how Kennedy's security detail operated. The man behind the wheel kept the car in drive and the guy in the shotgun seat jumped out and scanned the area a full 360 degrees. Only then did he open the director's door. Kennedy emerged from behind the heavily tinted windows and a moment later the blond, almost white head of Steven Rapp appeared from the other side of the car. Mitch smiled briefly. His brother had always had that effect on him. Steven Rapp was one of those rare individuals who were funny without having to try.

Mitch Rapp was six feet tall and weighed 185 pounds. Steven Rapp was five six and couldn't have weighed more than a buck thirty-five. Mitch had black hair; Steven had blond hair. Mitch had square broad shoulders; Steven had a slightly concave chest. Where Mitch had brown eyes, Steven's were a brilliant blue, and so the contrasts went. There had been a lot of mailman and milkman jokes while they were growing up and who could really blame the wiseasses—Mitch himself had wondered how these two opposites could have come from the same womb. Their mother for years laughed about it and claimed it was because Steven was undercooked by a full five weeks in the womb, whereas Mitch didn't want to come out and was two weeks late.

Where Mitch had been blessed with athletic ability, Steven had been blessed with intelligence, and not just your average Mensa high-IQ type intelligence. Steven was a certifiable genius with a master's degree in quantum theory from MIT. For the past four years he'd been running the hedge fund department for Salomon Brothers in New York City. His annual bonus last year had been a cool twenty-seven million dollars. Mitch had been giving him money to invest for nearly a decade, and Steven had turned several hundred thousand dollars into more than four million. He was extremely good at what he did, and Mitch was very proud of him. He was also very protective, which was why this next part was going to be awkward.

Even before their father had passed away so unexpectedly, Mitch had watched over Steven like an eagle guarding its nest. When their father died, Mitch pummeled any kid who so much as looked at Steven the wrong way. It got so bad that even Steven told him he had to find other ways to deal with his grief. This coming from his eight-year-old little brother. Even then the kid had been wise beyond his years. When their mother died of cancer, Mitch had made the extra effort to check in on him, to make sure his baby brother didn't feel alone in the big city, but Steven just kept plugging along. His work was all-consuming and that was at least something he could identify with.

Tommy Kennedy entered the room and stood next to Mitch. Rapp put his arm around the boy.

Tommy looked out the window and said, "My mom says your brother is really smart."

"Yep."

"Do you think he'll want to check out my Game Cube?"

Rapp grunted, amused by the question. Steven was the original video gamer, crushing all takers in Pong, PacMan, Asteroids, and all of the original video games. His apartment in Manhattan had a separate room just for gaming, replete with two custom chairs and a fifty-inch, high-definition plasma screen. Rapp nodded and said, "My brother will definitely want to check out your Game Cube."

Rapp made his way toward the front door. Most of the aches and pains he had felt when he finally got out of bed in the morning were now gone. His right thigh hurt a bit, and his ribs were still tender, but other than that, he felt pretty good. The wood-paneled door had one six-inch titanium dead bolt. Rapp turned the dead bolt with his left hand and opened the door with his right. A beeping noise sounded in the hallway behind him. Rapp knew that an employee of the CIA was sitting in a small security room under the horse stables noting the fact that the door was open.

Rapp was dressed in the clothes Coleman had brought him: jeans, a T-shirt, and hiking boots. The white cast on his right arm was the only outward sign of his ordeal.

Kennedy clutched her purse against her left side and allowed Steven to catch up. Rapp's brother was wearing loafers, khakis, a white dress shirt, and a blue blazer. His black eyeglasses helped him look a bit older. He looked up at Mitch, who was standing under the portico, and pushed his glasses up on his nose a notch. "I'm sorry, Mitch." Steven climbed the steps and wrapped his arms around his brother. "She was an awesome woman."

"Yes, she was."

"I'm so sorry," Steven said again as he squeezed his brother tight.

"I know." Rapp put his arm around his brother and kissed his forehead. "I'm glad you came. It means a lot to me."

54

The stolen Mercedes ML 500 had only 8,456 miles on it. It was black and had dark tinted windows just as Tayyib had requested. He had seen quite a few of the mini sport utility vehicles since he'd arrived in America. They were fairly common, but still expensive. Tayyib thought it would be a good vehicle to both blend in and remain above suspicion. After leaving the shop in Alexandria, he had taken the expressway out toward Dulles International Airport. From there he'd taken the Hirst-Brault Expressway north toward Leesburg. About six miles south of the town he took a detour and headed west. He came upon the horse farm a few minutes later and kept his speed at 55 mph as he drove along the edge. Trees dotted the fence line and obscured the house that sat atop a hill a good four hundred yards off the road. The main gate had cameras mounted on both the left and the right. Tayyib guessed Castillo and his people would have little trouble getting past it.

He continued down the county road for a few more miles and then turned around to head back to town. It was twilight and he needed to get into position. On the way into Leesburg, Tayyib drove past the Loudoun County Sheriff's Department. He'd found the address on the internet and printed directions from MapQuest. Six cruisers and a Suburban were parked in the lot along with another half dozen civilian cars. He continued into town and did a slow pass of the government center and the police department. He noted three police cars in the lot and another one pulling out. He had no idea when the shift changes took place but he doubted it was at 9:30 on a Saturday night. He drove slowly through the quaint town. It was filled with antique stores, bed and breakfasts, and a smattering of coffee shops, ice cream parlors, bars, and restaurants.

Tayyib parked on the street around the corner from a café. He walked back to the café and was greeted by an overly enthusiastic and under-dressed young woman. He ordered an espresso to go and looked around the place. There were three other patrons inside: two teenagers making out near the front window and a young man pecking away on his laptop computer. Tayyib felt like slapping the young couple but reminded himself he had more important things to do. After paying in cash he went and stood in front of the café until the time was right. The air seemed a bit chilly, but none of the locals seemed to mind it. A woman in a tank top passed by walking a dog, and a couple of teenage girls sat in front of the ice cream parlor in skirts that barely made it a third of the way down their thighs. Across the street he could hear loud music spilling out of a bar, couples were out and about, and a few teenagers whizzed by on skate-boards. They all seemed to be having a grand time. *Well, that's about to end,* Tayyib thought to himself.

Tayyib was standing next to a small tree. He studied the branches for a second and picked his spot. After checking his watch one more time, he drained the rest of the espresso and threw the cup to the ground. Turning to the side so the two young lovers couldn't see what he was doing, he reached into his left jacket pocket and pulled out a hand grenade and a coil of fishing line. Tayyib turned his back to the café, looked to his left and his right, and then took the grenade and slid the spoon over one of the branches. The grenade dangled there like a piece of fruit—its matte green finish not quite blending in with the bright fall colors. Tayyib grabbed the end of the fishing line. One end was tied to the pin and he wrapped the other end around two fingers, dropping the loose coil to the ground. Casually, he started back for the car. A middle-aged couple passed him on the sidewalk and he edged closer to the street so they wouldn't get their feet tangled in the line. The last thing he wanted was a bunch of shrapnel in his back.

When Tayyib reached the corner he stopped and turned around. He could only make out the first few feet of the fishing line and then it dis-appeared in the shadows. The middle-aged couple were almost to the café and two women were approaching from the other direction. *The more mayhem, the better,* Tayyib thought to himself. He grabbed the coil firmly in his hand and continued around the corner. Once he was shielded he drew in the slack and gave the line a good yank. The line popped free and Tayyib dropped the loose bundle of fishing line to the ground.

He started for the car, counting the seconds in his head. He got to five, and then it happened. A loud explosion ripped through the still night air. Tayyib unlocked the Mercedes, climbed behind the wheel, and put the car in drive. He drove down Plaza Street and two blocks later stopped for a red light. When the light turned green, he continued past the police station and headed out of town, careful to maintain the posted speed.

Tayyib reminded himself that the important thing was to stay calm. He put on a pair of gloves and grabbed a black ski mask from the passenger seat. A few minutes later he turned onto Catoctin Circle and pulled up in front of the Sheriff's Department. Nothing had changed. The same vehicles were parked in the same spots. Tayyib pulled the ski mask over his head and threw the Mercedes in park. He calmly got out of the car, walked around to the rear of the vehicle, and popped the tailgate. Inside was an oily tarp from the garage. Tayyib moved it out of the way and grabbed a Chinese-made rocket-propelled grenade. It was loaded and ready to go. He shouldered the weapon and turned to aim it at the front door just as two deputies were rushing out. Tayyib widened his stance, put most of his weight on his back foot, and squeezed the trigger. The 40mm round traveled at a speed of 400 feet per second and Tayyib was a mere eighty feet from the building. There was a split-second delay and then a swooshing noise followed almost immediately by the detonation of the grenade.

Thousands of shards of glass flew in every direction. Tayyib lowered the weapon and looked at the two deputies. They were both on the ground just his side of the door. Neither was moving. Tayyib assessed the damage that had been done by the RPG round. Smoke was pouring out of the building and he could hear people screaming from inside. He dropped the RPG to the ground, and it clattered on the asphalt. In a nearly robotic fashion he pulled the last grenade from his pocket, yanked the pin, and threw the grenade through the shattered entrance, over the bodies of fallen deputies and toward the chorus of panicked voices. He turned, closed the tailgate, and was at the open driver's door when the grenade detonated. He didn't even flinch. He got behind the wheel, put the car in drive, and calmly pulled back out onto the county road.

Tayyib removed the ski mask and checked his watch. Castillo and his men would be moving into position and starting their attack any minute. As tempted as Tayyib was to go monitor the situation, he knew he needed to get rid of the vehicle as quickly as possible. He stepped on the gas and headed south for Dulles International Airport.

55

Steven carried the conversation during dinner, regaling Irene and Tommy with stories of what Mitch had been like growing up. His quirky, self-depreciating sense of humor helped take everyone's mind off the tragedy for a short while. Even so, there had been moments during the meal where Mitch would get that faraway look in his eye. To his brother, it was obvious he was thinking of Anna. Steven would respond by saying, "Remember that time . . ." and then he would be off telling another story.

The meal wound down, the wineglasses were drained, and young Tommy let out a yawn. Irene took this as an opportunity to give the two Rapp brothers a moment alone. She had decided since it was a Saturday night and Mitch was up and moving around that it would be best if they all stayed over. Steven had agreed. "It looks like someone is ready for bed."

Tommy shook his head. "No. I don't have school tomorrow."

"It's still late."

"But I didn't get a chance to show Steven my Game Cube."

Kennedy looked up at the grandfather clock in the corner of the dining room. It wasn't yet 9:30. Before she could respond, Steven Rapp asked, "You have a Game Cube?"

Tommy nodded enthusiastically. "Yep!"

"What games?"

"Tony Hawk Pro Skater Four, Star Wars . . ." Tommy rattled off a half dozen titles.

"How much money do you have on you?"

Tommy looked confused, not quite understanding why the question was being asked.

"Hundred bucks a game. You and me."

Tommy's eyes got big and he looked at Mitch, who was shaking his head. Mitch looked at his brother and asked, "You like picking on an eight-year-old?"

"You sure had no problem doing it when I was his age."

Mitch just shook his head rather than go down that road again.

"All right," Steven said, "a buck a game, and I'll spot you as many points as you want."

"First we do the dishes," Irene insisted. "Come on, Thomas, help me clear the table." Irene stood. "Would anyone like any coffee?"

Both men declined.

"Why don't you two go into the living room and relax?"

As Irene and Tommy picked up the dishes, Mitch grabbed another bottle of wine from the sideboard and opened it. He filled his glass and offered some to Steven.

"Why not?" his brother said. "I'm not driving tonight."

They walked into the formal living room. It had a distinctly feminine feel: yellow walls; white enameled woodwork; blue and yellow floral patterned drapes; an ivory-colored couch with a mishmash of pastel pillows, matching side chairs, and white carpeting. Like most of the house, it looked like it hadn't been decorated since the mid-eighties. Mitch sat on one end of the couch and his brother took the other end.

There was an awkward moment of silence and then Steven asked, "Have you made any plans for the funeral?"

Rapp stared off into space and shook his head. "Her parents are handling all of that."

"Don't you think you should have a say in the matter?"

"I got their daughter killed, Steven. I think that disqualifies me from having a say in anything."

"Have you talked to them?"

"No."

"Don't you think you should?"

"I'm going to see them tomorrow." Mitch looked into his wineglass and added, "I have no idea what I'm going to say. She was their only daughter. They adored her." His eyes misted over. "They were so damn proud of her." He thought of the pain they must be in. Their beautiful daughter was gone forever.

Steven was at a loss for words.

Mitch looked up with tear-filled eyes. "I'm fucking falling apart. I never felt more helpless in my life."

"I don't know . . . you were in pretty rough shape after Maureen died." Steven was referring to his brother's girlfriend who had been aboard the Pan Am flight that had been blown out of the sky over Lockerbie, Scotland.

"That was nothing compared to this. I was a kid back then. I didn't know what real love was."

"That's a lie," Steven said a bit forcefully. "You and Maureen were in love, and that's not taking anything away from Anna. It's simply the truth. You survived her death, and you'll survive Anna's. It's not going to be easy, but you owe it to her." Irene had explained to Steven that his brother was nearly catatonic over his wife's death. One of the doctors had recommended putting him under suicide watch. Steven had never hidden a thing from his big brother and he wasn't about to start now. "The last thing she'd want is for you to take your own life over this."

Mitch made a face that suggested his brother's concern was an insult. "Steven, I would never kill myself. That's not my problem. It's what I'm going to do when I get out of here."

"How do you mean?"

Mitch didn't get to answer the question. There was a noise from outside that caught his attention. His face turned to the ceiling, his ears focusing intently on the slightest sound. The solid construction gave the house great insulation, but even so, Mitch had spent so much time on gun ranges, indoors and out, that there was no mistaking what came next. The muffled crack of a rifle.

"Irene!" Mitch screamed at the top of his lungs. There were several more shots and he sprang to his feet. "Where are your bodyguards?"

Mitch grabbed Steven by the arm and yanked him out of the chair. More muffled shots rang out. They moved quickly from the living room, through the dining room, and into the kitchen.

Kennedy was at the kitchen sink, Tommy at her side. She had a dishtowel in her hand and a confused look on her face. "What's wrong?"

"Gunfire outside!"

"I didn't hear a thing."

"Trust me. Where are your bodyguards?"

"They're outside."

"Shit!"

Mitch grabbed mother and son by the arms and moved them quickly across the kitchen. Kennedy had the presence of mind to grab her purse from the counter.

"Get to the tunnel and head over to the interrogation facility." Rapp opened the door to the basement and started moving the Kennedys and his brother down the stairs. "When you get over there lock yourselves in one of the cells. Go!" Mitch yelled.

"But what are you—" Kennedy started to ask.

There was an explosion outside that shook the house. "Go, dammit!" Rapp screamed. He slammed the door shut and raced across the kitchen for the back stairs. He bounded up the first two steps, ignored the instant pain from his thigh injury, and continued up the steps two at a time, grabbing the handrail as he went. At the small landing there was another explosion. As Rapp reached the second floor he heard machine-gun fire from the rear of the house and wondered if he'd made the wrong decision to stay behind.

56

Castillo rode in the first Suburban. A mile short of the house he told the men in his vehicle to get ready. A short while later the gate came into view, and Castillo hit the switch for the emergency lights. The driver crossed over into the oncoming lane, down onto the shoulder, and then jerked the vehicle to the right and skidded to a stop directly across from the tall black gate. The second Suburban pulled up alongside the first, and the third one continued just past the entrance, came to a sudden stop, and then backed up. Two men in blue coveralls and FBI baseball caps jumped out and wrapped a heavy chain around the center of the gate. They hooked the other end to the trailer hitch on the truck and scrambled out of the way. The vehicle lurched forward in four-wheel drive, slowed for a second as the gate resisted, and then there was a loud screeching noise as the metal began to twist. One after another, the anchor bolts that held the gate to the stone columns popped free and the gate came crashing down. The truck dragged the twisted black bars out of the way and the two waiting Suburbans raced up the long driveway.

They were going close to 60 mph by the time the house came into full view—their engines roaring and the red, white, and blue emergency lights flashing their official warning. A man in a suit was waiting for them at the edge of the circular drive. He had a radio in one hand and his other hand rested on the butt of his still-holstered gun.

Castillo smiled and told his driver, "Run him over."

The heavy Suburban took the turn, its wheels squealing and emergency lights flashing. The man in the suit was still under the illusion that he was about to have a confrontation with a fellow federal employee. He'd been told by Kennedy that Director Ross wanted to put Rapp under protective custody. At the last second the driver jerked the wheel to the right, blew through a three-foot hedge, and hit the guard with the Suburban's front right fender. The passenger-side rear wheel came to a stop on the man's chest. Every door on the Suburban flew open except the driver's. Five men, all dressed in matching coveralls and baseball caps, jumped out. Castillo was barely out the door when a second guard came around the corner of the house. This man had his gun drawn. Castillo raised his Uzi submachine gun with one arm and pulled the trigger.

Castillo wasn't the only man who had seen the guard. Within two seconds the man was hammered to the ground by no fewer than ten bullets. A third guard was dispatched in roughly the same manner as he came around the other side of the house. One of Castillo's men dropped to a knee to line up the first RPG shot on the house. Castillo banged his fist on the hood of the Suburban and yelled at the driver to move the vehicle farther away. Two seconds later the truck was clear and the first RPG was fired.

Four men, three of them with machine guns and one of them with an RPG, were headed around to the back of the house. Castillo surveyed the scene. So far everything was going according to plan. The debris from the first RPG was beginning to settle and the third vehicle had just arrived after getting rid of the gate. Castillo looked at the door. As far as he could tell, it was still intact. "Hit it again!" he yelled.

A second round was loaded. Castillo checked the area behind the man to make sure no one was standing in the back blast zone, which was a good way to get killed or severely burned. "Shoot!" he screamed.

The round hit the door squarely and a large section of the portico's ceiling broke free and crashed to the ground. Castillo ran along the sidewalk and up the three steps. He covered his mouth against the cloud of dust and gave the door a solid kick. He might as well have been kicking the side of a mountain. The door didn't budge an inch. As more of the dust settled Castillo bent over to examine the damage done by the RPGs. There were two holes in the door not quite big enough for him to fit his fist through. The wood was splintered away but beneath it, he could see the rough edges of bent steel. "What the fuck?" he exclaimed.

The Salvadoran ran his hand along the door and gave the handle a twist. This was when he noticed that the door opened out, not in. Aware that he didn't have all the time in the world, Castillo ran back to the driveway and grabbed the RPG from his man. "Give me that damn thing!" He loaded another round, took careful aim and squeezed the trigger. There was yet another explosion, and more of the porch ceiling came crashing down. Castillo's men were now firing at the windows and fanning out around the house. When enough of the dust had settled, Castillo was happy to see that there was a hole where the door handle used to be. He barked at one of the drivers, "Grab a crowbar and go open that thing."

Castillo realized his ears were ringing and he worked his jaw from one side to the other to see if it would help eliminate the harsh noise. It was then that he noticed the pock marks the bullets were making on the windows. "Why am I fucking around with this door?" he asked himself. "Here," he handed the RPG to the man standing next to him, "reload this thing."

How stupid, Castillo thought. He heard an explosion from the rear of the house and hoped the other men were making better progress.

57

Rapp raced into his bedroom and didn't bother with the light switch. There was no sense letting them know where he was. The bag of stuff Coleman had brought him was on the floor next to the bed. Rapp dropped down a little too quickly and pain shot through his left knee. He swore under his breath as he screwed the silencer onto the end of the Glock, slammed in a magazine, and chambered a round. He grabbed the two extra magazines and stuffed one in each back pocket. Training, skill, instinct, and a little bit of luck was what kept people alive in these situations. It was his training that told him to grab the earplugs, the tactical knife, and the flashlight.

Holding the earplugs in his hand, he paused for a split second, his mind registering that something didn't seem quite right. He'd been through enough of this stuff before to know what certain types of battles sounded like. This one was decidedly not covert, and although Rapp had yet to stop and think of who might be attacking a CIA safe house, he had noted that something seemed out of place. Professionals preferred silenced weapons for three reasons. The first was that they drew less attention and they allowed you to sneak up on people. The second was to differentiate yourself from the opponent. If everyone on the team used a silenced weapon and you heard an unsuppressed weapon fired during an operation, you knew the bad guys were on to you. The third and last reason was practical. Silenced weapons saved your hearing.

With that in mind, Rapp put in his foam earplugs and crawled over to the window. He stayed off to one side and peeked down onto the patio area around the pool. The first thing he noticed, he'd expected. There were four men, three of whom were firing machine guns at the house. They were all dressed in dark coveralls. A fourth man was loading an RPG and doing a very clumsy job of it. Rapp looked beyond the men toward the stables and was relieved to see no one paying any attention to the place. Irene, Tommy, and Steven should be safe by now. Rapp turned his attention back to the four men and noted again that something wasn't right. Tactical teams didn't use RPGs. They used shaped charges to blow open doors and windows. The RPG was an infantry weapon, originally designed to be used against tanks. The next oddity that Rapp noticed was that these guys were standing way too close to one another, and they were firing their weapons from the hip. Rapp's eyes and brain were experiencing what a fine art dealer goes through when he looks at a reproduction of a well-known original for the first time. From a distance everything looks fine, but upon closer inspection all of the details are wrong. He noticed for the first time that the men were wearing FBI baseball caps. Rapp knew his fair share of FBI agents. They had a certain demeanor about them, and none of these guys fit the bill.

Rapp reached out and turned the lock on the window. With his hand as close to the edge as possible he slowly pushed up on the bottom half of the double hung window. The din from outside rushed into the room along with the chill night air. Rapp was on his right knee, his left foot planted firmly on the ground, the sill of the window at his chest. He took a quick peek, noted the position of each man, and then raised the silenced Glock and held it next to his face, the thick black silencer pointed at the ceiling. They were approximately fifty feet from the house and standing still as they fired at the house. This was going to be like shooting fish in a barrel. Rapp took in a deep breath, extended his left hand through the open window, and revealed only a third of his body as he moved into firing position. As was his habit, he started on the left and moved to the right.

The night sights on the Glock were neon green—two dots on the rear sight and one dot front and center. Rapp had done this so many times he didn't even have to think about it—it was pure instinct. The front sight fell on the first target, the glowing green dot covering half the man's head. Rapp squeezed the trigger with a steady, even pull—the dot remained perfectly still and in focus, the target's head a slight blur. The trigger tripped the hammer and a hollow-tipped bullet spat from the end of the weapon. The front sight instantly fell on the next target, and Rapp repeated the process three more times in rapid succession. In less than two seconds all four men were down on the brick patio, limbs askew, weapons nearby, bullet holes in the center of their heads, and very much dead.

Rapp closed the window, left the room, and crossed the hall into another bedroom. An explosion rocked the house just as he was approaching the window and he heard something crash to the ground on the first floor. He quickly stepped off to the side and peered around the heavy drapes. He counted eight men, all dressed like the four he had just dispatched in the backyard. There were three black Suburbans parked in the driveway with emergency lights flashing.

Rapp again noted the poor tactics and discipline, and asked himself, "Who in the hell are these clowns?"

A second later Rapp noticed Vince Delgado, the head of Kennedy's security detail, lying on the ground. Rapp assumed he was dead. His jaw momentarily clenched in anger, and then he noticed one of the men barking orders at the others. He was holding an Uzi submachine gun in his right hand and looked really pissed off. The guy pointed his gun toward the west side of the house and yelled something at two of the men. Rapp started to move before they did. He backed away from the window and out of the room. As he moved quickly down the hallway, he caught a whiff of cordite that must have been coming from downstairs. If they got inside the house with all those guns, things might get a bit hairy. Rapp reached the small study at the end of the hall and went straight for the window. He twisted the lock and opened it. He heard voices almost immediately. A second later two men appeared beneath him, moving at a fast walk and talking to each other in Spanish.

Rapp frowned. Absolutely none of this was making sense. He let the men pass beneath him, leaned out the window, and shot each one through the top of the head from about fifteen feet. Rapp took a quick look around. No one else was in sight. He closed the window and wondered just what in the hell a couple of guys speaking Spanish were doing coming after him.

He hustled back to the bedroom at the front of the house and looked down to find only two men in sight. They were standing in front of the closest Suburban. One held a gun against his hip like some bored prison guard and the other an RPG. There had been eight before, minus the two that he had just killed. That meant there were at least four more men that he couldn't see. Rapp decided to thin the herd a little more and slowly opened the window. He heard a voice come from almost directly beneath him and assumed that the other four men were on the front porch trying to get the door open. The guys by the Suburban were at least eighty feet from the house, and the angle of the shot required him to kneel down. Rapp leveled the silenced pistol and squeezed off two quick rounds. Both men dropped to the ground, one of them propped up against the front tire of the nearest Suburban.

Rapp closed the window and did a quick magazine change, placing the partially used one in his back left pocket. The smell of cordite was growing stronger, and Rapp wondered if a fire had started on the first floor. He left the room and went for the center staircase. The explosions had knocked out the lights in the front entryway and the living room. A faint stream of light spilled down the hall from the kitchen, and Rapp thought he caught the glow of a small fire coming from somewhere in the living room. The smoke was definitely getting worse. A fresh volley of gunfire erupted, and Rapp heard rounds thudding into the bulletproof glass in the living room.

He was about to start for the back staircase when he noticed the holes that had been punched in the front door—undoubtedly from armor-piercing rounds. Rapp had an idea and moved down the main staircase as quickly as his injured legs would carry him. He eased his way up to a hole in the center of the doorway just as they started banging on the window in the living room. He peeked through a soda can–size opening, and sure enough there was a man standing no more than eight feet away with his back to him. Rapp figured they'd given up on the door and were trying their luck with the windows. He placed the silencer in the hole and nestled his head in behind the rear sight. The man's head looked as big as a beach ball at this distance. Rapp squeezed the trigger and sent a round straight through the guy's ear. The guy went limp as a noodle and right as he fell another guy came into view. The man watched his friend fall to the ground; the why hadn't yet registered with him. He was starting to open his mouth to sound the warning when Rapp sent a shot straight through his right eye.

The guy took a tumble off the porch into the bushes and someone started yelling in heavily accented English. Rapp decided two things at that moment. It was time to move to a new spot before these guys pumped another RPG through the front door, and he needed to take one of these morons alive so he could find out who in the hell they were and who had hired them. Staying in a crouch he hightailed it down the center hall to the kitchen. By his count there were at least two guys left on the porch and maybe more. He took a left through the kitchen and crossed the dining room. Straight ahead he saw a small fire in the corner of the living room and decided to scrap his plan. He went back to the patio door in the kitchen. The backyard was still flooded with security lights and he stopped to make sure no one was waiting for him. Rapp undid the lock and stepped onto the back patio, closing the door behind him. He decided to go left since that was the side of the house where he'd killed the two men who'd walked under the window. The other direction was the garage, and he had no idea what the situation was like over there. He stayed low and worked his way between the bushes and the house.

58

Castillo stood near the edge of the porch with a man on each side. He was getting more frustrated by the second. This was supposed to be easy. Slam a couple of RPGs through the front door, rush the house, and let loose with the machine guns. Just like *Scarface*. That's what he'd told his posse. There wasn't a guy in the gang who hadn't seen the movie at least ten times. "Shoot anything that moves," he'd told them, "other than each other." That had been his only real worry—that and getting back to the city without the cops stopping them. The tricked-up Suburbans would take care of that, though. They'd already deceived the stupid guards. The one dumb son of a bitch was so fooled he hadn't even drawn his weapon. Castillo realized that was about all that had gone right so far. They were supposed to have been inside the house almost five minutes ago. The boys had been pumped. He'd told them they'd all get $10,000 cash for a night's work, and get to kill a bunch of feds in the process.

One minute into the operation Castillo had been counting his money, and now things weren't looking so easy. Having given up on the door after four shots, he fired his last RPG round through the window. It created a nice clean hole, but other than that the window was still intact.

Castillo pointed his Uzi at the window and asked, "Are you guys ready?"

The two men raised their Car 15s and nodded. Castillo opened fire and the other two did the same. In less than five seconds they'd drained their magazines. Castillo yelled for them to reload as he inspected the pockmarked and spider-veined glass. When everyone had reloaded, they unleashed another volley at the window. Shell casings littered the porch along with chunks of plaster that had fallen from above. The men themselves were sprayed with tiny shards of glass that had chipped under the deluge of bullets. There wasn't an unblemished spot left on the window, but it was still intact.

"Goddammit," Castillo screamed. His Uzi was jammed. "Where in the hell are those two idiots?" Castillo had sent two of his men around back to get a couple of RPG rounds. He had five and the team around back had five. He couldn't be sure with all the noise, but he swore he'd heard only one explosion from the back of the house. "Give me that crowbar!" he yelled to one of his men.

Castillo set his Uzi down on a chair and grabbed the three-foot steel bar with both hands. He took a couple of huge swipes at the window. The glass made a cracking noise. Castillo redoubled his effort and put all of his weight into it. The upper left corner began to peel away and he was finally making some real progress when one of his men started screaming obscenities. Castillo turned around to see what the man was so exercised about and saw one of his guys lying on the ground with a pool of blood growing around his head.

"What the fuck?" Castillo barked.

"I think you guys killed him."

"What the fuck are you talking about?"

"The bullets! They bounced off the window."

Castillo actually considered this for a second, and then he saw the boots of another one of his guys. The man was lying in the bushes with a hole where one of his eyes used to be. Castillo's ears were ringing from all the gunfire, and his head was starting to hurt. He moaned out loud and wondered where in the hell his luck had gone. Leaving them here would be stupid. Their bodies were covered with MS-13 tattoos. He looked up toward the vehicles to tell Hernandez to load the bodies into his truck, and that was when he saw two more of his men laying down on the job. The very next thing that popped into his head was a vision of $500,000 vanishing into thin air.

"Fuck." He pointed to the two dead men on the ground next to the Suburbans. "I suppose they were killed by ricochets too." Castillo tossed the crowbar to the man and said, "Open that window." Looking back at the other two guys he said, "One of the guards must still be alive." He was looking one of his men straight in the eye when the guy's face literally exploded, showering Castillo with blood and chunks of brain and skull. Castillo froze, his eyes trying to comprehend what had just happened, everything slowing down for a second or two, and then suddenly he snapped out of it and lurched for his Uzi, which was resting on a chair only a few feet away. He almost had his hand on the grip when he remembered the thing was still jammed. He kept reaching and then something slapped his hand away. Castillo looked down in shock, his brain not yet registering that a bullet had torn through his hand. To his left and right he noted two more of his men falling to the ground as he clutched his shattered hand. By the time he looked up a man was already coming at him from the far end of the porch, his gun extended. Castillo recognized the eyes. They belonged to the man he'd been sent to kill.

59

The moon floated over the Pacific Ocean casting a shimmering wake that danced straight across the bay to her balcony. The hotel was beautiful, only thirty-six rooms, almost all of them suites, each with its own private gravity pool and unobstructed view of the tranquil bay. Under normal circumstances the setting would have been extremely romantic. The humid tropical air, the waves lapping at the cliff beneath her balcony, a gentle breeze blowing in off the salty water, a small cluster of sailboats anchored for the night rocking gently in the water. Down on the beach couples were out walking in the surf.

Claudia had never been to this particular hotel before, but she had been to many others like it, and always with Louie. The mere thought of him, the man she thought she knew, brought the tears back. How she had gotten to this point in her life, she wasn't sure, but she knew she had never felt so alone, and so utterly disgusted with herself. She looked back on the last six years with a clarity that can be reached only when the journey is over. When you have told yourself there is no going back. It was resolution inspired by pain, the type of thing that steeled the psyche against future assaults. What had caused her to reach this tipping point, she hadn't been sure of when she arrived at the hotel a day and a half ago. The reflective solitude of the place coupled with her own isolation left memories and aspirations to battle it out in her mind, debating her possible salvation, and whether or not she ever deserved it.

Claudia Morrell had been raised a devout Catholic, by a beautiful, gentle, and traditional mother. Her father, a lifelong military man, was a ruggedly handsome soldier who had barely enough time for his wife let alone his children. Claudia knew now why she had chosen this drastic course. Ten years ago she would have laughed at any shrink if they'd told her she had been lashing out at her father—making him pay for his years of neglect. Looking back on it now it was obvious. She got back at him by dating one of his junior officers. She saw her father in Louie, there was no denying it. When her father tried to sabotage their relationship by having Louie transferred, that was the beginning of the end. It was the catalyst that had set things in motion. That much she understood.

He had driven her away, but it was she who had chosen this morally corrupt life. The transformation from a God-fearing Catholic to this wasteland of ethical ambiguity did not take place overnight. It was, like most lives of crime, one that had started off small. At first her role in the partnership was nothing more than moving money around to make sure it wasn't tracked, and that it was tucked away in a place where certain governments couldn't get their hands on it.

Sure enough, though, it progressed. She'd begun to guess what Louie was up to. All of the secrecy, and his vigilant, almost paranoid behavior, was not without reason. When she'd discovered that Louie was a contract killer, she had been surprisingly unaffected by the revelation. She supposed it had its roots in the fact that her father had killed men in battle. In Louie's case, it was not a stretch to feel ambiguous about him killing sociopaths, capitalist pigs, corrupt politicians, and unethical businessmen. But this Mitch Rapp was a different story. She had felt it was wrong from the moment she heard his name, but she had not protested enough.

Alone, looking back on her decisions with a healthy dose of self-loathing and maturity, she knew that the simple embarrassing truth was that she had been raised better. She had been given the tools to know right from wrong and she had consciously chosen not to use them—to ignore that little voice that told her every step of the way what she was doing was wrong. She'd used her own issues with her father as an excuse to discard the moral compass she'd been given as a child. And her lame excuse was that her father had not given her enough attention.

Claudia looked up at the moon and wiped the tears from her face. She was filled with self-loathing. Her childhood had been good. Her parents had taken good care of her. They had never hit her or screamed at her. They were still married, and they still loved each other. Claudia had no excuse for why she had allowed herself to sink so low. She had rationalized condoning Louie's actions for a very long time but no longer. The moment she'd met with the German, she did not trust him. She'd known it was wrong to target Rapp. The undeniable, harsh truth was that she had allowed herself to sell every ounce of her morality, everything her parents had taught her about right and wrong, for ten million dollars.

That was her price tag, and now she found herself embroiled in this Greek tragedy, bloodstained hands and all, a life growing inside her, sired by a man who had just killed a pregnant woman and had not shown an ounce of remorse. Louie's complete lack of shame, or even regret, had been the thing that woke her up from this bad dream. She understood that mistakes were made, but to be so headstrong as to not even acknowledge them was repulsive. For the first time in all the years she'd loved him she did not like what she saw. In her eyes Louie had turned into a monster.

What the gods had in store for her and her unborn child she was too afraid to even consider. Somehow, though, she knew she needed to make things right. There was the past, and there was nothing she could do about that, but she could try to make amends. She doubted she could redeem herself, but maybe she could make things right for her baby. She could not bring Anna Rielly and the beating heart of her baby back, but she could repent and do her best to make things right. Claudia now knew with complete conviction what she must do.

Wiping the tears from her face she stood and walked into the living room. She hit the space bar on her laptop to bring it out of sleep mode and then logged onto the Internet. There were two more messages from the German. She read them quickly. They were essentially angrier versions of ones he'd already sent. Abel wanted the money back or the job finished. If they didn't comply he was going to hunt them to the ends of the earth. The German was lucky Louie wasn't here to read them, because if he had, he'd get on the next plane to Europe and Abel would be dead before Monday morning arrived. Claudia had already decided he wasn't going to get the money back. In fact, Abel was about to have much bigger problems.

Claudia had found the person's e-mail account earlier in the day. It had not been difficult. She simply punched in the person's name and then added @cia.gov. The initial try didn't work, so she added a period between the first and last names and sent it again. This time it went through. With her fingers poised above the keyboard she took a deep breath and began typing. Claudia worked on the message for nearly an hour, and then deleted nearly everything she had written. There was too much. She would have to start out slow, with a simple apology, and see where it went from there.

Claudia maneuvered the arrow until it rested on the send tab. Her finger remained poised above the pad ready to tap it and send the message on its way. Claudia hesitated a moment, and then the little voice in the back of her head, the one she had ignored for the last six years, told her to do it. Claudia tapped the mouse pad, and the laptop beeped. The words MESSAGE SENT popped up on the screen, and she knew there was no turning back.

60

What do you mean, he's gone?" snapped Ross.

Kennedy regarded him carefully, jammed her fingers into the pressure points on each palm and told herself to stay calm. "He's gone, Mark."

"I heard you." Ross brought his hands up like he wanted to choke someone. "How in the hell did he just vanish?"

"Maybe we should wait for the president," Kennedy said in a reasonable voice. She didn't want to have to repeat herself, and she had no doubt that Ross would be more civil with his boss in the room.

It was Sunday afternoon, and Ross had just finished playing eighteen holes with the president, the party's chairman, and one of the party's chief fundraisers. Kennedy had been tempted to call the president after the attack, but by the time she'd caught her breath it was past midnight, and as a general rule she never disturbed the president's sleep unless she needed him to make a decision. She'd thought about calling Ross, thought about how the call would go, and knew immediately that the longer she could put off bringing him into the loop the easier her life would be. There was too much to do, and he would want to be calling the shots.

So she had delayed it as long as she could, and now she was here to deliver the bad news and watch Ross freak out. Kennedy had not slept a wink. In addition to her professional duties, she had to contend with her son and how he was handling the trauma. Fortunately, Steven Rapp had understood that she needed to manage the situation and that Tommy needed someone to reassure him that everything was all right. So while she tried to sort out the mayhem, Steven and Tommy were escorted back to her house by a beefed-up security detail. The most difficult part had been explaining to Tommy that Vince Delgado and Mike Burton had been killed.

She'd arrived back at her house a little before ten in the morning. Tommy woke up, came down the hall, and the first thing he asked her was what happened to Vince and Mike. They had been on her personal protection detail for more than a year and she knew Tommy was attached to both men, especially Vince. She would break the news to their family members herself, but it would have to wait until she took care of a few things.

Ross was her chief concern. There were several things that she had done in the last fourteen hours that he would not like, but he was not someone who was well suited to consider the long-term needs of the CIA. She had timed her arrival at the presidential retreat to coincide with them getting back from their golf outing. She'd been waiting in the Aspen Lodge by herself for a little more than fifteen minutes, which had given her some extra time to think about how she would handle Ross. It was during this brief calm in a tumultuous week that she stumbled upon the key to dealing with Mark Ross. She was a little surprised she hadn't thought of it before, but she was not the type of person who tried to play her superiors.

Ross had no intention of waiting for the president and he pressed Kennedy by asking, "When did this happen?"

Kennedy glanced over Ross's shoulder toward the door. "Last night."

"When?"

"Around ten o'clock."

Ross's jaw went slack and his eyes narrowed. Now it was his turn to look over his shoulder. When he was sure they were still alone he turned his angry eyes back to Kennedy and said, "It is two in the afternoon. Would you mind telling me why in the hell it took you so long to inform me?"

Vanity, Kennedy thought to herself. *That's the key.* "Mark," she leaned in and spoke as if they'd known each other for years, "you know what's going on here today?"

Ross looked confused.

"No one is thrilled with Vice President Baxter's performance." Kennedy paused and let the innuendo hang there for a few seconds. "He's been a drag in the polls, and there's been a lot of talk about replacing him on the ticket." She moved in even closer and whispered, "I know there was a reason the president asked you to play golf today."

Ross took in a deep breath and nodded.

Kennedy could tell by the expression on his face that he'd already thought of this. It didn't matter that he didn't know the president wasn't running for reelection and it wouldn't matter in a month when he announced that he wasn't. Ross would take that news as an opportunity. He'd just have to wait and see who was going to be the front-runner and get them lined up in his sights.

"You're on the short list, Mark. Today was your interview. I didn't want to screw that up by dropping this on you right before you teed off, or worse, cut your round short."

Ross was speechless for a moment and then just as he was about to comment on Kennedy's revelation the president entered the room.

"Irene," Hayes said as he came over to them. He was dressed in a golf shirt, sweater vest, and slacks. "I'm sorry to keep you waiting. What's the problem?"

Kennedy shared a brief look with Ross and then said, "Mr. President, one of our safe houses got hit last night." Kennedy explained to the president and Ross that she had picked up Steven Rapp and brought him to the safe house so he could see his brother. They had just finished dinner, it was around 9:30, she was in the kitchen with her son cleaning up, when suddenly they heard gunshots and several explosions. Rapp rushed herself, her son, and his brother into the basement. Kennedy took a moment to explain the physical setup of the safe house, and how they took a tunnel over to the subterranean interrogation facility and locked themselves in a cell. About an hour after the incident had started, a CIA quick response team arrived on site and secured the facility. Kennedy explained with some difficulty that two men on her security detail had been killed, as well as two other CIA guards who were tasked to the facility. She ended the summation by telling them that Rapp was gone.

"What do you mean, he's gone?" Ross asked in a far more subdued tone than he would have five minutes ago.

"He literally wasn't there," Kennedy answered. "We assumed the worst at first . . . that he was captured and taken away, or killed and taken away, but then we ran the security tapes." Kennedy stopped, and it was obvious by the expression on her face that there was more to the story.

"And?" Ross asked, his curiosity fully piqued.

"The house was hit with a total of seven RPG rounds and over a thousand bullets. In addition to the four CIA employees killed, there were thirteen other bodies discovered."

"Thirteen?" Ross was shocked by the number.

"They were the men who we think were hired to attack the facility. They used three black Chevy Suburbans equipped with emergency lights." Kennedy turned to the president. "Like the kind the Secret Service uses to get through traffic. They tore down the main gate, and then drove up to the house with their emergency lights flashing. They were wearing blue coveralls with FBI baseball caps. My bodyguards didn't even draw their weapons. I think they thought it was the FBI showing up to place Mitch under protective custody."

"Back up a minute," said Ross, "or move forward. You said the four guards were killed. There were other guards, right?"

"No."

"Then what happened to these thirteen guys?"

The president looked at Kennedy and said, "Mitch was what happened to them."

Kennedy nodded. "Each man was killed with a single nine-millimeter shot to the head." Kennedy frowned and added, "Here is where it gets interesting. There was a fourteenth individual. The tapes show Mitch putting him in the back of one of the Suburbans and leaving."

"Why?" asked Ross.

"Why do you think?" Kennedy replied. "Somebody has now tried to kill him twice, and his wife is dead. He's going to squeeze everything he can get out of this guy and find out who hired him."

Ross didn't like the sound of this. "So we have no idea where he is?"

Kennedy shook her head.

"Have you identified any of the thirteen?" asked the president.

"We think they are members of a Latino gang based out of Alexandria."

"A Latino gang," Ross said. "Why in the hell would they want to kill Rapp?"

"Since we don't have anyone to interrogate, I'm going with the assumption that they were offered cash. Mitch has never operated in Central America. A gang like this would have no reason to go after him."

"What does the FBI have to say?" Ross asked.

Kennedy hesitated briefly. "I haven't brought the FBI in on this."

"What?" Ross was shocked.

"Mark," Kennedy said, "we don't need this kind of publicity. This facility is off budget. With your political career still ahead of you, it would be wise for you to stay as far away from this thing as possible."

"But we have four dead federal employees and thirteen dead . . . citizens. I assume these men are citizens."

"Mark," Kennedy shook her head, "the murder of my people will not become an issue. These families are briefed about this type of possibility and they will not make a stink."

"It's a domestic federal facility, though. It falls under the FBI's jurisdiction."

"If we bring the FBI in on the investigation, we'll end up with reporters crawling all over this and you will end up sitting in front of a committee on the Hill answering some very uncomfortable questions, and all for what?"

"What about the . . ."

"Mark," Kennedy said with an edge to her voice, "we have thirteen dead gangbangers who killed four federal agents and we have it on tape. The punishment for killing a federal agent is the death penalty. Citizens or not, these thirteen guys have already been punished. Bringing in the FBI will accomplish nothing more than putting this whole sorry mess on the front page of every newspaper in the country."

"What about the fourteen guys?"

Kennedy took a step back and shrugged. Her nonverbal answer was clear. She could care less what happened to them.

Ross started to speak, but the president reached out and placed a hand on his forearm. "Mark, trust me on this. Sometimes you're better off not asking questions. Let Irene take care of it."

It was clear Ross was struggling with this concept. He drew in a breath through clenched teeth and said, "Fine, but we need to find Rapp and make sure he doesn't embarrass this country."

Kennedy expected this. "Why?"

"Because we are a nation of laws, and we can't have a federal employee running around other countries killing people."

Really, Kennedy thought to herself, *what do you think Mitch has been doing for the last fifteen years?* She shared a quick look with the president. "Mark, I want you to be real careful here. Think about how this would be done, and what type of unwanted attention it will bring us. For starters, we can't charge him with anything."

"How about the thirteen dead Latinos?"

"Mark," the president said in a forceful voice, "forget about what happened last night. I don't want to hear it brought up again."

"Fine," Ross said, backing off a bit, "but we have to do something."

Kennedy saw her opening and said, "I think I have a solution."

"Let's hear it," said Ross.

"For now, we only alert our station chiefs abroad. I can send out a flash message telling them if they are contacted by Mitch, or they hear anything about him, they are to pass it on to me ASAP. I can stipulate that I want him brought in for questioning."

"What about the embassies?" Ross asked.

Kennedy thought he would suggest this. "I would prefer to keep it within the Agency."

"Not a big enough net." Ross shook his head.

Kennedy looked to the president to see if he'd back her up.

"For now," Hayes said, "let's alert only the Agency people." The president noted that Ross didn't like this and added, "Mark, he's not going to reach out to anyone from State. If he comes up for help, he'll contact one of his Agency connections."

"But can we trust those people to turn him in?" Ross asked.

Both the president and Ross looked to the director of the CIA. The truth was that they could not trust the station chiefs, but Kennedy wasn't about to admit that. This was all about telling Mark Ross what he wanted to hear, so Kennedy said, "I'll start calling select station chiefs immediately, and I'll make it very clear that they are to report any contact whatsoever, or they'll spend the rest of their careers burrowed in the basement of Langley purging outdated files."

This seemed to satisfy Ross, and Kennedy decided that having accomplished what she'd set out to do, now was a good time to leave. "I know you two have an important lunch scheduled, so I won't keep you waiting. If there are any new developments I'll let you know, otherwise, I'll have a more detailed briefing ready for tomorrow morning."

The president thanked Kennedy, which inspired Ross to do the same. Kennedy left the lodge and was ferried to the helipad in a golf cart. As soon as she was tucked away in the back of her helicopter, she pulled out her secure satellite phone and punched in a number. After several rings a man answered on the other end and Kennedy said, "I just bought you a little more time."

61

The G-3 executive jet descended through the thin mountain air toward the old Soviet-era airport. They were in Northern Alliance territory; a small section of the country that had refused to be ruled by the Taliban. It was Sunday night. There were no clouds and a three-quarter moon bathed the rugged landscape beneath. It was almost 11:00, and from the air you would have no idea that Mazar-e Sharif was a city of over 100,000. There were only a few streetlights here, and an occasional floodlight. Very few cars were on the move. Even the runway lights appeared in spotty condition. Considering the sketchy shape of runways in this part of the world Scott Coleman had relieved one of his men and taken over the controls. If anyone was going to ruin his fifteen-million-dollar plane it would be him.

He'd received the call from Rapp just before 11:00 p.m. He had been expecting to hear from him, just not so soon. They'd spent the morning and early afternoon together at the facility talking about where they would start once Rapp was in good enough shape mentally and physically. Coleman had left that meeting and called his team. He knew they were already in—they had all individually approached him to offer their services. "Anything Mitch needs, just ask and we'll be there." The guys—Charlie Wicker, Dan Stroble, and Kevin Hackett—were all former SEALs, and they had all worked with Rapp before, as recently as the op they'd run in Canada.

Everyone had been assembled by midnight, and they were wheels up by 1:00 a.m., streaking across the Atlantic at nearly 40,000 feet. They'd stopped in Germany long enough to refuel and were back in the air in under thirty minutes. No customs to clear, no hassles to deal with. Operators like Coleman and his men were used to a lot of hurry up and wait. Deployments, such as this one, where they literally had to fly to the other side of the world, took some time. For this reason Coleman kept the plane well stocked with DVDs, paperback novels, and magazines. Coleman was happy they had them, because after Wicker, Hackett, and Stroble had offered their condolences to Rapp, which was before they even got off the ground, none of them knew what else to say. Special Forces operators like these guys were not exactly in touch with their feminine side. They had no problem discussing death when it was some guy they'd blown away in combat, but when it was someone's wife who had been tragically killed, they were at a complete loss for words.

Coleman and Hackett took turns flying, and everyone else either slept or tried to sleep on the way to Germany. The second leg of the journey was spent watching movies, reading books, and talking to Rapp about anything other than his dead wife. With the landing lights on, Coleman made a diving pass at the runway to see if there were any unusually large craters he should try to avoid. He was surprised to see the strip patched up and in relatively good shape. No doubt, courtesy of the U.S. taxpayers. He circled around and came in on his final approach. The G-3 touched down and settled at the far end of the runway.

Coleman leaned into the center aisle and looked back into the cabin. "Where to now, Mitch?"

Rapp had a satellite phone up to his ear. He covered the mouthpiece and said, "South end of the terminal. There should be a fuel truck and a Toyota 4Runner." Rapp removed his hand and said, "Sorry about that, Irene. You were saying?"

"Ross agreed to keep the State Department out of it for now."

"And the FBI?" Rapp asked.

"Yes."

"Good work."

"That remains to be seen. Last night someone set off a grenade in downtown Leesburg injuring five people. Two of them seriously. Five minutes later an RPG was fired into the Loudoun County Sheriff's Department."

"A diversion?"

"I would assume so."

"Has anyone asked about the racket at our place last night?"

"Yes. Local nine-one-one received a complaint at nine thirty-eight last night. They finally got around to calling this morning."

"And?"

"We told them we had a corporate event and shot off some fireworks."

"They bought it?" Rapp asked.

"So far."

"What about the house?"

"The front gate is being replaced this afternoon and the house is covered in scaffolding and tarps. They've already started sandblasting the bullet marks from the brick and replacing the doors and windows. All the evidence will be gone by tonight."

"The bodies?"

"Incinerated."

"And what about my prisoner?" Rapp asked.

"Dr. Hornig is working on him."

Rapp considered that for a minute. The Agency had two principal interrogators with distinctly different approaches. Dr. Jane Hornig was one; Bobby Akram, a Pakistani immigrant and a Muslim, was the other. Hornig had advanced degrees in both biochemistry and neurology and was considered the foremost expert in America on the history and evolution of human torture. She specialized in experimental drugs and exotic techniques. Bobby Akram, on the other hand, wore his subjects down by manipulating Maslow's Hierarchy of Needs and putting them through tough, well-researched interrogations. Rapp liked Akram, but he didn't like Hornig. She gave him the creeps, but when time was short, no one was better.

"Has she found out who hired him?"

"Not yet, but we found an interesting link. Two years ago, the DEA arrested a Saudi immigrant who was importing heroin through his contacts in Afghanistan. It turns out the guy used to work for Saudi Intelligence. While he was in jail, his lawyers started working on a plea bargain. The lawyer said that his client could provide proof that his former employer provided training to several of the nine-eleven terrorists and helped plan the attack."

Rapp frowned. "What does this have to do with some Latino thug?"

"Castillo, that's his name by the way. Anibal Castillo. He says back then he was approached by the same man that hired him to kill you two days ago. He paid Castillo a hundred grand to have MS-13 kill this former Saudi intel officer while he was in the federal pen. I made a few calls and it all lines up. This former Saudi was ready to start singing and the day he was supposed to sign the plea bargain he was killed in his cell."

"Who hired him?"

"We don't know yet, but we have Castillo looking through our database of Saudi intel officers."

The plane lurched to a stop, and Rapp said, "Listen, I have to run. Call me as soon as you find out."

"Are you going to tell me what you're up to?"

"You don't want to know." Rapp peered out the small window.

"Yes, I do, Mitchell. I just lied to my boss and the president to protect you."

"I thought the president was on board."

"All right . . . Ross, then."

"Yeah, well . . . tell Ross if he gives you any more crap I'm going to add him to my list."

Kennedy was tempted to take him up on the offer. "I have one last thing for you." There was a pause and then Kennedy asked, "Have you ever heard of an Erich Abel?"

Rapp thought about it for a second. "No. Why?"

"East German–born. Worked for the Stasi during the eighties and early nineties."

"Does he go by any other names?"

"Not that I know of, but I'm looking into it."

"Why the sudden interest in this guy?"

"I'm not sure, but I'll let you know when I find out."

"All right. I've gotta run." Rapp punched the end button and tossed the phone on the leather seat as he stood.

Coleman was already down the steps and supervising the refueling. Rapp made his way down the small steps carefully. His legs were sore from the long flight. He walked stiffly across the tarmac.

Jamal Urda was waiting for Rapp. Urda was the CIA's station chief in Kabul. He had worked with Rapp the previous spring on a nasty bit of business, and although things had started off a bit rocky between the two men, Urda had a lot of respect for Rapp. Urda extended his hand. "Mitch, I'm sorry about your wife."

"Thanks." Rapp shook his hand. "I appreciate it."

The two men stood in the chill air for a moment while Urda tried to figure out how he should transition from the personal to the professional. He was relieved when Rapp spoke first.

"What's the situation?"

"My deputy just called from the embassy."

"Yeah?"

"He says we received a flash communication from Langley, saying if anyone comes in contact with you they're supposed to report it right away."

Rapp nodded.

"Then Irene called me and told me to ignore the message."

Rapp knew that Urda could be a bit territorial, and he had hoped to avoid any problems. He had just wanted to land, pick up what he needed, and be on his way. "Do you have a problem with that?"

"Nope." Urda looked over his shoulder. There were a couple of people sitting in the 4Runner. "My ex-wife." Urda shrugged. "I don't even like her, but I'll tell you right now, if one of these jackasses killed her, there'd be hell to pay." Urda pointed to the ground. "Stay here. I'll go get him."

Urda returned a moment later, leading a bound and hooded man. "I had them clean him up a bit for you. I guess he smelled pretty bad."

Rapp waved Wicker over and handed the man off to him. "Buckle him in." Rapp turned back to thank Urda. "I appreciate you doing this."

"I know you'd do the same."

Rapp nodded.

Urda started to leave and then stopped. "As far as I'm concerned, you were never here."

"Good." Rapp took a moment to stretch and then got back in the plane. The prisoner was wearing the local tribal garb. Rapp snatched the hood from the man's head and studied his face. It was him all right. A little thinner for sure, but it was him.

The man squinted for a moment trying to adjust from total darkness to the faint light of the cabin. Upon seeing Rapp, Waheed Ahmed Abdullah's face became a twisted mask of fear. "What do you want with me?"

"Nothing," Rapp lied. Waheed had been part of a terrorist plot to detonate nuclear warheads in both New York City and Washington, DC. Rapp had captured him in Pakistan the previous spring and interrogated him personally.

"I don't believe you."

"Your father is a man of great influence. He has secured your release." In a way Rapp was telling the truth. Waheed's father was a man of great influence in Saudi Arabia. He had also placed a bounty on Rapp's head, which in a roundabout way ended up getting his son released from the hellhole of a prison he had been in. Rapp was not about to tell Waheed that his father thought he was dead.

"Just relax," Rapp told Waheed as he pulled the hood back over his head. "If you behave, you will see your father tomorrow." Rapp retrieved a hypodermic needle from his jacket pocket and removed the protective cover. He grabbed Waheed's bound wrists and said, "I need to give you a sedative. When you wake up, we'll be in Saudi Arabia." Rapp stabbed the needle into his prisoner's thigh and depressed the plunger.

62

ZIHUATANEJO, MEXICO

Claudia hovered over the keyboard, wondering if she had lost her mind. One e-mail was bad enough; the reply, risky, but anticipated; the follow-up, downright stupid. Now here she was composing her fourth message to the director of the Central Intelligence Agency. This new repentant attitude was waging a fierce battle with Claudia's tactical training, and so far the repentant attitude was winning. She was taking standard precautions: changing servers and bouncing around the Web delivering her messages from different locations, but still, she was dealing with the head of the world's most powerful spy agency. There was no telling what tricks the woman might have up her sleeve.

The first message, sent nearly twenty-four hours ago, had been a simple heartfelt apology. *Anna Rielly was a mistake. I am sorry. I deeply regret taking the job. If you would like to know who hired me, I am willing to discuss.* Claudia struggled over whether she should write the note for both her and Louie, but in the end decided Louie hadn't shown the slightest sign of remorse, and was in fact at this very moment trying to finish the job. By including him in the apology she would have continued to delude herself. She sent the message and went to bed. It was late Saturday night, and she did not expect to hear back from Kennedy until possibly Monday. She woke up on Sunday famished and ordered breakfast in her room. She managed to keep it down, and took it as a good sign, so she ventured out and took a long walk on the beach. She thought mostly about her father and mother, and tried not to think about Louie. She considered calling her parents for the first time in three years and when she made it back to her room she decided she would do just that.

She checked her various e-mail accounts first and discovered Kennedy's reply. It read: *How do I know you are the real person and not some imposter?*

Claudia half expected this. She logged off and thought about her response for a minute. When she was ready she typed, *We put trackers and bugs in her car, and found out he had knee surgery scheduled that morning. When they left for the hospital we filled the house with gas and waited for them to return. My partner was hiding in the woods across the street from their house. She was not supposed to be harmed.*

After logging back on, Claudia sent the message and then logged off. For the next two hours, she checked the account every fifteen minutes until she finally received a reply. It read: *Who hired you and why?*

Claudia typed her response while online. *Erich Abel. He is a former Stasi officer, and he resides in Vienna. He was acting as a middleman. For whom I do not know, but I suspect the Saudis. I have never worked with him before.* She hit the send tab and logged off. Claudia stood. She was slightly short of breath, and surprised to find herself sweating.

It had been almost eight hours since she had sent the last reply and she had checked her in-box only once. The note she found from the director of the CIA asked simply, *Why are you doing this?*

Good question, Claudia thought, *but not very easy to answer.* For nearly three hours she had struggled with her reply, wondering if she was divulging too much and then simply not caring. It rambled on, page after page of her deepest thoughts and regrets. She explained that she was disgusted with herself for having any part in the matter. That she and her partner had parted ways over the debacle. She added two final points to the e-mail. The first were the names of the five Swiss banks from which Abel had transferred the money. Claudia listed the relevant routing numbers, dates, and dollar amounts, knowing that it was likely either that Abel's name was not on the accounts or that he had used an alias. She did not know if she would have the courage to include one last piece of information.

She struggled with it for well over an hour, through fits of tears and pangs of guilt, until finally she surrendered herself to that voice of her youth—the voice of her conscience. It called to her over and over, telling her it would be difficult, but that in the end she would feel better, and it was right. The second she sent the e-mail she felt as if a weight had been lifted from her burdened heart.

Claudia turned off her computer and wiped the tears from her face. She knew nothing could bring Anna Rielly back, but she hoped that she had made it clear that she was deeply sorry for what had happened. She had gone further than she'd wanted to, and revealed far more than she should have. The lengthy final message gave away too much. It flew in the face of everything she had learned—everything that had kept her alive. Part of her didn't care anymore if she was caught. A massive burden had been lifted, and she was ready for what life would hand her. She would go back to the beginning. To her roots. She would go home to her parents, have her child, and start over.

There was a knock on the door, and Claudia froze. She immediately assumed the worst. She should have changed hotels. They had found someway to track her, some new piece of technology she was unfamiliar with. She was wearing a white tank top and a pair of cutoff jean shorts rolled up several inches at the hem. Her professional instincts kicked in momentarily and she searched the room for a weapon. After a second she thought better of it. If the CIA had found her, there would be no escaping. If Louie had been here, maybe they could fight their way out, but she wasn't a killer. Claudia imagined them on the other side of the door—men in black with big black guns waiting to bust the door down. She glanced over her shoulder in the direction of the patio and gravity pool. It was at least a thirty-foot drop to the jagged rocks and the surf.

Claudia collected herself and wiped her nervous palms on the front of her shorts. She stood tall and walked across the room. She would accept the inevitable. She would not run. Claudia didn't bother with the peephole. She unlocked the door and opened it. She was prepared for anything other than what she found.

"You're a hard woman to locate," Louie said. "Do you have any idea how many hotels there are in Ixtapa and Zihuatanejo?"

Claudia was speechless.

"I'm sorry, darling. You were right. I was wrong." Gould handed her a bouquet of flowers. "We should have never taken the job."

Claudia took the flowers, a raging storm of conflicting emotions battling within. She had been so ready to move on only a minute ago and now here she was being pulled back. Her mind struggled to find the proper meaning in all of this. She tried to gauge the depth of her feelings and the sincerity of Louie's words.

"I can't bear thinking of life without you," Louie continued. "Will you please forgive me?"

It was his simple plea for forgiveness that got to her. It was something the nuns had drilled into her as a child. *To receive forgiveness, one must be willing to grant it.*

63

Zurich, Switzerland

Kennedy had had her doubts about the first e-mail. It got her attention, certainly, but the CIA received thousands of e-mails every month from crackpots and conspiracy theorists. Rarely were they sent to her directly, but the nut-jobs were on her mind as she read the message. The second e-mail pulled her in. There had only been minor mention of Mitch's knee surgery in the press and no mention whatsoever about the killer hiding out in the woods across from the house. As far as the press was concerned, the explosion was still being reported as an accident.

Kennedy received the third message on the way to Camp David. One phone call to Langley confirmed that an Erich Abel had in fact worked for the East German Stasi. The possible Saudi connection fit with the information that had been passed on by the Jordanians. Kennedy called her associate deputy director of Intelligence and ordered a full workup done on Abel. She wanted to know everything the Agency had on the man, and Sunday afternoon or not she expected a briefing the moment she returned from Camp David.

The briefing had been held in her office at 4:15 on Sunday afternoon. Present were the associate deputy director for Intelligence, the head of the Office of Russian and European Analysis, and the deputy director of the Counterterrorism Center, or CTC. One other person arrived late. He was Marcus Dumond, who was CTC's resident computer genius. Dumond informed Kennedy that the effort to track down the mysterious e-mailer had run out of gas in the Netherlands. Kennedy had pretty much expected this to be the case.

Kennedy was shown a sixteen-year-old photo of Abel and given twenty-plus minutes of information that, like the photo, was at least fifteen years old. She further learned that Langley's resident expert on East Germany, and the Stasi, had retired six years ago and was living in Arizona. They had tried to reach him, but he was busy playing golf and wouldn't be home for another hour. An address for Abel in Vienna had been confirmed and the Agency's people at the embassy in Austria had been put on standby and told to await instructions from the director.

Kennedy did not like that last bit of news. She wanted a low profile on this thing. If her people got too excited and started beating the bushes, this Abel might get spooked and run for it. She called the Vienna station chief herself and gave him explicit orders. She wanted passive surveillance and only passive surveillance to begin immediately. That meant parabolic mikes and drive-bys. No stakeouts with two guys parked in front of Abel's apartment waiting for him to show. Under no circumstances was anyone from the Agency to contact Abel directly or take any risk. It was approaching midnight in Austria. Abel should be at home sleeping, and by the time Monday morning arrived, Kennedy planned on having one of the Directorate of Operations' top surveillance teams in place.

Kennedy handed out some new marching orders. The information was old. She wanted to know what this Erich Abel had been up to for the last ten-plus years, and she wanted all of it on her desk by 6:00 a.m. Before leaving the office, Kennedy sent one last e-mail. She wasn't sure she'd get a reply, but she knew she had to try and keep the dialogue going. Her question to the mystery e-mailer was straightforward: *Why are you doing this?*

Kennedy had her suspicions. In her mind this was all about what Coleman had predicted. Tell the media Rapp is dead. The killers will get the rest of their money, and then when it is announced that he is still alive, the person or persons who did the hiring will demand that either the job is finished or that their money is refunded. Kennedy sensed they were turning on each other. This Abel was the middleman. If the e-mailer could be believed, and it was the Saudis who were behind this, Abel would be under great pressure to get their money back. He would in turn be demanding that the assassin finish the job or give the money back. Kennedy wondered if the assassin or assassins were using her to eliminate Abel.

Kennedy went home to check on Tommy and try to get some sleep. Steven Rapp had returned to New York. Her mother was with Tommy along with twelve heavily armed men from Langley's Office of Security. Tommy was tired, having not slept more than six hours the night before. Even so, he had a lot of questions about Mitch. Kennedy explained, as she always did, that she couldn't talk about work, but she could tell him that she had talked to Mitch and he was doing fine. Tommy fell asleep in her arms a few minutes past 8:00, and she carried him to bed. After talking to her mother for about thirty minutes she checked her e-mail one last time before heading off to bed herself.

As she began reading the lengthy message any thought of sleep vanished. The rambling two-page letter was beyond surprising, and Kennedy had to force herself to read the entire thing without stopping. Kennedy had a healthy sense of skepticism. In her business, information had to be checked and rechecked before it could be believed. This confession was filled with facts that would be exceedingly difficult to verify, but even so Kennedy already suspected the information was accurate.

She was left with two options. The first involved bringing the State and Justice Departments into the loop, and for several reasons she hated the mere thought of it. First of all, this was a CIA problem. Someone had tried to kill one of her people, and the CIA would take care of the problem on its own. Langley was more suited to play rough, which was what this would take. If she brought Justice and State in on it, they would spend the next five years in Swiss courts, and the only outcome would be a few forfeited bank accounts. No individual would be brought to justice and punished for Anna's death. Her second option was to get on a plane, fly to Zurich, and deal with this situation quickly and quietly.

In addition to a six-person security detail she brought Marcus Dumond. They left shortly after ten in the evening and with the time change between DC and Zurich, and the flight time, it was nearly ten in the morning when they arrived. Kennedy did not inform the U.S. ambassador that she was in the country, and she did not inform Ross or the president that she was leaving the country. The president would understand, but Ross would not. At this stage of the game it was better to ask for forgiveness than permission.

Kennedy did, however, inform her Swiss counterpart and ask that he help her skirt customs once she landed. She explained to him that they had important matters to discuss and that it would be better if there was no official record of her visit. Two of the Agency's people stationed in

Zurich were waiting on the tarmac at the airport with August Bartholomew, the head of the Swiss Foreign Intelligence Service. Kennedy rode with Bartholomew and managed to keep the conversation away from the purpose of her visit during the relatively brief ride to her hotel. She had no idea if Bartholomew had the car wired, or if he was wearing one himself, but either way she could not afford to take the risk. When they got to the hotel she would explain to him what was going on. Kennedy was sure he had already guessed that her visit had something to do with one of the two things the Swiss were famous for, and it wasn't chocolate.

The Swiss took their banking and their neutrality seriously, and for good reason. Anything that could sway Swiss objectivity or damage the reputation of Swiss banks was considered a threat to national identity and long-term security. The war on terror had done just that. Armies of lawyers, diplomats, law enforcement officers, and intelligence officers had descended upon Bern and Zurich after 9/11 demanding that the Swiss government hand over any and all records that had anything to do with al-Qaeda and its various members. It was a very uncomfortable experience for the Swiss, due in great part to the fact that they did a massive amount of business with the Saudis and al-Qaeda was almost entirely financed by Saudi dollars. The Saudis liked their privacy and they made it very clear they would take their banking elsewhere if the Swiss broke their vow of secrecy.

Diplomatic talks dragged on. Lawyers for both the U.S. Justice Department and those representing the families who had lost loved ones clogged the Swiss courts with lawsuits and motions. In the end, almost two years later, the sanitized records of Osama bin Laden were handed over and almost nothing else. More than once during the drawn-out legal battle Bartholomew had told Kennedy that there was a better way to handle this. A more delicate way. That in the future she should not hesitate to pick up the phone and call him if there was a problem. She had decided to do just that, and with or without his help, she was not leaving Zurich without the information she'd come for.

The presidential suite at the Hotel Baur Au Lac was secured for one night at a cost of 5,000 Swiss francs. Kennedy did not plan on spending the night. The suite consisted of three bedrooms, two separate living rooms, an office, and a verandah that overlooked Lake Geneva. Bartholomew and Kennedy entered the suite after the CIA security team had swept it for listening devices. Kennedy apologized in advance to

Bartholomew and then had one of her security people wand him to make sure he wasn't wired. An intelligence professional, Bartholomew took it in stride.

Kennedy ordered coffee service and then sat down to explain to her counterpart what she was about to do. There were a few details that she left out, but for the most part she was truthful with him. When she was finished explaining her plan she handed Bartholomew a list of men whom her office had already contacted. Appointments had been set up in thirty-minute intervals. The first man was due to arrive shortly. The five men were the presidents of some of Switzerland's most reputable and powerful banks. Kennedy asked Bartholomew if he would like to stay. It took him all of two seconds to decide. He thanked Kennedy for her courtesy and then excused himself.

Getting the men to take the meeting was easy. These banks hated bad publicity, and when the office of the director of the CIA called and told you it was in your best interest to take a private meeting with the head of the world's most well known spy agency, you shuffled your schedule and took the meeting. Kennedy did not underestimate these men. They were very smart, very cool customers. Her arsenal of threats varied greatly, and she would have to be very careful how she used them. These men were bankers. Some of the world's best. They had their reputations to consider, and the reputations of their banks to consider, but in the end, there was one thing that would trump all.

Sometimes the solution to a problem is so simple it is easy to overlook. Kennedy had considered telling these men that Mitch Rapp was uncontrollable and if they didn't give her the information she needed, he was likely to pay them a visit they would not enjoy. Another option was to threaten a massive campaign against them using the press, and the full force of the United States government. The problem with this was that they knew Kennedy didn't want the press covering this any more than they did. The third option which she was prepared to use against some of them, if things got ugly, was to wage a full-scale cyberattack against their banks and watch their business transactions come to a screeching halt. This tactic she would keep in reserve to use against anyone who was unusually stubborn.

What she had finally decided to do was state the case as she knew it, and ask them to voluntarily turn over all information associated with the account numbers she had been given by her mystery e-mailer. If they balked, she was prepared to drop the bomb. She would show them a list of their largest U.S. depositors. The mere fact that she had such a list would unnerve them. For Swiss banks nothing was more sacrosanct than their client lists. For more than a decade the CIA had been carefully gathering information on the Swiss banking industry by hacking into their networks. They had amassed a giant database. It was a myth that all Swiss bank accounts were numbered. Many were, but there were also plenty of accounts where the person's name was listed. With Dumond's help Kennedy had gone over the list on the flight over and identified over seven billion dollars in U.S. corporate and individual deposits in the five banks. Kennedy's ploy was relatively simple: give her the information she was looking for, or the list of depositors would be called by the president himself and told to dump their Swiss banks.

The first two meetings went fine. The men were actually appreciative that Kennedy had chosen this route rather than dragging them into court. The third meeting went very poorly. Even Kennedy's threat to scare off the bank's U.S. depositors did not work, so she excused herself, walked into the other room, and ordered Dumond to crash the bank's network. Kennedy waited a few minutes and then returned to her guest. Within a minute the man received a call from his bank telling him their entire computer system was down, and they had no idea how long it would take to get the system up and running. Kennedy told the man, who she had taken an extreme disliking to, that she had ordered the cyberassault and would continue to bombard his network every day until he handed over the information or she ran him out of business. The man relented.

The fourth banker handed over the information so readily that Kennedy assumed he had already spoken with one of the other bankers who she'd met with. The fifth and final banker put up a bit of a fight, lecturing Kennedy that confidentiality was his sworn duty to his clients. It was no different from the doctor–patient relationship or the attorney–client relationship, he claimed. Kennedy listened politely, and then handed the man a piece of paper. On it was a wire transfer between his bank and a bank in the Bahamas for one million dollars. The man held his ground and said that on principle alone, he could never reveal who was behind the transfer.

Kennedy nodded and then pointed out that the bank's largest depositor, to the tune of nearly a half billion dollars, also happened to be a close personal friend of President Hayes. The banker wanted to know how she had obtained such information. Kennedy didn't bother to answer the question. She told the banker if he didn't hand over the name of the account holder involved in the transaction and every scrap of information that pertained to the account, the president would get on the phone this very day and tell his close and very patriotic friend that his bank was protecting terrorists. He would go on to tell his friend that both he and the country would consider it a favor if he would find a new bank. Kennedy then rattled off another half dozen names and told the banker that they would also be receiving calls from the president. The banker jumped off his ethical high horse in near record speed. Five minutes later Kennedy was reading a fax that contained everything she needed to know.

64

The blue digital display on the rearview mirror said the outside temperature was 102 degrees. The white van had no windows on the side; just two small, dark-tinted portals on the back cargo doors. The vehicle was very inconspicuous, which was exactly what Rapp wanted. Waheed Ahmed Abdullah lay on the back floor bound, gagged, and blindfolded. So far Rapp had treated Abdullah with respect and care, which was no easy thing considering the man's past crimes and his father's suspected role in the death of Anna Rielly. "Suspected" had been Kennedy's choice of words. She wanted time to verify that Saeed Ahmed Abdullah was in fact involved in the attack and not just shooting his mouth off. Rapp needed no further proof. He was at war, and he should have never let his guard down. The second he had heard about this bounty placed on his head he should have flown to Saudi Arabia and killed Saeed Ahmed Abdullah, but he had instead mistaken the information for loudmouthed Arab bravado.

Looking back on it now, it was a good thing that he had spared the son's life six months ago. His rationale at the time had been straightforward. After being tortured, Waheed had given Rapp crucial information that had helped stop nuclear attacks against Washington, DC, and New York City. In the emotional hangover that followed the foiled attacks Rapp had decided not to execute the zealot. He found the Saudi to be a bit of a simpleton and rather than shoot him, he stuck him in a Northern Alliance jail with the thought that maybe, over time, he would lessen his extreme positions and in ten years or so he could be released. For good reason they decided to tell the Saudi government that Waheed was dead. Waheed's father had too much influence, and too much money. If it was known that the son was alive, the father would stop at nothing to get him back. What Rapp had failed to see at the time was that the father would also stop at nothing to get his twisted revenge. Rapp had gone with the false assumption that the father would blame the son for getting involved with al-Qaeda and for being up to his neck in a plan to kill millions of innocent civilians and unhinge financial markets, but he was wrong. The father was a Wahhabi and a jihadist to the core. Kennedy could look for her proof, but it wouldn't matter a bit to Rapp. He could not bring Anna back, but he sure as hell would punish those responsible for her death.

Rapp had popped a couple of pills and had managed to get a few hours of sleep on the flight from Mazar-e Sharif to Qatar. The journey had taken several hours longer than was necessary because they had to detour around Iranian airspace. By the time they landed in Doha, the sun was coming up over the Persian Gulf. Coleman kept an office and airplane hangar at the airport in Doha that he used as a forward staging area to bring his people and equipment into the region. He pulled the plane into the hangar, and the large doors were closed. By the time the local customs official, whom Coleman had on the take, showed up, Abdullah had already been transferred to the back of the rented van. The official took a moment to look at everyone's passports. He applied the proper stamps, handed them back, collected an envelope from Coleman, and was gone.

Rapp wanted to get on the road as soon as possible. The drive from Doha to Riyadh would take a good five hours and he wanted to be there by noon. This was where things got a little hairy. Coleman wanted to follow Rapp into the city. Rapp flat-out said no. He and Coleman got into a serious argument. Coleman insisted that he have backup every step of the way. Rapp told Coleman that his blond hair and blue eyes made him stick out like a sore thumb in the region, whereas Rapp, with his flawless Arabic and dark complexion, had no problem fitting in. Waheed was drugged, and Rapp would have no problem handling him. He did not plan on getting caught, but if he did, things would be particularly nasty. Ally or not, the Saudis were not known for their humane treatment of prisoners. Rapp was very appreciative of the help he'd received so far, but this was something he wanted to do on his own, and he did not budge. Coleman, for his part, knew Rapp well enough to know that there would be no changing his mind, so he finally stepped aside and let him go. They would meet him on the outskirts of Riyadh, where Rapp would ditch the van.

Waheed was stripped naked while still unconscious and dressed in a fresh set of clothes including a vest and robes. He was then placed back in the van and given one more shot that would keep him unconscious for roughly three more hours. Rapp wanted him out when he crossed the border, but semialert by the time they reached Riyadh. Long Styrofoam coolers packed with seafood and dry ice were then placed all around Waheed until he was entombed. Rapp gave Coleman his fake U.S. passport and a few other things for safekeeping. He concealed his gun, silencer, and extra ammunition in the bottom of one of the coolers, as well as $10,000 in cash, a change of clothes, and a separate set of IDs and credit cards.

Crossing the border was easy. Rapp had a well-worn Yemeni passport as well as a worker's visa for both Qatar and Saudi Arabia. There was a decent amount of traffic that traveled back and forth between Doha and Riyadh, and the border guards were not worried about anyone trying to sneak into Saudi Arabia. The border guard glanced briefly at the passport and then waved Rapp through. Twice between the border and Al Hufuf, Rapp pulled over in remote areas to check on Waheed and get rid of a few of the coolers. He would need the extra room in back when they got to their final destination. Between Al Hufuf and Riyadh, he stopped to fill up on gas and check one last time on Waheed. He was awake but groggy. Rapp removed his gag and gave him some water and a few bites of a candy bar. He kept Waheed's hands bound and the blindfold on and explained to him how the exchange would take place. Waheed for his part remained docile and a bit out of it. This worried Rapp a little. He needed the Saudi to be able to stand on his own and walk.

If Waheed was unable to walk, Rapp would have to come up with another plan. He was trying to figure out what he'd do when the oasis of Riyadh appeared on the horizon. A moment later his satellite phone started beeping. It was Kennedy. Rapp answered and listened intently as she briefed him on what she'd found in Switzerland. All in all, twenty-two million dollars had been transferred from a Swiss account owned by Saeed Ahmed Abdullah to five separate Swiss accounts owned by Erich Abel. Kennedy had found her proof.

"Who is this Abel guy?" Rapp asked.

"I don't know much more than I told you last night. I ordered a full workup done on him and I expect an update within the hour."

"Any idea where he is?"

"No, but we're watching his apartment in Vienna and tracking his credit cards."

Rapp looked past the windshield at the vast barren landscape. "Something doesn't add up, Irene."

"Like what?"

"These e-mails you received . . . we're missing something. People in this line of work don't just sprout a conscience one day. I think it's like Scott said." Rapp had discussed the anonymous e-mails with Coleman on the flight from DC to Afghanistan. "These guys all thought I was dead. They got the balance of the contract, and then the news broke that I was alive. Saeed went nuts and wanted his money back, so he crapped all over this Abel guy and he in turn crapped all over the hired gun. Rather than give the money back . . . the hired gun turns in Abel with the hopes that I'll kill him and he can keep his money."

"Your line of logic works, but there are a few things I haven't told you."

"Like what?"

"I received a fourth e-mail last night. It was quite long. From it I've discerned a few things."

Rapp looked over his shoulder to see what Waheed was up to. "I'm listening," he said into the phone.

"Abel hired two people for the job."

Rapp nodded. "No big surprise."

"Well . . . this will be." Kennedy sighed. "This morning, one of those people deposited five million dollars in a Swiss bank account under your name."

Rapp wasn't sure he'd heard her right. "Say again."

"One of the people Abel hired to kill you deposited five million dollars in a Swiss bank account that was set up by this person in your name."

"Why?" was all Rapp could think to say.

"It's a little complicated, but I'll try to give you the brief version. The team hired to kill you had a bit of a falling-out. One of them didn't want to take the job in the first place. Not surprisingly, this is the one who's been corresponding with me. When Anna was killed by mistake, things got ugly between the two, and they went their separate ways."

"So how does that explain the five million dollars?"

Kennedy sighed, "The woman is pregnant."

"Woman?" Rapp said in a confused voice. He'd been sure they were talking about two men.

"Yes, a woman. It turns out she is pregnant and knows that Anna was pregnant. She feels a tremendous amount of guilt over her role in this."

Rapp was only half listening. His mind was searching for something. Something that he knew was supposed to be important. The blow to his head had scrambled certain memories, and some of the things that had happened in the days preceding the attack were a bit sketchy.

"She's a woman," Rapp said more to himself than Kennedy.

"Yes," Kennedy replied. "Typically they are the ones who get pregnant."

Rapp ignored her remedial tone and said, "And her partner is a man."

"I would assume so," Kennedy sighed. "And quite possibly the father of the child."

The scene flickered across Rapp's mind like a homemade movie. He muttered, "I saw them."

"What?"

"I saw them on the road the day before my knee surgery. I was coming back from a run and came around the corner and there they were." Rapp had a clear picture of the two of them. He suddenly recalled that the man gave him a bit of concern. He had that lean, athletic quality that is so prevalent with the Special Forces guys. Kennedy was saying something, but Rapp wasn't listening. He was focused on the replay of what had happened. The man had said something to him. Rapp could hear the voice. He had said that she was pregnant. The woman was throwing up. He remembered the man's glasses and wishing he could get a look at his eyes. He'd asked them a few questions and the guy had done all the talking and then finally the woman stood up and said something. There was something unusual about what she said. Rapp struggled to remember what it was and then it hit him. It wasn't what she said, it was how she said it. The woman had a French accent.

65

Louie kissed Claudia on the forehead and slowly pulled his arm from under her neck. She stirred and rolled onto her other side. Carefully, he flipped back the sheets and slid out of bed. He went to the bathroom to relieve himself and then decided to go out to the patio. Looking out at the ocean he leaned over and rested his forearms on top of the wall. Sunrise was fast approaching. The sky above him was gray, and the sky to the west was black.

Louie was glad he'd come to his senses and abandoned the idea to finish the job. Losing Claudia after all they'd been through would've been extremely stupid. He'd recognized before it was too late that it was his ego that had been driving him to finish the job. The desire to be known someday as the man who had defeated the great Mitch Rapp mixed with his need to finish everything he started had blinded him to the reality of the situation. The professional in him kicked in when he was clearing U.S. customs at the Houston International Airport. He had one set of identification, one credit card, no weapon, and just under $8,000 in cash. The likelihood that he could successfully get to Rapp, who would now be alert and protected, was not good. The odds that he could kill the man and get out of the country without leaving a trail were next to nothing.

Ultimately, though, it was that one memory of Rapp the day they had accidentally bumped into each other on the road that had forced him to come to his senses. Louie had spent the entirety of his adult life around soldiers. Men who were trained to go off and fight. They came in a variety of shapes and sizes. Some had overpowering physical presence, but were as dumb as a potted plant. Louie had used these men in the same way one used pack mules. He had them carry heavy machine guns or mortars. Other men were wiry and small, but had great instincts or organizational skills. These men became clerks, or if they had endurance they were trained to be snipers or scouts. Muscle could be added or heft could be taken away. Basic skills could be drummed into the stupidest of men, but instinct was something that could not be taught. It could be discovered and nurtured, but you were either born with it or you were out of luck.

Standing in the Houston airport waiting for the flight that would take him back to DC, Louie remembered the way Rapp had looked at him on that morning, and the way his hand had hovered just above the fanny pack that undoubtedly concealed a gun. They had found out later, from listening to the wife's conversations, that he had been hurt on that morning. Louie remembered hearing the wife tell a friend that she had never seen her husband in so much pain. At the time Louie was thinking in terms of how he could use the injury to his advantage and hadn't bothered to connect the fact that despite being in great pain, Rapp's instincts had still detected something wrong that morning on the road by his house. Like any highly developed predator, Rapp was acutely in touch with his senses and his surroundings at all times.

As the departure for the flight to DC neared, Louie began to lose his nerve for the first time he could remember since almost drowning in a scuba training accident at the age of twenty-one. His subsequent trips to the ocean had been terrifying, and if it hadn't been for his fellow paratroopers standing right next to him he had no doubt that he would have quit. The only thing worse than his fear of the water was his fear of letting down his fellow brothers in arms. But now, alone in an airport filled with strangers, there was no esprit de corps. His thoughts turned to Claudia and the child that was growing within her. Without any further thought he returned to the Continental ticket counter and exchanged his ticket to DC for a flight to Ixtapa.

Louie looked down at the waves breaking against the rocks beneath him and smiled. He was confident that he had made the right decision. To think that he had almost abandoned Claudia when she'd needed him most embarrassed him. Louie had always sworn that he would never be like his own father. Leaving her like that in the airport, pregnant and traumatized, was just the thing his father would have done.

Louie watched the sailboats gently rock back and forth on the water. This place was special. It was too bad they couldn't stay here and raise a family.

Just then Claudia came up from behind him and wrapped her arms around his waist. "What are you doing up so early?"

"I got up to go to the bathroom and decided to come out here and look at the water." Louie stood up straight and grabbed her hands. "How great is this place?"

"Much better with you here."

He undid her hands and stood next to her. His arms wrapped around her shoulders and hers wrapped around his waist, they stood there looking out across the bay. With a sigh, Louie said, "It's too bad."

"What?"

"That we're going to have to leave."

"Why?" she asked, her voice filled with disappointment.

"You know why. It's too risky to stay in one place for too long. Especially right now."

Claudia's heart sank as she remembered the difficult road that lay ahead. She had yet to tell Louie what she'd done in the days they were apart and it was beginning to weigh heavily on her. There was no telling how he would react when she told him, although one thing was certain; the longer she waited to tell him the harder it would be. Claudia rested her head against Louie's bare chest, and started to speak but suddenly lost the courage.

Louie noticed something was bothering her and asked, "What?"

She held him tight and asked, "Do you love me?"

"You know I do," he said with a slight laugh.

"I have something I must tell you." She kissed his chest and added, "But I want you to think about what I am going through while I tell you this."

Louie grabbed her by the shoulders and took a step back. He knew Claudia well enough to be warned by her tone. "What did you do?"

She looked him in the eye, wavered, thought she might not have the courage, and then blurted out, "I have been in contact with the CIA."

Louie searched her eyes for the truth. She was not lying to him. In as calm a voice as he could muster he asked, "Why?"

"It is complicated. It started out as a way to say that I was sorry for what happened to the woman. On top of that you know I don't like Abel. I didn't from the moment I met him."

"I don't care about Abel. I want to know what you did."

"After we parted ways, Abel sent several more threatening e-mails. I decided if that was the way he wanted to play I would give the CIA his name and see how he liked it when Mitch Rapp showed up looking for him."

Louie nodded slowly. A part of him admired Claudia for the move. He had warned Abel to watch his step. The man was in no position to threaten them, but he supposed the German was under a great deal of pressure to get the money back. The type of pressure that sometimes causes people to do very foolish things. "The CIA is a big place," Louie said. "Who did you contact?"

"Director Kennedy."

This surprised Louie momentarily. "When you say you've been in contact, what exactly does that mean?"

"We have e-mailed each other."

"How many times?" Louie asked, his chest tightening.

"I sent her four e-mails."

Louie released her shoulders and nearly bit off his own tongue. "Why four?"

Claudia's big brown eyes welled with tears. She could see Louie struggling to contain his anger. She ignored the question and moved onto the part that was really going to send him through the roof. "Please stay calm for a moment so I can get this all out, and then if you want to leave me I'll understand."

"I'm not going to leave you," he said, almost as if he was convincing himself.

Claudia grabbed his hands. "We've always split everything . . . Right?"

He nodded.

She knew of no easy way to say it so it just came out. "I put five million dollars into a Swiss bank account under Rapp's name."

Louie thought his head was going to implode. "Five million dollars." He was doing everything in his power to stay calm. He loved this woman standing before him. If he didn't care for her, he would have simply chucked her over the wall and taken great joy in watching her head split open as it hit the rocks. "Why?"

"Our baby."

"What does giving Mitch Rapp five million dollars have to do with our baby?" Louie's voice started to rise.

"I wanted to try and make things right . . . and buy some time."

"Buy some time." Louie frowned. "How does this buy some time?"

"You know he's going to come after us."

"Let him," Louie said in a quiet but angry voice.

Claudia shook her head. "You don't mean that. This is not some normal man. We killed his wife. His pregnant wife. What would you do if some man killed me right now?" Claudia watched him intently for a moment. "We both know you would stop at nothing until you had killed him with your own bare hands. If Mitch Rapp finds us, he will kill us both."

"And you think just because you gave him five million dollars he will forget about us?"

"No," she said, "as I told you, it will only buy us some time."

"Time?" he asked with a frown, still not comprehending what she was after.

Claudia placed his hand on her stomach and said, "I asked for nine months. I asked for him to spare our baby. I want to give birth to our child and hold it in my arms, and then whatever he does to us I will accept." She sensed some understanding in Louie's face. "That five million dollars isn't even ours," she said with disgust in her voice. "I never wanted the job, and we didn't finish it. If I had it my way, we would give him all of the money."

"We need that money," Louie said in a surprisingly calm voice. He was just now comprehending the maternal forces that had been at play. Her words had stirred his own sense of paternity—a need to protect Claudia and their unborn child. He disagreed vehemently with what she had done, and how it may have exposed them, but there was no undoing it. Her motives had been pure.

Louie kissed her on the forehead and said, "I still love you."

Claudia melted in his arms. "Thank you, darling."

They stood there, not speaking, for several minutes and then Claudia said, "Let's go back to bed."

Louie shook his head. "No."

"Why?" she asked, suddenly afraid that he would in fact leave her.

"We need to get out of here immediately. Pack your bags."

66

His first reaction was to think they were being played, fed some fake information that would lead them on a wild-goose chase and waste a lot of time and resources. He also didn't want to associate a single noble characteristic with his wife's killers. In the face of all of that, though, there was the five million dollars sitting in an account under his name. There was also according to Kennedy a very heartfelt confession, apology, and plea written by this woman whom Rapp had seen throwing up on the side of the road near his house. Rapp had been through a lot over the years, experienced a lot of strange things, but this one left him shaking his head. It didn't make any sense. If he had the time he could attempt to sort it out. He could analyze what he knew, investigate what he was unsure of, and ultimately decide what was subterfuge and what was the truth. He could gauge real intentions and weigh the possibility of an ingenious deception on the part of the real killer or killers. He told Kennedy to have Dumond empty all of Abel's bank accounts and keep an eye on the banks. Rapp didn't care how carefully the guy was hiding, when he found out eleven million dollars of his money was gone he would want some answers. In the meantime, though, Rapp needed to focus on reuniting a father and son.

Rapp arrived in the capital city of Riyadh as the call to noontime prayer was being sounded. Traffic was light, and then there was no traffic at all as shops were shuttered and closed and the streets were cleared. Kennedy had confirmed through a source on the ground in Riyadh that the father was where Rapp expected him to be. Saeed Ahmed Abdullah was a devout follower of the ultraradical Wahhabi sect of Islam. He had built countless mosques, orphanages, and religious schools all run by Western-hating Wahhabi clerics. Many Saudis follow the tenets of their faith when in the Kingdom, but as soon as they leave the country they partake in the forbidden fruits—gambling, booze, sometimes drugs, and especially sex. Not Saeed Ahmed Abdullah, though. He was different. He was a pious Muslim at all times. Not only did he pray five times a day, as was pre-scribed by his faith, but he did so in a mosque with the exception of the *Isha,* or nighttime prayer, that was said before going to bed.

Running a billion-dollar corporation was not easy. There were lots of demands on Saeed's time, so to help ease that pressure, and stay connected to his faith, he had mosques built directly across the street from his home and his office. A report by the Jordanian Intelligence Service said he at-tended the *Fajr,* presunrise prayer, and the *Maghrib,* post-sunset prayer, at the mosque near his house. The *Zuhr,* or noontime prayer, was said at the mosque by his office as well as the *Asr,* or late afternoon prayer. The Jor-danians had kept an eye on Saeed for some time. In addition to building mosques, schools, and orphanages, Saeed also liked to donate large sums of money to Hezbollah, Hamas, and several other Palestinian terrorist or-ganizations that specialized in suicide bombings. The Jordanians did not like the Saudis pouring gas on a fire that they had been trying to put out for decades, so they tried their best to find out who was doing it and then pass the information on to sympathetic ears in the royal family and the U.S. government.

The suicide bombers and terrorists were bad enough, but on a cer-tain level Rapp at least respected them for having the balls to do it them-selves. Men like Saeed, however, who sat back and gave money to these zealots like it was some hobby, they were reprehensible. They knew ex-actly where their money was going. They knew they were funding sui-cide bombers who would get on buses and kill innocent men, women, and children, and worse, they were proud that they had a hand in it. Proud and blinded by the demented belief that they were doing God's work.

Rapp clutched the steering wheel and drove on through the well-kept business district. His tears were long gone, dried up and replaced with a white hot anger that focused his sense of mission and purpose. For most people, seeking revenge for the murder of a loved one was an entic-ing, but ultimately impossible notion. Apprehension overtaking another life, no matter how guilty the person might be, would weigh heavily on most people. For Rapp there would be none of that. This was another day at the office, only quite a bit more personal. Over the last fifteen or so years he'd killed a lot of people. A few he'd pitied, but most he'd despised. They were men who clung to their arcane, sexist, and bigoted perversion of Islam while the rest of the world passed them by, men who believed in the nobility of suicide bombers, who wantonly killed tiny children.

Rapp had always avoided that, always done everything in his power to make sure that innocent people did not get caught up in the violence, but today would be a test. Men like Saeed always traveled in entourages, with cousins and nephews and assistants and servants and friends. How many of these men who surrounded Saeed were directly involved in the death of his wife, Rapp wasn't sure, but it was likely that many if not all were complicit through their knowledge of the plan. Was that enough to execute them? Rapp had struggled with the question. These men were the enemy, after all. They were all Wahhabis who constantly called for jihad and cheered the beheadings of innocent civilian contractors in Iraq. Men who kept their wives locked up at home. Men who had probably cheered the death of Rapp's wife. The thought of them celebrating the murder of his Anna tested all restraint. Rapp decided that he would visit upon these pious men the same type of ugly, brutal mayhem they so glibly sponsored.

He slowed the van and took a right turn. The van was the only vehicle on the street. The call to prayer could be heard thrumming out its hypnotic beat in the midday heat. Rapp saw one man, coming toward him. He was wearing a white headdress held in place by a simple black rope and a white kaffiyeh. If the suit and tie was the uniform of the American businessman, this was the Saudi equivalent. The man had a black beard and was wearing dark sunglasses. He appeared to be in a hurry and several times looked over his shoulder to see if anyone was following him. Normally, this behavior would have caught Rapp's attention, but it was easy to figure out why the man was acting this way. He was afraid he would be caught by the religious police, and chastised for not praying.

Rapp slowed as he neared the other end of the long block. The mosque and the headquarters of Abdullah Telecommunications stood out for no other reason than their size and location. The office building was a minimalist block of concrete, entirely forgettable if not for its sheer size. The mosque, however, was one of the most ornate Rapp had ever seen. Four towering minarets marked each corner and a massive gold dome dominated the center of the building. Rapp suspected that the gold was real. Up ahead, at the corner of the building, he noted a security camera aimed to cover the area around the front door.

Rapp went straight at the light and then took a left turn. He drove around the block twice and settled on a spot that was not covered by the security camera. It also was shaded and afforded a view of the mosque. He turned off the engine and climbed into the back to check on Waheed. Rapp sat him up and then leaned him against the side of the van. He pulled the blindfold off his face and in Arabic asked him how he was doing. Waheed told him he was thirsty. Rapp placed a hand under his bearded chin, tilted his head back, and gave him some water.

"Better?" Rapp asked.

Waheed nodded.

"Do you think you can walk?"

"I'm not sure."

Rapp pulled open a blade and sliced the white plastic flex cuffs around Waheed's ankles. He told him to move his legs around a bit and asked if he'd like another candy bar. Waheed nodded eagerly. Rapp took off the wrapper and let him hold it in his bound hands.

"We are parked next to your father's office." Rapp noted Waheed seemed surprised. "Your dad does not know the exchange is going to take place. Do you understand?"

Waheed nodded.

"There is a man out there who will have a gun on you at all times. If you do anything other than hug your father he will shoot you. We don't want to make a big scene. Do you understand?"

"Yes."

Rapp looked at his watch. There was no man with a gun of course, but Waheed would never know that. "Are you ready to take a walk?"

"Yes."

Rapp cut the flex cuffs on Waheed's wrists and said, "You know I'd just as soon kill you, so don't do anything stupid." With his knife still in hand Rapp acted as if he was straightening Waheed's robes. His free hand slid between the folds and checked something on the Saudi's vest. Rapp put the knife away and opened the back door. The mosque would begin to empty in a few minutes. He helped Waheed edge his way to the back tailgate. With his sunglasses, dark skin, robes, and black beard Rapp fit right in. He let Waheed sit there for twenty seconds, his feet resting on the ground. Rapp did not give him sunglasses. He wanted Saeed to recognize his son. Grabbing him under the arm, Rapp helped him to his feet. In the shade the heat wasn't too bad and in fact Rapp hoped it would help speed the bloodflow to Waheed's legs.

The first step was not good. Waheed's legs buckled and Rapp had to move quickly to get under him so he didn't drop to the pavement. Rapp stood him up against the back of the van, closing one of the rear cargo doors.

"Small steps," Rapp said. He moved Waheed away from the van and closed the other door.

Waheed put one hand against the side of the van and started to walk while Rapp had a firm grip on his left side. He made it past the van to a palm tree and stopped there for a few seconds.

"Remember . . . nothing stupid."

Waheed's eyes were slowly adjusting to the light. "Why are you doing this?"

"Let's just say the king likes your father and leave it at that."

Waheed smiled, proud that his release had been secured by none other than the king of Saudi Arabia. This news seemed to give Waheed a much-needed boost in energy. They made it to the corner of the building. A security camera was mounted above their heads. Rapp wasn't worried. Waheed stood up on his own for the first time. He looked across the street at the beautiful mosque has father had built and was overcome with emotion.

He started to weep and Rapp said, "Come on. There'll be time for that later. Don't fuck this thing up."

Rapp led him around the corner. There was a fountain in front of the building ringed by stone benches. If for some reason Waheed was unable to stand, Rapp would leave him there and let the father come to him. They stood by the fountain for a minute. Rapp pulled out a bottle of water and gave the Saudi another drink.

"How do you feel?"

"Better." He blinked repeatedly under the bright Saudi sky.

The front door to the mosque opened and two men appeared. "It won't be long now," Rapp said. "You are to stay on this side of the street. Do you understand?"

"Yes."

"If you try to cross the street you will be shot. Do you understand?"

"Yes."

Rapp thought he detected a faraway, drugged-out look in Waheed's eyes. "What will happen if you cross the street?"

"I will be shot."

"Good." Several more men came out of the mosque. Rapp felt his pulse begin to quicken. He was carrying his silenced Glock 9mm, two extra clips, forty-nine rounds total, and the knife. Rapp felt Waheed begin to sway and he firmly grabbed hold of his bicep. "Do you need to sit?"

"No. I'm fine." Waheed widened his stance.

There was now a constant stream of men coming out of the mosque. Rapp had only seen pictures of the father before, but even if he'd met him in person he wasn't sure it would have done any good. All the head-dresses, white robes, beards, and sunglasses made it difficult to get a good look at anyone. That was also why the security camera gave Rapp little concern. As Rapp had predicted, though, the father traveled with an entourage. Both doors were opened for him and he left the mosque with a man on each side and a procession of people following him. Rapp felt Waheed stiffen. He turned to see if there was recognition in his eyes. There was.

"Stay calm," Rapp told him. "When he's halfway across the street I will leave your side. That will be the signal for your people to release the hostage. If you take a step in any direction other than to greet your father you will be shot."

"What hostage?" Waheed asked, suddenly confused over this new twist.

There was no hostage, but Rapp wanted to keep Waheed's mind occupied. Speaking out of the side of his mouth Rapp said, "You don't think I'd give you back without getting something in return, do you?"

The father spoke briefly with several people and then started across the street with a trail of at least a dozen men. Rapp stood his ground. If the father continued on a straight line, he would pass five feet to Rapp's right. Rapp checked Waheed one last time. "Remember, no sudden moves. Once he's all the way across the street and on the sidewalk you may go to him. Not a moment sooner." The father was halfway across the street. Rapp stepped away from Waheed and said, "Good luck." Under his breath he whispered, "I hope you and your father enjoy hell."

Rapp had noted the slow pace of the father. He moved away from Waheed at a brisk pace, but not anything that would attract attention. Exactly four paces away, Rapp retrieved a remote detonator from his pocket. He glanced down at the remote and pressed the first button on the left. The bars lit up on the small screen, telling him the signal was good. The trickiest part about setting off a remotely detonated bomb was usually arming it. That was why he had waited until the last possible moment.

The plan was straightforward. Waheed and his father would be killed in the favored manner of the terrorists they sponsored. Everything Rapp needed had been waiting for him when he landed in Qatar. A khaki-colored tactical vest, a ¼-inch sheet of C-4 plastic explosives, ball bearings, primer cord, a blasting cap, and remote detonator. The sheets of C-4 were made with a peel-and-stick side. The tactical vest had Velcro straps on the side and a solid front. There was a large pocket across the chest to hold a chicken plate, or ceramic breast shield designed to protect the heart during combat. Rapp had cut out three squares of C-4; two for the large lower pockets of the tactical vest and one to fit into the pocket where the chicken plate was supposed to go. He peeled off the wax paper backing on the C-4, pressed ball bearings into the dough like explosive sheets, put the sheets into the pockets, and then connected them with primer cord through the lining. Waheed was a walking claymore mine.

Rapp glanced over his shoulder after the tenth pace. The father was just stepping onto the curb. Rapp continued moving away from them. He looked straight ahead for a few seconds and then over his shoulder again. Waheed had his arms extended and his father stood frozen in shock at the sight of a son he thought dead. Waheed rushed forward and the two men embraced. Rapp was almost to the corner of the building; he watched father and son for a split second, the memory of his wife flashed across his mind, and then he turned away. The security camera was just ahead and above him.

Rapp kept his chin down. He glanced at the remote detonator in his right hand and then raised his left hand and extended his middle finger at the camera. Rapp pressed the button, and a thunderous explosion ripped through the warm, dry afternoon air. He never broke stride, never bothered to look back. He was already trying to decide how he would find Erich Abel, and how he would kill him.

67

Nawaf Tayyib was not the type of man to obsess about his career. He believed in duty, loyalty, and success, all the things he had learned playing on the elite soccer teams of Saudi Arabia as a youth and then as a young man. These qualities along with his size and speed had carried him out of poverty and into the inner sanctum of one of the most powerful men in the kingdom, the very man he was going to see at this moment. Prince Muhammad bin Rashid was going to be very disappointed.

Tayyib remembered blowing out his knee at the age of twenty-five, and how he had laid there on the field looking at his leg. It was a night game, as most of them were. To play a soccer match in the midday heat would have been suicide. Tayyib played defense, and his size and roaming ability enabled him to cover a lot of ground. The first rule for a defender was to never let an opponent get behind you. There was one exception which involved a good deal of risk. Usually once or twice a game Tayyib would be back on defense and he would perfectly anticipate an opponent's pass. They always underestimated his speed. He would lull them into thinking he was moving one way and then when he saw his opening, he would dart forward and pick the pass perfectly. He would catch the entire opposing team leaning toward his own goal and Tayyib would be off like an Arabian thoroughbred, racing to the other end of the field with everyone chasing him.

On this last night of his career, he had made it practically the entire length of the field, the goalie had come out to cut down the angle, Tayyib made a fake to his right, and then kicked the ball from the right center over to the left center. The goalie was caught completely out of position, and Tayyib had an open net. He let up for just a second; it was the easiest of shots. He planted his right leg to deliver a booming kick with his left foot and then from out of nowhere an opposing player came in high and fast and rather than take him out at the ankle, took Tayyib out at the knee. With all of his weight on his right leg, his knee folded like a cheap umbrella in a gale. Tayyib hit the turf, rolled, and when he lifted his head his thigh was straight, but his foot was off to the side at a right angle. Tayyib knew his soccer career was over before he'd even registered the agonizing pain.

Now, as he walked down the wide, opulent marble hallway to Prince Muhammad's office, he had the same feeling as he had had that day. None of this had been his idea, but that didn't matter. He believed in Prince Muhammad. He trusted the man's vision to expand Islam under the banner of the Wahhabis—the only true followers of the faith. Their religion was under a constant onslaught by the West. To protect Islam they needed to expand and retake the southern shores of Europe as a buffer. He so believed in the cause that he planned on offering his resignation. Tayyib's career was over. He had failed a man who did not accept failure.

After firing the RPG through the front door of the Sheriff's Department on Saturday night, Tayyib had gone back to Alexandria and waited down the street from the car garage. He had $500,000 sitting in the trunk and had never been so eager to give money away. As the clock inched toward 11:00 he expected the three black trucks to come pulling up any second. At 11:15 he started to worry. By 11:30 he was crawling out of his skin. He waited until midnight and dialed the phone he'd given Castillo. After eight rings he got a recording. Tayyib started the car and left. On the way to the embassy, he wiped down the phone, removed the battery, and chucked it out the window.

He didn't sleep that night. He tried, but he couldn't. Two scenarios kept playing on a loop in his brain. In the first Castillo and his men took the $500,000 they already had and were out having the time of their lives laughing at the stupid foreigner who had handed them such a large amount of money. The second scenario was that they had gone to the safe house and failed. The more he thought about it, the more he hoped they had taken the money and flown to Las Vegas. If they had been caught trying to kill Mitch Rapp, it might create some problems. Tayyib doubted

Castillo or any of his men knew he was a Saudi, but they might be able to make a link with the witness he'd had them kill the year before.

The Sunday morning newspapers were delivered to the embassy at 5:00 a.m. There was no mention of anything happening in Virginia. Tayyib supposed they'd had to go to press before the story could be written. He turned to the TV to see if he could learn anything. At 7:00 a.m. one of the local affiliates led with the story of the explosions in Leesburg. There were reporters on site giving live updates, and there was an announcement that the sheriff would hold a press conference at 12:00 noon. Tayyib checked the twenty-four-hour news channels. Fox mentioned the explosions on the crawl at the bottom of the screen, but that was it. Tayyib got on the Internet to see if he could learn more. There was nothing. The press was not equipped to handle stories that broke late on a Saturday night, but by the time the sheriff held his press conference three of the twenty-four-hour news outlets and all of the local affiliates were covering the story.

Tayyib watched the press conference in his room, sitting on the edge of his bed. He listened intently to everything that was said. At no time did anyone mention an attack on a federal facility in conjunction with the attacks in Leesburg. Tayyib spent the afternoon trying to learn something, anything. He drove by the garage three times, half expecting to see police cruisers and yellow crime scene tape, but there was nothing. He took this as a bad sign. A very bad sign. Tayyib jumped on the last nonstop flight of the day from Washington, DC, to Riyadh.

He had a first class ticket so he was able to sleep through most of the flight. He landed in Riyadh a little before 1:00 p.m. He did not want to face Rashid, but he knew he must. Tayyib wasn't a man to shake responsibility or blame. A car and driver were waiting for him. As soon as he'd settled into the backseat of the Mercedes sedan he called his office to get an update on what was going on with the Leesburg story. Nothing had changed since he'd left Washington. Something else had happened, though. Tayyib listened carefully and then asked the man on the other end if he was certain. He said he was. Tayyib hung up, looked out the window of the Mercedes sedan, and closed his eyes. He had been back in the country for a little more than thirty minutes and the situation had gone from bad to disastrous. The car pulled up in front of the Ministry of Islamic Affairs. Tayyib got out and put on a white robe over his suit.

He took the elevator up to the top floor and stepped into a wide hall with Carrara marble floors and alabaster stone columns every twenty feet on the right and the left. Deep burgundy fabric hung on each side of the columns, creating semi-intimate nooks. There were eight of them. Four on the left and four on the right. Each nook contained a desk. Behind each desk sat a man. No women worked in the building. The hall served as the outer office for the Minister of Islamic Affairs.

Tayyib marched down the hall, his gaze straight ahead, more intent than usual. He did not bother to look at any of the gatekeepers and they did not bother to stop him. He stopped in front of the last desk on the right and said, "Is the minister alone?"

"No."

"Clear the office." It was a command.

The administrative assistant looked at an appointment book on his desk and hesitated.

Tayyib leaned his six-foot-four-inch frame forward and placed his large hands on the man's desk. "It is not a request. It is an order. Unless the king is in there, I suggest you clear the office or you will be out of a job."

The man jumped to his feet and scurried into the office. Tayyib followed.

The office was eighty feet long by fifty feet wide. There was no desk anywhere in sight, just clusters of chairs, couches, and pillows. Rashid was at the far end of the room sitting on an oversized chair that was almost, but not quite, a throne. Five men, well into their seventies, were gathered around Rashid on a group of three couches. The assistant scurried ahead at a pace just short of an all-out run. Tayyib made him nervous.

He approached Rashid and whispered in his ear. Rashid nodded and then informed his guests that he was most sorry, but he would have to cut their meeting short. The men got up and filed out of the room at a snail's pace. Tayyib stood off to the side clenching and unclenching his fists.

When they were finally gone and the door was closed, Tayyib bowed at the waist and said, "My prince, I apologize for the intrusion."

Rashid stared down at him with his slightly hooded eyes. He'd known Tayyib for eleven years now, since the man's early days at the Saudi Intelligence Service. Tayyib built a reputation as someone who got things done and kept his mouth shut as well. There were plenty of men who got things done, but few knew how to keep quiet about it. Tayyib was not a lighthearted individual, but neither was he someone prone to melancholy, fits of rage, or any other outward expression of emotion. He was serious and steady, and that was why Rashid liked him. That was also why the look on Tayyib's face gave the prince cause for concern. "I assume things did not go well in America."

Tayyib blinked, his business in America already a distant memory. He dropped to a knee. His bad one. He lowered his head and said, "Prince Muhammad, I am sorry, but I have some terrible news."

Rashid exhaled through his nostrils and nodded for the man to continue.

"On my way here from the airport I received a call from my office." Tayyib lifted his head and glanced up at the prince. "There was an explosion in Riyadh just a short while ago."

"Where?" Rashid asked in a guarded tone.

"In front of the headquarters of Abdullah Telecommunications."

"Abdullah Telecommunications," Rashid said absolutely shocked. "What kind of explosion?"

"A suicide bomber."

"A suicide bomber," repeated a confused Rashid. The Kingdom was very good at exporting suicide bombers. Occasionally one would strike within the Kingdom itself, but it was always against Western targets, usually the Americans. "Was anyone killed?"

"I'm afraid so." Tayyib looked down. "Saeed Ahmed Abdullah."

Upon hearing the name of his childhood friend, Rashid was speechless. After a moment he regained his composure and asked, "How did this happen?"

"Witnesses say that Saeed was leaving noontime prayer and was walking across the street to his office. The man was waiting for him. He came up and hugged Saeed and then blew himself up."

Rashid was dumbstruck. "Who was the bomber?"

"We don't know yet."

"Why would a suicide bomber want to kill Saeed?"

Tayyib had been wrestling with this same question.

The prince stood and gathered his robes, one folded over each arm. "Rise," he said as he stepped down from the platform. His mind had stumbled upon a horrible possibility. "And what of our business in America?"

Tayyib stood and said, "I have failed you, my prince." He had thought about his answer on the long flight. The truth was he didn't know what had gone wrong, but that in and of itself was proof of failure. "The men I sent to take care of the job never returned."

"What happened to them?"

"I do not know."

"So Mitch Rapp is still alive." It was a statement not a question.

"I think so."

"And my good friend Saeed has just been killed." Rashid walked across the marble floor from one Persian rug to the next until he was looking out a small window. He could think of no reason why a Muslim would kill Saeed. Rapp on the other hand had plenty of motives. Rashid remembered he had warned his old friend to keep his mouth shut. The Americans had found out about the bounty, and Rapp was already in Saudi Arabia killing those responsible for his wife's death.

"I know what you are thinking, my prince, but I do not see how Rapp could have left America and put this together so quickly. Who would he find to be a suicide bomber?"

"Maybe he blew himself up?" Rashid asked in a hopeful tone.

Tayyib thought about that for a moment and then announced, "I have studied Rapp. The man would never commit suicide unless he had to. He would have simply shot Saeed."

"Then tell me why a fellow Muslim would want to kill Saeed?"

"Maybe it wasn't a Muslim."

Rashid frowned. "There is no such thing as a non-Muslim suicide bomber. Do you see any Jewish suicide bombers? Even the Irish during their war with the British never resorted to suicide bombings. The Japanese are the only other culture to employ the tactic in modern history, and I doubt the Japanese killed Saeed."

"I'll grant that the timing looks bad, but I don't see how Rapp could have left America on Sunday and orchestrated something like this. I myself left Sunday evening and I arrived only an hour ago."

"What about Abel?"

Tayyib considered the possibility. "We still can't find him. As of Saturday I know he had not returned Saeed's money, but again where is Abel going to find a suicide bomber?"

"Then what happened?"

"I am reluctant to guess with so little information."

Rashid turned away from the window and said, "Guess anyway." It was a command.

Tayyib stood off to the side and tried to come up with anything that was plausible. "Saeed has many militant ties. It is possible that a rival to one of these groups decided to kill him."

Rashid scoffed at the idea. "You don't find it at all coincidental that

Saeed paid twenty million dollars to have Mitch Rapp killed? The killers miss him and end up killing his wife, and now Saeed is dead. You don't find that odd?"

"Of course I do, but with all respect, Prince Muhammad, men like Rapp don't blow themselves up."

Rashid thought about that for a second. He had a point, but things had changed. "His wife was killed. Who knows what he is capable of now?"

Before Tayyib could respond his phone rang. Tayyib froze. The prince hated phones, and had a steadfast rule that when in his presence they were to be turned off. He struggled to get it out of his pocket and silence the ringer. His large hands fumbled with the tiny buttons. The screen told him it was his office. Tayyib hesitated. The call could be important. He looked at Rashid, held up the phone and said, "I'm sorry. This is my number two. He might have more information about the explosion."

Rashid nodded reluctantly.

Tayyib answered the phone and listened intently. After about thirty seconds he said, "Are you sure?" He listened to the man for a little bit longer and said, "Call me if you learn anything more." Tayyib shut the phone and exhaled.

"What?" Rashid asked impatiently.

"Several of Saeed's sons were there. They had accompanied him to prayer and they were walking back to the office together when it happened. After they'd overcome the initial shock of the bombing they began cursing the body of the suicide bomber. They were spitting on it and kicking it when one of them suddenly realized he recognized the bomber."

"Who was it?"

"It was their brother Waheed."

"Waheed?" Rashid said in utter disbelief. "That cannot be. He is dead."

"He is now," Tayyib said, not trying to be funny.

"Rapp killed him six months ago," the prince insisted.

"Apparently not." Tayyib folded his arms and thinking aloud said, "The body was never returned."

"Why would Waheed kill his own father?"

"He may not have." Tayyib knew something the prince didn't.

"You just said he did," Rashid snapped.

"He may not have known what was happening. There is a security tape. It shows Waheed being led by another man. The two stop in front of the office building and wait there for several minutes. Then as Saeed starts to cross the street from the mosque to go back to the office the man leaves Waheed's side and walks away. He looks over his shoulder once and then looks down at something in his hand. We think it was a remote of some sort. A second before the explosion the man raises his hand to the camera like this." Tayyib held up his middle finger and made the gesture toward the wall, away from Rashid. "Then there is an explosion, and Saeed is blown in half."

"Can they tell who the man on the tape is?"

"They are going to try, but it will be difficult. The man was wearing a kaffiyeh and sunglasses."

Rashid looked back out the window, his mind running down the list of possibilities. "That gesture is very American."

Tayyib nodded. "The Americans and the French."

"What is your assessment now?" the prince asked.

"Six months ago, Mitch Rapp captured Waheed Ahmed Abdullah in a mountain village on the Pakistani-Afghan border. Shortly after that the U.S. government informed us that Waheed was dead. Now Waheed shows up back from the dead and ends up blowing his own father to pieces." Tayyib shook his head.

"Who was the man in the surveillance video?"

"I don't know. I haven't seen it."

Rashid scoffed. "You know who it was."

Tayyib nodded. "It was more than likely Mitch Rapp. I don't know how he did it, but it was probably him."

"You must find Abel," Rashid said in a slow, methodical voice. "I don't know how the Americans know that Saeed was behind this, but my guess is that Saeed was too talkative about his role in the matter."

"I warned you about that."

"I know you did and I talked to him, but he did not listen. There is only one way we can be linked to this."

"Abel," answered Tayyib.

The prince nodded. "You must find him and kill him."

"I will see to it myself."

"Good. I am leaving for Spain tomorrow morning. The dedication of the mosque is on Friday. This is very important to me. Find Abel before then, interrogate him to find out if he has talked to anyone, and then kill him."

"What about Rapp? If he is in Saudi Arabia you might not be safe."

Rashid pursed his lips and looked out across the flat rooftops. "Maybe I will leave for Spain tonight."

"I think that is a good idea. I will make arrangements to have your security detail strengthened."

"Good." Rashid had an idea. "In the meantime, I will call America and see if I can make things more difficult for Mr. Rapp."

68

Abel never got on the cruise ship. In the end he stood there on the pier and looked at all of the plus-size people being led onto the ship like cattle being led away to slaughter and balked. He was a man of great wealth now, and he reasoned that hiding at a five-star hotel would be every bit as effective as trying to blend in on a cruise ship. So he turned around and went right back to where he'd come from. Well, not exactly. Instead of returning to Venice proper he took a ferry to Lido, the skinny eight-mile-long island that runs south of Venice and forms a barrier between it and the sea. Abel thought if anyone was lucky enough to follow him to Venice, the last place they would look would be out on one of the outer islands. So he booked a suite at the sumptuous Hotel des Bains.

Saturday and Sunday were spent strolling up and down the beautiful sandy beaches of the island, enjoying the unseasonably warm October weather and trying to figure out where he would buy his villa. He was back to that now. Rapp was alive, the assassins had failed, Rashid was trying to track him down, and his future was clear. He would have to divest of everything he owned, and start over with a new name and identity. He'd done basically just that when he'd immigrated to Austria twelve years ago. He'd kept his name, but nothing else, and he had done it with limited resources. This time he had eleven million dollars plus, he estimated, another million or so once he sold the two apartments and a few other things.

He had decided to keep Saeed's money. The assassins had yet to send their six million back, and in a way they'd made Abel's decision for him. He had no way of tracking them down quickly enough, and he wondered how wise it would be to even try to find them. They knew far more about him than he did about them, and the man had warned him that he would kill him if he tried to discover their true identities. Abel never again wanted to feel that man's hot breath on his neck. He would let them be. Let them keep the six million, and since Saeed was no longer honoring their original agreement by asking for the entire twenty-two million back, Abel felt no need to honor any aspect of the deal either. It was every man for himself.

The other deciding factor had been his worsening relationship with Rashid. Things always ended badly with men like Rashid. The key was knowing when to get out. Abel had felt for some time that he was disposable in the prince's eyes. Now that this thing with Rapp had ended in failure, he had no doubt that Rashid had ordered his henchman Tayyib to find him and kill him. Giving Saeed his money back would change none of that, so it was with complete confidence that he had decided to keep the money and start a new life.

The apartments he didn't care about, but the Alpine house would be difficult to part with. Maybe he could keep it and see how things went. He had used a lawyer and a front company to purchase it. He'd always envisioned it as a place that he could hang on to if things got bad. Over the years, however, he'd brought people like Petrov there, and for that reason alone he could not totally rely on it as a safe haven. For now, though, he would keep it.

It was a big world with lots of nice places, but Abel preferred Europe. Especially the areas around Switzerland: northern Italy, southern Germany, Austria, and France. On the other hand, South America was probably the logical choice. Largely untouched by terrorism, they still had not modernized their customs and immigrations agencies enough to make it difficult to obtain entry with fake passports. The major cities, though, the ones like Rio and Sao Paolo, places where a European could disappear, were filled with some of the worst poverty he'd ever seen. Poverty was something that irritated Abel. He didn't like crowds, and he yearned for order. The complete lack of self-control displayed by the masses, the way they lived on top of each other in the most unseemly conditions and spat out child after child like rats in a sewer, disgusted him. South America might be the smartest choice, but Abel wasn't quite ready to surrender so easily. There had to be a better way.

Monday morning arrived with Abel desperately searching for a way to stay in Europe. The warm weekend weather gave way to a cool front coming in off the Adriatic and Abel found himself practically the only man on the beach. He took a long walk all the way to the southern tip of the Lido, which from his hotel was about four miles. The idea of changing his identity had grown on him. It was time—time to start a new chapter in his life. Paris, Milan, and Zurich had some of the world's best plastic surgeons. He wouldn't do anything drastic. Maybe a chin tuck, a new nose, and one of those new micro face lifts. Nothing too drastic. Just enough to make him look younger. The rest he could accomplish with a new wardrobe. For the last twelve years he'd cultivated a European aristocratic look. Maybe the metro chic look would suit him better? The younger women appeared to be more drawn to that.

Abel made it back to the des Bains a little after 1:00 in the afternoon and took lunch in the garden. He ordered a light salad and a cup of bean soup. He'd been eating rich foods for five days now and decided he'd better get back to his old ways or he would have to portray a fat man in the next life. He knew a good forger, a man who used to work for the Stasi. He was in his seventies now, but had kept up with the technology of his trade. The man had moved to Vienna and set up shop. As he finished his soup, Abel decided he would have the plastic surgery, convalesce for a month until the swelling went down, and then go see the forger. He would be a new man, and if he was careful enough in building his history, he might be able to stay right in Europe. Maybe the South of France or Monaco. He could hide right in plain sight with all of the other jet-setters.

Abel wiped the corners of his mouth and sighed. He had time and he had money. The world was a big place. Surely he could disappear. The waiter took away the finished dishes and asked if he'd like anything else. Abel ordered a cappuccino and then decided to check on his finances.

He turned on his PDA, and held it in front of his face cupped in both hands, his thumbs working the small keys. He logged onto the Internet and then pulled up a list of sites that he commonly visited. All of his banks were near the top. Abel scrolled down to the first bank and clicked on it. Five seconds later he was entering his account number and lengthy password. Five seconds after that he was staring at his balance.

Abel blinked several times. It was impossible. His heart started to race. There had to be a mistake. Abel logged off the Internet and was about to call the bank directly when he thought better of it. He logged back on and checked another account. He gripped the small plastic device and willed it to connect faster. When the second account appeared on the screen, he stood up so quickly his wrought-iron chair fell over and landed loudly on the stone patio. Abel ignored the waiter, who had come to see if everything was all right. He rushed into the hotel, cursing under his breath, the veins on his forehead bulging. His thumbs worked furiously to verify this horrible news. He pulled up the third account and then the fourth. By the time he reached his suite there was no denying it. All five accounts had been emptied. His balance was zero in each one. Just like that, eleven million dollars was gone.

Abel paced back and forth across the wood floor of his twelve-hundred-dollar-a-night suite. He screamed once at the top of his lungs, for just a few seconds, and then he got control of himself. He had to think this through. There had to be a mistake or a way to fix it. He knew all of these bankers personally. What had happened was impossible, but then again it wasn't. Saeed was worth billions. His pull at these banks could be immense. The Swiss were cautious and Abel knew of situations where they had placed money in escrow accounts until the two parties could sort out their differences.

Abel was as mad as he'd ever been. He'd had it all planned out and he was damned if he was going to let some amateur like Saeed get the best of him. In the end Abel had the leverage, not Saeed and not Rashid. He was nobody. A professional intelligence operative who could disappear. They could not.

Abel opened the room's safe and turned on his encrypted satellite phone. As soon as he had a signal he dialed the number for Rashid's office in Riyadh. When the man answered on the other end, Abel identified himself and said that he would wait exactly ten seconds for him to put the prince on the phone. Any longer than that and he would hang up. Abel knew Rashid was looking for him and guessed correctly that the call would be put through in a speedy manner.

He was on nine when the prince answered.

"My friend, where have you been? We have much to talk about."

"You're damn right we do." Abel had never spoken to Rashid in such a manner. "Tell Saeed that he has until the close of business today to put that money back in my account or I will make sure Mitch Rapp finds out he was the one who took out the bounty on him."

"I think you're a bit late," Rashid said in a no-nonsense tone.

Abel detected no false bravado. "What do you mean?"

"Saeed was just killed in an explosion."

"When?"

"An hour ago."

"Where?"

"In front of his office."

"By who?"

"Who do you think?"

"I don't know," growled an angry Abel.

"Mitch Rapp."

Abel stopped pacing. "How? That's impossible."

"Apparently not."

Abel could feel a monstrous headache coming on. He started pacing again, looking at the floor as he went from one end of the room to the other. "I want my money back," he blurted out.

"I don't know what you're talking about."

"The eleven million dollars Saeed paid me to have Rapp killed."

"Rapp is still alive."

"I don't care. The deal was I keep the deposit whether he was killed or not. I want my money back."

"Come to Riyadh and we will talk about this."

"Rashid, don't be a fool. I will never set foot in your country again." Abel had never spoken to him in such a discourteous manner. It was always prince this or prince that.

"Then come to Spain. I am leaving for Granada tonight. We can discuss your money and figure out how we will deal with Rapp."

"No," Abel said firmly. "You will pay me eleven million dollars by five o'clock Zurich time today, or I will tell Rapp this was all your idea."

There was a long silence and then Rashid said, "Don't be foolish. Two can play that game. If you do that you will be signing your death warrant."

"Maybe, maybe not. I am nobody. A single individual who can disappear. You are the powerful and wealthy Prince Muhammad bin Rashid." Abel spoke the name with disdain. "Rapp will have a hard time finding me. You, on the other hand, will be easy to find."

"Erich, think about what you are doing. You do not want me as an enemy."

"And you don't want to end up like your friend Saeed, so you'd better give me the eleven million dollars by five or I promise you, Rapp is going to find out that you orchestrated this whole thing. I'll send your assistant wiring instructions for the money."

"Give me until five tomorrow. I am wealthy but not in the way Saeed was. I need time."

"Noon tomorrow! That is all you have."

Abel hit the end button on the phone and threw it on the bed. He clasped his hands behind his neck, took several more laps around the room, and then grabbed his suitcase. He had to get moving. He needed cash, but he couldn't trust the banks. That meant he had to get to the Alpine house. He had close to $100,000 in the safe. It would be enough to get the surgery done and buy a new set of identification. Hopefully Rashid would see the light and give him the money. He did not want to spend the rest of his years looking over his shoulder for Mitch Rapp.

69

Kennedy's armor-plated sedan pulled up to the Southwest Gate. The Secret Service officers were accustomed to her coming and going, but checked the undercarriage and trunk nonetheless. Kennedy had been to the White House so many times she'd stopped counting years ago. There were still moments, though, like now, when she could feel her pulse quicken and her stomach tighten. Most of these visits were simple, standard intelligence briefings. Occasionally there was a crisis to handle, but more often than not her duty was to inform and advise the president and the rest of the national security team as was needed.

This afternoon was going to be different, though. Nothing boring, benign or otherwise. It was going to be a high stakes game, and the players were some of Washington's most powerful. Three people in particular wanted her head on a platter—the director of National Intelligence, her supposed boss; the secretary of state; and the attorney general. On top of it all, her recent travels had tired Kennedy out. DC to Zurich and back in less than sixteen hours. Add to that the murder of Anna Rielly, the attack on the safe house, and a boss who had no idea what he was doing and you ended up with a frayed and worn-out director of the CIA. Kennedy would have preferred to go straight home to see Tommy and then go to bed early, but there was no postponing this meeting. They were too upset, and to be completely honest, there was a devious side to her that was looking forward to it. She'd learned from Rapp. Sometimes it's best to let it fly. Especially when the deck is stacked in your favor.

Kennedy checked her watch. It was 5:18 on Monday. Fortunately, she'd managed to get a few hours' sleep on both the flight over and the flight back. When she'd decided to follow the lead to Zurich, she did so with the comforting knowledge that the president would at least privately support her. She was always prepared to play the game and kiss the ring fingers and curtsy, in order to keep the Cabinet members and other important types happy. She herself, after all, was one of the important people, but that wasn't going to help her out on this one. These people were above her and she had committed the ultimate insider's sin. She had kept them out of the loop and she had stepped all over their toes. In the end, at least in their eyes, she had made them look bad. That was the problem. This group didn't like being made to look bad.

Kennedy left her large briefcase in the backseat and grabbed a brown leather folder. She stepped from the car and stood on the curb for a second. Her shoulder length brown hair was pulled back in a simple black clip that matched her black pantsuit and black shoes. Kennedy slid a hand between her blue blouse and her pants waist to make sure the shirt was tucked in. She adjusted her glasses and then set off through the door and into the West Wing where she was stopped by another Secret Service officer. Kennedy flashed her badge and signed her name in the logbook. From there she went upstairs and straight to the president's gatekeeper, Betty Rodgers, a DC native and extremely competent assistant.

Betty's office was small, like most of the rooms in the West Wing with the exception of the Oval Office and Cabinet Room. Betty looked up at Kennedy over the top of her reading spectacles. She was in her early fifties, but she already had that grandmotherly look. She pursed her lips as if she had something to say and then stopped.

Kennedy liked Betty, which was important. As the president's top assistant she got to see some of the country's most treasured secrets. She was someone who needed to be tough and discreet. She was both.

"Good evening, Betty."

"Irene, what have you been up to?" Betty asked in a friendly but accusatory tone.

"Very little."

"That's not what I've heard, honey. You've got some very angry people in there. They've been burning up the phones all day."

Kennedy cared about their reaction, but she was most interested in getting a read on the top boss. "How is the president?"

"Different."

"How do you mean, different?"

"I don't know . . . he just hasn't been himself lately. It has nothing to do with your little trip to Switzerland. He's actually been pretty calm about that. It's the other ones who've been raising a stink. They all called individually to complain and then they came over here together at lunch to do it all over again." Betty took her glasses off and let them hang from the chain around her neck. In a hushed voice she asked, "I hope you got what you were looking for, because they want to burn you at the stake."

Kennedy smiled and patted her brown leather folder.

"Good." Betty looked at her watch. "Get in there and give them hell. And be quick about it. I have dinner plans."

Kennedy thanked her and entered the Oval Office. They were all waiting for her. The president, Ross, Secretary of State Berg, Attorney General Stokes, and even Vice President Baxter. Baxter and the president were sitting in the two chairs directly in front of the fireplace. The power chairs. Ross, Berg, and Stokes were lined up on one couch like a firing squad. The identical couch opposite was empty. That was where they wanted her to sit. Isolated, like some child being called to the principal's office. Kennedy gladly accepted her seat of solitude. She set her leather folder on the glass coffee table and leaned back, confident that their argument would be emotional whereas she had some pretty damning evidence on her side.

Ross was the first to speak. He was wearing another one of his perfectly tailored Brooks Brothers suits. It was dark blue, almost black, and made out of a light wool. He had on a white shirt with some type of special weave, the kind that costs more than some people's monthly rent. His silver tie complemented his silver and black hair. Just two weeks ago Kennedy remembered thinking the man was handsome. Now all she saw was a man obsessed with his own vanity.

Ross shifted his position on the couch and straightened up a bit. He looked at Kennedy with a no-nonsense glare and asked, "Do you have anything to say for yourself?"

Kennedy shook her head. She wanted to draw them out.

"Well, let me tell you how my day went," Ross said in an irritated tone. "Shortly before lunch I got a call from Secretary of State Berg. She wanted to know if I knew you were in Switzerland." Ross glanced at the president and then back at Kennedy. "Do you think it's acceptable to leave the country and not inform me?"

"You're a busy man, Mark. I didn't want to bother you."

"Not a good move."

Kennedy shrugged.

Ross was visibly irritated by her casual attitude. "Do you have any idea the problems you've caused today? The Swiss foreign minister called Beatrice this morning," Ross pointed to the Secretary of State, "and raised holy hell over your unannounced visit."

"What did he want?"

"He wanted to know what in the hell you were doing in his country meeting privately with five of his top bankers."

Attorney General Stokes leaned forward. "I have a major case pending in front of the Swiss courts right now. We have been working on it for years. So help me God, if you've screwed it up, you and I are going to have some big problems."

Stokes was clearly upset. Kennedy figured he and Ross had been feeding off of each other's anger. They were the two career politicians, and next to the vice president the two men who would more than likely run for president at some point. Kennedy found it interesting that Secretary of State Berg was sitting out the first round.

"Do you know what happened in Riyadh today?" Ross asked.

"Yes."

"Do you know anything about it?"

"That's a pretty open-ended question."

"Do you know who was responsible?"

"Maybe."

"Would you care to share?"

"No."

"Dammit, Irene," Ross snapped, "do you think this is some game?" Ross flipped open a folder he had on the coffee table. There was a black and white, eight-by-ten surveillance photo inside. "This was sent to me by Prince Muhammad."

Ross spun the photo around so Kennedy could see it. There was a man dressed in traditional Saudi garb walking down a street. Someone had drawn a red circle around him. His arm was extended and he was flipping the surveillance camera the bird. The photo was pretty grainy. Kennedy studied it. He was about the right size, but other than that it was impossible to tell who it was.

"Any idea who that is?"

Kennedy shook her head.

Ross angrily tossed another photo her way. This one showed two men about to embrace. "The man on the left is Waheed Ahmed Abdullah. I assume you know who he is, at least?"

Kennedy nodded.

"Why did we tell the Saudi government that he was dead six months ago?"

"Is this the same Waheed Ahmed Abdullah who was a top lieutenant for al-Qaeda?" Kennedy's tone was one of false confusion. "The same Waheed Ahmed Abdullah that helped finance and plan a terrorist attack earlier this year? An attack that involved smuggling two nuclear weapons into this country?" She studied the photo. "The same Waheed Ahmed Abdullah who wanted to vaporize Washington, DC, and New York City?"

"You didn't answer my question."

"And you didn't answer mine. Have you read the file on Waheed?"

"I don't need to. I want to know why we're lying to one of our staunchest allies."

"If you think Saudi Arabia is one of our staunchest allies, I humbly suggest that you offer your resignation to the president immediately."

Ross's face flushed with anger. "And I suggest you watch your step, Dr. Kennedy. You are on very thin ice." Ross glanced at the president once again, as if to say, I told you so. He looked back at Kennedy and asked, "Where is Mitch Rapp?"

"I don't know."

"You're lying," barked Ross as he stabbed his finger at the first surveillance photo. "That's him right there. What did we tell you? There was a right way to handle this and a wrong way. Having a vigilante on the loose setting off bombs in Saudi Arabia is most definitely the wrong way."

Kennedy grabbed the third and last surveillance photo. She held it up for Ross and the others. "Who is this man right here? The one Waheed is about to hug?"

"That is Saeed Ahmed Abdullah," Ross answered angrily. "Waheed's father and one of Prince Muhammad bin Rashid's closest friends."

"Really," Kennedy said with feigned surprise. Ross had just put his nuts on the chopping block. She opened her own folder and displayed a series of financial transactions. "Is this the same Saeed Ahmed Abdullah who earlier this month paid a former East German Stasi officer twenty million dollars to have Mitch Rapp killed?" Kennedy let the multiple sheets spill forth onto the coffee table. "I'm pretty sure we're talking about the same guy."

Ross, Berg, and Stokes all leaned forward to take a page.

Kennedy looked to the president. "The bankers were actually quite cooperative. Several of them told me in the future they would prefer to handle things this way rather than waging these public battles in the courts." Kennedy turned to Attorney General Stokes. "Battles that take a lot of time, resources, and money. By the time we get the information we're after, the money has all been moved and the information is so old it is all but useless."

Stokes was about to offer a lame protest, but Kennedy cut him off. "The information I was given today is generating other results. My cyber people have begun looking into other Swiss accounts used by Saeed Ahmed Abdullah. In just eight hours' time we have identified over one hundred million dollars that he has given to al-Qaeda and other terrorist accounts in the past year alone."

"One hundred million dollars," was all Attorney General Stokes could think to say.

"Beatrice," Kennedy said to Secretary of State Berg, "the next time you talk to the Swiss foreign minister tell him that I will pass on his complaint to Mitch Rapp. Tell him that Mitch would be more than happy to fly to Bern and sit down with any Swiss official and listen to them explain why they feel it is so important to protect the confidentiality of terrorists like Waheed and his father."

"And, Mark," Kennedy said to Ross, "when you had breakfast with Prince Muhammad bin Rashid the other day, did you happen to mention that Mitch Rapp was still alive?"

Ross started shaking his head before he had time to think about the question.

"You didn't say anything about him convalescing at a CIA safe house?" Kennedy acted like she had some proof, but in truth she was operating off of a hunch.

"I didn't talk to him about anything like that."

"Well, when you speak with him again, ask him if he knew his closest friend took out a twenty-million-dollar bounty on my top counterterrorism official. And while you're at it, ask him how he feels about Saeed Ahmed Abdullah giving over a hundred million dollars to terrorist organizations in the last year."

"Are you trying to say he's involved in this?"

Kennedy shook her head and stood. "Not yet, but trust me, the man is rotten. He is no ally of ours." Kennedy picked up her folder. "The next time you talk to him, tell him that I have a feeling he had a hand in this somehow, and that if I can prove it, he can expect a visit from Mitch Rapp." Kennedy started for the door.

"Wait a second." Ross shot up out of his chair. "We're not finished here."

Kennedy paused and looked over her shoulder with utter confidence. "Yes, we are. I'm exhausted. While the three of you were busy trying to appease questionable allies, I flew halfway around the world and accomplished in one morning what a hundred lawyers from the Justice Department and another hundred State Department officials have been trying to do for the past two years. I'm going home, and I'm going to bed."

"Stop," Ross said. "You need to bring him in."

"Sorry . . . can't do it. He's out of my control."

"That's a lie! You don't want to bring him in."

Kennedy stopped with her hand on the doorknob. She turned slowly and said, "Mark, Mitch Rapp has done more to secure this country against terrorism than everyone in this room combined, and if you ask the president he will tell you the same thing. Maybe you should start helping him or at a bare minimum get out of his way."

"The man is reckless, Irene. He needs to be brought under control."

"Good luck . . . but while you're at it you might want to think about whether or not you want to be on Mitch Rapp's bad side."

"Is that a threat?"

Kennedy shrugged. "It's a fact. They killed his wife. There's no controlling him. He's going to kill anyone who had anything to do with this and if he finds out that you're siding with the Saudis while we have clear evidence that Saeed paid twenty million dollars to have him killed . . . well . . . let's just say I wouldn't want to be on your security detail."

Kennedy opened the door and left.

70

No one moved. Ross stood like a statue in front of the couch and just in front of the president. His cheeks were red and his fists balled up tight. He blinked several times, as he struggled with whether or not to take Irene's threat seriously.

"She just threatened me! She can't do that."

Everyone in the room had a law degree. Such was the state of politics. Attorney General Stokes, however, was the only one who had seen the inside of a courtroom. He shook his head and said, "She gave you an opinion as to what Rapp might do. It wasn't a threat."

That was not the answer or support that Ross expected from his friend. He turned to the president and said, "I can't work with her anymore. Something has to be done."

"Sit down, Mark." President Hayes crossed his legs and looked at his newest Cabinet member. The onset of his illness had given Hayes cause to become more reflective. Gone was his yearning desire to drive and shape the debate. It had been replaced by a tactic that he found far more productive. He would sit back and listen. Let the monumental egos of his advisors battle it out. Over the last forty-eight hours he had come to the conclusion that Ross was in fact the wrong man for the job, but replacing him was pretty much a nonstarter. A man like Ross would not go quietly. He would leak to the press like a sieve. He would make it his personal mission to destroy Kennedy. She didn't deserve that, and Hayes didn't want her distracted. Her job was too important. It was time to rein in the egos and remind them who they worked for.

Hayes cleared his throat and said, "I'd like to be very clear on something. If it wasn't for Mitch Rapp, I believe this city would have been destroyed by a nuclear explosion six months ago. That means pretty much everybody in this room would have been killed." Hayes took a moment to make eye contact with each person. "The lengths to which he went to stop that terrorist attack . . ." Hayes shook his head and his voice trailed off. "You don't even want to know what he had to do, but let's just say it wasn't pretty. We owe the man our lives, and that is no small thing."

"I know that, but . . ."

The president held up his hand and in a firm voice said to Ross, "Don't interrupt me. All of us are either elected or appointed. That means our time in our particular position is limited. Cabinet members last on average about three years. Presidents and VPs, we get four, and we're really lucky if we get eight. People like Kennedy and Rapp, they've devoted their entire lives to the war on terror. They were fighting it before most of us even knew there was a war." Hayes paused and folded his hands over his knee. "I for one think they deserve our support on this one."

"But, Bob," Ross said, "it's more complicated than that. We have alliances and relationships that are at stake here. We cannot have an employee of the CIA running around blowing people up."

"We can't?" Hayes asked provocatively, with an arched brow.

"No!" answered an appalled Ross.

Hayes sized up Ross while he slowly nodded his head. He stopped, pursed his lips, and said, "Do you know what I think. . . . I think we are the United States of America and we need to start acting like it."

The three Cabinet members stared back at him not sure what to say. The vice president knew better than to speak.

"If the Saudis want to make an issue out of this, they will lose. Mark, I want you to call Prince Rashid, and tell him that I'm extremely upset. You may tell him exactly what Irene said. If we find that he had any knowledge of his friend placing a bounty on one of my top counterterrorism people, I will personally sign the executive order that authorizes his assassination."

"Mr. President," said an uneasy secretary of state, "he is a member of the royal family. The king would be extremely upset."

"The king hates his half brother," the president said with a frown. "He knows Rashid would love nothing more than to become king and undo everything he has worked for. I will call the king myself and discuss the situation. I will guarantee by tomorrow all of this will be a nonissue."

Hayes stood and buttoned his coat. Everyone jumped to their feet, Ross a little slower than the rest, Hayes noticed.

"Mark, do you have a problem with any of this?"

"No, sir," he replied without enthusiasm.

"Good. And, Bea," Hayes said to his secretary of state, "when you talk to the Swiss foreign minister, tell him I appreciate his cooperation on this issue. If he persists in raising a stink, tell him I'm going to make it my personal goal in life to call every billionaire I know and tell them to divest any holdings they have in the Swiss banking industry."

The secretary of state swallowed hard and nodded.

Hayes walked over to his desk and checked his appointment book. He glanced up. No one had moved. He picked up the handset of his secure phone and said, "If you'll excuse me, I need to make a call to the king."

71

It was Tuesday morning, and the surveillance team had been in place for a little less than twenty-four hours. So far there was no sign of Erich Abel. They'd spent most of Monday trying to get a better feel for just who the man was and watching the apartment. That's what they were best at—waiting and watching, and of course not being noticed. They obtained an updated photo off his driver's registration as well as twelve years of driving history. Not a single ticket or parking violation in all that time, which said a lot about the man. They ran his credit report and found out where he banked in Vienna, and what credit cards he used. The credit cards were checked for activity and to no one's surprise they hadn't been used in nearly two weeks. They checked phone records, for the apartment, the office, and any mobile phones they could link to him. Back at Langley a team of specialists were poring over the numbers he'd called, trying to connect them to a company or a person. There were a lot of Saudis on the list.

Late Monday afternoon they'd sent a man into the apartment. It was a nice building that fronted Stadt Park just south of old Vienna's inner ring, no more than a mile from his office. There were fifty-two units in the building. It didn't totally reek of money, but it was definitely high-end. There was a doorman and security cameras, so they had to be creative. They sent two agents through the front door posing as a couple. They were lost, and looking for an old friend who they thought lived in the building. Thirty seconds into the charade the male agent remembered the correct name of the building they were looking for. A name that just happened to sound like this one, but was in fact the name of a building three blocks away. When the doorman stepped outside to point them in the right direction, two men with a lock pick went through the back door.

They didn't bother planting bugs to start with. Abel had gone underground, and it was highly unlikely that he would be returning anytime soon. This was an information grab. The agents spent nine hours going through every square inch of the two-bedroom apartment. They took nothing, but photographed anything that might be of consequence; old address books, handwritten notes, files, and photographs. Then everything was downloaded onto a laptop and relayed to the team for immediate analysis. They opened every book and leafed through them page by page. Every appliance was pulled out and inspected, every scrap of food, dry, frozen, or refrigerated, was checked to make sure it was real. Then they went room by room checking the floor, walls, and ceiling for hidden compartments.

They'd done this many times before. Where and how a person lived said a lot about them. These agents, in their fifteen plus years with the CIA, had rarely seen a place so clean, so organized, and so sanitized. There was no doubt about it, this Abel was a professional with obsessive-compulsive tendencies. They'd suspected thirty minutes into the sweep that they wouldn't find any bombshell. Subjects like this were too cautious to keep the important stuff at home. They used safe deposit boxes, or other offsite storage that would be hard to link to them. Shortly past midnight one of them left through the front door while the other stayed and planted a few bugs just in case. He waited twenty minutes and also left through the front door. There was a new doorman on duty. He would think they'd been visiting one of the owners.

Rapp, Coleman, and the guys got to the hotel a little before eleven in the evening. The drive from Riyadh to Qatar had been uneventful. The plane had been waiting, fueled, and ready to go. They were wheels up by six in the evening and on their way to Vienna. Through a fronted travel agency that was actually owned by the CIA six separate rooms had been booked at the Europa. The two connecting rooms were held under a single reservation and were being used as the command post. The other four rooms were under separate bookings that coincided with the fake passports used by the surveillance team. These rooms were used for sleeping.

Milt Johnson was the team leader. Now in his sixties, he was no longer an in-house employee of the CIA. He was a civilian contractor, which for him was just fine, because it meant he collected his full pension plus a salary that was thirty percent more than what he'd made during his last year. Milt typically ran his team in three eight-hour shifts, or two twelve-hour shifts to start with. If things got really hairy, which they usually did, he needed his people rested, because he would have to put them all into the field. The tricks of Milt's craft were fairly standard. They rented the most common cars they could find in the host country, they kept them filled with gas at all times, and he always had at least one man on a scooter or motorcycle. Unless the situation called for it, he never hired people who were too tall or too short, or too pretty or too handsome. His people carried things like reversible jackets, hats, and sunglasses or clear eyeglasses. He always had a makeup artist on hand and he never let his people drink coffee. Coffee meant bathroom breaks and too many bathroom breaks could lead to losing the target. Milt knew firsthand because he'd blown a major surveillance operation one time.

It had been during the mid-seventies, and the United States had had a mole in the Berlin embassy. Milt was part of a team that had zeroed in on the deputy ambassador. He was on the night shift all by himself, drinking coffee like a fiend so he could stay awake. Every hour on the hour he was getting out of the car and ducking into the alley to relieve himself. In the morning, the deputy ambassador was gone, and Milt was left having to explain how the man had slipped out from under his nose. He hadn't had a cup of coffee since.

Milt had worked with Rapp a lot over the years, but until just a few years ago he'd never known his real name. He'd read about the explosion at the house and the death of Rapp's wife. He had been very sorry about it. When Rapp arrived in the hotel room with Coleman, Milt casually took Rapp by the elbow and led him into the connecting room. The rooms were sizable and elegant. It was a turn-of-the-previous-century hotel that had either been kept up remarkably well or completely renovated. There were two double beds, an antique desk, and a massive armoire that doubled as an entertainment center, dresser, and in-room refrigerator.

Milt closed the connecting door and said to Rapp in a somber voice, "I'm very sorry about your wife."

Rapp nodded. He appreciated the sentiment, but didn't want to talk about it. "Thanks, Milt. I appreciate you getting on this so quick."

Milt nodded. He was four inches shorter than Rapp and had gray wispy hair that had receded at least a quarter of the way back from its youthful starting point. "We'll find this guy. Don't worry."

"Anything so far?"

"Nope. And to be honest I wasn't expecting to. I've read his file. These Stasi guys were pretty good, and this one seems above average. He's a smart little fucker but we'll catch him."

"The apartment was a bust?"

"Yep, but we had to cover it."

"The office?"

"First thing in the morning."

"Expectations?"

Milt shrugged. "We might find something, but I'm thinking the banks will be the key. This guy likes nice things. He just bought a brand-new hundred-plus-thousand-dollar Mercedes." Milt smiled. "When he finds out you drained his accounts he's going to come unhinged. If he calls the banks to sort it out, we'll be on him. If he doesn't, he's going to be low on money and he'll have to surface sooner rather than later."

Rapp thought about that. "What about putting the word out? Unofficially of course. Offer a million dollars for him and see if he contacts any of his old Stasi buddies for help."

"I thought about that, but I think we should wait a few days. Let's see where tomorrow takes us and then we'll decide. In the meantime, I want you to get some sleep. You look like shit."

"I feel like shit."

"That's to be expected." Milt put a hand on his shoulder. Sleep was a strange thing. The more you needed it, the harder it was to get. And Milt could see that Rapp desperately needed some sleep. "Mitch, have I ever let you down before?"

Rapp shook his head.

"And I'm not going to let you down now. I'm not going to stop until I find this Abel guy, and then I'm going to find the people he hired. You can count on it. Now go to bed. I have a feeling tomorrow is going to be a big day."

72

Tayyib had met the woman on two occasions, both times in Abel's office. Rashid had sent him there unannounced, for no other reason than to make Abel uncomfortable and to let him know that the six-foot-four Tayyib with his haunting eyes and impassive demeanor knew where Abel worked. Rashid had made up some inconsequential reason for the visits, but the message was clear enough. Tayyib did not like women. Especially large-breasted blond women who were trying to make him stray from the path. That was what he remembered most about Greta Jorgensen—her impossibly large breasts and the tight sweaters she had worn on both occasions. He would not have known her name if it hadn't been displayed on a placard sitting on top of her desk.

The men he sent to find Abel had reported that he was not at the office on Monday. Tayyib asked them what excuse the secretary had given them and they reported that there was no secretary. The office was closed. No one was there. Tayyib asked them if Monday had been a holiday. They said it wasn't. That meant Abel had talked to her and told her not to come into work. And that meant she knew how to communicate with him. Finding out where she lived did not prove difficult. Outside of the Kingdom, the Saudi Intelligence Service was strongest in Vienna, the home of OPEC. There were only two Greta Jorgensens in the phone book and three G. Jorgensens. Tayyib estimated the woman to be in her late thirties and either divorced or single. She hadn't been wearing a ring. The intelligence people at the embassy eliminated three of the Jorgensens straightaway and with a little more checking they eliminated the fourth.

The fifth and final woman lived in a bland apartment building north of the Danube not far from the Wiennord train station. They had one of the interpreters from the embassy call her apartment to see if she was in. She answered on the fourth ring and in perfect Austrian German the interpreter asked for Johan. She explained that no Johan lived there and the interpreter told her he was sorry.

Twenty minutes later Greta Jorgensen was sitting in front of her computer making the final arrangements for her trip. That was what her boss wanted her to do, and she loved to travel. Her bags were packed and she was leaving in the morning. It was almost midnight when she heard a faint knock on her door. She had a neighbor who was a waitress. Sometimes when she got off work, she'd stop by to see if Greta wanted a glass of wine and a cigarette. Greta had told her about her sudden trip and asked her to come along. The friend had said she couldn't afford it. Greta hoped she had changed her mind. She opened the door without bothering to look through the peephole and was surprised to find a very tall serious man standing there instead. Greta tilted her head to the left and studied the face that she vaguely recognized, but couldn't place. Before she could make the connection, the man punched her in the jaw and everything went black.

73

Rapp and Coleman stood shoulder to shoulder behind Milt and watched him orchestrate the movements of his team. On the desk in front of him, three laptops were open and powered up. The one on the left showed the exterior of Abel's office building, the one in the middle was a live feed through the windshield of a car that was moving through morning traffic, and the last one had a map of Vienna on the screen. Everyone on Milt's team wore a transponder. Each agent's location was marked on the screen with a neon green dot and a number. This way Milt knew where all of his people were at every moment and like an air traffic controller he could look at the screen and vector them into position as was needed.

The plan this morning was simple. The building where Abel's office was located was near Parliament, which meant there would be a fair amount of cops in the neighborhood. The building was five stories, made out of stone, and like nearly everything else in Vienna, it was in immaculate shape considering it had been built a full century ago. Abel's office was on the third floor, sandwiched between two attorneys. The place was well organized and occupied mostly by professionals. That was why Milt had wanted to wait until morning. There was no need to push it if they didn't have to. Buildings like this received visitors all day long, but overnight they shut down. The place had decent security and was staffed by a watchman. It would be far easier to walk in under their nose in broad daylight.

Standing in front of a fountain across the street, one of the agents called in that everything was clear. It was two minutes before nine and people were streaming into the building. The sky was patchy with clouds and the temperature was mild. It looked like rain was likely.

Milt flipped the mike arm up on his headset and announced to the two men standing behind him, "The weather is perfect."

He yanked the mike back down and asked, "Sarah, how are you feeling?"

"Good." The voice came out of a small black speaker on the left of the desk.

"All right. Why don't you head in. Nothing fancy. No big risks. We've got all morning." Milt never liked to rush unless he had to.

THE HOTEL WAS only a few blocks from the office. A black A-4 Audi pulled out into traffic and less than a minute later it stopped in front of Abel's building. A brunette with dark, horn-rimmed glasses got out of the car and closed the door. Milt never worked with blondes. They stood out too much. The agent's shoulder-length black hair had a slight wave to it and on her right side it partially covered her face. She was wearing a stylish black nylon trench coat that stopped midthigh and could be reversed to light gray. Underneath, she was wearing a dark gray pantsuit with a white blouse. Very monochrome. Very forgettable. At least that was the intent.

Sarah had a wireless, pin-sized fiber-optic camera in her glasses. She stayed right on the heels of two men and headed for the elevators. A medium-sized black purse was slung over her right shoulder, and a newspaper was folded in quarters and clutched in her left hand. She kept her chin down in case there were any cameras. There were three elevators. The doors to the middle one opened, and she followed some people in and stepped off to the side. Three had already been pressed so she retreated even farther into the elevator. She wanted to be the last one off. The elevator lurched straight to the second floor and a few people got off. At three the doors opened, and one man hurried off. Sarah paused for a beat and then pressed her way to the front. A man held the door for her and she stepped off and took a right. The other man had gone to the left.

"Remember your bailout," Milt said softly. "If it isn't right, you've got a bathroom and a staircase at the end of the hall."

The building was U-shaped with an inner courtyard. Sarah continued down the hall to where it stopped and took a right. Abel's office would be on her left, midway down. Number 318. So far everything was clear. In the right pocket of her trench coat was a small black object shaped like a gun. It was actually a lock pick. It would take her less than two seconds to get in. She rounded the corner and immediately sensed something was wrong. Up ahead, about where Abel's office should be, there was a cluster of people. Sarah gave them a good look and then glanced down at her paper. Milt was already talking in her ear.

"Give me a slow drive-by and keep on walking."

Sarah was already planning on doing just that. She glanced up again and counted three heads. All men, one very tall and two of average height. She looked down at her paper and actually slowed her pace a touch. There were still four doors ahead on her left. Sarah looked up as she passed the next office so they could get a number off the door. It said 312. The men were standing in front of Abel's office. Her pulse quickened and she wondered if Milt had already figured it out.

His voice came over her wireless earpiece in a calm and slow tone. "I think they are crashing our party. Would you please get me a close-up of their faces and then head into the ladies' room?"

Sarah did just that. When she was only four paces away, she looked up and smiled. She noticed for the first time that there was a woman standing in the middle of the three men. All Sarah saw was a shock of blond hair between two of the men who were facing her and then they closed ranks and the woman disappeared. Everything about their body language and the expressions on their faces was wrong. It was as if they were angry that she would even dare look at them. Sarah knew instantly that they were Saudi.

RAPP LEANED OVER Milt's shoulder as he rewound the footage. Milt worked the touchpad while he talked to Sarah, who'd had a bad experience before with some Saudi intel officers. "I know you hate them. Just sit tight."

"I swear," the agitated female voice came from the small black speaker. "If they come in this bathroom I'm going to kill them."

"Sarah," Milt said, as the footage jumped back ten frames at a time, "I would really prefer it if you didn't kill anybody." Milt paused the playback on the most clear picture of the two men. One tall and one average. Milt blinked several times and said, "I'll be damned."

"What?" Rapp asked.

Milt shifted to the third computer, closed out the map, and opened a file that Langley had sent him during the night. He'd forgotten to show

Rapp. A composite drawing came up on the screen. It was a dead ringer for the taller man that Sarah had just passed in front of Abel's office.

"Who is he?" asked Rapp.

"I don't know." Milt shrugged. "It came addressed to you with a note that said this is the man who hired the Salvadorans."

All at once Rapp recognized what was going on. "What do you have for nonlethal?" Rapp asked urgently.

"We have Tasers."

"Where?"

"In that black case right there."

Rapp grabbed the hard black case off the floor, tossed it on the bed, and popped the clasps. He threw one of the high-voltage stun guns to Coleman.

"Let's go."

"Radios!" Milt half yelled. He grabbed two small black Motorola secure digital radios, clip-on wireless mikes, and tiny, flesh-colored wireless earpieces. "They're charged and ready to go."

Rapp and Coleman stuffed the radios in their jacket pockets, clipped the mikes to the inside of their collars, and put the earpieces in. They started for the door.

"Milt," Rapp said over his shoulder, "tell Sarah she's not allowed to kill anyone until I get there. And send that guy's photo back to Langley and have them verify that he's the one I'm looking for."

"What in the hell do the Salvadorans have to do with this?" Milt watched them leave. Rapp didn't bother to answer his question. "Why do I get the feeling I'm going to have a mess to clean up?" Milt pulled down his lip mike and got busy repositioning his team.

74

Tayyib was beginning to wonder if the woman knew much of anything. They'd taken her from the apartment, shoved her in the trunk of a car, and taken her back to the embassy. Tayyib had started with the fingernails on her left hand. He'd torn them off one at a time. Her story started to change after the third one. She had gone from saying she didn't know where her boss was to telling him that he might be in Italy. Where in Italy, he wanted to know. She sobbed that she didn't know where, just that she thought she overheard him say something about Italy. That was when he decided to let two of the men rape her. They had been eager enough, and Tayyib knew they would be grateful. Tayyib would not defile himself in such a way, but he knew with women, this type of subjugation could put them into the proper frame of mind.

He left the basement storage room and found the kitchen. He gave them an hour. He ate a sandwich, drank a glass of milk, and thought about what questions he would ask her when he started up again. Abel was a man who embraced technology. Tayyib had first met him five years ago. Even then he was carrying one of those combination handheld computers and cell phones. His office would be the key. There would be something there that would tell him where Abel was. Some piece of information stored on a computer. Tayyib could not disappoint Rashid. He had to find the German or the prince would never trust him again.

When he went back downstairs the men were finishing up with her. They had her stripped and bent over a table with her arms tied to the far legs with brown extension cords. She was there for him to take. He felt a rush of excitement and was seconds away from giving in. He forced himself to silently recite the salat ul-jumuah. *Allahu Akbar, Allahu Akbar . . . Ashahadu an la ilaha ill allah . . . Ashahadu anna Muhammadar Rasulullah . . . God is greater, God is greater. I declare there is no god but God. I declare Muhammad is the messenger of God . . .*

The prayer, however, did not subdue his desires and he knew that he could no longer be in the presence of the temptress. One of the men laughed that she had begged them to stop. That she had mentioned something about a safe in the office. It was already past four in the morning. Tayyib angrily ordered the men to rape her again. Going to the office right now might arouse too much suspicion. They would have to clean her up and take her to the office in the morning.

75

Rapp and Coleman took the stairs. Coleman was down them like a shot. Because of his stiff knee and thigh bruise Rapp fell slightly behind. Coleman waited for him on the street and they walked side by side, quickly, but not so fast as to raise unwanted suspicion. They passed one police officer on the way and paid him no attention. Rapp began gesturing with his hands and speaking to Coleman in French. They were both in jeans. Rapp was wearing his black Polartec jacket, and Coleman was wearing a dark brown bush jacket with oversized pockets. It was one long block and one short block. They arrived at the front door of the building in just under three minutes.

"Taser the big guy," Coleman said as they walked up the steps.

"Yep. I want him alive."

"And the other two?"

"Depends on what they do. You worry about the big guy. I'll handle the other two. Milt," Rapp said into the tiny microphone on his collar, "tell Sarah to give us a quick look. We're headed into the building right now."

Coleman nodded as Rapp began speaking in French again. They passed through the large heavy brass doors and continued across the lobby, straight to the elevators. They managed to catch one by themselves and on the way up, they listened to Sarah as she left the bathroom and walked past Abel's office. "The door is closed, and I think they're in there."

"Wait for us, by the elevators," Rapp said.

Five seconds later the door opened and Rapp and Coleman charged out. They met Sarah halfway down the hall and huddled.

"We go in fast. I'm first, Scott, you're second, and Sarah, I want you to stay by the door. You're silenced, right?"

"Yes."

"Stay low. I don't want any errant shots passing through a wall and hitting one of us. If we find someone in the outer office and they don't do anything stupid, Scott and I will go right past them and it's up to you to secure them. If the guy doesn't do exactly as you say, shoot him." Rapp looked into her eyes to see if this would be a problem. "Are you okay with that?"

She nodded, but then said, "Why don't we get a fiber optic up here and have a peek under the door?"

Rapp shook his head.

"She's right, Mitch," Coleman said. "It'll take five minutes tops."

"I don't want to waste five minutes, and we don't need to make this complicated. We move fast and this whole thing is over in five seconds not five minutes. Shoot anyone except the girl and the big guy."

"Fine."

Rapp started down the hall and turned right at the end. Rapp was picturing the layout in his head. There would be a small reception area and then either a door straight ahead, or on the right or left that would lead to Abel's office. When he was five paces away from the door his left hand slid around and underneath his jacket. His fingers found the hilt of the 9mm Glock and drew it from his waistband. With the silencer attached it was a long draw. Rapp stopped just short of the door and looked over his shoulder to make sure Coleman and Sarah were with him. He held up his right hand and then leaned forward and placed it on the doorknob.

Everything stopped for that instant. Rapp closed his eyes, dropped into a slight crouch, took one more deep breath, and then twisted the knob while leaning into the door with his left shoulder. He did it in one smooth motion with his gun extended. He found himself standing in an outer office that was approximately ten feet wide by fifteen feet long. It had a desk on the right, a couch on the left, and a door straight ahead. Rapp could hear hushed, male voices from the other room. He crept slowly across the room and then he heard something said in Arabic. He slowed for a second and leaned one way and then the other to see if he could tell where they were. He told himself this was no time to stop. They wouldn't have their guns drawn and if they did, they would be at their side.

Rapp charged into the room, checking his left quickly and then sweeping to his right. The three of them were standing behind a large desk. A section of the bookcase was pulled out and behind it was a gray steel wall safe. None of them bothered to turn around so Rapp said, "Hey, guys."

They all flinched in surprise, including the girl. Rapp's eyes checked the hands of each man in less than a second. He saw one gun, the man on the far right, and that was where Rapp directed his aim. He was just about to say "Don't even think about it" when the man moved. The gun was resting flat against his thigh. Rapp was looking him in the eye, but he saw the movement. The gun started to come up. It never got above his waist. Rapp squeezed the trigger and drilled the man right between the eyes. His head snapped back against the bookcase and he crumpled to the ground.

Coleman was already in the room, his Taser up and ready. He took aim at the man on the far right and pulled the trigger. A pair of fishhooks shot out from the end of the weapon and attached themselves to the man's chest. Twenty thousand volts of electricity shot through the man's body and he did the herky-jerky for a second and then collapsed to his knees, his face twisted in pain. Through the connecting wires Coleman hit him with another charge, and the man fell facedown on the rug, unable to move.

Both Rapp and Coleman took aim at the taller man while Sarah closed the door to the hallway.

"Don't do anything stupid." Even as Rapp said it he knew they had a problem. The woman was standing too close to the man. Rapp could have shot him easily, but he wanted him alive. The man stepped quickly to the side and put the woman between them. He grabbed her by the throat with his right hand and the hair with his left.

"Drop your weapons."

"Or what?" Rapp said.

"I'll crush her throat."

Rapp watched as the man increased pressure and the woman's eyes began to bug out of her head. Rapp assessed his options. The guy had himself almost completely concealed behind the woman. His eyes danced around the periphery of the silhouette and he found his spot. Rapp dropped his muzzle three inches and squeezed the trigger.

The 9mm round hit him in the right elbow and shattered the socket. The response was instantaneous and gratifying. His right hand fell limply to his side, and his left hand released the woman's hair. The man's brain was on override, and his left hand came across his chest to aid his semi-attached right forearm. At the same time the woman doubled over on the desk gasping for air. That was when the fishhooks sunk into his chest and he was hit with the burning electrical charge.

76

Abel stepped off the train, covered his mouth with a handkerchief, and thanked a God he didn't believe in for the formation of the European Union. Gone were the days of customs and immigration checkpoints at every border and port of entry. Now they were all one big happy family and they could pass freely from one country to the next without going through any hassle. This all suited Abel's new lifestyle very well. He'd taken the train from Venice to Milan where he spent the night in a completely forgettable hotel near the train station. He'd dined by himself at a small café. Gone were the expensive wine and food and hotels. If Rashid didn't come through with the money by noon all of his hard work, and this entire gamble, would be for nothing.

He'd taken the first express train north in the morning. Fortunately it was far nicer than the run-down, soiled Ferrovie dello Stato train he'd taken from Venice. They made one stop at Chiaso and then crossed the border. The train continued on its way, rumbling through the beautiful countryside all morning long, winding its way north, coming out of the mountains and making a straight run for Zurich. Abel devoured five separate newspapers looking for information on Saeed's death. All of the articles were thin on facts. It was too early to know for sure what had happened, but Abel knew it had been Rapp.

The train pulled into Zurich a few minutes before noon. His eyeglasses were in his pocket and his handkerchief covered his face as he passed under a tinted security camera pod. Abel walked briskly with his medium-sized wheeled suitcase rolling behind him. He did not go straight for the taxi line. He crossed the street and walked south down Bahnhofstrasse toward the lake. Abel knew the city as well as any in the world. He kept an apartment here that doubled as an office. He wouldn't be going anywhere near the place, though.

After a brisk ten-minute walk he was in the heart of one of the world's most upscale shopping districts. Abel turned east and took one of the low-slung bridges across the Limmat. He found a bench on the east bank and turned on his PDA. While he waited for the color screen to come to life he glanced up at the sky. It was a blanket of gray. No clouds, just flat gray blotting out the warm sun. A cool gust of wind kicked off the river and Abel turned up the collar of his trench coat.

The screen sprang to life and the tiny speaker announced that the device was ready with a few musical notes. Abel's thumbs began working furiously. He found the bank's Web site, entered his account number, and passed through three separate security portals until the account balance appeared on the screen. Abel paused, frowned, and then swore. The amount in the account was one million dollars. Not eleven.

Abel stood, took several laps around the park bench, and then sat back down and typed out the instructions to his banker. He wanted the money moved out of the account before he made his next call. He sent the instructions with all the proper passwords and then logged off. He called Rashid's office. The prince was not in, but he was expecting the call. The assistant gave Abel a number to dial. Abel hung up without thanking the man and turned off his phone. He wondered if this was some kind of a trap. He decided to use a pay phone to make the call.

Half a block away he found one and punched in his calling card number followed by the new number. After a series of whirs and clicks a man answered on the other end.

"Prince Muhammad, now."

"May I ask who is calling?"

"Just put him on the phone," Abel snapped. He looked over both shoulders, up and down the riverbank, and counted the seconds.

"Erich?" the prince asked. "Where are you?"

"I'm in Vienna," he lied. "Where are you?"

"Southern Spain."

Abel shook his head. Rashid loved to talk about Spain and how someday again it would be Muslim. "I just checked the account. You are ten million dollars short."

"I have some bad news for you. The Americans already know that you were working for Saeed."

"You are lying."

"No, I am not."

"Who told you?"

"Their director of National Intelligence . . . Ross."

"I don't believe you." Abel tried to sound calm even though his head was pounding.

"It is true. In fact I don't think Vienna is a good place for you to be. Fly to Saudi Arabia and I will protect you."

Fly to Saudi Arabia and you'll kill me, Abel thought to himself. "How did the Americans find out about me? Saeed would have told them nothing."

"The assassins you hired have been talking."

"They were caught?" Abel asked in disbelief.

"No. Not that I know of. All I was told was that the CIA has been in contact with the banks that you and Saeed used. Director Kennedy herself flew to Zurich and met with the bankers. Saeed did not take your money. The CIA did."

"I don't care who took my money. Our deal still stands. Eleven million dollars. You owe me ten."

"Yes I do," Rashid said in a reasonable voice, "and you will get it. Every six months I will wire you another million."

"That'll take five years."

"Exactly, and during that time I will sleep well knowing that you have an incentive not to betray me."

"No! We made a deal yesterday."

"Deals get modified. Fly to Granada. I'll send my plane. We can discuss your terms."

Abel took the hard plastic handset and banged it against his forehead several times. He was in no position to negotiate. "Six months from today, I want to see a million dollars deposited in my account or I give the Americans everything on you. Not just this stuff about Rapp, but everything. And just in case you've decided to send that goon Tayyib after me, you'd better know I took out an insurance policy."

"What insurance policy?"

"I put everything on an encrypted disk and gave it to an attorney." Abel was lying. "If I fail to call him by a specific date each month he has instructions to send the disk to the FBI. I want my million dollars every six months, Rashid, and if I see any sign of Tayyib or any of his people I will call Mitch Rapp personally."

Abel slammed the phone into its cradle, and spun around. He grabbed his bag and started off down the street. He hadn't made arrangements with an attorney yet, but he would the first chance he got. Rashid's renegotiated deal was hard to argue with. If he'd been in his shoes, he would have done the same thing. Abel still didn't trust him and that was why he was going to have to proceed with plan B. It was a bit risky, but it was better to do it now than wait another day. The Americans were sure to find out about his mountain retreat at some point. He'd left his new Mercedes in a private garage, before he'd left for Venice. He would pick it up, dash across the border to his Alpine house, and empty out his safe, which had over $500,000 in cash, plus a few weapons, several sets of identification, and some very important files.

77

VIENNA, AUSTRIA

The two Saudis were on their backs, their ankles and hands bound with white flex cuffs and duct tape stretched tightly over their mouths and eyes. The bigger man's elbow wound had been bandaged, not because they were concerned for his health, but because they didn't want to have to clean up any more blood. It had taken an entire bag of cat litter just to soak up the puddle of blood that had poured out of the third man's head. Milt's team was used to this stuff. Within minutes they were running around town purchasing a vacuum, cleaning solutions, a two-wheeler, cat litter, duct tape, rolls of heavy plastic, and even a fifty-inch projection TV. The TV was left in an alley not far from where it had been purchased, and the box was saved.

Rapp looked on, as the guy he'd shot in the head was wrapped up in plastic, duct-taped, and then placed in the large TV box. None of them were carrying IDs, but Rapp was willing to bet the farm they were Saudis. The big guy with the busted elbow was left on the floor while the other guy was knocked out with a needle full of Xanax to the thigh, and tossed in the box on top of his dead friend. Milt's guys resealed the box with clear packing tape and took it away on the two-wheeler. The dead guy would be chopped up into pieces and dropped into vats of industrial acid. The second guy they weren't sure what they'd do with, but after listening to the woman tell them how she'd been brutally beaten and raped, Rapp was tempted to cut the guy's balls off, shove them down his throat, and let him choke to death.

Coleman and Sarah were in the other room trying to talk to the woman. They'd given her a much smaller dose of Xanax to help calm her down. She was making too much noise. She told them how she had answered her apartment door the previous night and the big man had been standing there. The next thing she remembered was waking up in a basement somewhere and then the beating started. They wanted to know where her boss was. So did Coleman and Sarah, but they didn't push it. After all this woman had been through she was not going to respond well to rough or even assertive behavior. They listened and asked a few gentle questions to help nudge her in the right direction. When was the last time you spoke to your boss? Have you ever seen any of these men before?

She explained that her boss had called her on Thursday of the previous week and told her not to bother coming in for a while. She decided to take the time to travel. She was going to leave this very morning and then these men showed up at her apartment. At this point she had a meltdown, and it took several minutes and a little Xanax to calm her down. One of the men she recognized. The tall one. She was pretty sure he was a Saudi. Her boss did a lot of work with the Saudis and several of the other Arab countries. She explained that Vienna was home to one of the three United Nations headquarters and also OPEC. Coleman pressed her on the type of work they did. Mostly lobbying, and some risk assessment. Coleman asked her if she knew her boss had worked for the East German secret police. She said she did not, and he believed her.

Meanwhile Rapp was going through the contents of the safe. It took one of Milt's guys less than two minutes to open it. They'd found some interesting stuff in there, like a copy of *Alice in Wonderland*. A leftover from his old days with the Stasi no doubt. Probably given to him by his KGB supervisor. Rapp opened it to the title page and sure enough it was addressed to Abel. The inscription was in Russian and since Rapp didn't understand a word of it he handed it off to one of Milt's people so it could be boxed up and taken back to Langley for deeper analysis. It was an old trick of the KGB to use books as keys to decipher coded messages. There was also a 9mm H&K P2000 with a silencer. Rapp inspected the weapon, turning it over in his hand and checking it from several angles. It was spotless, but not from cleaning. Rapp guessed the weapon had been fired fewer than a hundred times. There were a few disks that were coded. They were sent straight over to Milt so he could begin working on them with Marcus Dumond back at Langley. Other than that, there were a few files, 10,000 euros, and a fake passport and matching credit card. All said, there was nothing that was going to tell them where Abel was right now.

Rapp had attempted, briefly, to interrogate the big guy, but he began screaming like all hell and Rapp had been forced to pistol-whip him across the side of the head to shut him up. The guy was just coming out of it and Rapp was anxious to try again. He wanted to find out just who in the hell he worked for.

Coleman came up and tapped him on the shoulder. "You might want to come talk to her."

"What's up?"

"She's talking about some place that didn't show up on any of our checks. Some Alpine house. I guess it's a mountain retreat that her boss uses to get away."

"Has she ever been there?"

Coleman shook his head. "I guess he's pretty private about it, but over the years, she's heard bits and pieces."

"Does she know where it is?"

"Not specifically, but she says it's in the Tyrol Region near a city called Bludenz."

Before Rapp could ask just where in the hell Bludenz was, Milt Johnson's voice came squawking over the secure digital radio. "Mitch, are you there?"

Rapp had taken out his earpiece. The radio was clipped to his belt. He snatched it and thumbed the talk button. "What do you need, Milt?"

"Did I tell you this guy dropped one hundred and twenty-five grand on a brand-new Mercedes a week ago?"

"No."

"Well, I think I just found it."

Rapp stared at the radio for a second and shook his head. "Am I supposed to be impressed?"

"Not yet. You're supposed to ask me how I found it."

"Milt, how did you find it?"

"I'm glad you asked me that. These high-end cars all come with GPS. We hacked into the Mercedes database, entered the vehicle number that we got off the registration, and came up with the car's GPS locater. I kicked it over to the NSA this morning and they just let me know where the car is."

"Let me guess . . . it's parked at the Vienna International Airport."

"No. It was actually parked in Zurich, but six minutes ago it started moving."

Rapp paused and looked at the little black radio again. "Where is it headed?"

"South is all they said. Out of the city."

Rapp didn't press the transmit button right away. He knew Zurich well and was trying to picture what lay south of the city. The lake was dead south. Everything flowed around it either to the east or west. He hit the button. "Is the car headed southeast or southwest?"

It took a few seconds for Milt to reply. "Southeast."

Rapp's mind was racing ahead. Southeast was either the Austrian border or Italy. "Milt, I'm on my way over. Get me a fast helicopter, and find out who we have on the ground in Zurich."

Rapp clicked off and looked at Coleman. He pointed at the bound Saudi on the floor. "He's coming with us. Tell them to get that box back up here and get him down in the van ASAP."

78

Abel was not worried about tracking devices. The car was new, and it had been stored and covered at a local garage while he was gone. There was no way for anyone to know that he had kept the car there. Still, his years of spycraft made him cautious. On the way out of Zurich he got off the autobahn twice and doubled back. When he was absolutely sure no one was following him, he set out for his destination like a rocket. The 493 hp engine propelled the silver Mercedes down the Swiss autobahn at speeds sometimes approaching 150 mph. That was only on the straightaway, though. The police were fine with fast driving, but not reckless. When he made his way into the mountain passes, the winding, climbing, and then falling road caused him to reduce his speed greatly. The trip from Zurich to Bludenz took two hours and forty-seven minutes.

Abel pulled into the quaint town and was immediately hit with a feeling of melancholy. He loved this place and it made him sad that he would be denied its simple pleasures because of some sadistic Saudi and a crazy American. On impulse, he stopped the car in front of the small grocery store. He was hungry and he might as well pick up some of his favorite foods. Abel walked in the front door, and a bell chimed to announce to the owner that a customer had arrived. Abel breathed in the smells. The pastries, the meats, the fresh coffee, this place was heaven.

The butcher was standing at his post behind the meat counter, a fresh white apron tied around his waist. Abel watched him carefully for any type of reaction, any hint that strangers had been in town asking about him. Who knew what the Americans might do? With their new war on, it was very possible they would alert Interpol and the state police in both Switzerland and Austria.

The butcher smiled warmly at him. He looked Abel directly in the eye and although he did not know the customer by name, he told him it was good to see him again. This was all a relief to Abel. He was one step ahead of the people looking for him. He asked for several links of sausage and then picked up some vegetables, a few small wedges of cheese, milk, fresh coffee, a couple of pastries, and a few eggs. By the time he checked out, he was considering spending the night. He knew he shouldn't, but he also knew this would be the last time he would see his beloved Alpine house for some time.

Abel drove the silver SL 55 AMG Mercedes up the switchback road with the sunroof open and the windows down. It was chilly outside, but he didn't care. It felt so good to breathe in the clean mountain air. Abel would miss the majestic views and the quaintness of the village. If only there was a way to stay, to simply hide out here in the Alps and hope that no one discovered him. Petrov knew about the place, though, and the Americans would eventually find out that Petrov had been his handler all those years ago when the Iron Curtain still divided Europe.

Abel looked back on it all and wondered where he had made his mistake. Was it when he agreed to take the job from Saeed? Was it when he pushed the assassins and threatened to hunt them down? At the time, it seemed like his only option, but looking back on it now, it had been a foolish and emotionally inspired move. He had no idea who they were, and they knew far too much about him. It was clear now what they had decided. He had threatened them, and rather than hunt him down themselves like the man said he would, they decided to put the CIA and this monster Mitch Rapp onto his trail. It was a brilliant move on their part, and one that Abel should have foreseen. His second mistake was leaving the money in the accounts. He should have moved it. It pained him to no end to think that he had let eleven million dollars slip through his hands.

Abel rounded the last switchback. There was no guardrail, just a tiny stone ledge and then a steep drop over the edge. His place was ahead on the right. The tires left the pavement and moved onto the crushed rock | of his driveway. He skidded to a stop in front of the house and looked around. It appeared at first glance exactly as he had left it. He grabbed the keys and got out, standing there for a moment, looking back up the hill through the thick branches of the pine trees and the golden fall leaves of the aspens. Other than the slight rustle of dry fall leaves there wasn't a sound.

Abel left the groceries in the backseat and entered the house. He locked the door behind him and went straight downstairs. The house was built into the side of the mountain, so the basement had an earthy, musty smell. A single door with triple windows offered a shaded view of the valley. The deck from above cast a shadow. It was not quite 4:00 in the afternoon. The German went to a door at the back of the basement, opened it, and turned on a light.

A furnace and water heater sat in the far corner. The cement floor was painted a burnt red and was cracked. Skis and poles were hung on a set of pegs. Boots, gloves, goggles, and hats, and a variety of other outdoor accessories were neatly placed on two shelves. A wood pallet with paint cans stacked on top sat in the corner opposite the furnace. Abel grabbed one of the slats and dragged the pallet to the middle of the room. He took a small crowbar hanging on the wall and wedged the straight end into a small crack in the floor. A small section roughly the shape of Australia rose above the rest of the floor. Abel stuck his free hand under the lip and grabbed hold. He tossed the crowbar to the side and slid the section out of the way, revealing a large floor safe. He dialed the combination, jerked the handle clockwise a quarter of a turn and pulled up. He removed one black nylon bag and then a second, a third, and finally a fourth.

Everything was put back just as it had been and then he grabbed the four bags and went back upstairs. When he reached the front entryway he was breathing heavily and for a moment was concerned he'd stirred up some mold in the storage room and was having an asthma attack. He stood up straight, placed his hands over his head, and concentrated on taking deep, full breaths. After a half minute he felt better. It was nothing more than the thin mountain air. Suddenly, he remembered the groceries in the car. He was famished.

Abel threw the dead bolt and yanked open the heavy wood door. He crossed the timber porch and stepped down onto the crushed rock. He glanced to his left and right and then again up the slope of the mountain. It was his favorite place on earth. Maybe he could stay one last night. Cook a nice meal, build a fire, and sip a little cognac. He had a bottle of Louis XIII. It would be a shame to waste it. Abel made a note to clear out the wine cellar. There would be room in the trunk. He would stay the night and say good-bye the proper way.

Abel opened the back passenger door and grabbed the bag of groceries. He put them under his left arm, stepped away and closed the door with his right. As he turned to head back into the house he found himself staring down the length of a thick black silencer at the face of the last man he wanted to see. Abel dropped the bag of groceries, and said, "I can explain."

"I'm sure you can." Rapp took half a step back and then kicked Abel in the balls, dropping him to the ground.

79

It was the two exits off the autobahn and the doubling back that told them it was Abel behind the wheel. Milt had tapped into the Mercedes mainframe, and they were following the car's progress on a color screen that showed the exact road the car was on. It showed gas stations, churches, restaurants, rivers, lakes, parks, everything. As soon as the car doubled back for the second time, Rapp knew it was their man. Two of the Agency's people from the embassy in Bern had been camped in front of Abel's Zurich apartment for the better part of a day. They were pulled off their assignment and put into pursuit of a car they never caught up to.

Finding a helicopter proved more difficult than they would have thought, but that also didn't matter. An hour into tracking him, the car headed due east, straight for the Austrian border and according to the map a town called Bludenz. Milt worked the computers and found out they had a regional airport. By plane, the flight was less than thirty minutes. Rapp, Coleman and his men, and the big Saudi all took off for the airport. While in flight, Milt arranged two rental cars: a Volvo sedan and van. The vehicles were waiting for them when they landed. The only difficult part was transferring the Saudi. Rapp decided to leave him in the plane under the watchful eye of Stroble, rather than risk one of the locals seeing a bound and gagged man being stuffed into a rental car.

It took eight minutes to get from the airport into town. Milt had given them constant updates on the car's progress. It had arrived in Bludenz just before they'd landed and it had stopped for exactly seventeen minutes. It then headed north, up what Milt assumed was a residential road. He had been right. They took the Volvo slowly up the switchbacks, beyond where Milt said the vehicle had stopped. Rapp and Wicker got out and silently worked their way back down the hillside. They found the big, expensive Mercedes parked right in front of what they assumed was Abel's house. Rapp radioed Coleman to come back down and block the driveway while he picked his way from tree to tree. Wicker found a good spot and covered Rapp with a silenced special-purpose sniping rifle. Rapp maneuvered to a spot where the woods were closest to the house and then made his way onto the side of the porch and crawled to a spot near the front door. Before he could even check the lock, the door opened, swinging toward him, and then Abel appeared.

THE LIGHT WAS fading. The sky had gone from blue, to orange, to gray. Rapp stoked the logs in the large stone fireplace with a black iron poker, and then left the tip of it sitting in the midst of the blazing red coals. He took two sturdy chairs from the dining room and placed them in front of the fireplace. Coleman sat Abel in one and the big Saudi in the other. Their lower legs and ankles were duct taped to the chairs, as were their waists and chests. Both men were blindfolded and gagged. Neither knew he was in the other's presence. Rapp and Coleman had already searched the house and found nothing of interest other than the black bags, which were loaded into the trunk of Abel's Mercedes.

When Rapp was ready he asked Coleman to remove their shoes and socks and then told Wicker, Hackett, and Stroble to wait outside. When Coleman was done with the shoes and socks he gave him the option to leave. Coleman declined.

Rapp stood in front of the two men with his back to the fire. He reached out and grabbed the silver tape that covered Abel's eyes and yanked it off his face. Two thirds of both eyebrows stayed attached to the tape. Abel tried to scream, but his cry was muffled by the tape covering his mouth. Rapp yanked the tape off his mouth, and Abel began gasping for air. Rapp yanked the tape off the Saudi's eyes, and the man barely flinched. The Saudi had yet to utter a word other than when he was screaming in Abel's office and that had been because he knew his only chance was to have one of the neighboring office workers call the police. Since then he'd remained silent. Rapp could see it in his eyes. This one was a true follower. It would take months to break him, and even then the

Saudi might prefer to die. That was why Rapp kept the tape over his mouth.

Rapp held up a phone and said, "On the other end of this line is a man who has thoroughly read your KGB file. He has access to every database you could imagine. We know all about your time with the Stasi. We know how you started out as gay bait for Westerners traveling to East Germany, and we know about the blackmail operations you ran. You are only going to get one chance at this." Rapp held up the forefinger of his left hand and repeated himself, "One chance."

Rapp turned around and grabbed the hot poker from the fire. The tip was bright red. Rapp held it in front of Abel's horrified face and said, "We've talked to your buddy here." Rapp moved the poker over to the Saudi. "I think he lied to us. He blamed everything on you."

The Saudi looked at the tip with a frown.

The poker swung back in front of Abel's face. It was still glowing hot. Abel turned his head away. Rapp pulled the poker back and said very calmly, "Look at me. If I catch you lying to me . . . even once, this is what I'm going to do to you."

Rapp took the poker, held it vertically in his left hand, and jammed it straight down through the top of the Saudi's right foot. The Saudi's entire body looked as if it would break through the duct tape for a second. Coleman stepped up from behind and grabbed the man so he wouldn't tip over in his chair. Rapp yanked the poker free and held it in front of Abel. A hunk of charred skin hung from the end, and the room filled with the awful smell of burnt flesh.

"One chance," Rapp said. "That's all I'm going to give you."

That was all it took. Earlier, Abel had thought his biggest mistake had been threatening the assassin. Then he thought it was leaving the money in the accounts. Now he was convinced the biggest mistake he ever made was entering into a business relationship with Prince Muhammad bin Rashid. Abel sang and kept on singing for twenty solid minutes. He told how Rashid had sent for him. How Rashid had arranged the meeting with Saeed. How later he learned that this whole thing had been Rashid's idea. Abel didn't know that for a fact, but he suspected it. Rashid was a sick sociopath. He lived to manipulate people, and it was important to give Rapp someone bigger to go after. Some fresh meat. He'd already killed Saeed, and if this was the end of the road for Rapp, Abel was a dead man. If he could offer him someone like Rashid, someone who was really guilty, he might survive. He told Rapp that Rashid was in Granada, Spain, at his villa for the rededication of some ridiculous mosque on Friday. Abel had been to Rashid's villa before. He explained how the Saudi prince viewed himself as the new caliph for the reclaimed Muslim lands of southern Spain.

He spat on Tayyib and told Rapp everything he knew about the Saudi intelligence officer. He'd never liked the man. At one point the big Saudi tried to knock his own chair over and go after Abel. Rapp grabbed the red hot poker and held it up to the Saudi's groin. Tayyib instantly turned into a statue.

Rapp put the poker back in the fire and asked Abel, "Tell me about the assassins you hired."

Abel hesitated.

Rapp reached for the poker.

Abel answered, "A man and a woman. I met them in Paris. I had never worked with them before."

"How did you find out about them?"

Abel hesitated before answering. "Rashid had heard of them."

Rapp saw the lie. He could tell by the way the man had looked quickly down and to his right before answering. It was the first time he'd done it. Rapp grabbed the poker, held it out in front of Abel, and then jammed it through the top of his right foot.

Abel howled in pain and began screaming.

Rapp told Coleman to get some ice from the kitchen and then said to Abel, "I told you not to lie to me. Now, how did you come to hire the assassins?"

Abel had tears streaming down his anguished face. Coleman returned with the ice wrapped in a kitchen towel. Rapp tapped the other foot with the hot poker and said, "Last chance."

"Petrov . . . Dimitri Petrov."

Rapp had also read the file. "Your old boss from the KGB."

Abel nodded.

Rapp set the bag on top of his foot. "Now tell me everything you know about the assassins."

"I never saw the man. I only spoke with him. He spoke perfect French and English. His Russian was also very good, but not as good."

Rapp remembered the man's perfect Americanized English from when he'd run into him near his house. "What do you remember about the woman?"

"Very beautiful. Black hair, high cheekbones, very nice skin."

"Eyes?"

"I never saw them. She never took her glasses off."

"Nationality?"

"French. I am almost certain."

That jibed with what Rapp had guessed. "Do you think they were a couple? Beyond the business end of things?"

"Definitely."

Rapp stopped asking questions for a moment.

Abel grew nervous. He knew once Rapp had gotten what he wanted from him, it would likely be the end. "I would like to say that I was nothing more than a courier. I was never told who Saeed and Rashid wanted killed. I simply handed over an envelope to the assassins."

Rapp placed a hand on the fireplace mantel and looked at Coleman. "Why don't you drag our other friend outside and leave us alone for a minute?"

Coleman grabbed the Saudi's chair, tilted him back and dragged him across the hardwood floor and out the front door.

The door closed with a thud and Abel said, "I am very sorry about your wife. They went too far."

Rapp felt like shoving the hot poker through Abel's heart for even mentioning his wife. "Nothing more than a courier, huh?"

"That's right."

"A courier who got paid eleven million dollars." Rapp's eyes were locked on Abel's. Once again he looked down and to the right and then he looked back at Rapp with pleading eyes.

"Please, you must believe me. All I did was deliver an envelope. Nothing more, nothing less."

Rapp pushed himself away from the fireplace and walked into the dining room. Coleman had found the bottle of Louis XIII cognac. Like the modern-day pirate that he was, the former SEAL wanted to keep it. Rapp told him maybe. Now he had a better idea for it. He walked back in front of the fireplace, the ornate bottle in hand. Rapp took off the cap and thought about taking a swig. He thought about his wife and the life they had had together. He thought about the child they would never have. Then he thought about how their entire future had been ruined by this greedy prick sitting before him.

Abel was really nervous. When men like Rapp got quiet, nothing good ever came of it. He had to keep him talking. "We are both professionals, you and I. I know the rules. Professionals never harm each other's families."

"You were a Stasi pig who used to kidnap people and hold them for ransom. You were never a professional." Rapp brought the bottle to his lips and took a big gulp. It went back smooth and then bit his throat with a mellow burning sensation.

"How old is this place?" Rapp looked up at the timber rafters.

"It was built in nineteen fifty-two," Abel answered, a confused expression on his face.

Rapp nodded. "I bet the wood is pretty dry at this altitude." Rapp turned the bottle on its side and some of the cognac spilled onto the wide plank hardwood floor and then onto the carpet. Rapp splashed out a little more.

"What are you doing?" Abel yelled.

"Arranging your funeral pyre." Rapp splashed a little more liquid on the carpet by Abel and then some close to the fireplace.

"No!" Abel screamed. "I know more!"

"I'm sure you do. More lies." The cognac splashed into the flames and caught fire. It shot out from the stone hearth and spread to the rug. Rapp bent over and grabbed the side of the copper kettle that was filled with kindling. He dumped it onto the floor and it caught fire almost immediately.

Abel was screaming. Pleading for his life. "You can't do this!"

"Oh yes, I can," Rapp said as he started toward the door. He opened the heavy wood door and never bothered to look back. Didn't even bother to close the door. He figured the air would be good for the fire.

Rapp took one more swig of the cognac and then handed it to Coleman. "I'll drive."

The other guys got into the rented Volvo van, and Rapp got behind the wheel of Abel's Mercedes. Coleman climbed in the passenger seat.

The former SEAL took a sip of the $2,000-a-bottle cognac and sighed. "Where to now?"

Rapp put the car into reverse and said, "Granada, Spain."

80

Rapp looked up at the country estate on the hill and assumed the bastard Rashid was hiding behind its walls. It was mid-afternoon on Wednesday. They'd arrived in the city of 300,000 late the previous evening and rented two minivans. The first order of business was to find a hotel and get some sleep. Langley had confirmed what Abel had told them; that Rashid was in the Spanish town to rededicate an old mosque that had been converted into a church. The ceremony was to take place on Friday. Rapp decided that they would start their reconnaissance in the morning.

They found the country estate right away. It was impossible to miss. It sat high on a hill just to the north of the world-famous Alhambra. Rapp had toured Alhambra in his early twenties. The part citadel/part palace was built by the Nasrid Kings, the last Moors to rule southern Spain. This was where they took their last stand in 1492 before they were defeated by the forces of Spain's Catholic monarchs Ferdinand and Isabella. According to the report provided by Langley, Rashid had bought the country estate in severe disrepair and had poured millions of dollars into it and every other Muslim landmark he could find in the historic town. Abel had said that this was all part of Rashid's grand plan to retake southern Spain and claim it for Islam.

Rapp was sitting behind the wheel of a dark blue minivan. He looked down at the laptop balanced on the center console, and read the report the researchers at Langley had sent along. The house that Rashid bought even had a name. The place dated back to the twelfth century and in Arabic it was called al Yannat al-Arif—*the garden of lofty paradise.* Rapp picked up a set of binoculars and looked at the place high up on the hill.

"That's as close as you're ever going to get to paradise, Rashid."

Rapp lowered the binoculars and looked up the street at a small outdoor café. He was parked on the Carrera del Darro. Coleman was sitting at a small table negotiating with a man who looked like he could have been his brother. They were the same height, the same build, the same fair hair, and about the same age. Rashid had called in the reserves. On the first reconnaissance sweep of the morning they noticed the men in the blue coveralls, with the berets and Enfield rifles. It was immediately obvious that these guys were no rent-a-cops. The way they carried themselves, their berets, their Enfield rifles all pointed to one thing—these guys were British commandos. Probably former SAS guys, some of the best soldiers in the world.

Their presence presented a real problem tactically. They would not be easy to get past, and even more importantly, neither Rapp nor Coleman had any stomach for killing men they saw as comrades in arms. They had both worked with the British before and considered them America's best ally. Stuck in this seemingly no-win situation Coleman came up with an idea. He ran his own security company. Almost all of his men were former SEALs, Delta Force, Green Berets, Rangers, or Recon Marines. They were almost always guys who got out because they were tired of the bullshit that went along with being in the service. That and the fact that they could make six to ten times more in a year what they were getting paid in the military. Personal protection, guns for hire, it was a pretty specialized field. There were a few pretenders, but most of the players were real, and they were all interconnected, either from their military days or the time they spent hanging out in crappy Third World bars while they either protected diplomats or plotted to kill terrorists and thugs.

Coleman had contacts in Britain, and he got on the phone. Within an hour he had a pretty good idea which company had taken the job guarding Rashid. It was an outfit called Shield Security Services, and as they'd guessed, it was run by a couple of former SAS guys. Coleman called the office directly, and a nice young woman answered. He explained who he was and that he was in the business. He asked to speak to the owner, a guy named Ian Higsby. The woman informed him that he was on assignment at the moment. Coleman pressed her for details telling her he needed to subcontract a job and that he'd heard good things about the company.

The prospect of new business did the trick and she gave Coleman Higsby's mobile phone number.

Coleman called him up straight away, introduced himself, and gave the commando his military credentials. Higsby had heard of him. By the tone of his voice, Coleman got the idea that this was not good. Coleman saw no point in bullshitting the guy, so he came straight out and asked him if he was in Spain. The dead silence on the line said it all.

"Granada," Coleman said.

The man still didn't answer.

"We need to meet," Coleman told him. "Face to face. As soon as possible."

"Why?"

"You ever heard of a guy named Mitch Rapp?"

"Most certainly. I was just given a picture of him and told to shoot him on sight."

"How do you feel about that?"

"Wasn't exactly thrilled. It was dropped on me after I took the job."

"Well . . . like I said. We need to meet. I think we can help each other out."

They agreed on a place in the Albaicin neighborhood and set a time.

Rapp had been watching them for the better part of an hour and was starting to get frustrated. It appeared to be going well, but enough already. Finally, the two shook hands, and Coleman got up and walked down the street. Rapp watched the Brit head the other way. Coleman got in the van and gave Rapp the thumbs-up.

"It's all taken care of."

"It was that easy?" Rapp asked, surprised.

"Higsby had read about your wife. He offers his condolences."

Rapp started the car and said nothing.

"He received a call on Monday and was offered fifty thousand to do five days of security. He's got an eight-man team, and Rashid sent a plane for them. The job was five days in southern Spain babysitting some Saudi billionaire. He takes ten grand off the top and the rest of them get five grand apiece for what they thought was going to be a cakewalk. Then they got here and the head of Rashid's security detail showed them a picture of you and told them to shoot you on sight."

"How'd they like that?" Rapp asked as he pulled out into traffic.

"They didn't. Some of these guys have served over in the sandbox, and they've had friends killed by Saudi suicide bombers. They consider you an ally and Rashid the enemy. Higsby told me he practically had a mutiny on his hands."

"So did he agree to play ball?"

"Yeah, he was a little worried about what this might do to his reputation. None of us like to lose a protectee. It's not exactly good for business."

"Did you offer him the cash?" Rapp was referring to the money they'd taken from Abel's Alpine house.

"One hundred thousand euros. Plus I told him I'd make sure the U.S. government sent some contracts his way. I'll leave it up to you to tell Irene."

Rapp nodded. "No problem. I'll take care of it. What's the plan?"

"He's eating dinner tonight with the mayor. Up at the house. Seven o'clock. Higsby said he went to bed at nine last night so he doesn't expect him to stay up late." Coleman unfolded a piece of paper. "He gave me a layout of the place and showed me where he sleeps. He also offered a uniform."

"Good." Rapp stared straight ahead. "I'll go in alone as soon as the mayor leaves."

81

They sat and waited. They watched the mayor arrive, or at least they assumed it was him. Who else would travel with a local police escort? The cars pulled up to the main gate just before seven in the evening, just as the sun was disappearing and the light was fading. The temperature began to drop like a stone. They knew it would be a while so they got something to eat and went over the plan one more time. All the gear was stowed and Hackett was sent to the airport to get the plane ready in case they needed to make a hasty departure.

The mayor left shortly after nine, and they roused Tayyib from his drug-induced slumber. He'd already been cleaned up, and put in a fresh set of clothes and a new suit. His blindfold remained on and he was placed in the back of the van with Stroble. Rapp sat in the front passenger seat. Rapp had shaved his beard and cut his thick black hair down to a bristly flattop. He was wearing blue coveralls and a beret. The same as Higsby and his men. Coleman and Stroble were dressed in the same manner.

Rapp turned around and looked at Tayyib as the van wound its way through the narrow streets. He didn't look too bad considering what he'd been through, but most of his wounds were covered by his clothes. In addition to the shattered right elbow and the nerve damage done to his right foot, Rapp had also sliced all the tendons on Tayyib's left wrist, rendering his hand useless, and leaving him with only one fully operational limb—his left leg. People reacted differently to drugs and this guy was pretty big. If he came out of it too quick, Rapp didn't want to have to wrestle with him.

Coleman pulled over before reaching the road that led to the hilltop estate. He pulled out his mobile phone and called Higsby. The Brit answered and Coleman listened to him for fifteen seconds and then said, "We'll be right there."

Coleman hung up and looked at Rapp. "He's praying."

"Good. Let's go."

They'd gone over it all in the plan. There was a small mosque on the property, located closer to the main gate than the residence. Rashid had anywhere from three to six of his own bodyguards near him at all times. Rapp hoped they were all with him. It would make things easier.

"What about the bodyguards?"

"Three of them are standing outside the mosque. The other three he's not sure about."

Rapp frowned. He turned around and looked at Stroble, silently communicating that it was Stroble's job to make sure the other three bodyguards didn't show up unexpectedly. Stroble nodded. They'd gone over it all in the permission briefing. Wicker was already on site. He'd scaled one of the perimeter walls and had slithered onto the rooftop of the tallest building. From his perch he could cover the entire length of the inner courtyard that led from the main gate to the three-story main house.

The engine groaned as the van continued up the steep hill. Suddenly, Higsby and one of his men were visible in their headlights standing in front of the main gate. Coleman pulled over and turned off the van. Everyone got out, including Tayyib, who practically had to be carried, which was just fine. Stroble got under one arm and Coleman the other. Rapp led the way past Higsby and his man without a word.

The three of them plus Tayyib went through the main gate and took the walkway to the left. Up ahead on the left side of the open-air court Rapp sighted three men in suits. They were all smoking.

Rapp headed straight for them, stopped ten feet away, and in his best British accent said, "This man just showed up at the main gate asking to see Prince Muhammad. He said his name is Nawaf Tayyib."

The men froze for a moment, their cigarettes dangling in their mouths.

"He keeps saying that the *Malik al-Mawt* is here." *Angel of death*. "The man named Mitch Rapp that you spoke of."

One cigarette fell to the ground and the other two were thrown. All three men grabbed their guns. Two of them ran forward to grab Tayyib, and the third went into the small mosque to get Rashid. The blindfold was yanked from Tayyib's eyes and he howled in pain as one of the men grabbed him by his right elbow.

Coleman and Stroble were already retreating, their silenced MP-5 submachine guns aimed down but gripped firmly in both hands. Rapp had only his silenced 9mm Glock and a knife, which were both still holstered. He too began to retreat. His whole plan could fall apart any second and if that happened, the shooting would start and Higsby and his men would be forced to answer some very difficult questions.

Rapp started to step back. One of the men holding Tayyib got on a radio and started yelling in Arabic. Rapp took another step back slowly. Tayyib was trying to talk. Rapp heard his own name mentioned. Five seconds later three men burst through a door on the opposite side of the court and dashed across a path lined with sculpted cypress trees.

"Bees to the honey," Rapp said to himself as he continued his slow retreat. He looked toward the door to the mosque wondering just what in the hell was taking Rashid so long. Rapp couldn't wait much longer. He extracted the remote detonator from his pocket. This time rather than using a vest, Rapp had simply wrapped Tayyib's entire torso in C-4 and covered every square inch with ball bearings. Rapp made it to a pillar and stopped. He looked over his shoulder quickly to check on Coleman and Stroble. They were standing next to each other one more pillar back. Rapp jerked his head for them to get behind it.

He looked back just as the bodyguard reappeared from the mosque and said, "Prince Muhammad wants to know if you've checked him for explosives."

Everybody froze. Rapp hadn't really thought he'd be able to get away with it twice, but the bomb would still serve its purpose.

The men on each side of Tayyib pulled back his suit coat and the man standing in front placed his hands on Tayyib's waist. Rapp stepped behind the large stone column and pressed the button on the remote. There was a loud explosion, followed almost immediately by the sound of breaking glass as hundreds of ball bearings were hurled outward by the force of the explosion.

Rapp counted to three and peered back around the column. All six bodyguards were down and Tayyib was in two pieces—head and shoulders pointing toward the door to the mosque and his legs and ass pointing the same way. The other six men, and much of the courtyard, were covered in what used to be Tayyib's torso and arms.

Rapp stepped over the bodies and went straight for the mosque. He stood next to the door and counted. He knew curiosity would get the best of Rashid and by the time Rapp got to seven Rashid proved him right. His pointy black beard poked its way into view followed by a pair of shocked brown eyes.

Rapp's left hand shot out and grabbed Rashid by the end of his beard. He yanked him forward and at the same time brought his left knee up, delivering a vicious blow to the older man's solar plexus. Rashid fell to the ground right on top of one of his nearly decapitated bodyguards. Rapp rolled him over and placed his boot on the man's chest.

He looked him in the eye and said, "Why?"

Rashid had a fire in his eyes. He spoke in Arabic and said, "Because you are an infidel."

Rapp shook his head with disgust. "And my wife."

There was no smile, no fear, no pleading, there was nothing other than total conviction in the man's eyes. "She was an infidel. You are all infidels."

Rapp nodded and said, "And you are going to hell." Rapp grabbed a phosphorus grenade from the cargo pouch on his right thigh. The incendiary device reached a temperature of 2,000 degrees in less than two seconds. Rapp lifted his boot from Rashid's chest and sent it crashing down once more, this time into Rashid's stomach. The Saudi's mouth opened wide, gasping for breath. Rapp was ready. He was holding the grenade by the top third, and he brought it crashing down with such force that it shattered Rashid's front teeth and wedged itself firmly in his mouth.

Rapp got right in his face and said, "Fuck you! And fuck your sick, twisted, perversion of Islam." Rapp yanked the pin and walked away. Three seconds later there was a pop followed by a blinding white flash, and then Rashid's head literally melted from his body.

EPILOGUE

Rapp watched them for three days from a house on the hill over-looking the beach, which was probably one day too many. Coleman didn't say anything. Didn't make any observations. Didn't offer any advice. It had been nine months, one week, and three days since Rapp's wife had been killed. Wicker was with them, as were Hackett and Stroble. Wicker could have ended it more than a dozen times with his rifle. The winds were calm in the morning and the evening. It was just under 800 yards from one terrace to the other, and the trajectory was steep. For most people it would be an impossible shot, but for Wicker it was business as usual. The sniper waited for the word, but it never came.

The hunt had changed Rapp. With each passing day over the past months he had grown quieter and retreated from all but Kennedy, her son, Coleman, and the O'Rourkes. Liz O'Rourke was Anna's best friend from college. They were the only people other than Kennedy that he re-ally confided in. Even with Coleman it was all about the hunt. He spoke with his brother a few times, and Steven had come to the memorial ser-vice in Washington—a service that Mitch ended up skipping. The priest waited for thirty minutes, and then Kennedy and Liz O'Rourke told the priest to start without him. Neither woman held out much hope that he would show. He was too private a man to show his grief in front of so many people whom he barely knew.

The new house sat unfinished and the old house on the Chesapeake, a house that Anna had grown to love, remained a charred ruin. Coleman went to Kennedy. He wanted to bring in an excavator and have the mess cleaned up. She thought about it for a second and told him no. It was Mitch's decision. When he was ready, he would do it himself. They all waited. Waited for Rapp to come out of his shell and get on with his life, but it didn't happen. The days ticked by and then the months. Rapp rented a house in Galesville on the bay, just up the road from where Anna had died. He didn't want to leave the water. He was afraid to lose that connection.

Almost every day he drove to the charred wreckage on the bay that had been their home. Sometimes he stayed in the car. Sometimes he got out and walked around. Every single time he sobbed uncontrollably over the memories that had been and the dreams that would never be. He never got to see his baby, never got to cradle the little infant in his arms. He never got to find out if it was a boy or a girl. He never even got to say good-bye to the woman of his dreams. He'd failed to protect her when she'd needed it most, and it was eating him alive. The unfulfilled dreams and the yearning to hold her one more time, to look into her beautiful, stunning, green eyes and smell her hair, was more painful than anything he'd ever experienced, but even so, it wasn't as bad as the guilt he felt over causing her death.

When he went in to work, it was only to be updated by Kennedy and Dumond on what they had learned about the assassins. Other than that he stayed away from Langley. What he was doing nobody knew and no one dared ask. The first break came from the Russian named Petrov. Kennedy had been stationed in Moscow earlier in her career and she had many contacts. Through several of Petrov's old colleagues she talked him into sitting down. Word had reached him about Abel's demise. It had been reported as an accidental death, but Petrov knew better. Men like Abel didn't die in chance house fires.

She told him that Abel had been hired by several wealthy Saudis and given a twenty-million-dollar contract to kill Mitch Rapp. Petrov was genuinely surprised by the amount. Kennedy told him what he already knew—that Abel had hired two assassins who were recommended by none other than himself. Then she told him something he didn't know. The assassins had missed Rapp and killed his wife by mistake. Petrov winced at the news. Families were off limits and a man like Mitch Rapp would stop at nothing until he hunted these people down and killed them.

This was a mess Petrov did not need. He could either tell Kennedy what little he knew, or risk Mitch Rapp paying him a visit in the dead of the night. The decision was easy. He told Kennedy what he knew about the assassins, which wasn't much, but proved to be crucial. The woman was in fact French and so was the man, Petrov suspected. He also suspected he was former military, and at one point had lived in America, probably during his teens. When Kennedy pressed him on this, he explained that the man's English was too good. Too colloquial. He had all the idioms and slang down. The type of thing you can pick up only by living in a country. Petrov handed over the phone numbers and e-mail addresses he had used to contact them over the years.

Kennedy flew from Moscow to Paris and sat down with her counterparts who ran France's DGSE and DST, the country's premier security and intelligence organizations. While many of France's politicians could be considered weak on terrorism, the same could not be said of the DGSE and DST. They were among the world's best and most effective counterterrorism organizations. Both men were fully aware of what had happened to Rapp and his wife. Rapp had worked closely with the DGSE before and the director said he would do everything in his power to find out who these people were. The head of the DST made the same commitment. Kennedy returned to the States and waited.

The break came three weeks later, nearly five weeks after Anna's death. The DGSE sent Kennedy two dossiers. The man's name was Louie Gould, and the woman was Claudia Morrell. Everything about the dossiers made sense. Gould was a former French paratrooper and the son of a French diplomat who had done two tours in Washington. Morrell's father was a general in the French Foreign Legion. He and his daughter had had a falling-out over Gould, and the two had disappeared off the map a little more than five years ago. Both French intelligence services promised Kennedy that they would join in the hunt.

The big break came nine months and one week after Anna's death. Kennedy had come up with the plan. They knew the woman was pregnant. She had asked Kennedy to let her live long enough to give birth and hold her baby. Kennedy had the FBI put out a worldwide bulletin on the couple and they got the allied intelligence services involved. They focused on hospitals. Specifically, doctors who delivered babies. Every month they sent out a new wave of e-mails and faxes as a reminder. They contained actual photos of Gould and Morrell and then computer-generated renderings of how they might have changed their appearances.

The couple was wanted for questioning in a capital murder case, and a toll-free number was included, along with a reward for $100,000. They received hundreds of phone calls, none of which panned out. Many of the early ones were ruled out because the delivery dates didn't match the timetable. As they got to the seventh month, though, each lead had to be run down. When the phone call came in from the hospital in Tahiti, a French overseas territory, they all held their breath. An agent for the French DST rushed over to the hospital in Papeete and donned a pair of surgical scrubs. Within an hour the agent called and said he was almost positive the woman was Claudia Morrell.

Rapp looked down at the house. It was early in the morning, their third sunrise on the island. He'd been standing like a statue for nearly ten minutes, staring at the house. He glanced down at his watch. It was almost 7:00. Less than a minute later Gould appeared on the terrace below. He was in shorts and running shoes. He stretched for several minutes, and then bounded down the steps and started running up the beach in the opposite direction.

Rapp watched Gould for a long moment and then said, "I'm going in by myself."

"I don't think that's very smart."

Rapp ignored him. "If anything happens to me, finish the job."

He was dressed in a pair of khaki cargo shorts and a loose-fitting, faded blue T-shirt. Rapp walked to the front entry of the rental home. Coleman, Wicker, Hackett, and Stroble watched him. Rapp slid into a pair of flip-flops and grabbed his sunglasses. He stepped outside and fired up the Vespa scooter that came with the place and took off down the hill. He didn't want to think about this any more than he already had. The scooter was quiet, especially when it was going downhill. Rapp coasted his way down the lush hillside. The road was very narrow. After several hundred yards it emptied onto a slightly wider road that could accommodate two-way traffic. The beach house was up on the right a short distance. The closest neighbor was about five hundred feet away.

Rapp turned off the scooter and stashed it in the bushes near the end of the driveway. He checked his watch. The man had returned between 7:25 and 7:30 each of the two previous mornings. Rapp picked his way through the jungle until he was even with the house. He then entered the side yard, which was some type of broad-bladed grass. He continued around to the beach side and drew his silenced Glock from his back waistband. The weapon felt light in his hand.

The house was stucco with a red Spanish style roof. The patio that overlooked the beach had a thick three-foot wall that ran along the perimeter with steps in the middle and on the side where he was. Rapp grabbed the digital radio from his cargo pocket and pressed the transmit button.

"Any sign of him?"

"Not yet."

Rapp peered around the corner. The patio was empty. "Don't try anything with Wicker."

"It would be a hell of a lot easier. Not to mention safer."

"Stand him down. If I need help I'll let you know."

Rapp put the radio on silent mode and climbed the stairs in a crouch. There were French doors immediately on his left. Rapp paused and glanced in. It was the living room. The woman would still be sleeping with the infant. Rapp had learned every detail he could about the two. He had been tempted to talk to their parents, but it would have been foolish to tip his hand that way. It was better to let them fall into a false sense of security. Rapp moved onto the next set of doors—the ones off the kitchen and dining room. The ones he suspected Gould used to come and go in the morning. He turned the knob. It moved and the door pushed in quietly.

Rapp stepped carefully over the threshold and closed the door behind him. The fact that the door was unlocked spoke volumes about their state of mind. Not that a lock would have stopped him, but it would have at least slowed him down. Rapp was completely healed. At least physically. His knee felt better than it had in years, and the cast on his right arm was long gone. He glided across the dark stained wood floor and moved to the right, toward the hallway that led to the bedrooms. There were doors on the right and the left and one at the end of the hall. The two on the sides were closed, and the one at the end was slightly cracked. Rapp guessed Gould had left it like that so as to not wake them when he returned.

Rapp placed his right palm on the door and kept his gun up and ready. Slowly, he pushed the door open and stepped into the room. The woman was lying on her side in bed, her dark hair offset against the bright white sheets and pillows. The infant was cradled in her arms and her lips rested softly against the impossibly small child's head. Rapp wavered for a second and almost lost his nerve. He was struck by how beautiful the woman was and how absolutely peaceful she and her young child appeared.

Rapp shook his head and regained his composure. He stepped silently across the dark wood floor and extended his gun. He placed the tip of his silencer against the woman's left temple and watched her eyes flutter open. She slowly turned her head until the silencer was pointed at her forehead. Rapp's right hand slid under her pillow and checked for a weapon. There was none. He checked the drawer in the nightstand, but it was also empty.

She looked up at Rapp almost as if she had been expecting him and said, "Thank you for letting me give birth to my daughter."

Rapp backed up a step and motioned for her to sit up. She did, and then picked up the sleeping baby and held it in her arms. Rapp checked his watch and grabbed the radio.

"Any sign of Gould?"

"He's coming back up the beach. ETA two minutes."

Rapp crossed the room and put the door back to where he'd found it and then checked the nightstand on the other side of the bed. He found a 9mm Beretta, emptied it, and then went back to the woman's side of the bed where French doors led out onto the patio. They were covered by thick curtains. The morning sun crawled in around the edges and backlit the room. Rapp kept his gun on the woman and then pulled back the curtains enough to get a peek. He stood in the corner with his back to the wall, the door on his left and the woman in front of him, and he waited.

She tried to talk several times, but he shook his head.

"If you want your baby to live . . . keep your mouth shut and don't say a thing."

"You would never kill this baby, or any other baby."

She said it with such calm conviction that it surprised Rapp. "No, I wouldn't, but I would kill you, so if you'd like to see your baby grow up, be quiet." Rapp looked at his watch and added, "There is a sniper outside, and he's very good. The best I've ever seen. If you say a word, he will run, and he will be killed before he reaches the beach."

She shrugged. "Then why did you come in here? Why didn't you just have him shot on the beach?"

"Because I'm not a coward. Because I don't have other people do my work for me. I do it face to face. I don't blow up houses and kill innocent bystanders."

Claudia looked away and swallowed hard.

Rapp checked one more time and then turned the radio off. Half a minute later, Rapp felt the door in the other room open. The bedroom door moved slightly with the air that rushed out of the house and then settled. Rapp kept the gun pointed at the mother's head and whispered, "Don't say a word or you both die."

She closed her eyes and kissed the baby's head.

The door to the bedroom opened slowly and Gould poked his head in. He saw his wife sitting up in bed and smiled. They had married. He stepped into the room and said, "What are you doing up?"

Claudia looked to the corner of the room and he followed her eyes.

"If you so much as twitch you're dead."

Gould was dripping with sweat from his run. He looked at Rapp and very slowly raised his hands above his head. "I'm sorry about your wife."

Rapp didn't reply. Now that he was in front of the man, he was at a loss for words.

Gould looked at Claudia and dropped to one knee and then the other. His hands were folded behind his head.

To Rapp it was almost as if this had been rehearsed. Like they had discussed what to do if he ever found them.

"I'm sorry," Gould said again, his voice cracking. "Please understand, Claudia had nothing to do with it."

"Did you know she was pregnant?"

Gould slowly nodded, as if he was deeply ashamed. "I knew. Claudia didn't know until after. She cried for days."

Rapp glanced at the woman. She was crying now. A tear fell and splashed on the baby's face. She squirmed in her mother's arms.

"I know I'm in no position to ask for anything, but . . ." His voice trailed off.

"Let's hear it."

Gould swallowed hard and took a deep breath. "Would you please spare Claudia, and if you don't, would you please bring the baby to her parents in France?"

Rapp kept the silencer leveled at the man's head. He wasn't going to kill the woman. Any thought of that vanished the second he saw the baby in her arms.

"Anything else?" Rapp asked.

"I'm very sorry for everything I did to you. I should have never taken the job. Claudia was right."

Rapp acted bored. "Is that it?"

"May I please kiss my baby and my wife good-bye?"

Rapp's eyes narrowed and he nodded slowly.

Gould kept his hands behind his head and he got up slowly. He stepped over to the bed and sat next to his wife. He wrapped his arms around Claudia and they both cried. Gould stroked her hair and told her how much he loved her. He then bent down and kissed the infant on the head.

"My sweet Anna," he said, "I am lucky to have seen you born and to have held you in my arms . . . even if it was only for a few days." Gould's shoulders began to shake and he wept over his baby. Claudia wrapped her arms around him and kissed the top of his head just as she had kissed the baby earlier.

Rapp stood there in the corner of the room with his gun pointed at the father, mother, and child. *What have I turned into?* he asked himself. This was his life, or what it would have been, if only Anna had lived. The pain of the last nine months came rolling back and slapped him with the memory of his wife and his unborn child. Standing there, his resolve teetering, he asked himself one simple question: *What would Anna do?* It was her life he was avenging, not his own. He could hear her calling out to him as if she were alive and standing right next to him.

The baby woke up and started to cry. "Anna, don't cry," the father said. "Everything will be all right. Your mother will take care of you, and I will love you forever."

Claudia looked up at Rapp, her eyes red and moist with tears.

"You named her Anna," Rapp said.

"After your wife."

Rapp nodded and slowly lowered the gun. He took a deep breath and left the room without saying another word. He stepped out onto the patio and went straight down the stairs to the white sandy beach. He never looked back. He never feared for his life for a second. He would give Anna, both of them, what they surely wanted. If Gould was still the calculating killer that he had been, he wouldn't be far behind. There would be other weapons in the house. He would grab one and he would step outside and that would be the end of it. Wicker would shoot him in the head before he ever got off a shot. If he truly loved Claudia and that little girl, he would stay right where he was and hold them until the sun went down.

Rapp stood in the surf with his gun in his hand and counted. He got to a hundred, thought of his wife, thought of the baby, and smiled. It was the first genuine smile he'd had in over nine months. He glanced down at the gun and then tossed it up in the air, catching it by its thick black silencer. Rapp hesitated for a moment, and then threw the weapon end over end into the ocean.